fiction

WHAT REVENGE HIDES

By

Lucy Alvarez

© **2025 Lucy Álvarez**
All rights reserved.

This is a work of fiction. Names, characters, places, and incidents are either products of the author's imagination or are used fictitiously. Any resemblance to actual persons, living or dead, or to actual events is entirely coincidental.

No part of this publication may be reproduced, distributed, or transmitted in any form or by any means —electronic, mechanical, photocopying, recording, or otherwise— without the prior written permission of the copyright holder, in accordance with applicable copyright laws.

Intellectual property registration: 00765-02896834
ISBN: 9798274931953
Second edition: 2026
Copy editor: Kylie Patterson

To my family

You helped me through my most difficult times
and showed me how to find the light.
Thank you.

CHAPTER 1

London, 18th March 1787

Abigail Clarkson felt her eyes burn with tiredness as she read the words of the book her father had recommended. *It will be good for your education*, he had told her, as he placed the thick volume in her hands. But a book on marine insurance was not the best way to keep her awake.

After all, she was exhausted. Getting her mother to drop her insistence on attending at least one ball that season had been in vain. And although it was the only reason they had extended their stay in London, Abbie didn't share her mother's obsession with seeing her married.

She closed the book, blew out the candle next to her bed and lay down. She lay her head on the pillow, releasing a scent of fresh linen that filled her senses, enveloping her with the pleasant aroma.

As she drifted off to sleep, a clamour coming from the floor below made her sit up straight in bed. Listening into the darkness, with her head turned to the door, Abbie's heart pounded with force. The silence broke again when a shrill sound echoed through the room, followed by the unmistakable cry of a woman, sending a shiver through her as she recognised her mother's voice.

Abbie jumped out of bed and ran to the door, but as she got closer, she heard footsteps and a man's voice, followed by a thud that sounded like a sack of flour falling to the ground.

She pressed her ear to the door, trying to hear what was happening on the other side. As the footsteps approached her room, she stepped back and stared at the door. The line of light coming from the hallway dimmed as the sound of the footsteps got closer and closer. The doorknob began to turn slowly.

Abbie looked around for a place to hide. She saw the dressing screen and ran to hide behind it, flattening herself against the wall. She stayed as still as possible. Her heart was pounding so hard she could feel it echoing in her head.

She looked across the room, but from that angle, she couldn't quite see the entrance. Fixing her attention on the dressing table mirror, the door became visible in the reflection as it opened. It revealed the shape of a man so large that his body filled the doorway frame, allowing only a few beams of light to filter through the spaces left by his bulky form.

Holding her breath, Abbie hoped the intruder wouldn't realise where she was hidden. But instead of leaving, he headed directly to her bed. Giving the sheets a yank, he pulled them away to find it empty.

She could see how his muscles tensed as he released a growl and lifted his head to look around the room. Although the insufficient light didn't quite allow her to see him clearly, it was enough to reveal his abrupt face and evil gaze. She could see his angry expression, desperately running his eyes through the room. He walked further into the bedroom, and his reflection disappeared from the mirror as he did.

Abbie looked around for something to defend herself with and grabbed a marble figurine in the shape of a dove from the small table beside her. She could hear his footsteps getting closer and closer until silence fell in the room. She lifted her head and froze. A pair of small, round black eyes stared back at her, framed by a twisted smile and half-rotten teeth, radiating with the satisfaction of having found her.

Abbie tightened her fingers around the dove, and with all the strength she could muster, she smashed the bird against the man's head. His desperate cry echoed through the room. He clutched his head, but the blood began to slip through his fingers, dripping into his eyes. Blinded, he rubbed at his face, smearing it across his skin.

Abbie shoved him out of the way and raced towards the open door without wasting a second.

'Bitch!' He growled. Before Abbie could reach the door, he grabbed her by the hair and yanked so hard that she fell back, crashing into the dressing table. A sharp, searing pain spread across her cheek.

She touched her face – it burned hot beneath her palm. Dazed, she shook her head, trying to clear the fog clouding her vision. But he grabbed her hair again, jerking her to her feet. She screamed, disoriented, clawing at his wrist to ease the pressure, tearing at her scalp.

Abbie tried to release her hair from his chubby hands, scratching him with her nails until she felt the skin break.

'Let me go!' Abbie kept fighting with all the fire she had inside her.

'Bloody whore!' She managed to stand, but he spun her around and slammed her against the wall. The brutality of the impact knocked the air from her lungs. Gasping for air, she froze as she felt the blade of his knife sharp against her neck.

'Stop movin', or I'll slice yer throat!' Barely able to breathe, Abbie stopped fighting and locked eyes with him.

His eyes were dark and narrow, a sharp contrast to the

round, broad, and ugly face, already marked with numerous scars, one of which crossed his right cheek to the edge of his bottom lip. His nose, crooked to one side, had been broken more than once and now leaned at an unnatural angle, making him the most terrifying man she'd ever seen.

She held his gaze, desperate not to show how terrified she was. His putrid breath turned her stomach as he leaned closer.

'Try somethin' that stupid again, and ye'll not live. Do ye understand?' She was scared, and he could see it in her eyes. She didn´t answer, but her trembling lip gave her away. 'Good.'

His eyes lowered to look at her body. The lower he went, the wider his smile grew. She wore only a thin white nightgown. She could see the lust in his eyes, and it made her sick to her stomach for whatever thoughts he might have; she was sure they were as vile as he was.

He stepped closer, lowered his head to her neck, and breathed her in. The stench of rot made her stomach lurch, forcing her to shift her head to the other side, trying to escape his rancid breath. He stayed in that position briefly before whispering against her neck,

'Ye smell good.' He moved away from her a few inches.

Abbie flinched. 'You smell disgusting.' She snapped, lifting her chin.

At her four and twenty years old, she had plenty of suitors coming to her father's door to know about the desires of the flesh, but the look in this brute's eyes was entirely different from the noble behaviour of the gentlemen who had courted her.

He smiled, dismissing her comment and turned her around, pushing her towards the door.

'Now walk, yer ma and da are waitin' for ye do'nstairs.'

As he said these words, a gunshot cut through the air. Her blood froze instantly, and she looked back at him. She could see he was just as surprised as she was. 'Bloody 'ell!' He mumbled and tightened his grip on her. 'Or maybe they ain't...' He said it like it didn't matter if her parents were alive or dead.

'What was that?' she asked, looking back to the door, unable to move, but he shoved her again, this time harder as he shouted.

'I SAID WALK! And keep ye mouth shut!'

They stepped out of her room and turned right towards the stairs. Jacob – the family´s loyal butler who had been with them since she could remember – lay unconscious outside her door.

'Jacob!' She cried, dropping to help him. But her captor dug his fingers into her shoulder until she yelped with pain. Catching her breath, she managed to whisper, 'Is he…?' She couldn't find the words to finish the sentence.

'Naw. Not yet.' the man growled. 'But if ye don' do wha' I say, everyone in this house will be. Ye understan'?' She nodded, desperate for the well-being of the whole household. 'Keep walkin'.'

They reached the staircase, and although her head swam from the blow to her cheek, the fear for what was happening to her mother overpowered the pain. Gripping the bannister to steady herself, she began the descent, closely followed by her captor. When they finally reached the staircase hall, her legs could barely hold her up.

The door to her father's study was open, and as she approached, he shoved her so hard that she lost her balance and fell to her knees. When she looked up, the scene paralysed her.

Her father cradled the inert body of her mother in his

arms, tenderly rocking her, whispering in her ear in a desperate attempt to bring her back with the sound of his voice, brushing her hair with his hand. Her soft skin was devoid of any colour, her lifeless eyes wide open. Her beautiful nightgown was soaked in the blood that flowed from her chest.

Her father raised his gaze to look at the man before him. Those sweet eyes that she knew well were now filled with anger and hatred towards the man who had stolen the love of his life. The intruder was tall and thin, with long, greasy, dark hair. His clothes looked like they had been pulled from a rubbish dump – torn, filthy, and reeking of neglect.

With the pistol still aimed at her father, Abbie caught the smirk on his face - a look devoid of remorse, untouched by the murder of an innocent woman.

'You will pay for this!' he spat. She had never seen this side of her father. He was always so calm and kindhearted, but she couldn't recognise this man before her.

'Skinny! What the 'ell happn'd here!?' Her captor asked from the doorway.

Without looking back and still locked in her father's gaze, the man shrugged. 'She tried to escape.' He said, lifting his shoulders. As if the fact that he had just taken a life, her mother's life, wasn't important.

'Ye bloody halfwit! I leave ye alone an' ye start killing? We need 'em alive!' he growled. He stepped forward, grabbed Abbie's arm, and pushed her towards her parents. It was only then that her father seemed to realise she was in the room.

'No! What is she doing here? Leave her out of this—she doesn't need to be involved. Whatever this is!' he shouted. As soon as she was close enough, he seized her arm and pulled her closer, setting her behind him, shielding her from the men standing before them.

He studied her face and saw the blood trickling down her cheek, already starting to dry. 'Are you alright, darling? Did they hurt you?' He asked softly, holding her chin gently to turn her face, lifting her chin to examine the nasty cut.

She wanted to hug him and cry like when she was a little girl, but she didn't want to worry him further than he already was. Instead, she took a deep breath and nodded. 'Yes, Papa. I'm fine. It's just a small cut.' She said, blinking, fighting back the tears that clung to the corners of her eyes.

She was afraid to look at her mother's lifeless body, but when she did, the tears that she had held back welled up effortlessly. 'Mama...' Her hand moved to touch her mother's cold face. She kissed her on her forehead and gently closed her eyes. Turning her attention to her father, she whispered. 'What's happening? Who are these men and what are they doing here, Papa?' Her voice trembled.

'I don't know, darling', he said. 'But we need to stay calm. Don't move– and stay behind me, no matter what.' Abbie nodded.

'That's my girl', he said, tenderly caressing her cheek. Their attention shifted back to the men in the room.

'Pay it no mind, Jack; she was gonna' die anyway,' Skinny sneered, turning to glance at Jack. Skinny's eyes widened when he saw the state of his face. 'What the hell happen'd to ye?' pointing at the bloody gash on his forehead.

'This whore happen'd.' He said, motioning towards Abbie with his knife.

Skinny raised an eyebrow. 'A fiery one, eh? I like tha'.' His pig's eyes ran down her body, filthy with intent. But her father stood between them, protecting her body from his lascivious gaze.

His father looked at the captors, now standing in front of them, side by side. 'You bastards, leave my daughter out of this! Take whatever you want! I'll give you anything.'

Jack's mouth twisted into a grin. 'Oh, don't worry about that ol' man, we'll take whatever we want.' He looked at Skinny with a twisted smile.

'Then take it and leave!'

'You see ol' man, we cannee leave until ye give us what ye stole.'

Alan Clarkson frowned. 'I haven't ever stolen anything in my life. What on earth are you referring to?'

'That ain't what me patron is sayin'.' Jack replied, his voice low. 'You 'ave some documents an' he wants 'em back. If I go back empty-handed, I'm done for.'

Her father's eyes narrowed, and Abbie realised he knew exactly what they meant. 'What are they talking about, Papa?' she asked, her voice unsteady.

Jack saw the look in her father's eyes, too, and grinned, flashing his yellow, rotting teeth.

'Oh, doll, he knows alright what we are talkin' about,' he said. 'Tell us where they are, and maybe we'll let ye and yer precious daughter live. I've got patience, but me friend 'ere…' – he gestured to Skinny – 'he enjoys watchin' people die.'

His words didn't give Abbie any reassurance that he would keep his promise.

'What you seek is not here,' her father said. His voice was cold as ice. 'Papa?'

Skinny stepped closer and moved the pistol from her father's head to Abbie's. 'Where is it?' Abbie couldn't tear her eyes away from the pistol pointing straight at her.

'Stop wasting me bloody time and hand over the bloody documents!' Skinny was growing impatient.

The cold steel pressed against Abbie's forehead; her

eyes clamped shut, waiting for the pistol to go off at any moment. She felt how the vein in her temple throbbed, beating like a drum, anticipating that something horrible would happen.

'It's not here!' her father cried. 'It's in our home in the country. I'll give it to you– just don't hurt her – please!'

She stayed frozen, waiting for the shot – but nothing happened. Slowly, she opened her eyes. The man was staring at her. 'Jack,' he said, 'I don't believe him.' He pressed the pistol harder against her temple.

'Noooo!' Her father pushed her aside and threw his body between her and the weapon. The gunshot rang out, a loud crack buzzing her ears, as they both fell back.

Pain struck through Abbie's arm. Lifting herself slightly, she turned – only to see her father clutching his throat. The bullet had passed through his neck, causing blood to spurt out uncontrollably, soaking his white shirt.

'Papa!'

She scrambled to his side, placing her hands over the wound. She tried to stop the flow of blood, but it poured from the hole in his neck, slipping through her fingers and tainting her white shirt with a dark red.

'No, no, no! Please stay with me. Papa! Don't go!'

Tears streamed down her cheeks as he reached up and gently squeezed her hand. His eyes, filled with love and pain, met hers.

'I'm so sorry, darling.' He exhaled one last breath, and his eyes closed.

'No! Papa!' She held him tightly against her chest. Grief swallowed her whole – but when she looked up at the men before her, rage blazed through the horrible pain, burning in her chest

'Bloody idiot,' Jack snapped, 'ye killed him! How are we gonna find it now? He'll have our 'eads!'

'How was I to know the idiot was to jump in front of

her?' Skinny barked, 'It was his fault. I wasn't gonna shoot.' He showed no remorse whatsoever.

'We need to leave. Now,' Jack growled.

'Not yet, we can't leave her alive. She'll talk.' Skinny's eyes were locked on her. Abbie's mind raced. She needed to do something – and fast.

'Fine. Kill her,' Jack said coldly. Skinny began reloading his pistol, and Abbie saw her chance. She lunged upward, knocking his arm aside as he finished. The pistol slipped from his grasp and skidded across the floor. But he recovered quickly. With his left hand, he struck her hard across the face, so hard she hit the ground, pain flaring through her temple. Dizzy and dazed, she watched Skinny scan the floor in search of the weapon but could not find where the pistol had landed; he turned to his partner. 'Give me your knife!' he shouted to Jack, 'I'll slit 'er throat!'

Her blurry vision sharpened just enough for her to catch the glint of metal under the sofa. With every ounce of strength she had left, Abbie stretched out her arm and grabbed the pistol's handle, gripping it so tightly her knuckles turned white.

Skinny's hand clamped around her ankle like an iron shackle, yanking her towards him with brutal force.

'Come 'ere, ye fucking wench! I'll show ye what is done to filthy rats like you.'

Abbie screamed, kicking and thrashing, but it was useless. For a man who looked like he hadn't eaten in days, he was shockingly strong – or otherwise extremely determined to harm her.

A door slammed somewhere behind them. The noise startled him, and he loosened his grip just enough for her to break free. She rolled onto her back, holding the pistol with both hands and locked eyes with him.

The fear turned to fury. Without hesitation, she pulled

the trigger.

The shot rang out.

His expression shifted from rage to disbelief. He touched his chest, stared perplexed at the blood dripping through his fingers, then looked up again– eyes wide, stunned.

He collapsed like a puppet whose strings had been cut. He landed in a heap, eyes still open, still staring at her. Abbie's hands began to tremble as she realised what she had done. *It was necessary*, she told herself, *I had no choice.*

But even when she could find truth in her actions, she felt the weight of it settle in her chest. She had taken someone's life – and she knew it would haunt her forever—no matter the reasons.

The room began to darken as if the candles were being snuffed out one by one. She heard a gunshot, glass shattering, distant voices, but every sound was like she was submerged in deep water, coming from far away. She couldn't make sense of the words.

Strong arms wrapped around her. 'Abigail! Abigail! Can you hear me?' The last thing she saw was a pair of deep blue eyes, filled with fear and desperation.

Then everything faded, and she vanished into the shadows, his voice still echoing in her mind.

***

Lord Alexander Crawford arrived at his best friend's house late at night. A home once brimming with music and laughter now stood silent, cloaked in darkness. He looked at the magnificent structure that had been in the Everleigh family for generations, and now… the place was empty.

Stephen Kensley, the 3rd Duke of Everleigh, had died not but a week ago in a horse accident. How? Alexander still couldn't comprehend it. Stephen had always been an exceptional horseman, better even than himself. He shook his head. No, Stephen had been better than him in every way: a better rider, a better husband, a better friend.

A better man.

And now he was gone, leaving behind his most precious treasure to him. – his seven years old daughter Georgina.

A part of Alexander felt deeply honoured that Stephen had trusted him to be her guardian. But another part of him whispered doubts: *What was he thinking?* He knew nothing about raising children. Could he really be the best option for the seven-year-old girl? He loved Georgina; there was no question, but being a father was another matter entirely.

That was why they had been staying at Georgina's grandmother's house for the past week. She was, after all, the last family the little girl had left. And it still felt too soon to bring her back to the house where they had lived.

He climbed the wide stone steps to the house, angry at himself, but also at his friend.

'What were you thinking, Stephen?' He muttered aloud. He pushed open the front door and stumbled over something on the floor. It rolled away across the entrance hall. He walked in and grabbed the oil lamp resting on top of the small oak table. Alexander opened the drawer, found the flint box he knew would be there, and lit the lamp.

As the flame flared to life, the scene before him came into focus – the house had been ransacked. He stepped inside, heart pounding, and made his way into Stephen's study. All the drawers in the room were open. Books and documents littered the floor in chaos.

It was then that the idea began to take hold – Stephen's death might not have been an accident. And if someone had wanted him dead, there was only one person who wanted to harm him.

And not just him, but also his business partner, Alan Clarkson.

Alexander turned back to the door and shouted out to John, his most trusted man, at the same time as he climbed onto the carriage's front seat beside him.

'To Alan Clarkson's house! Hurry, John! – Don't stop for anything until we get there.'

The moment the carriage stopped outside the Clarkson's residence in Berkeley Square, Alexander leapt out and sprinted to the gate. The front door was ajar.

Instinct kicking in, he drew his pistol and glanced back at John, still in the driver's seat. He nodded sharply. Alexander beckoned with his head to follow him inside. John grabbed his own weapon and jumped down to follow him.

He hurried across the path in quick strides and took the steps two at a time until he reached the door. At the threshold, he paused, listening carefully to the sounds coming from the house. There was an argument between two men– angry, heated – though he couldn't make out the words. It wasn't friendly, of that he was certain.

He pulled a second pistol from his boot and braced himself. Then, with his shoulder, he nudged the door open. As soon as he set foot inside the house, a gunshot rang out. The sound crashed through the house, shaking the walls.

Every muscle in his body tensed. He sprinted down the corridor towards the source of the sound at the end of the corridor. Just as he reached the door, a voice barked, 'I'll slit 'er throat!'

Alexander didn't hesitate. He kicked the door hard – it slammed open, crashing against the wall behind it.

The horrific scene that met him when the door flew

open made his heart clench. Two men stood over the bodies on the floor. Alan Clarkson and his wife lay motionless, their skin pale, their clothes soaked in blood.

Shock rooted him for just a moment – until rage surged through his veins.

Snapping into action, he raised his pistol and aimed at the man closest to the door, who now turned to face him, a knife glinting in his hand. A gunshot rang out, jarring them both – but it wasn't Alexander who fired.

He watched as the thin man dropped to his knees, a look of disbelief on his face.

Without wasting time, the man spun and bolted for the window. Alexander's pistol followed him, and before he could reach it, he fired the weapon just as he reached it. The shot struck his arm, but it wasn't enough. With a guttural cry, the man dove through the window and vanished into the night.

Alexander glanced at John, who was now standing next to him. No words were needed. John nodded and took off, out the door to chase after the fugitive.

Left in the quiet aftermath, Alexander turned back towards the room to look at the chilling picture – and that's when he saw her. Abigail Clarkson, Alan's daughter, laid on the floor, blood staining her white chemise, a pistol still clutched in her trembling hands. He had only seen her once before, a few months back, but he recognised her instantly. Her long blonde hair fell free over her shoulders as she stared blankly at the man she had just shot. Her whole body trembled. With her body shaking and her eyes lost in a trance, he watched as her fingers started losing their grip around the pistol and slowly dropped her arms to either side of her body.

Alexander crossed the room in two strides and dropped to his knees, gently taking the pistol from Abbie's hand. He wrapped an arm around her and pulled her limp body against his chest. Her head rested on his shoulder; her eyes barely open.

'Abigail,' he whispered, 'Can you hear me?' he called her name repeatedly, trying to keep her awake, but with no response. 'Abigail!'

She looked at him, though it was clear she didn't see him. Her gaze was distant, lost somewhere far from the room, until finally, her eyes fluttered closed.

'No!' Alexander bent his head, panic rising – then exhaled in relief when he felt the faint brush of her breath against his cheek.

A sound behind him made him twist around, aiming his remaining pistol at the door while shielding Abbie with his body.

Jacob stumbled into the room. The butler's eyes widened at the sight of the scene before him.

'Oh, my Lord,' he breathed, his voice trembling.

'Jacob,' Alexander said sharply, 'there's no time now. Please see to Alan and his wife.' The butler knelt beside him, eyes brimming as he looked at the couple lying still next to Abbie. He bowed his head and crossed himself slowly, reverently.

Then, he looked up at Alexander, shaking his head slowly from side to side. The silent gesture said everything.

His heart ached with pain and anger. Alexander turned back to Abigail; he would not let her end the same way, not if he could help it. Sliding one arm under her shoulders and another under her knees, he lifted her into his arms.

'Show me to her chamber,' he said.

Jacob led the way up the stairs. As they entered the room, he lit the candles around the space. Alexander rested Abbie's lax body carefully on the bed, brushing her blood-matted hair away from her face.

'Bring a candle closer,' he instructed, 'then send word to Doctor Walshman at once – you'll find him on New Bond Street, above Sotheby's. Tell him Lord Crawford requires his presence immediately.'

He paused, suddenly aware of the silence in the rest of the house. 'Where is everyone? Why is no-one awake with all this commotion?

Jacob placed a candle on the bedside table. 'I don't know, sir. I'll find out and I'll fetch the doctor myself if need be.' He hurried out of the room to follow Alexander's instructions.

Alexander turned his attention back to Abbie. The most visible injury was the cut on her cheek, and the bruises beginning to form around her eye. Bastards. They must've struck her hard for the bruises to show that soon. He examined the rest of her, trying to determine where the blood had come from. He wasn't sure how badly injured she would be. Most of it had pooled around her stomach and right arm. He carefully tore the sleeve of her blood-soaked nightgown to find a bullet embedded in her arm; the wound was still bleeding profusely. Thankfully, the bullet hadn't penetrated deeply, but it was enough not to be able to be removed easily; he would have to wait for the doctor.

Tearing the already damaged sleeve, he used it to make a tourniquet to prevent further bleeding. Abbie winced when she felt the pressure, but didn't wake up.

The front of her nightgown was stained crimson. He ripped a hole in the centre, exposing her pale stomach, and exhaled in relief. There were no other visible wounds.

The blood on her stomach wasn't hers. Satisfied she had no more injuries, he gently pulled the sheets over her to cover her body. Pain and fury surged through him at the sight of her so bruised and bloodied.

He had only seen her once but could never forget her golden hair or those honey-coloured eyes. It had been the day that he and Stephen visited Alan Clarkson's home. She was on her way out with her mother, and her father briefly introduced them before leaving.

He swore and ran a hand through his hair in frustration. Stephen was gone. Now Alan and his wife were dead.

Looking down at her battered face, he brushed a strand of hair from her cheek. Rage stirred again just thinking about what she had endured – witnessing her parents' murder, and still fighting for her life.

Just then, Jacob returned, followed by Doctor William Walshman.

'Doctor Walshman is here, sir.' Jacob announced.

Alexander stood and offered his hand. 'Thank you for coming so quickly, William.' The two men shook hands. They had known each other for several years. Shortly after Alexander enlisted in Her Majesty's service, the doctor was assigned to the same ship, which was fortunate for the entire crew, as his medical knowledge surpassed that of any doctor in London.

'Please, tell me what happened,' William said.

Alexander stepped aside, allowing him access to Abbie's bedside. The doctor sat and placed his bag on the bedside table. He examined the tourniquet on her arm while Alexander explained the events of the night.

'Two men broke into the house,' he said grimly. 'They killed Mr and Mrs Clarkson and tried to do the same to her. She's been shot in her right arm – the bullet is still inside. No other major wounds, aside from the cut on her cheek and the bruises on her face as far as I could see,' he added.

The doctor nodded, then turned to the butler. 'Jacob, could you send for hot water and clean cloths, please?

Jacob responded promptly. 'Of course, doctor.'

Before he left, Alexander stopped him. 'Where are the other servants, Jacob?'

Jacob's expression turned grave. 'When I went to the stables, I found Simon asleep. An unusual deep sleep, and it took effort to wake him. He seemed disoriented... I believe he was drugged, sir.' He lowered his voice just for Alexander to hear. 'I managed to wake him up, but he was in no condition to ride, so I fetched the good doctor myself and sent Simon to find the others. When I returned, everyone else seemed to be under the same effect. All have been accounted for – except the coachman, sir. He's nowhere to be found.'

'Find out whatever you can about him.'

'Yes, sir,' he added.

Alexander nodded. 'Thank you, Jacob. And once the doctor has finished here, see that he treats the rest of you as well.'

'Yes, milord. I'll check on them and ask Suzie to assist the doctor.' Jacob hurried out.

Alexander turned back to the doctor. 'How is she?' William looked up from his inspection and saw the worrying look on his face. 'She'll survive,' he said. 'But we need to remove that bullet as soon as possible.'

'Any other injuries?'

'No. The bruising on her cheek could have caused her to lose consciousness. Combined with blood loss, it's no surprise she hasn't woken.'

A few minutes later, Jacob returned with a disoriented-looking maid carrying clean cloths. Alexander took them from her and gently encouraged her to sit.

'Alexander,' the doctor said, 'please hold her arm. She may wake. This is going to hurt terribly, and I need her to be still; any movement can cause more damage.'

Alexander braced her body as the doctor extracted the bullet with a pair of tweezers. Abbie stirred, her eyes snapping open. She screamed in agony – then collapsed again into unconsciousness.

When the bullet was finally removed, the doctor bandaged the wound and cleaned the cut on her cheek. He looked at those present in the room.

He turned to the maid. 'Are you feeling better, girl?' Suzie, visibly recovering the colour on her face, nodded.

'Good. Bring fresh linens and a clean nightgown. Let's get her changed.'

Suzie began gathering the items while Alexander and the doctor stepped outside the room, giving her privacy.

Outside the door, William turned to him. 'She will heal. She needs rest. I will come back tomorrow to see how she is doing. It would be good if someone could stay with her all night. Send word when she wakes up.'

Alexander nodded. 'We'll see to it.' He shook his friend's hand. 'Thank you again, William. Before leaving, can you see that everyone else is tended to?'

The doctor smiled. 'Of course.'

Jacob appeared at the top of the stairs. 'I will take you to them, Doctor.' The two men descended together, leaving Alexander alone in the hall outside Abbie's chamber.

Alexander stood just outside the room, waiting for Suzie to finish changing Abigail. He would not leave before seeing her. He wanted to erase the memory of her bloodied body, the screams of pain, but he knew those images would stay with him for a long time. Just then, John came running up the stairs.

'Did you find him?' Alexander asked. 'No, sir. I followed him as far as Piccadilly, but I lost him there.'

'Damn it!' Alexander clenched his jaw, growing impatient. 'How did they get in? Did you search the house?'

'Yes, my lord. Every room. None of the windows or doors were forced – someone must have let them in.'

Alexander nodded grimly. 'Jacob said the coachman is missing. He's the only one unaccounted for. Is everyone else awake now?'

'Yes,' John confirmed. 'They're still dazed, but other than terrible headaches, everyone seems to be unharmed.'

'Good. At least no-one else was seriously hurt. Talk to the others. Find out what they know about that coachman – where he's gone. We need to know whether he is involved with what happened tonight.'

'Yes, my lord.'

As John turned to go, Suzie stepped out of the room, holding a bundle of bloodied clothes in her arms.

'Thank you, Suzie,' Alexander said gently. 'Now go and let the doctor look at you. John, help her, please.'

John took the garments from her and offered his arm. 'Come. Suzie, is it?' The maid nodded, tired but grateful. 'Yes.' He gave her a small smile, gently guiding her. 'I'm John.' She smiled faintly in return, allowing him to guide her down the stairs.

Alone again, Alexander entered the room. Abigail was sleeping. He sat quietly beside her and caressed her cheek, brushing a lock of her forehead, careful not to hurt her with his touch. 'I'll find them', he whispered. 'And they'll regret ever laying a hand on you.' He leaned forward and pressed a soft kiss to her forehead.

He meant every word. He would find them, no matter how long it took. And he would not rest until every single one of them was dead.

CHAPTER 2

Abbie's nightmares began to fade as she emerged from the depths of sleep. But the fear and despair lingered in her heart – a heavy weight on her chest – because deep down, she worried that what she'd lived through wasn't just a dream at all. She tried to open her eyes, but gave up almost immediately, her eyelids heavier than stone. Her head throbbed, a sharp ache pulsing in her temple, echoing like a drum.

A ray of light burned across her face like a naked flame close to her skin. She tried to raise a hand to shield herself, but a sudden, excruciating pain tore through her arm, and she screamed as she attempted to lift her arm.

Someone stirred beside her.

'Miss Abbie?' came a soft voice. A gentle hand touched her shoulder. 'Don't move, miss – you'll hurt yourself.' Abbie slowly parted her lips, but even the slight movement made her flinch. Her entire body ached as though she'd been trampled by a horse.

She managed to open her eyes just enough to see Suzie leaning over her with a worried expression. But the light stung too much, and she closed them again. She heard Suzie run to the door and call out with urgency.

'Mrs White! Mrs White! She's awake!' She shouted by the door and hurried back to sit by her side, taking her hand gently.

Abbie winced at the loud noise, and Suzie lowered her voice, noticing her discomfort.

'How are you feeling, Miss Abbie?' she whispered.

Abbie cracked her eyes open again just enough to see the worrying look on Suzi's face. 'Can I bring you something, Miss?'

Abbie took a deep breath and whispered. 'Water, please', she said with a hoarse voice.

'Of course.'

Suzie poured the water from the jug into a glass and helped her drink slowly, supporting her with care. She drank slowly and then gave the glass back to Suzi. 'Suzie?' Abbie whispered. 'Yes, miss?'

'What happened?'

Suzie hesitated; her face shadowed with pity. But, before she could explain, Mrs White appeared at the door. 'Oh, my dear child!' she cried, rushing to the bed and taking Suzi's place beside her.

Mrs White had been part of the family since she was only five years of age. Hired alongside Jacob when her father's company began to prosper, she had become like a second mother.

Her thoughts turned instantly to her parents. The ache returned, and tears began to form in her eyes.

'Mrs White?' Her voice cracked. The memory was still hazy, but the dread settling in her chest told her the truth she was trying not to face. Fear struck her, afraid of the answer to the question she was about to ask, even when she already knew the answer.

'Mrs White...my parents?'

The older woman's eyes filled again, her voice trembling. 'I'm so sorry, child. I'm so very sorry.'

Abbie let out a shuddering breath. 'No...' Her lower lip quivered. Tears spilt down her cheeks uncontrollably.

Mrs White wiped away the tears running down her face, whispering soothing words to comfort, but nothing could take away the pain tearing through her. Abbie took another deep breath, heavier this time. The need to know what happened that night overcame the fear of hearing the truth from Mrs White's lips. She needed answers – even if they hurt.

She tried to reach for Mrs White's hand, but as she lifted her arm, a fresh wave of pain stopped her short. She looked down to see the bandage, darkened with dried blood. 'What happened to me?'

'There were two intruders last night,' Mrs White said quietly. 'We… we don't know what they wanted. They…' her voice faltered. she could see how the woman struggled to say the words aloud. 'They hurt your family, dear.'

The memories came back like lightning flashes: the man in her room, the study, her mother's lifeless body on the floor, her father's scream, the gunshot.

'My father…' She looked back at her arm. Her father used his own body to shield her from them. 'Where are my p…' Her voice faded before she could finish the question, but Mrs White answered anyway.

'They're downstairs,' she said softly.

Abbie blinked away tears. Her voice was steadier now, though hollow. 'Is everyone else alright?'

A new image surfaced. Jacob – lying on the floor outside her room. 'Jacob?'

Abbie grabbed her arm. Mrs White placed a hand over hers. 'He is fine, dear – just a headache. We tried to get him to rest, but you know how stubborn he is. The others are recovering. The doctor saw everyone last night after tending to you.'

Abbie frowned. 'What do you mean by everyone? Were they all injured?'

Mrs White sighed. 'Daniel brought wine for the household staff last night. We believe he laced it with something. We can't remember anything, not clearly.'

'Daniel? Papa's coachman?'

'Yes, miss. Jacob was the only one who didn't drink. The rest of us didn't realise what happened until he came to wake us all up.'

Abbie's brow knitted. 'You said two intruders?' Abbie dug into her memories; she knew someone else was in the house that night. 'But I saw someone else.'

A new voice answered her. 'Yes, miss.' Jacob stood in the doorway, his head wrapped in a bandage. He looked tired, older somehow, and Abbie could see the exhaustion and pain in the butler's eyes.

'It was Lord Crawford who found you.'

The name stirred something in her memory, but it was blurry. She tried to remember where she'd heard it before, but the pain throbbed in her skull at the effort as she tested her memory.

He stepped into the room and stood beside Mrs White. 'You need to rest, miss,' he said gently. 'There will be time for questions later.'

Part of her wanted to press on, to understand everything, but the exhaustion was too intense. She felt nauseous just being awake.

She let her head sink back into the pillow and turned her eyes to Jacob.

'You should rest too. Please, Mrs White – he needs to rest.' And with that, the shadows crept in again, taking her back into the quiet.

As she drifted, one last image lingered. A pair of piercing blue eyes – the most intense she had ever seen – staring straight into her soul.

***

She didn't know how long she had slept, but the sun was already setting when she finally opened her eyes.

Glancing around, she found Suzie still by her side. The young woman had become more than a maid to Abbie – she was a confidant, a friend.

They were the same age, and for Abbie, it had always been inconceivable to treat Suzie as anything less than an equal. Suzie sat slumped in a chair, her head dropped to one side – she had fallen asleep too.

Poor thing, Abbie thought.

She pushed herself upright with a soft moan, pain flaring in her injured arm and across the bruises that mottled her body. Suzie stirred and opened her eyes. 'Miss, how are you feeling?' She rushed to help her sit up straighter.

'I'm sorry, Suzie. I didn't mean to wake you. You must be exhausted.'

Suzie fluffed the pillow and gently guided her back.

'I'm not the one who was shot, Miss Abbie. You need rest far more than I do. I only have a mild headache, and it's already fading. Let us take care of you now, alright?'

Abbie smiled at her. She was lucky to have her. Still, it was unfamiliar, allowing someone to take care of her. She had always been the one doing the caring. But today, she had no strength or will to resist.

A loud grumble from her stomach broke the silence. Suzie heard it and grinned. 'Shall I bring you some food?'

Abbie gave a sheepish smile. 'Yes, please.'

Suzie turned towards the door, but Abbie caught her hand. 'Send Jacob up, will you? I… I need to speak with him.'

Suzie placed a warm hand over hers. 'Right away, miss.' And she left the room.

Alone again, Abbie looked around. There was no trace of the previous night. Everything was in place, as if nothing had happened the night before. But it did.

The ache in her chest returned, and tears welled in her

eyes – until a soft knock at the door pulled her back.

'Miss Abigail? It's Jacob.' Said the butler from the corridor.

'Come in,' she said, though her voice was barely more than a whisper. He entered and bowed, waiting near the door.

'Please, Jacob, come in.'

He approached slowly and sat in the chair Suzie had just vacated. 'How are you feeling, Miss Abigail?'

'As well as I can be, Jacob,' she said softly.

His eyes, always so gentle, held a paternal kindness. He had always treated her with respect and care, like a second father.

'You called for me. How may I assist you?'

Abbie took a breath. It was time to be brave.

'I need you to help me fill in the blanks, Jacob. I need to know what happened last night. All of it. Please don't leave anything out; I want the truth.'

Jacob nodded solemnly.

'Last night, Daniel brought wine for the staff. He said he'd found it at the market and poured a glass for everyone. I declined – on account of the doctor's advice. My health doesn't allow it. We stayed in the kitchen for a while, but everyone grew tired, so I sent them to bed. I made my final rounds – closing doors, blowing out candles in the house. Your father was still in his study. He said he'd be working late and told me to retire for the night. I went to my rooms to write some letters. But a few hours later, I heard strange noises. I thought it was someone stirring in the bedrooms. When I went up the service stairs, someone struck me. There was a sharp pain in my head, and then… nothing.'

Abbie gasped. 'You didn't see him?'

Jacob shook his head. 'No, miss. I could not see the man who attacked me. I felt the pain in the side of my head, and shortly after, I lost consciousness. I do not know how long I was in that state; when I started to come around, I heard a gunshot. I forced myself to go downstairs. And when I reached the study...' His voice caught, and his pale face grew even paler.

'I'm sorry to make you relive it, Jacob,' Abbie said gently. She reached out and touched his arm.

The butler breathed deeply and looked at her. He brought his hand to his head, and Abbie touched his arm to encourage him to continue.

'The door to the study was open. I steadied myself and went in. Mr and Mrs Clarkson were on the floor. There was a stranger – dead – and Lord Crawford was there too.'

Abbie blinked. 'Lord Crawford? Who is he? You mentioned him before.'

Jacob nodded. 'He was an acquaintance of your father, Miss Abigail.'

A faint memory returned – a tall man, whom her father had introduced her to as she was leaving the house with her mother. 'He was here a few weeks ago, wasn't he?'

'Yes, he came with Lord Everleigh.'

She remembered now. That was a name she knew. 'Lord Everleigh of Oxfordshire?'

'The very same.'

'Did they have business together?'

'I believe so, but I can't say for sure, miss. I know he knew Mr Clarkson and Lord Everleigh, but that visit was the first time I saw Lord Crawford.'

Abbie frowned. Something didn't sit right. 'Then what was he doing here last night?'

'I don't know,' Jacob admitted. 'With everything that happened, I forgot to ask.'

Abbie nodded. 'Do not worry, Jacob. Continued,

please.'

He nodded and proceeded with the difficult narration of the events. 'He must have thought I was one of the intruders; he raised his pistol at first. But once he recognised me, he asked me to check on Mr and Mrs Clarkson. It was too late.' He paused, voice breaking. 'I am so sorry, Miss Abigail. I was too late.'

He buried his face in his hands. She had never seen him so broken, but no one in this house had gone through such traumatic events.

This had been a house of joy and laughter where every resident was treated with respect and affection. 'You do not need to apologise for something that wasn't your fault, Jacob,' she said, gently. 'Those men did that. Not you. Even if you'd come sooner, you could've been killed too.' He looked at her, his eyes expressed the sadness in his heart, heavy with grief. He was a good man, and Abbie knew how deep his pain was.

'Tell me, what happened next?' she asked.

'Lord Crawford told me to show him to your room. After that, I tried to wake Simon to fetch the doctor, but he was in a deep sleep – drugged, I suspect. I went to look for the good Doctor myself, and when I returned with Doctor Walshman, we roused the others. It took us a while to wake them from their deep sleep.'

'What happened to them?'

'The doctor believes the wine Daniel gave us was laced with opium. Enough to make them all sleep and not hear a sound.'

Abbie's brow furrowed. She knew about the effects of opium only through books, and she also knew it wasn't an easy thing to find or a cheap one either. Daniel certainly couldn't have afforded to pay for it himself. 'He must have had help.'

Jacob nodded. 'I believe so.'

'You mentioned a doctor Walshman?'

'He's a friend of Lord Crawford's. He treated you first, then checked on the rest of us. No one was badly hurt, thank God'

'And Lord Crawford?'

'He stayed until the doctor finished. Then he left.' Jacob flinched as he moved. His head must still be aching.

'You should rest now, Jacob,' Abbie said. 'I've kept you too long.'

'I'm fine, miss.'

She gave him a knowing look. 'Let Mrs White take care of things for the day. I do not want you to get ill. Please?' She begged.

He hesitated, then nodded. 'Alright, miss. I'll lie down.' Abbie squeezed his hand and gave him a half-smile.

As he turned to go, she courageously asked the painful question. 'One more thing, Jacob…Where have they taken my parents?' The words barely made it past the knot in her throat.

He looked at her, eyes soft. 'The constable took them to the morgue. Doctor Walshman arranged everything. He will prepare them for the funeral. Shall I make arrangements for Oxfordshire? I thought you might prefer to bury them near Redwood House.'

'Yes,' she whispered. 'Thank you, Jacob. I also think my parents would prefer to rest in the countryside rather than here in London. Besides, I wouldn't want to stay here much longer. As soon as I'm well enough to travel, I'd like to return to Redwood House.'

'I will prepare everything for our departure, miss.' When he closed the door behind him, Abbie let the tears fall freely.

The funeral. She would have to plan the funeral.

Her heart ached as if someone was squeezing it in their fist. The grief seized her, sharp and merciless. She sobbed for her parents and the loss of the most profound love she had ever felt, love that would no longer be there to comfort her.

She curled beneath the sheets and let the darkness surround her, letting the sorrow consume her as she drifted, once more, into sleep.

CHAPTER 3

Abbie tightened her cloak to ward off the shiver that ran through her body. She didn't know if it was caused by the cold wind, stubbornly refusing to yield even at the threshold of spring, or by the sight unfolding before her eyes.

'We are here today to celebrate the life of Alan Clarkson and his beloved wife…'

She tried to listen to the priest's words, but they felt distant, like echoes in another world. He stood just a few feet away, yet she could barely hear him. Her focus remained fixed on the engraved headstone surrounded by beautiful white flowers – a striking contrast to the cold, grey stone. She read the words silently to herself.

In memory of Alan and Victoria Clarkson, loving father and mother of Abigail. Departed this life 18th March 1787.

She blinked, dismissing the tears threatening to run down her cheeks, and drew in a steadying breath to recompose herself. She had to stay strong. Not only for her, but for her parents.

Weakness is something people feed on, Abbie. Never show them your weakness, for they will use it against you.

Her father's words echoed in her mind. He had built a fortune from nothing with his hard work, but envy was a dangerous force. And she couldn't shake the thought out of her head that it was precisely envy that had caused them to now be buried in front of her.

There was still no trace of the man who had attacked

her – the one who had left her bruised and broken. No one had seen him flee the house, and in a city like London, a man like that could vanish without a trace. He could be hiding anywhere, and with no clues to follow, there wasn't much anyone could do. Still, she refused to give up. Not after what she'd seen in her father's study at Redwood House, the whole place turned upside down. It was almost certain that whoever the bandit was, he was looking for the damned documents for which her parents were killed.

'I swear I'll find out who did this, Papa,' she whispered to herself.

Standing next to her was her Aunt Agatha. She had lost her only sister, and Abbie knew the woman's grief was just as deep as her own, for she would forever miss not only her sister but her best friend. Aunt Agatha was a small woman with an incredibly tender heart. Her long silver hair was neatly pinned at the back of her head, framing a gentle, heart-shaped face. Abbie had never known anyone more generous or selfless. She always put others before herself – even her intolerable husband.

Only days earlier, Abbie had argued with Uncle Harper. He was a short-tempered and arrogant man, a man raised in wealth his entire life, who disregarded everyone he felt was inferior to him.

When she decided to bury her parents in Oxfordshire near the family home, he ranted endlessly about the cost of transporting the bodies from London. As if, for Abbie, that would be something that mattered. She knew her parents would want to be buried in the place where they had built their little family, and that was the most important thing for her. Who cared how much it would cost?

Abbie thought with sadness in her heart of the injustice of life. Her grandparents had cared only for the money her uncle could offer, not the happiness of their daughter. Aunt Agatha had always been too good for him – too kind, too gentle. Not like him, a man who only thought about himself. He hadn't even attended the funeral with her, choosing instead to sulk at home.

Aunt Agatha squeezed Abbie's hand. 'What did you say, darling?'

Abbie placed her hand over her aunt's and smiled faintly 'Nothing, Aunt.'

Abbie glanced up at the gathered crowd around the grave. Many familiar faces who had come to pay their respects were present – neighbours from the area, family friends, and even a few from London, stood out in the crowd with their fine coats and elegant gowns. It wasn't surprising. that so many people had come to their funeral.

Her mother, as well as her aunt Agatha, were actively involved in charity work, often organising fundraisers for children in need. For that reason, she was well known in the social circle. As for her father, his rapid wealth growth, due to his excellent eye for business, earned him a reputation and status in London circles. Not just in the trading world but also in society, for association with well-positioned business partners and nobility friendships.

Abbie had no doubt people respected him, but she knew that with money came false friendships, and she saw a number of those among the crowd. People who had come not out of love, but for appearances.

One figure stood apart from the rest.

Separated from the rest of the funeral entourage. A man of striking bearing lingered at the edge of the gathering. Even from a distance, there was something oddly familiar about him. His long, dark brown hair, loose in an uncommon fashion for the time, framed his angular features, for Abbie could not deny he was extremely handsome, and she couldn't, or better said, she didn't want to stop looking at him.

He looked back at her without any reservation, his eyes locked on hers with quiet intensity. For a moment, it felt like time itself had stopped, and they were the only two souls in that cemetery.

Then the crowd stirred, around her, drawing her back to reality, realising the service had ended. She looked at those who began approaching her to offer their condolences.

And when she looked back to where the man was, he was gone.

'Abigail?'

Startled, she turned her head, surprised to see Uncle Harper standing behind her. *Where did he come from?* Aunt Agatha visibly tensed next to her. The sharp stench of whisky hit Abbie's nose, and she instinctively leaned away quickly, avoiding inhaling more of its stinky aroma. Not even for his own sister in law's funeral, had he resisted drinking – though at least she had to be thankful he had bathed, masking the reek of whisky a little but not enough to eliminate it.

He tilted his head towards a stranger approaching. The man wore a powdered wig tied with delicate silk lace, contrasting oddly with the cold expression on his face. His beady, round eyes looked at her most disturbingly, provoking a feeling of uneasiness that did not please her.

He took her hand without asking, trapping it between his own, not leaving her a choice but to wait for her release. 'Miss Clarkson, allow me to introduce myself. I'm Phillip Braxton. I was acquainted with your father.'

Abbie nodded, just praying for the man to leave and give her hand back. 'My condolences. Your father was a fine man. If there is anything I can assist you with, please don't hesitate to ask.'

He bowed and pressed a clammy kiss to her gloved hand. Abbie silently thanked Aunt Agatha for her good sense of propriety and for insisting she wear gloves – it spared her the full feel of his damp lips over her skin. She suppressed a shudder. After all, the man was offering his condolences, but still, a chill ran through Abbie's body.

Carefully, she withdrew her hand as discreetly as possible so that he wouldn't realise how uncomfortable it made her feel. Decorum demanded grace, even in the most unpleasant situations.

Holding her hands together, she said, 'I appreciate your kind words, Mr Braxton,' she said with a tight smile. 'And thank you for attending the funeral.'

She looked to the next person waiting to talk with her. He moved aside with a bow, but added before leaving, 'Remember, I'm here if you need anything.'

There's something not right about that man. She thought, ignoring the comment as graciously as she could.

The line of mourners stretched on. She kept accepting condolences from the funeral attendees for what seemed like an eternity when she just wanted to go back home and hide. Collapsed in her bed, buried her face in her pillow and tried to forget the past week had ever happened.

Finally, and with immense relief, the last familiar faces approached – Mr and Mrs Bates.

Mrs Bates's kind features helped lessen the tightness in her heart. 'Mrs Bates.' Abbie greeted the woman warmly, embracing her. She turned to the man beside her, looking at her with paternal love. 'Mr Bates.' She held her hand and squeezed it softly.

The couple had lived for years in a modest home on the edge of the estate, tending the crops and livestock for her father with unwavering loyalty.

'Thank you very much for coming,' she said, forcing a smile to lessen the worry in the woman's eyes.

Mrs Bates took her hands. 'Oh, child, I'm so sorry. Your parents...' her voice cracked.

Abbie held her hands, understanding her pain because her heart was also aching.

'They were good people,' Mrs Bates continued. 'They didn't deserve what happened to them.'

The woman touched her bruised cheek with maternal care. 'Neither did you, my dear. You poor thing.' Her voice trembled.

Even a week later, her cheek was still a bit swollen. The colour had changed from black to purple, and now, green was surrounding the side of her face and her left eye.

She had been so good at controlling her emotions today, but her soft touch melted her heart. A tear slid down Abbie's face, unable to prevent it.

'Your parents will be missed, Miss Abbie.' Mr Bates said quietly. 'They were exceptional people and loved by everyone in the area. My most sincere condolences.'

'Thank you.'

The man placed his hands on his wife's shoulders to gently guide her away. 'Come, darling, I'm sure she would like to go home and rest; she must be tired.'

Abbie nodded, holding Mrs Bates's hand. 'Thank you both for coming here. Seeing you has done me good. I'll visit you soon.' Mrs Bates smiled at her and kissed her hand in a maternal gesture before she left.

Once everyone had gone, she turned back to the grave. The gravedigger was nearly finished covering their grave with soil. She drew a long, deep breath and turned toward Aunt Agatha, who stood beside a now swaying Uncle Harper, moving like a pendulum, unable to hide how drunk he was any longer.

'Let's go home now, please,' Abbie said softly. 'I'm tired and in need of rest after this morning.'

She looped her arm through her aunt's, and they walked together to the waiting carriage, Uncle Harper stumbling after them.

Inside the blue velvet interior, Abbie contemplated the vast fields from her seat by the window. The breeze gently waved her blonde curls that had slipped from her tidy bun at the bottom of her head. Normally, she enjoyed the countryside ride – but today, the short travel from the graveyard to the house felt like an eternity with Uncle Harper's voice rambling in the background. The smell of alcohol invaded the carriage, turning her stomach.

The handkerchief she held against her nose did little to block the stench of his breath. She had to resist the urge to stuff the white fabric in his mouth to silence him.

Because of this reason, a headache bloomed behind her eyes, and she tried to ignore him until one word cut through the fog: *marriage*.

She turned to find him staring at her, waiting expectantly for an answer.

'Well, girl? What do you have to say?' He said, dragging the words.

'Pardon me, Uncle Harper, but I did not hear what you said.'

Abbie looked back at him. He snorted, pushing his stinky breath in Abbie's direction once more. 'I said,' he slurred, 'you need to wed – and soon.'

Abbie straightened in her seat, not wanting to believe what she had just heard. 'No, I don't.' She said it with the certainty that she had always shown, looking directly into his eyes.

His face darkened. Her response clearly annoyed him, for he raised his voice in reply. 'You can't expect to remain unmarried for much longer, child! Someone must handle your father's affairs, and I would not have you depending on us.'

Abbie was about to unleash a flurry of insults when her aunt carefully placed a hand on her husband's arm.

'Harper, please, not now.' He shook her off with a grunt, eyes flashing. Those kinds of actions made Abbie's blood boil with rage.

Abbie needed to distract her uncle by directing his anger at her, knowing that her aunt would pay the consequences later if she didn't. She looked at her aunt, silently asking her to let it go, and then turned her attention to her uncle, who looked at her red with rage.

'Uncle Harper, I won't marry just to suit propriety,' she said evenly. 'I will marry someday – but not now. I'm in mourning ,and at this moment, it is the last thing on my mind. I just lost my parents. And regardless of what you believe, my father taught me well. I helped him run his affairs, and I'll continue to do so. because I have been doing it for some time with him. I don't need or want a husband, and I won't be forced into marriage.'

'You need guidance,' he snapped. 'I am your guardian now–'

'No, you are not! I am four and twenty, Uncle. I am legally free to do as I please. And I will not be forced into marriage!'

His eye twitched, and she knew she had struck a nerve. It almost made her laugh. Abbie saw how his previous bravery had given way to insecurity. He leaned back in his seat, turning his head to look through the window, muttering, 'We'll see…'

Abbie didn't reply. She knew this conversation was far from over, but for now, she just wanted peace. She put a curl behind her ear and turned back to the window, desperate for quiet.

The carriage began its ascent up the long road towards Redwood House. She watched the white stone walls come into view.

The house was large and elegant, its majestic windows always made her feel proud to call Redwood House her home. The beautiful country house was of a considerable size. With ivy trailing from the grand entrance in thick green strands, Abbie loved the stunning contrast between the white stone and the green of the ivy leaves. Many had urged her father to cut it back, but he had refused simply because she loved it. It was a house quite unusual for a man without a title, but her father had worked hard to give his family a home.

Looking at the place she grew up, she knew that the moment she opened the front door, everything would be different. The house that knew so much love will now be empty.

There would be no mother to greet her at the door, wrapping her in her tender arms, kissing her forehead and telling her that her hair was all messy after her horse rides, laughing with her. And no father to guide her through the roughness of the world, to teach her about math, literature, science… she will cherish those precious moments forever. She could not have wished for better parents, parents who loved her until their last breath.

The carriage pulled up to the front steps, and Abbie watched Jacob hurry down the steps from the front door to open the carriage door. Unsurprisingly, her Uncle Harper ignored all sense of decorum and shoved his way out of the carriage first, offering no help to her or her aunt. Abbie shook her head in disbelief, but one glance at her aunt's sad expression made her regret the gesture. The poor woman bore enough already, carrying the weight of having such a disgraceful husband, to add to the embarrassment she must have felt for his constant behaviour.

Abbie leaned forward and took her hand. 'Come, Aunt Agatha. Let's go inside. It's been a long day.'

Her aunt nodded, forcing a shy smile as her eyes brimmed with sorrow. 'Yes, dear. It has indeed.'

Jacob offered his hand as Agatha descended, and Abbie followed, accepting his help.

'Thank you, Jacob,' she said.

'Miss,' he replied with a respectful bow, as she used his hand to help descend the last step from the carriage.

They walked together to the front door. Abbie paused before stepping inside. The house had never been so quiet, so empty. It had once echoed with the sound of her mother's piano, laughter drifting from the drawing room, but not this time. Now, there was only silence.

Her aunt gave her arm a gentle squeeze to give her courage, and together, they entered.

Mrs White was already waiting. She had arrived earlier with the other servants and stood just inside the drawing room. Without saying a word, she opened her arms. Abbie allowed herself to be folded into the familiar embrace of the woman who had cared for her like a second mother, spoiling her and reprehending her every time she misbehaved, something that happened often when she was a young girl.

Feeling her strength slip away, Abbie stepped back with a small, trembling smile. Tears rolled down the housekeeper's cheeks.

'Oh, Mrs White... I know you miss her too.' Abbie placed a comforting hand on her arm.

'I surely do, child. I'll never forget her.' Mrs White dabbed at her face with her apron, sniffed, and tried to compose herself. 'Come, are you hungry?' she said, touching her cheek.

'Not so much,' Abbie admitted, 'but I think some tea

and biscuits would do my aunt some good – if it's not too much trouble.'

'I'll see to it. But you must eat something as well, child. You look pale as chalk.' She touched Abbie's cheek. 'I'll bring you some of those little sandwiches Jane does for you. You've never been able to resist them!'

At the mention of Jane, Abbie managed a more genuine smile. It had been days since she'd crossed more than three words with her childhood friend, the best baker in the region.

Jane's mother was their cook, Mrs May, and they had come to their house when Jane was a baby. Despite the age difference between the two young women, their friendship blossomed through the years. Jane had inherited her mother's talent and far surpassed everyone's expectations when her interest grew towards baking. She had become an incredibly skilled young woman.

Mrs White continued her soft reprimand: 'You will fall ill if you keep going on like this, child. You have been eating like a mouse and need to put something in that belly of yours.'

Knowing there was no point in arguing, Abbie nodded and smiled. 'Thank you.'

She led her aunt into the drawing room. Aunt Agatha sank into the sofa while Abbie walked to the glass doors overlooking the back garden.

Her mother's garden.

She had personally taken it upon herself to ensure that it was among the best in the region. Daisies, lilies, roses, and even flowers from other countries had caught her mother's eye when she strolled through Covent Garden. Beautiful flowers of different colours and shapes filled the garden with life.

She remembered their walks at an ambling pace,

enjoying the mutual company, arms intertwined, and talking about life, the future, the garden, everything and nothing in particular. A tear slid down her cheek, one of many in recent days. She hadn't felt like herself since that awful night. The light inside her had dimmed, and her laughter had gone; they had simply disappeared with the death of her parents, and she didn't know if she would be able to get them back.

Her aunt's voice pulled her from her thoughts.

It had been happening to her constantly for days. Losing herself in the memories without paying notice to anyone around her.

'She loved sitting here,' she said softly.

Abbie came to sit beside her and wrapped her arm around her shoulders. With a sob, her aunt started crying, and Abbie knew she couldn't do anything but hold her in her arms and wait. Wait, until the pain tightening her chest eased.

The door burst open to let the chubby figure of her uncle through. Her aunt quickly sat upright, wiping her tears away. Abbie turned a cold gaze on the intruder. He scowled at her with disdain and took a sip from the glass in his hand. By God, it wasn't even noon yet, and he was already drinking. He was going to drink his way through her father's wine cellar in less than a week if she didn't get rid of him soon.

'We need to finish our conversation,' he said, slumping in a chair opposite them, nearly spilling his drink. The chair sank profusely under his uncle's weight.

'And which conversation are you referring to, Uncle?' Abbie asked coolly. She would not tolerate his rudeness.

'Why, your marriage, of course!'

Abbie exhaled sharply and stood from her seat; tiredness reflected in her voice. 'I already told you, Uncle Harper, I'm not getting married. You can save your breath.'

His face flushed red. 'Do not talk to me in that tone, child!'

Abbie's temper threatened to spiral out of control. Why now? Couldn't he wait until she had time to grieve? Not that she would change her mind on the subject, but this wasn't the time to talk about this, not when she had just buried her parents. 'I am not a child,' she snapped, barely holding back the fury in her voice. 'And you know very well that my father never forced me into marriage. You couldn't even wait until they were buried to start contradicting his wishes.'

'I'm your uncle!'

'Which doesn't give you any authority over me.'

'How insolent!' He said as his face turned into shapes of red that Abbie had never seen before.

'Insolent?' she echoed, stepping forward. 'Insolent is arriving drunk at your sister-in-law's funeral. Insolence is ignoring your family for years, except when you needed money. And now...' her voice dropped, cold and pointed. 'Now you dare come here and pretend that you care about me when the reality is that you are in this house just to see what you can get out of here. I wouldn't be surprised if you already had a husband picked out – someone who'd benefit *you*.'

Her temper finally erupted. Years of biting her tongue in the name of peace exploded into the room.

She shook her head. 'I don't have time or inclination to have this conversation with you, so please, uncle, let me be.' The anger she had contained all her life, out of respect for her parents, went out without any control.

A part of her shouldn't have been surprised by her uncle's reaction, who shot to his feet as if the sofa was on fire and approached her in a threatening manner.

Her aunt, until then silent, stood. 'Enough, Harper!'

Both turned to her, stunned.

Abbie had never seen her react like this, with such strength and certainty.

'You do not talk to me like that, woman! When we get home…'

'She's not going anywhere with you,' Abbie said, stepping in between them, protecting her aunt. 'I think it's best you leave now. You are no longer welcome in this house.'

The raised voices must have stirred the rest of the household, for Jacob and Simon appeared in the doorway, followed closely by Mrs White.

Uncle Harper's eyes blazed. stretching his neck to look over Abbie's shoulder. 'You'll regret this, Agatha.'

'I doubt she will,' Abbie said. 'Jacob! Please see that my uncle leaves the house immediately.'

'With pleasure, Miss Abbie.' The butler smiled faintly. He despised any man who drank that much and behaved in such a manner.

As Jacob and Simon escorted the grumbling man out, Abbie felt a wave of relief at the sound of the door shutting behind him, and the shouting stopped. Her aunt collapsed into a chair, burying her face in her hands. 'Oh, Abbie… what have I done?'

Abbie sat next to her. 'You've done nothing wrong. He's a miserable rat who doesn't deserve you!'

Her aunt looked up, startled and shocked by her words. 'Don't look at me like that,' Abbie added. 'I kept silent because Mother told me we shouldn't interfere, but I could no longer refrain from speaking my mind.'

What Abbie saw in her eyes was absolute terror 'But when I return, he will be furious.'

She finally realised what her aunt meant. 'Has he ever hurt you, Aunt?' Abbie asked gently.

Tears spilt down her aunt's cheeks.

Abbie's anger rose once more. 'You will not go back to him. Ever.'

'But I must go back! He'll come for me. I have never defied him before... And what if he hurts you? I will never forgive myself if something happens to you because of me.'

'All the more reason not to return,' Abbie said, gripping her hands. 'I'll hire guards to protect us if I must, but that miserable excuse of a man will never lay a hand on you ever. He will not harm you again!'

Abbie held her trembling hands. 'Come, Aunt, let's get you to bed. Mrs White will bring you something to eat upstairs.' Mrs White was at the door, and the housekeeper nodded, disappearing towards the kitchen.

Aunt Agatha let Abbie guide her to her rooms. Once in her bed, she covered her with a blanket before returning to the drawing room.

Mrs White was waiting for her back at the bottom of the stairs.

'Jane is preparing a lemon balm to help calm Mrs Agatha's nerves. And your refreshments are in the drawing room. I know you said you weren't hungry, but you *must* eat something, dear.' She took Abbie's hand. 'Please, child. For me?'

Her begging eyes melted her heart. 'I promise, Mrs White.' The older woman smiled, clearly sceptical.

On the table beside the sofa sat a tray with tea and sandwiches. As promised, Abbie poured herself a cup of tea and took a bite of the delicate triangles. 'See? I'm eating.'

The housekeeper smiled back at her and, raising a brow, she asked. 'What was all that shouting about?'

'Nothing to worry about, Mrs White.'

'Don't try to fool me, child. That man doesn't have a good bone in him. Poor Mrs Agatha was shaking when you took her up the stairs. What did he want?'

Abbie took another bite of her biscuit, followed by a sip of the warm tea. She left the cup back in the tray and leaned back on the sofa. She rubbed her temples to stop the headache that threatened to break out. 'He wants me to marry.'

The housekeeper's hands flew to her hips. 'What nonsense is this! I will not tolerate this madness!'

Abbie chuckled softly. 'Do not worry, Mrs White. I won't be marrying anyone my uncle suggests. But I doubt he will give up his intentions so easily. I think he has already decided who I am going to wed.'

Mrs. White huffed. 'Then we must do something.'

'I know. I need to go over Father's affairs and speak to his lawyer.'

'Fine. But before you bury that head of yours in the books, you will finish eating. It'll help you think better.'

Abbie nodded. 'I will, Mrs White.' She took another biscuit and grinned. 'Here – I'm chewing,' she said with her mouth full. Satisfied, the housekeeper left the room, closing the door behind her.

Alone now, Abbie realised just how hungry she was. She hadn't eaten much for the past five days and was starting to feel the weakness in her legs. She poured another cup of tea, adding a splash of milk; the beverage comforted her instantly, and the warmth soothed her. When she finished, she closed her eyes and drew a deep breath. It was time.

She knew she needed to start what she had been delaying. She had been thinking about what her father said that horrible night. *The documents are not here; they are in our home in the country'* Abbie felt her body heavier than ever, but she stood and crossed to the door that led to her father's study.

The room was still in disarray from whoever had been

here searching for the elusive documents, but truthfully, it didn't look much different from how her father usually kept it. Papers were scattered across his desk and the floor, books stacked in uneven piles on every surface. A few drawers hung open, and one chair was tipped over, but the space still felt like his – lived-in, cluttered, familiar.

It had been decorated especially for him. Her mother had known him well and ensured everything suited his taste. The walls were adorned with a rich green wallpaper, and the dark oak furniture lent the room a masculine feel. A matching crimson damask sofa and armchair were arranged in front of the fireplace, where her father had spent many afternoons lost in thought, a glass of cognac in hand. Everything about the room reminded her of the beautiful life they had shared.

Her father had never been one for tidiness. He liked to call it 'organised chaos', and somehow, he always knew exactly where everything was. Her mother had often tried to tidy it, only to be told he'd never find anything again if she moved a single paper. Abbie could almost hear them bickering about it from opposite ends of the hall.

She walked slowly to the desk and ran her hand over its worn edge. This was where he'd taught her to read a balance sheet, how to calculate shipping costs, how to think like a merchant. He used to light up when he spoke about trade, as though every ledger was a map to something bigger. He used to tell her stories of how he started trading wool from a little town in Shropshire to the big city of London. After working hard for many years, he had finally saved enough money to start his own company. He was a man who loved the excitement of big business deals and the risk that came with them, which some people didn't like. However, her father was born for it, and he thrived on the rush of what could happen next. That was something she always admired about him. She knew how lucky she had been to spend that time with him and will remember them forever.

Abbie looked down at the scattered papers and exhaled. She took a deep breath and focused on the task ahead. She dropped to her knees and began sorting through the papers, creating small, neat piles, separating them between invoices, letters from different merchants, and shipping records. It would take time, but perhaps something among them would help her discover what had really happened. What those men had been after.

She wasn't ready to let go. Not of this house. Not of her father. And not of the truth.

This was going to take longer than she thought.

Well, Abbie, you better start working, ' she said to herself, determined to find the answers she needed.

CHAPTER 4

Abbie woke on the sofa to the first light of dawn, a blanket tucked gently around her – undoubtedly Mrs White's doing. She pulled it up to her chin and snuggled beneath the soft fabric.

It had been a long night of sorting through the endless piles of documents. She must have dozed off, and neither her aunt nor Mrs White had had the heart to wake her. At least she'd had the sense to fall asleep on the sofa rather than the floor. Her eyes drifted over all the clutter still spread across the room, and the frustration of the past few days returned in full.

Despite all her efforts, she had made no progress whatsoever. It was the only thing she had thought since arriving at Redwood House, and it was beginning to suffocate her.

She needed to clear her mind. As things stood, all she could see was a wall that she couldn't get past. Not a single document had offered a clue. Nothing had brought her any closer to understanding what those men had been looking for.

A break was necessary to clear her head and look at the problem from a different perspective because, right now, she felt stuck. And there was no better way to do that than with a ride on her favourite horse Hettie.

Stretching her arms above her head to ease the stiffness in her back, she glanced down at her black dress, now rumpled from sleep. Time to get changed.

She left the study and found Jacob waiting at the bottom of the stairs.

'Good morning, Miss Abbie. Would you like something to break your fast?'

'Just a cup of tea, Jacob. I'm going for a ride – I don't like to ride with my stomach full' she smiled, softly. 'Could you send Suzie to my room?' The butler bowed and went to fetch her maid.

Once in her room, she opened the curtains of the lofty windows to let the first morning light spill across the room. The bed remained untouched. Her room at Redwood House was utterly different to the one in London. This one still had the touches of her childhood. A little girl obsessed with flowers and dolls. Abbie always thought there were too many good memories attached to her dolls to disregard them, but since she was a grown woman, most were now stored away in a box in the attic, save for one, that still held a place of honour on her bedside table.

A soft knock on the door preceded Suzie's voice. 'Miss Abbie?'

'Come in, Suzie.'

'Good morning, miss.' Suzie entered carrying a tray, steam curling from the ceramic teapot. She placed it on a table by the window and began pouring the tea. 'You fell asleep in the study last night. We didn't want to wake you up. You looked so tired – and you haven't been sleeping much this past week – so. So, I thought. *We should not wake her up.* That's what I said to Mrs White. Yes, I did! And she agreed.'

Abbie accepted the cup of tea from her hands with a grateful smile. She loved her company; such a cheerful character would make anyone's day.

'Thank you, Suzie. I needed that rest. But tonight, I'm sleeping in my bed. My neck won't survive another night on that sofa!' They shared a smile. Abbie sipped the tea and started unbuttoning her dress.

'I'll need to freshen up. Would you send some water up, please?'

'Of course, miss. I already asked the cook to boil it. I'll bring it right away.' With that, she disappeared, closing the door behind her.

Abbie slipped out of her dress and white chemise, leaving them on the bed, and pulled on her robe. She paused in front of the full-length mirror. The bruises still covered her face, and neck had faded into pale green shadows, but they still carried the weight of what happened. She turned away quickly from the mirror, for every time she saw them, a heavy weight oppressed her heart, remembering the pain from just a few days ago.

Suzie returned with the basin and placed it on the dressing table with a cloth neatly folded.

'Here, miss. It's still warm.'

The water was a balm to her sore muscles.

'Suzie, can you lay out my riding dress?'

Suzie nodded and headed to the dressing room, but she stopped before going in.

'You don't have any black riding dresses, miss.'

'I'll wear the dark blue one.' Abbie knew what was crossing the maid's mind. 'With a black shawl over it, no one will notice. I don't even know if riding is appropriate during mourning, but I need to get out of the house. I need fresh air and a bit of exercise, and I am sure Hettie needs it, too.' And through her best convincing smile at the woman who frowned in response.

'That horse is not to be trusted, miss. She's too nervous. One day she'll go crazy and throw you off the saddle!'

Everyone said the same about poor Hettie, but that was what Abbie loved the most; was her temperament.

The mare would only misbehave if others tried to ride her. With Abbie, she was loyal to the bone.

'Oh, come now, Suzie. She just has more character than the other horses.'

Suzie shook her head. in disproval. 'Not even your father could stop you.' She immediately looked regretful. 'I'm sorry, Miss Abbie. I didn't mean–'

Abbie walked over and placed a gentle hand on her arm. 'It's alright, Suzie. The only way to keep their memory alive is to talk about them.'

'You're right, Miss.' Suzie smiled and laid a hand over Abbie's. Then she fetched the dress and hung it neatly on the folding screen before following Abbie to the dressing table and began combing her hair.

First, she braided her hair and tied it up in a nice low bun with a black ribbon to ensure her hair would not go loose on the ride. Suzie knew how wild Abbie could be when she was riding her horse. The maid smiled at her creation. 'All done, miss. Ready for that wild horse of yours.'

They smiled at each other in the mirror, and then Suzi helped her into a clean chemise, stockings, and the blue riding dress. Abbie pulled on her most comfortable boots, and for the final touch, she wrapped the black shawl across her chest. Suzie offered her a hat, but she waved it away.

'Thank you, Suzie, but I won't be wearing it. We're in the country now. I doubt that I'll cross paths with anyone but sheep – or maybe a fox!' She said over her shoulder as she left the room and made her way to the stables.

She walked through the large wooden gates, giving a weary creak as she pushed them open. Simon, the stable boy, was forking hay into neat piles, humming softly to himself, concentrated on his task. When he noticed her, he welcomed her with a joyful smile.

'Good morning, Miss Abbie! How are you today?'

He was a cheerful young boy with his curly brown hair and warm brown eyes. Simon had worked in the stables since he was twelve years of age, brought in by his father, Owen Brown, the stable master.

He wanted the boy to learn the trade at a young age, so he brought him to work with him as soon as the boy was tall enough to lead a horse. But Abbie suspected Mrs Brown refused to let the boy out of her sight before then.

Simon had become a great stable boy. He had a natural touch with horses and was now learning how to train them as well.

'Good morning to you, too, Simon. I'm well, thank you. I thought I'd take Hettie out for a ride. How is she this morning?'

Simon dropped the fork he was using. 'Of course, Miss. Right away! I just finished brushing her. I'll saddle her up for you in no time, Miss. She has been a little distressed, but I think it is because she needs a run.'

They walked together towards the stable yard to Hettie's stall. The mare let out a soft snort in greeting.

Her glossy brown coat gleamed. The only colour was a white stripe running down from her forehead to her nose. Thanks to Simon's care, her hair looked shiny and regal. She looked magnificent. She was, without a doubt, the best horse she had ever owned. Abbie stroked her gently, pressing her cheek to Hettie's warm face.

'Hi. Did you miss me?' she whispered, only for Hettie to hear. The mare pushed her head against Abbie's in response. 'I missed you too, girl.'

Simon brought the saddle and blanket, and together, they saddled the horse. Abbie adjusted the cinch strap, and once secure, she placed her foot in the stirrup and jumped to sit astride, with practised ease. 'Thank you, Simon.' With a nudge of her heels, she whispered. 'Come on, girl, let's have some fun.'

And with the short command, Hettie leapt forward with eager energy, and they took off into the morning light, galloping across the wide, open fields as if nothing else in the world existed.

***

After an hour of riding around the estate, Abbie slowed Hettie's pace to a gentle walk and eventually came to a halt. The mare snorted softly beneath her and Abbie leaned forward to stroke her neck.

'Let's find you some water, girl.'

As she looked around, she spotted Mr and Mrs Bates' cottage in the distance – and an idea took shape. Mr Bates had worked alongside her father since they moved to Redwood House. If anyone might know something – anything – that could shed light on the mysterious documents, it was him.

'Come on, girl,' she murmured. 'Let's go and see the lovely Mrs Bates. I am sure she'll have some treats for you.'

Hettie seemed to perk up at her voice and trotted eagerly in the direction of the little house nestled between the trees.

As they arrived, Abbie dismounted and tied Hettie to a post by the front porch. The door swung open, and Mrs Bates appeared, wiping her hands on her apron.

'Miss Abbie!' she exclaimed, descending the steps to greet her. 'What a delightful surprise.' She took her hands in her own and studied her face with care. 'You're looking much better today, dear.'

Abbie smiled. She had the pinkest cheeks Abbie had seen. White hair was taking over the brown from her youth, but that gave her an even more amicable look.

'Thank you, Mrs Bates.' She knew she looked exactly the same as the day before but the older woman's kindness warmed her heart all the same.

'Come in, come in. I've just finished baking some biscuits.'

'Oh, I could never say no to one of your biscuits, Mrs Bates. Or maybe two?' she added playfully.

They chuckled together as Mrs Bates led her inside.

The house was modest but warm, filled with the unmistakable comfort of a well-loved home. The affection between the couple who lived there lingered in every corner. It was a place of peace. They had enough space for the two of them and one spare room – once belonging to their son, Jeremy. But the boy had grown to be a man now and, with the help of Abbie's father, who had bought an apprenticeship as a lawyer's clerk, Jeremy had moved almost three years ago into Lincoln's Inn. The Bateses couldn't be more grateful for her father's influence in the matter, and they were immensely proud of their son.

Abbie followed Mrs Bates into the kitchen, the scent of freshly baked biscuits greeted her like an embrace. Abbie's stomach growled in response.

'Hungry, are we?' Mrs Bates asked with a twinkle in her eye.

Abbie pressed a hand to her stomach, sheepish. 'Too obvious? I only had a cup of tea before leaving, and your biscuits smell delicious! You hardly can blame me, for it is your baking that had brought my appetite back.'

They both laughed as Mrs Bates set the kettle on the hook's fireplace to make some tea and returned moments later with a tray of golden-brown biscuits. She sat beside her and offered Abbie the plate. 'Here you are, dear. Eat as many as you like.'

Abbie didn't hesitate. She took one and a generous

bite. Still warm, it melted on her tongue – honey and butter flavours reached her senses in perfect harmony. Her eyes widened in disbelief.

'Oh, Mrs Bates! These are heavenly! I daresay you've outdone yourself this time.'

The woman blushed modestly, clearly pleased with the compliment. As the kettle began to whistle, she rose, poured the boiling water into a pot and allowed the leaves to steep before serving.

'Thank you, darling. Now,' she said, handing Abbie a cup. 'How are you, really? You looked so weary yesterday; we could see how tired you were.'

Abbie dabbed her mouth with a napkin, then sighed. 'That's a hard question to answer, for I do not know myself. Some moments I feel like I'm managing, and the next I'm in tears. I try to be strong, but the moment I'm alone, it all unravels. I feel like I'm two different people – one trying to keep everything together, the other falling apart, Mrs Bates.' She pressed her fingertips to her temple, feeling the weight of exhaustion. 'And then there are the questions. The mystery around my parents' deaths. I don't know if I have it in me to keep going.'

Mrs Bates reached over and touched her arm gently. 'I didn't mean to worry you, Mrs Bates.'

'You don't need to explain yourself, dear. Not to me. And you certainly don't need to do this alone. You're stronger than you realise, Abbie. Your parents would be so proud. But when your strength wavers, you let us help you. My Terry and I will always be here for you like your parents were here for us.'

As if summoned by her words, the kitchen door opened and Terry Bates stepped in, smiling broadly. His muddy boots showed he had been in the fields, probably preparing everything for the mid-summer harvest. Taking his hat off, he said. 'Miss Abbie, what a lovely surprise!'

'That's what I said!' chimed his wife.

He was about to walk into the room when Mrs Bates scolded him. 'Those boots aren't stepping into my kitchen, Terry,' she warned. 'So, you better take them out if you want to sit with us.' With a sheepish nod, he retreated to remove them. He returned a few minutes later without the muddy boots, and Mrs Bates had a fresh cup of tea ready for him.

He'd barely sat down when Mrs Bates said, 'Miss Abbie needs our help, dear.'

Mr Bates turned to her with concern. 'What can we do for you, miss?'

'I don't know if you could, but I thought… perhaps my father mentioned something to you. Anything out of the ordinary. Maybe, some business outside of his usual trade?'

He frowned slightly, confused, which told Abbie there wasn't probably much he would be able to tell. 'He never said anything to me. Why do you ask?'

She looked at the couple and knew she could confide in them, her worries and what had happened that night.

'The night that my parents were murdered…the men that broke into the house were looking for some documents.'

Mr Bates looked even more confused. 'What documents?'

Abbie raised her shoulders. 'I don't know. I've searched through my father's papers, but nothing stands out. There's so much to go through, and I don't even know what I'm looking for either, which is making the task even harder. Did he ever say anything to you?'

Mr Bates shook his head. 'No, miss… although–' He paused, brows drawing together.

'What is it, Mr Bates?'

'I don't know if it's related, but your father did come by a couple of weeks ago, asking after our Jeremy.'

'Jeremy?'

'Yes. He'd moved to a new lodging, you see, and your father wanted his address. Said he needed to speak with him about something. I do not know why he needed him or what business he wanted to discuss.' He said, seeing Abbie's questioning eyes. 'I gave him the address; that was the last time we saw your father.' He stood, fetched a slip of paper, scribbled an address, and handed it to her. She read the address out loud.

Jeremy Bates
Chancery Lane
Lincoln's Inn

'Thank you, Mr Bates. It's something – a place to start.' She held the piece of paper before placing it in her reticule for safekeeping, but she had already memorised the address.

'Tell him,' Mrs Bates added, 'that he had better start writing to his mother more often or I'll come to London myself and pull his ear like when he was a child!'

Abbie laughed. 'I'll be sure to pass along the message.'

She stood, embracing them both. It wasn't much, but it was more than she'd had before and hoped after seeing Jeremy, she would have more information than now.

'Please, don't talk about this with anyone. I still don't know what has happened or whether we're in any danger. Until I find out, it's better if it stays between us.'

'Don't worry, miss. We won't say a single word.'

Mrs Bates took a clean cloth and bundled all the remaining biscuits, tying them in a tidy knot. 'Take these with you.'

'Oh, I can't take them all!'

'I'll bake more tomorrow. Besides, Terry doesn't need them. His belly's growing so much that he can barely fit through the door!'

Mr Bates's eyes widened. The affected looked at his wife, stunned. 'Amelia!' The three of them laughed together.

'Thank you very much, Mrs Bates.'

'My pleasure, dear. Come by any time.' She hurried after Abbie and gave her an apple. 'And this is for Hettie.'

'She'll love it.' Abbie smiled, tucking the apple into the saddlebag with the biscuits.

Her spirits felt lighter as she mounted Hettie again. She gave the reins a soft pull, and they turned towards the riverbank to continue her ride heading to the old mill by the river.

She loved that place—quiet— with just the sound of the river enveloping her. Far away from everything – far from sorrow, from responsibility – it was the only place that still brought her peace.

The mill had been abandoned long before they moved to Redwood House. Her father had once told her that the previous owner had left it unattended after losing his fortune. Years of neglect had broken the wheel, and parts of the structure had since collapsed. Her father had never repaired it – he'd built a new one closer to the fields instead.

Dismounting, Abbie tied Hettie to a tree near the river and let her drink. Once the mare had satisfied her thirst, she offered her the apple Mrs Bates had so kindly given her, which Hettie devoured in one bite.

'You do love your apples, right?' The horse snorted in agreement. 'Let's rest for a bit. It's been too long since we had such an intense ride, and I don't know about you, but I am exhausted.' Abbie lay back on the grass, eyes following the clouds drifting above. There was something peaceful about seeing the cotton-like clouds fly across the sky. It was a sunny April day, and she could feel the sun warming her face. For the first time in days, she felt calm.

She wished she could be wearing lighter clothing. They were so restrictive! She removed the pins from her bun, letting her braid fall onto the grass. These few moments of stillness felt like a gift amid the chaos.

But there were still many things she couldn't understand, and it felt as if she was drowning in an ocean of questions. What did her father want with Jeremy Bates? Why consult a junior law clerk when he already had legal counsel? And what about Lord Crawford – what was he doing in their house that night? There was another mystery. The only thing Jacob was able to tell her was that he had seen him once in the house with her father and Lord Everleigh.

She had written to him before leaving London, but he hadn't responded. Was he avoiding her? What was he doing in her house? Was he involved in her parent's murder?

Her world was collapsing around her, and she didn't know how to stop it. Her father's secrets had died with him, and Abbie was left with only one thread to follow. She stared at the sky.

'Why did you leave me with this mess, Papa?' She threw the question to the sky as if he was listening from up there, watching over her. She wanted to scream so badly.

A sudden clattering sound startled her. It came from the half-ruined mill, followed by the desperate cry of a child. Abbie shot to her feet and ran to the building, climbing the wall to enter through the side. She knew the structure well; she had explored every corner as a child.

The floorboards creaked beneath her boots. She

moved carefully; she'd once fallen through a rotten plank here and hadn't forgotten the lesson. The steps on the left took you to the wheel engine, but she looked and couldn't see anything on the floor below. She passed the old pulley system and entered the grain room, dust rising with every step. The table and chairs left by the old tenants were covered in dust, and as she moved, it suspended in the air, making her cough. Some rays of light pierced the thatch above, bringing some light to the room and helping her see her way in.

At the far end of the room, the hooks that had once been used to raise sacks of ground grain to the mill loft hung forgotten. Abbie followed the ropes attached to the metal with her eyes upward and that's when she spotted a child clinging to the loft's support beam. A girl, no more than seven years old, eyes squeezed shut, shivering with fear.

Abbie approached gently, careful not to frighten her. 'Hello,' she said softly. The girl opened her eyes. Two big eyes were looking at her from the loft's edge.

'Hello.' She said timidly, still hugging the beam with all her strength. Abbie could see the relief in the little girl's eyes to see someone who could aid her. 'I can't get down.' Her voice trembled as if she was on the verge of tears. 'The ladder fell, and the boards up here are moving. I'm afraid I'll fall through and land like a big sack of potatoes.'

Abbie glanced down. The ladder lay against the wall, partially broken but usable. Enough for the girl to be able to climb down.

She dragged it over until she reached the side closer to the girl, and pleased with herself, she managed to land the ladder just a few inches from the girl. She steadied it beneath the loft. 'Now, you need to hold the ladder; can you climb down?'

The girl looked at the ladder and tried to reach it, then clutched the beam again. 'I can't.'

Seeing the fear in the girl's eyes, Abbie didn't hesitate. 'That's alright, I'll come up to you.' Abbie tied her skirt into a knot at the front to avoid stepping into her own dress and began to climb carefully. Reaching the top, she extended a hand. 'Take my hand.' The girl took Abbie's hand and slowly, she edged forward, moving between Abbie and the ladder. 'Good girl. Now it's time to start climbing down. I'm right behind you.'

They descended slowly, one slow step at a time. When they reached the floor, the girl breathed, relieved of touching the solid ground and threw her arms around Abbie's waist.

'Thank you! Thank you!'

She looked up, and Abbie smiled at her. 'You're very welcome... What's your name?'

'Georgina. What's yours?'

'Abigail. But most people call me Abbie.'

'Nice to meet you Abbie,' she said with a shy grin.

'Come, let's go outside. This place is stifling. I can barely breath.'

Georgina nodded effusively. 'Me neither!' Abbie grabbed her hand and helped her climb out. They stepped into the fresh air, relieved to see the shining sun. Georgina spotted Hettie immediately. 'You have a horse!' She ran over and started petting her enthusiastically.

'Hello.' She turned to look at Abbie. 'What's her name?'

'Hettie,' Abbie replied fondly.

Georgina's face lit up. 'I love that name! It suits her.'

'Would you like a biscuit, Georgina?'

The girl nodded eagerly. Abbie retrieved them from her saddlebag, and they sat on the grass. The girl stuffed her face with one of Mrs Bates's golden biscuits, devouring them in seconds.

'What were you doing in the mill?' Abbie asked.

She finished swallowing her biscuit before saying. 'Exploring! What about you?'

Abbie was fascinated by the girl's appetite. She grabbed another biscuit and gave it a generous bite. 'This is my secret spot. Or it was. I guess it is not a secret spot anymore,' she added with a smile.

The girl looked surprised. 'You live here?' Georgina looked around, confused. 'It's not a very cosy place to live, and you probably get wet every time it rains. There are holes everywhere! And there is no bed! Do you sleep on the floor? That must be really uncomfortable. I once slept on the floor, and it was really uncomfortable.' She paused to breathe.

Abbie bit her lip to hold in a chuckle. 'No, I don't live in the mill. I live in the house, Redwood House, that is. This is just the old mill. It's called Redwood Mill.'

The little girl looked relieved. 'Oh phew! That is good. I'm happy you have a bed. My uncle always says sleeping is really important. That's why I have to go to sleep every night – to grow. If not, I'll be wee forever.'

Abbie laughed. 'Forever? That is a long time.'

'I know, right? That's what I told him.' She paused, then said, 'So, this mill's not mine?'

'Yours?'

'What do you mean?' The girl lifted her head and looked at Abbie with sad eyes.

'Well, my father's, I meant. But he's not here anymore.' Her tone shifted but she kept talking. She gave another bite of her biscuit and continued talking before Abbie could ask. 'We live at the edge of the woods. I thought this was our land. I think Uncle Alex said it was... or maybe he said it wasn't. Now I can't remember.' She lifted her shoulders. The girl shrugged and gave a sideways glance. 'I think I've heard about you.'

Abbie raised an eyebrow. 'You have?'

Georgina nodded vigorously. 'Yes, my uncle was talking with a man, and the man said you would have to sell something because you didn't know something.'

The girl's words, although confusing, left no doubt as to what her uncle was referring to. And it didn't come as a surprise. She was expecting the neighbours to gossip about her—the orphan girl who inherited an estate without experience and no one to manage it for her. Everyone must be expecting her to fail. Probably best to marry her off, just as Uncle Harper had suggested.

It infuriated her that her own neighbours judged her without even giving her the chance to prove herself.

'Is it because you're a girl?' Georgina asked suddenly. Abbie tilted her head.

'I don't know, what do you think?' Georgina thought for a moment.

'Well… when I go climbing with Luke, he is our stable boy', she explained. 'I always win, so I think we can be better than the boys sometimes. And then he always wins me at horse riding. So, sometimes they can be better than us.' She lifted her shoulders. Abbie smiled.

'Very wise, Georgina.'

The girl beamed with pride. 'Thank you.' She said, smiling.

'Now, how about picking some wildflowers?'

'I'd love to! But I need to be back soon. My uncle will worry if I don't come back before lunch.'

'Then let's pick quickly. I'll take you home after, and we'll make sure you don't get into trouble with your adorable uncle.'

'How do you know my uncle is adorable?' Georgina chirped, missing the sarcasm completely.

Abbie smiled. 'Come on, let's get some flowers.' And

they both walked to the side of the mill.

Just over an hour later, Abbie rode to the Everleigh estate with Georgina perched in front of her on the saddle, cheeks glowing with laughter.

'I love Hettie,' she said, petting the horse. 'She's beautiful!'

'She was a birthday gift from my father. She's strong, fast, and a little bit wild, which makes her even more special to me.'

'We turn here,' Georgina said, pointing.

'Are you sure? That road leads to Everleigh Manor.'

'Yes, it does. It was my father's house.'

Abbie felt a pang. Of course – Lord Everleigh's daughter. She looked down at the small girl in front of her. Both had lost the people they loved most.

'I'm sorry for your loss, Georgina.'

The girl nodded, head low. Abbie hugged her, unsure if to comfort the girl or herself.

Changing the subject, Georgina said. 'I have one too, you know?'

Abbie wasn't sure of what she meant. 'One of what?'

'A horse, of course! Well, not a horse; I have a pony. Uncle Alex says I'm too little for a real horse, that I need to grow a bit more. That's why I sleep a lot.'

She giggled, then pointed. 'Look! That's our house!'

Sat atop the hill stood a magnificent house, about three stories high, with a tower in each corner, making it look like a castle. Two terrace levels framed the front of the house, and on the side, an enclosed courtyard was protected by high stone walls. Abbie felt intimidated by the size of the house. This could easily be twice the size of Redwood House. Her beautiful garden looked minuscule compared to this one. It was perfectly designed, and all the flowers were neatly planted in harmony and symmetry. The trees, perfectly aligned, guided the path to the house, their branches blooming with the first white flowers of spring. Abbie gently spurred Hettie to go through the gates into the yard.

They hadn't yet reached the front of the house when a man came running down the steps two at a time. He wore black breeches and a simple white shirt, the sleeves rolled to his elbows, the crisp fabric striking against the golden hue of his skin. His dark hair was loose, wind-tossed, and framed a face Abbie recognised instantly.

The man from her parents' funeral.

Abbie found herself holding her breath as he approached. His square jaw appeared to have been sculpted to resemble a Greek god. The man looked like an Adonis, capable of weakening any woman's knees, and Abbie feared she might be one of them.

But it was the concern in his piercing blue eyes etched into his expression that made her throat tighten.

He moved with urgency; his eyes locked on the girl. 'Georgina! Where have you been? I've had the whole county looking for you!'

He reached the horse and lifted the girl into his arms, holding her so tightly she began to giggle. 'Uncle Alex, I can't breathe!' He loosened his grip, but didn't let go, setting her against his hip, scanning her small frame for injury. 'It's the entire county looking for me? All of them?' Georgina's eyes widened.

Abbie noticed how he tried to hide his smile, but his worry was still palpable.

'Yes, the whole county. Every last one of them. You know better than to disappear like this. If something had happened to you, don't ever do this again. You nearly gave me a heart attack!'

Georgina lifted her hand to touch his cheek. 'Oh no, Uncle Alex! You can't die! I promise I won't do it again, but you mustn't die!' Her arms flew around his neck, clinging to him fiercely, her voice tight with fear, tears in her eyes.

Abbie watched something shift in his eyes – something raw and unguarded, as he realised how those words affected the girl. He held the child closer, pressing a kiss to her hair.

'I'm not going anywhere, sweetheart. I'll be with you always. That's a promise.'

Georgina pulled back and looked him dead in the eye. 'Promise?'

A smile tugged at the corner of his lips. 'Promise. But never scare me like that again. If you want to go on an adventure, you tell me, and I'll take you myself.'

She nodded solemnly. He brushed the tears from her pink cheeks with his thumb, his touch tender and soft.

Abbie stood frozen, struck by the intimacy of the moment – the fierce protectiveness in the man's embrace, the way he clung to Georgina like she was the last precious thing in the world. For a moment, he seemed like an entirely different man from the one she'd glimpsed at the funeral. But then he turned to her, and whatever warmth had filled his gaze vanished, switched to a questioning expression.

She couldn't tell if it was a surprise, disbelief, or perhaps both. His eyes darkened as they met hers, and the weight of his stare was impossible to ignore.

'Uncle Alex, this is Abigail – but everyone calls her Abbie! She rescued me.' Georgina said proudly.

Alexander looked between them. 'Rescued you? What happened? Are you hurt?'

'I went to the mill and climbed up to the loft, but the ladder fell, and I couldn't get down,' Georgina explained, her voice rising with excitement. 'So, Abbie climbed up and rescued me! Then we picked wildflowers! Look, I brought you some.'

His jaw clenched. 'You went to the mill?' Georgina lowered her head, suddenly sheepish.

Abbie stepped in, 'Sir, I believe she may have gotten lost.'

His gaze shifted to her eyes, and for a brief second, something passed between them. The air thickened. Abbie could feel the heat building up in her body. She wasn't sure how long they stared at each other until he turned back to Georgina.

'You little troublemaker. No dessert for you tonight.'

'Oh, Uncle Alex! But Emma made chocolate cake! And it's my favourite!' she cried.

He didn't concede to the innocent look she tried to pull. 'No dessert,' he said, firm but not unkind. 'Now go get changed, for lunch; you're covered in dust.'

He kissed her on the forehead before lowering her to the floor. Georgina ran a few steps, then spun around and retraced them.

'Thank you for rescuing me, Abbie! And thank you for bringing me home!' she added with a sweet smile at Hettie.

Abbie laughed. 'It was our pleasure.'

'Goodbye!' Georgina waved and skipped towards the house, her curls bouncing behind her.

The moment she disappeared, silence stretched between the two of them, expectantly. Abbie's heartbeat was loud in her chest, and she knew he could see the colour in her cheeks. She should have turned and ridden away, but his hands had settled on Hattie's reins, preventing her departure.

She met his eyes, refusing to look away, even as heat prickled her skin.

How could she be feeling anything but annoyance towards this man – the man who had questioned her capability to manage her own affairs.

And yet, every time he looked at her with those storm-blue eyes, her breath hitched and reason blurred.

No, Abbie, do not let his eyes melt your brain!

She said to herself. She needed to be angry and indignant with him, but it didn't seem like her body listened to reason. Finally, his deep voice broke the silence, bringing her back from her own thoughts.

'Thank you for bringing her home safe,' he began. 'I wanted to—'

She cut him off, her voice clipped and cool. 'No need to thank me. Georgina is a sweet girl with an admirable sense of adventure. And rather clever, too. She doesn't seem inclined to let anyone treat her as anything less than capable.'

She could feel her temper flaring beneath her skin. Pretending had never been her strong suit – and in that moment, she wasn't even going to try.

'If you'll excuse me, I have matters to attend to.' She pulled on Hettie's reins, leaving the man no chance to respond and gallop out of the courtyard.

'Miss Clarkson—'

But she was already turning the mare, guiding her swiftly through the gates. His voice trailed behind her as she rode away without looking back.

She knew her behaviour had been rash, perhaps even childish, but the damage was done. There was no taking it back, and no point in regretting her actions.

She'd have to learn to control herself around this mysterious man…or better yet, never see him again.

***

Alexander watched her disappear through the gates as if the devil himself was chasing her. He couldn't understand why she'd fled with such urgency, without even giving him a chance to introduce himself. It was clear she hadn't recognised him from that dreadful night – one that haunted him still – her body bruised and bloodied, the image seared into his memory.

At first, all he'd seen was Georgina's face – relief flooding through him at the sight of her safe. It wasn't until he had the girl in his arms that he had truly looked at the woman on the horse.

Her eyes were locked on his, golden-brown and burning with something fierce. Her hair, woven into a long braid that fell down her back, was streaked with loose, rebellious curls framing her oval face. Rosy from the ride, cheeks flushed, she looked alive in a way that struck him unexpectedly.

He had meant to ask her how she was healing. The bruises on her face hadn't fully faded; she must have still been struggling with some pain. Not just physically but emotionally too. And yet, she had looked at him as if he were the enemy. What had he done to provoke such hostility?

He shook his head, turning back towards the house, his thoughts churning. She hadn't recognised him. That much was clear. And still, there had been something in her tone – defensive, angry. As if she was bracing herself against him.

Inside, he found Georgina waiting for him, sitting at the bottom of the stairs, legs tucked up, chin resting on her knees. 'I know you don't like her Uncle Alex,' she said quietly, 'but I do. She's nice.' He dropped down onto the step beside her, puzzled.

'And why would you say I don't like her?'

She looked at him, guilt blooming in her wide eyes. 'Well... you were talking with that man the other day, and he said she wouldn't be able to handle her father's something, and she would have to sell something, and –

well, I don't know what that means exactly, but I *know* she can do anything. She *saved* me!'

Alexander sat back, groaning softly as he dragged his hand down his face. 'Please, Georgina – tell me you didn't mention that to Miss Clarkson.' Georgina winced and looked down at her feet.

'Maybe?'

He exhaled, long and slow. 'Oh, Georgina…' No wonder Miss Clarkson had looked at him like that. God only knew what she now thought of him.

The conversation she'd overheard had been with Lord Fairfax – a man whose views belonged in the previous century. Alexander had held his tongue during the entire exchange, not because he agreed, but because disagreeing would have drawn attention he couldn't afford. Fairfax and his ilk had come sniffing around in the wake of the Clarksons' tragedy, eager to gossip, speculate and position themselves to benefit if Abigail was forced to sell, the ambition to expand their fortune and buy Redwood House Estate for pennies. But that wasn't at all what Alexander wanted. In fact, the thought of it made him ill.

He stayed silent not out of cowardice, but out of necessity. If anyone suspected how closely he was investigating the Clarkson's deaths, or how determined he was to uncover the truth, it would put everything at risk – including Abigail's life. He couldn't afford to be seen as being aligned with her.

But now – thanks to Georgina's innocent meddling – Abigail believed he was just another man underestimating her, perhaps even threatening her position. She was never going to trust him. And without her trust, it would be much harder to protect her. He looked over at Georgina, who was slumped beside him, feeling sorry for herself. Her shoulders were drooping, and her gaze hadn't lifted up off the floor.

A year ago, if someone had told him that he'd be living in the countryside, playing guardian to a seven-year-old girl, he would have laughed. He didn't know what Stephen had been thinking, naming him Georgina's legal guardian. But then again, when he'd gone to see her after the news, and she'd looked up at him – those tear-filled green eyes trembling with grief – he'd known. He would do anything to protect her. Her mother had died bringing her into this world, and now Stephen was gone too.

He had already looked out for this family for most of his life. And now he felt like he wanted to do the same for Abigail Clarkson. Reaching out, he lifted Georgina's chin gently.

'I'm not angry, sweetheart.'

'I'm sorry, Uncle Alex,' she whispered. He brushed a finger down her cheek. 'Just promise me you'll stop eavesdropping behind doors.'

She nodded. 'I promise, Uncle Alex.'

'Good.' He tapped her nose. and the ghost of a smile returned to her lips. 'Now go upstairs and ask Paige to help you get ready for lunch.'

With renewed energy, she bounded up the stairs. He knew he'd likely have to tell her the same thing again before the week was out. But for now, it was enough. He rose slowly, casting one last glance through the window in the direction that Abbie had disappeared.

She had fire. He could see that now. Her father had said as much – intelligent, stubborn, headstrong. Alan had spoken of her with pride. The challenge now was to convince her he was on her side.

And he had no time to waste.

CHAPTER 5

Abbie woke up with the first light of day, her body heavy with exhaustion and her eyes puffy from another restless night. It felt as if she hadn't slept at all.

Forced by her aunt and Mrs White– who had threatened to drag her upstairs if she didn't go willingly – Abbie had finally relented. Too tired to argue, and in all honesty, they were probably right. She climbed the stairs without protest. Another night on the study sofa and her body might not have survived it. But even with the comfort of her bed, she barely slept a few hours, for as soon as she closed her eyes, the nightmares returned.

Every night, she had the same dream – her parents lying lifeless on the floor, unreachable despite how hard she tried to get to them. No matter how much she fought, her efforts were in vain. Her screams echoed into silence; her body paralysed. She was a mere observer as she watched their lives fade from their faces. Then, as always, the dream shifted; piercing blue eyes dragged her back to consciousness, forcing her to emerge from the darkness, bringing her back to life and staring at her with such intensity it felt as if they could see her soul.

She buried her face against the pillow and hugged it tightly, tempted to stay in bed all day and block out the world. She wanted to forget – the grief, the emptiness, the pain that clung to her like a second skin. But she knew she couldn't. She had to be strong.

You can do this, Abbie. If not for yourself, then for them.

That had become her anthem every morning as she opened her eyes.

Kicking off the covers, she sat up and swung her legs over the side of the bed. 'Come on,' she muttered to herself. 'You've got work to do.'

She crossed the room and pulled back the curtains, letting sunlight flood into the space.

Soon after, Suzie arrived with a basin of water for her morning ablutions and helped her dress. Abbie chose one of the new black gowns that had arrived the day before from London, ordered by her aunt. She'd been reluctant to accept them, feeling it unnecessary, but her aunt insisted that propriety demand it.

'You are in mourning, dear. Out of respect for your parents, you must show yourself properly. It's what your mother would have wanted.'

Abbie wasn't so sure. Her parents had never been strict about appearances. They would have preferred she live, not spend her time grieving. Still, she hadn't argued. Her aunt had enough to worry about, so she let her do as she wished.

She asked Suzie to braid her hair simply, tying it with a black ribbon at the bottom. The reflection in the mirror showed the fading, yellowing bruises still clinging to her cheekbone and jaw – ghosts of the assault that had marked her. Hopefully, within a few days, they would disappear completely. The shadows under her eyes, however, were another matter due to the lack of sleep. She pinched her cheeks to give them a bit of colour. 'Good enough,' she murmured.

'You look as beautiful as always, Miss Abbie,' Suzie said, placing a gentle hand on her shoulder.

'That's very kind of you, Suzie, but I'm aware my eyes have seen better days.' She ran a finger beneath one of them. 'I don't know how to get rid of these dreadful circles.'

'The best way is sleeping, miss,' Suzie replied with a smile.

'I'm trying. I promise.' Abbie said with a smile of her own. 'Is my aunt awake?' she asked, rising from the dressing table.

'Yes, miss. She's in the dining room. I believe Jacob just brought her some breakfast, though she didn't look well. I think she should eat more. The poor woman had barely eaten anything since she arrived at Redwood House.'

Abbie could not but agree with her. 'You're right about that. I'll speak with her. Thank you, Suzie.'

She made her way downstairs and found her aunt seated in the dining room, breaking her fast, a delicate teacup cradled in her hands, her expression far away.

'Good morning, Aunt,' she said softly.

She looked utterly spent – her skin pale, her eyes hollow with grief. Abbie's heart tightened. Abbie could have sworn she had aged in the last week. Since Abbie was an only child, she could not even come close to imagining what she must be feeling.

Abbie placed a light kiss on the cheek before taking the seat beside her, avoiding sitting at the head of the table. It would've felt wrong if she did. It was still Papa's place and would always be for her; no matter how much time passed, that place would always be her father's.

Her aunt blinked, returning to herself. 'Good morning, dear. How did you sleep?'

Abbie took her hand. 'As well as you did, I imagine.' Her aunt offered her a faint smile and reached up to touch her niece's cheek, her fingers careful.

'Not much, then?'

'No,' Abbie admitted. She avoided mentioning her nightmares for the same reason she hadn't shared all the details about the attack. It was unnecessary to let her know what her sister had endured in her final moments.

Her aunt had enough to bear. No need to burden her with horrors she couldn't change – especially when she already had a monster to contend with in her life.

'Have you heard from Uncle Harper?' she asked.

Her aunt's gaze dropped to her plate, where she toyed with her scrambled eggs. 'He sent a message this morning. He wants me to return to London.' She hesitated. 'And I think I should go….'

'No,' Abbie interrupted, her hand tightening around her aunt's. 'You are not going anywhere.' Her voice left no room for argument. 'If you go back, he'll hurt you. You know that as well as I do. How can I protect you if you return to him? The law won't help you. You know what it's like for women. Husbands are allowed to do whatever they want, without repercussions. You'll be trapped.' Abbie's voice was trembling now, shaking with fury and helplessness, for she knew the law established that the husband, being the head of the family, had the right to maintain order in his home, and that meant that he could use force to punish if he considered it necessary. Women could complain, sure they could, but that didn't do much good since, in most cases, it was dismissed because the man would suggest he had a reason to discipline her for her behaviour, whatever the husband considered deserved punishment.

Tears welled in her aunt's eyes. 'Oh, Aunt, I didn't mean to upset you,' Abbie said, softening her tone. 'But I can't bear the thought of you going back to him. Please, just listen to me. I will find a way. I'll do everything in my power to protect you from him, but you must give me time to see our options. Promise me you won't go back to him.'

Agatha dabbed at her tears with a linen napkin and

met Abbie's gaze. 'I promise,' she whispered. 'But what can you do, dear? And what if he comes for me? I couldn't fight him.'

'I don't know yet,' Abbie admitted. 'But I promise I'll find a solution. I'll hire extra help to watch the house if need be. I doubt my uncle will dare come here by force – but if he does, he won't get past me. I will protect you. Please, trust me.'

Her aunt nodded; her voice tight. 'I do.' Abbie gave her hand a last comforting squeeze.

'Good. Because I won't let him lay a hand on you – not ever again.'

If her parents had known the truth of her situation, they would have done something. They had suspected, perhaps, but never guessed the true extent of the abuse. Now, with them gone, it was Abbie's responsibility to act. And she would – whatever it took. She would not send her aunt back to be abused whenever he pleased.

***

The clock had just struck one in the afternoon, and still, Abbie had found nothing of significance. Nothing that would explain why her parents were murdered. She had searched every drawer in the study, rifled through every document, but as far as she could see, there was nothing worth killing for.

With the table long since overrun, she'd moved to the floor, arranging endless stacks of paper into piles. Now, feeling the weight of frustration pressing down on her chest, she lay back with one hand over her forehead, staring at the ceiling. What was she missing? A knock at the door interrupted her thoughts.

She recognised Jacob's voice on the other side.

'Come in!'

He entered scanning the room, instinctively looking towards the desk, expecting to see her there. When he realised she was sprawled on the floor, his brows lifted in surprise. Shaking his head, somewhere between amusement and mild disapproval, he made Abbie laugh. 'Everything alright, Jacob?' she asked, propping herself up on her elbows without bothering to stand.

He coughed softly into his hand, clearly suppressing a smile. 'Of course, miss. A message just arrived for you. It's from Lord Crawford.'

She promptly came to her feet and took the letter from Jacob's hands.

'From Lord Crawford?'

She retrieved the letter opener from the desk and sliced through the seal with urgency. She'd waited so long for word from him. Ever since she'd recovered enough strength to hold a pen, she had written to him – requesting a meeting. But he hadn't responded. No-one had seen him since that fateful night, and with every unanswered day, her questions only multiplied. He was the only one who knew what happened that night and probably the only person who could throw some clarity into what truly happened.

She unfolded the letter. His writing was neat and elegant.

Dear Miss Clarkson,
Please accept my apologies for the delay in my response. I have been absent from my home and only received your letter yesterday.
I would be most grateful for the opportunity to request a visit, at a time convenient to you.
Respectfully,
Lord Crawford

Abbie looked up at Jacob. 'He wishes to a visit. Is his

messenger still here?'

'Yes, Miss. Mrs White took him to the kitchen for some refreshment.'

'Perfect. I want to see him right away.' She was already marching towards the kitchen.

'Miss Abbie, I can fetch him for you,' The butler said, following her almost out of breath.

'Nonsense, Jacob. Besides, I need something to eat. And I've barely seen Jane since we got back.' Since she returned to Redwood House, she hadn't found time to spend with her friend.

They reached the kitchen to find a young man seated at the long wooden table. He had the most cheerful eyes Abbie had ever seen and a mop of unruly ginger curls. He was sipping lemonade and enjoying one of Jane's biscuits with evident delight. At the sight of her, he shot to his feet, nearly spilling his drink in the process.

'My lady!'

Abbie smiled warmly. 'No need for titles. I'm not a Lady, Mr.…'

'Luke, m'lady. Luke Finney.' He bowed awkwardly.

She decided not to correct him again. He was nervous enough. 'Well then, good afternoon, Luke. Thank you for bringing Lord Crawford's message.'

He dipped his head, cheeks pink with pride. 'My pleasure, my lady.'

'I see you've been enjoying Jane's pastries.'

His eyes lit up and nodded vigorously. 'Yes miss – they're delicious! Never tasted anything like them!' His lips were dusted with sugars crumbs left behind by the sweet dessert and Abbie couldn't help but smile.

'I'm glad you like them. Jane's the best baker in the region – —without question.'

Abbie glanced around the room. 'Where is she, by the way?'

'She left after she gave me the pastry, miss. Said she had to fetch something from the market.' Abbie nodded.

'Now, can you tell me where Lord Crawford is? Is he in London?'

Luke shook his head, making his ginger curls bounce with the motion. 'Oh no, miss. He's…' he hesitated, eyes darting to his hands. '…he's just a few miles away.' She paused, sensing his discomfort but put it down to nerves.

'Wonderful. Please inform Lord Crawford, I will receive him today at three o'clock.'

'Today, my lady?'

'Yes.' Her tone left no room for disagreement. 'There are matters we must discuss, and they can't be delayed any longer.'

The young man scrambled to his feet. 'Yes, my lady. I'll tell him right away.' He hurried out the door.

Abbie released a slow breath, steadying herself. She couldn't afford to wait any longer. Two weeks had passed, and she was no closer to the truth. Aside from a single address she'd received from Mr Bates, she had no real leads. She needed more.

Jacob was watching her carefully and tried to hide her desperation, but the butler knew her well.

'What if he doesn't have the answers you are looking for?' he asked gently.

'Then I'll keep looking,' she replied, lifting her shoulders. 'But I have the feeling he knows something. At the very least he can explain what he was doing in our house that night, Jacob.'

That was her first and most pressing question. Why had Lord Crawford been there? And could she even trust him? For all she knew, he might be involved in her parents' deaths. But until she had proof, she had to follow every thread.

They returned to the study. Abbie sat back down

among the piles of papers. Jacob hesitated in the doorway.

'Will you let me know when Lord Crawford arrives?' she asked.

'Of course, but, Miss Abbie…'

She looked up. 'Yes?'

He gestured at the floor with a slight frown. 'Wouldn't you be more comfortable at the desk?' She smiled faintly.

'There are too many documents, Jacob, and not enough room. Besides, I like the floor.'

Jacob sighed, resigned, and shook his head as he left her dive back into the endless piles of documents.

***

Hours later, Abbie was still immersed in the sea of paperwork when a knock sounded on the study door. Distracted, she murmured. 'Come in.'

Jacob stepped inside. 'Miss Abbie, Lord Crawford is here.'

'Mmm…' she nodded vaguely – then froze. 'What?' She exclaimed, turning her head to the longcase clock behind her. 'I told him to come at three!'

A deep, masculine voice answered from behind Jacob. 'It is three in the afternoon, Miss Clarkson.'

The voice was so familiar, it sent a jolt through her. She turned – and there he stood, framed in the doorway: tall, composed, exuding confidence.

Standing in her study like a figure from a myth – an Adonis draped in cobalt blue – was Georgina's infuriating uncle. But what disturbed her most was realising those deep blue eyes staring straight at her, were also the ones that haunted her dreams.

'You?' she blurted, stunned.

His dark hair framed a strong jaw, and that

insufferably perfect smile danced on his lips. The amusement reflected on his face confused her. *'Why is he looking at me like that?'* She thought to herself. Then she realised, with horror, that she was still sitting on the floor.

Scrambling to her feet, she smoothed down her dress with as much dignity as she could muster. She shot a wide-eyed look at Jacob, opening her golden-brown eyes in a silent question, who caught the silent reprimand.

'I did instruct him to wait at the entrance, miss,' Jacob said stiffly, casting a reproachful glance at the guest. He bowed and excused himself, leaving the door open behind him. Abbie took a deep breath, schooling her expression as Jacob disappeared down the corridor.

'My deepest apologies for the intrusion, Miss Clarkson,' Alexander said. The words were honest enough, but the smirk tugging at the sides of his mouth told a different story.

Abbie couldn't contain herself any longer. 'For the intrusion?' she echoed, advancing with her chin high, questioning the sincerity of his words. 'What about for not telling me you were Lord Crawford?'

He raised his hands in surrender and tilted his head to distance himself from her. 'In my defence, you ran off before I had the chance to introduce myself.'

'Well, clearly, you didn't try hard enough, sir!' she snapped. She was angry, or so she should have been, but looking into those ridiculously blue eyes, and that half smile that made him look even more attractive, if possible. The fire inside her began to flicker and fade like a morning mist. What was wrong with her? She had never reacted this way to any man. Her breathing quickened with his proximity, and she didn't know how to control it. She took a deliberate step back to reclaim some space.

'I truly am sorry for not introducing myself yesterday,' he said, more sincerely this time. 'I was focused entirely on Georgina's safety. I wasn't thinking clearly.' That, at least, was understandable. Still – yesterday was one thing – this morning was another.

'And what about this morning?' she challenged. 'Did you instruct your messenger to lie to me, Lord Crawford?' He shook his head.

'I didn't *instruct* him. I merely suggested it might be better not to mention where I was.'

'So… you tricked the boy into lying to me then?' Her eyes narrowed, and he met her gaze evenly.

'I assumed you might not be too eager to see me.'

'And what gave you that idea?' she asked, folding her arms.

'Georgina told me what she said to you,' he said, 'I'd like to clarify that what she repeated wasn't what happened; at least, it is not the whole story.'

'Oh? What was it then? Something along the lines of 'poor Miss Clarkson doesn't know what she's doing and will have to sell everything'?' She lifted her chin.

He winced and shook his head as he mumbled. 'Georgina…'

Abbie crossed her arms, trying to ignore the flutter in her stomach as he looked at her – really looked at her – with an intensity that made her spine tingle.

'The conversation was taken out of context,' he said. 'I certainly never doubted your abilities.'

'But you didn't contradict the man who did.'

'No,' he admitted. 'I didn't. But I had my reasons.'

'Do you always have an excuse for your behaviour?' He hesitated, and for a moment, she thought he might respond. But knowing that he could possibly hold the key to clear up her myriad questions, she cut him off with a dismissive wave of her hand. 'Never mind.' She gestured towards the sitting area. 'Let's hope you will be more forthcoming going forward.'

He inclined his head and waited for her to take a seat before claiming the sofa opposite. The tension between them was palpable, staring into each other's eyes until Abbie cleared her throat.

'I want to know what happened that night,' she said bluntly. 'Why were you in my house?'

'Straight to business, then?' he replied with a faint smile.

'That is why you're here, isn't it?' she said evenly. 'To explain what happened that night. To explain what you were doing in our house. I am sorry, Sir, but I fail to understand why you were in our home. I only remember seeing you once in our residence, and yet, on the night my parents were killed, you were there to save the day.'

'Are you implying that I had something to do with it?' His voice was calm, but something sharpened in his eyes. 'That I had anything to do with Alan's death?'

'Should my suspicions surprise you, my lord?' she said. 'I do not know anything about you. You disappeared from the face of the earth for two weeks! If the constable hadn't assured me you weren't a suspect, I'd have sent the police after you myself! So, you better have a good explanation.' Abbie's breathing quickened with every word. She needed to know if she should trust him or fear him. He ran his hand through his hair, visibly weighing up his words, which did not help to dispel her suspicions.

'Well?' she pressed. 'I'm listening.' He exhaled slowly.

'I went to your house that night because I feared your father could be in danger.'

Abbie blinked. 'And how did you come to that conclusion, my lord?'

He stood up and started pacing the room. 'That same night, I went to my friend's house – Stephen, Lord Everleigh. I found the front door forced open and the study ransacked. Someone had broken in, looking for something.'

Abbie couldn't stop looking at his muscular body, pacing from one side of the room to the other. She shook off her thoughts, trying to get back into the conversation. *Focus Abbie!* She said to herself, clearing her throat.

She arched a brow. 'Well, I hope your friend is well–'

'He is not,' Alexander said quietly. 'My friend, Lord Everleigh, died three weeks ago.'

Her breath caught seeing his eyes turned with grief. 'Oh,' Abbie was starting to understand. 'Georgina's father?'

He nodded.

'I am sorry for your loss, Lord Crawford,' she said, her voice softening. 'I didn't know him well, but my father always spoke highly of him. I know his death had a big impact on him. And he clearly did a wonderful job raising Georgina.'

Alexander nodded again, his voice rough. 'He was the finest man I've ever known. And yes, he was a fantastic father. Every time I look at little Georgina, I see him in her.'

They both paused, the weight of shared grief lingering in the space between them. Then Abbie leaned forward. 'But how is this connected to my father?'

'Lord Everleigh and your father were business partners.'

'I am aware of that,' she said. 'But they ceased their dealings more than a month ago. My father never told me why. I assumed there was a good reason.'

Alexander raised an eyebrow. 'I see you are acquainted with your father's business.'

She met his gaze, unflinching. 'Does that surprise you, Lord Crawford?' Abbie smiled and shook her head. She was used to this kind of reaction from people. 'Believe me, I am quite capable with numbers, and my father benefited from that on many occasions.'

'I don't doubt that, Miss Clarkson.'

She didn't know what to make out of the mysterious smile he was flashing at her. Silence fell upon the room until Alexander cleared his throat. 'They didn't stop their trading business.'

Her brow furrowed. 'You must be mistaken. I have been through every document in this house and haven't found any evidence that would support that.'

'You won't find it here,' he said evenly. 'You haven't found anything because all of the last month's transactions – shipping logs, contracts, correspondence – they're in my possession.'

Abbie blinked, stunned. 'Why would *you* have them?' She frowned. 'Also, could you sit, please? You're giving me a headache.'

He blinked at her, bemused and surprised by her bluntness, but obeyed, taking the seat again.

'Better,' she said with a small nod. 'Now, please explain.' His mouth twitched.

'Your father and Stephen met quite a few years ago, but it wasn't until recently that they decided to go into business together, trading with the Americas.'

'International trading? My father never dealt overseas, my lord. The furthest he ever shipped goods was from Hull to London.'

'That was true – initially. But after the first shipment proved successful, they took the bold step to expand. The next voyage was launched in January.'

'January?' Abbie blinked. 'But that was months ago! Why didn't he say anything?'

Alexander hesitated. 'Because things went wrong with that shipment.'

'What do you mean by wrong?'

A knock on the door interrupted her. 'Miss Clarkson, Mr Williams is here,' Jacob announced. They both turned towards the doorway.

'Here?' they asked in unison.

Abbie looked at Alexander, confused. 'How do you know my father's accountant?'

'It's… complicated.' Abbie exhaled in exasperation.

'Oh, my lord!' she said, rolling her eyes towards the ceiling, clearly not referring to him but as if appealing for divine patience. 'With you, everything is complicated!'

She turned back to Jacob. 'I haven't finished speaking with Lord Crawford. Tell him—'

'Wait, Jacob.' Alexander cut in. 'Miss Clarkson, please don't tell Mr Williams I'm here. He mustn't know we've met.'

'But why not?'

'I will explain later. Just – for now – keep this conversation private. And don't mention any details from that night. Please, trust me.'

Abbie hesitated; thrown by his urgency and the low, steady way he spoke. He had stepped towards her, lowering his voice. She could feel the warmth of him, the intensity in his eyes making her heart skip a beat. 'How can I trust you when I don't even know you?'

'Because your father trusted me,' he said gently. 'And just for that, please have a little faith that I'm being honest with you. Only for one more day. I'll come back tomorrow afternoon and explain everything.'

She wavered, torn between reason and instinct. Against her better judgement – perhaps because some part of her wanted to believe him, she nodded. 'Fine! But you'd better explain everything, my lord. You have one day.'

Alexander took her hand and placed a soft kiss to her fingers. 'As you wish, my lady.' He turned to Jacob. 'Keep him in the entrance hall while I slip out.'

Then, with a wink, he crossed to the window and unhooked the latch. Abbie's eyes widened in disbelief, fearing what he was about to do. 'Lord Crawford! What do you think you're doing?' She said, forcing her voice to whisper, trying not to shout.

'I'm leaving without being seen, Miss Clarkson.' He flashed that maddeningly cheeky smile at her. 'I will see you tomorrow. It was a pleasure to see you again.'

Tipping his hat, he jumped down. Abbie rushed to the window just in time to see him disappear into the stables.

She stood there for a moment, stunned and smiling. Shaking her head, she turned to Jacob, then quickly wiped the smile from her lips. There were more pressing matters at hand – namely, Mr Williams.

Damn these men who appear at the most inopportune moments.

She bit her lip while scanning the mess of the study, piles of documents littering every surface. The visit from Lord Crawford had only raised more questions, stirred deeper doubts, and left her with an inconvenient tangle of emotions that she hadn't yet begun to understand.

And now, she had to face her father's accountant completely unprepared – her mind still filled with the memory of Alexander's rogue smile. And instead of thinking about what she should say to Mr Williams, her mind only had space for the man who occupied her dreams.

Abbie! Collect yourself! She said to herself.

'Miss Abigail?' Jacob's voice brought her back.

She blinked. 'Right... Mr Williams.' She squared her shoulders. 'What was his excuse for coming unannounced?'

'He said he's just returned from London and needed to speak with you,' Jacob said, equally unimpressed. Now that Lord Crawford had seeded additional concerns, how could she discuss anything with the accountant? Everyone was a potential suspect for being involved.

Suspicions high, Abbie realised she had no choice but to improvise. 'Jacob, please show Mr Williams to the drawing room. I need a few moments to collect these papers.'

'I can help with that, miss.' he offered, stepping forward.

She stopped him gently. 'Don't worry, Jacob. Just keep him entertained while I clean up here and….' She looked down at her dress and ran her fingers through her hair. '…and myself.'

The butler nodded and left, closing the door to give her privacy. She quickly gathered the scattered documents and tucked them away in a drawer in her father's desk. In a rushed attempt at presentability, she twisted her braid into a bun and pinned it at the nape of her neck. She sat herself on one of the sofas in the centre of the room, smoothing her skirts with both hands. Just then, Jacob returned, ushering Mr Williams into the room.

August Williams' plump figure entered with his hat in hand, wearing a brown jacket that had clearly seen better days and a waistcoat that strained at every button. His round, too-wide-set eyes made his gaze unsettling, and there was something about the man that had always rubbed Abbie up the wrong way. She'd long suspected his awkwardness was an affection; his cold, calculating gaze often gave him away.

'G-good afternoon, Miss Cl-Clarkson,' he stammered, bowing with exaggerated deference.

His stutter came and went depending on how nervous he was. Sometimes unnoticeable, repeating only the occasional word, but sometimes so over-the-top that it seemed forced.

'Good afternoon, Mr Williams,' she replied, gesturing to the seat opposite. 'Please, have a seat.' She said, pointing at the sofa opposite her.

He did as she asked and sat himself onto the sofa with visible effort, his chubby form occupying almost half of the three-seated sofa. 'I-I'm s-sorry for your loss, Miss Clarkson,' he said, the familiar stammer getting stronger.

Abbie took a breath, steadying herself. The phrase had begun to grate after hearing it so many times in the past two weeks. Still, she nodded and murmured a polite thank you.

'Well, Mr Williams, I'm glad you finally came,' she said, adding a pointed emphasis to *finally*. 'But I must admit, I'm surprised you didn't inform me of your visit – and more surprised that you didn't attend the funeral.'

She couldn't go too hard on him if she wanted to find out more about what happened. Still, he would also notice if she suddenly went all soft and docile when he knew she wasn't that kind of woman and even less with him, for she never hid the aversion she felt for his father's administrator. Why her father hired him had always been a mystery to Abbie.

'What d-do you mean, Miss?'

'Well, Mr Williams, it has been two weeks since my parent's death, and I haven't heard from you. Do not think your absence at their funeral went unnoticed?'

'I c-can only apologise, Miss. I was unwell and c-couldn't leave my home for d-days.'

'Ah.' Abbie gave him a tight smile. 'Well, if that's the case, then it's certainly understandable.' *If* being the keyword, she noted the way his eyes flickered at her subtle challenge. Perhaps he wasn't as oblivious as he liked to appear.

Lord Crawford might be right in believing he was somehow involved. 'I trust you are feeling better now?'

She continued.

'Y-yes, Miss. Thank you.' He said, lowering his head and looking at her with sadness in his eyes, but Abbie could see the lie behind his gaze.

'So, let's get to it then. What is the nature of your visit today?'

'I j-just wanted to see if you would need any assistance with the s-sale.'

Abbie tilted her head. 'Which sale would you be referring to, Mr Williams?'

He shifted uncomfortably, hands fidgeting in his lap. 'The s-sale of the estate, Miss Cl-Clarkson.'

'And why would I sell?' she asked, arching a brow. 'The land provides sufficient income to support the house and its tenants. And I'm aware my father made several investments. Once I review everything, I fully intend to continue managing his affairs.'

Williams hesitated. 'I-I thought you knew...'

'Knew what, Mr Williams?'

'Your father... he invested everything in a shipping venture. The cargo was l-lost at sea. And since he didn't insure the shipment... I'm afraid he lost everything.'

Abbie's jaw tightened. 'My father would never make such a reckless mistake.'

'I advised him to get an insurer,' Williams said quickly. 'He refused. Said it wasn't n-necessary. Without coverage, there's no recourse. I am afraid you will have to s-sell and soon, Miss. Otherwise, the b-bank may seize the property.'

He reached into his case and produced several documents. She took them and scanned the pages. They outlined a substantial loan backed by a Royal Exchange underwriter. Her father's signature was there, along with Lord Everleigh's and a bank official's. Her stomach dropped.

So, it was confirmed that her father had business with Lord Everleigh; there was no doubt of that now. Her eyes widened when she saw the amount for the loan. 'Thirty thousand pounds?' she echoed. 'That can't be the cost of a single cargo?'

'There were two ships,' Williams replied. 'The first voyage covered the initial investment. The second...was attacked by p-pirates. They sank the vessel after stealing the c-cargo.'

'And what's the remaining debt?'

'Twenty thousand pounds.'

Abbie's heart jumped into her throat. It would be an impossible task to get that amount of money together.

Williams continued. 'If you want to c-cover the loan and still be able to live the life you're accustomed to, you m-must sell. Or you c-could lose everything.'

She couldn't hold back her snappy tone. 'Excuse me, sir, but are you suggesting my father put the house as collateral?'

'That is c-correct, Miss Cl-Clarkson.'

'How could he do that? And without insuring the shipment? It all seems so absurd.'

Abbie rose and crossed to the window, struggling to steady her breath. Nothing made sense. There must have been an explanation for her father to risk losing their home and everything he had worked so hard for. Her eyes drifted to the stables where Lord Crawford had vanished minutes earlier. *There must be more to this story... and he knows it.*

Her instinct told her Mr Williams was not to be trusted.

'I c-could find you a b-buyer,' Williams offered.

Her voice turned cold. 'There will be no need for that.' His round face was surprised by her determination.

'But Miss Cl-Clarkson—'

'I will not sell my father's legacy without a fight. I appreciate your concern, and I trust that you are suggesting that I sell for my own benefit, but you must understand, Mr Williams, I won't make such a decision until I've reviewed everything myself.'

'Of course, miss. I'd be happy to help you with all the paperwork…' He said, looking at her father's desk.

'That won't be necessary. I'm perfectly capable of reviewing the documents on my own. If I require your help, I'll send word.'

He sat awkwardly, reluctant to stand.

'If that's all, I have a full afternoon ahead.' She held his gaze until he rose.

'Of c-course. P-Please let me know if I can be of any a-assistance.'

'I will. Good day, Mr Williams.'

He turned toward the door, but before he reached the door, Abbie said.

'One more thing, Williams.'

He paused, glancing back.

'Never return to this house unannounced. If I wish to speak with you, *I* will send the word.'

His expression twisted briefly into something darker – an unguarded flash of anger. No more of the timid Mr Williams. But he quickly smoothed it into a false smile. 'It w-won't happen again. Have a g-good day, Miss Clarkson.'

He bowed and exited. Jacob was waiting to escort him out.

As the door shut behind them, Abbie stood by the window, arms crossed, frowning in thought. Her suspicion of Mr Williams had only deepened. And now, more than ever, she needed answers – Lord Crawford held the key.

She glanced at Jacob with disbelief. 'Why did Father

hire that man?' she muttered, more to herself than to him.

'I couldn't say, miss. But your father must have had a reason to keep him,' Jacob replied.

Abbie appreciated his loyalty; his devotion to her father was beyond question, and that meant more to her than any accountancy title. Still, she shook her head. 'But why keep him these last two years? Why not hire someone else? He clearly didn't trust him. If Lord Crawford's story is true, Mr Williams doesn't know a thing about it. And if my father didn't rely on him… then who was managing his legal affairs?'

Abbie couldn't understand why her father would keep someone he didn't trust close to him.

'I don't know, miss. I truly don't.' He bowed his head respectfully and left, closing the door behind him.

Abbie sat heavily on the sofa, one hand on her forehead. Her mind reeled, caught in a web of half-truths and hidden pieces. It felt like an unsolvable jigsaw – one where the pieces were slowly revealed one at a time but with no connection whatsoever. How could she know where to start?

Craving a reprieve from the endless questions, she made her way to the kitchen hoping Jane might be there. Perhaps baking would sooth her thoughts, if only for a moment.

Opening the sturdy door to the kitchens, she was immediately embraced by the warm, comforting scent of fresh bread, bringing her back lovely memories. The room bustled with activity. Large copper pots were hanging by the hearth, and in the centre of it all stood Jane, her face dusted in flour as she kneaded dough on the broad wooden table. So absorbed was she in her work, she didn't notice Abbie walked into the kitchen.

'What are you working on now, Jane?'

Jane looked up. 'Abbie!' Her whole face lit up. 'Finally,

you decided to grace us with your presence!' Abbie laughed at the cheeky tone in her voice – she had missed her.

'Jane! That's no way to address Miss Abbie!' Mrs May scolded from near the fire, giving Jane a sharp look. Abbie struggled to understand why she insisted on reprehending Jane every time she talked to her with no ceremony, for it was the reason why Abbie felt so comfortable in the kitchens and the certainty that she was being herself and not pretending to be someone else, just a real friend. Jane was left on Mrs May's doorstep when she was but a baby, and she raised her as her own. When Abbie and Jane met, they became friends instantly.

Abbie smiled and held up her hand. 'Mrs May, please don't tell her off. If she starts calling me 'Miss Abbie', I might just toss that flour she's working with back in her face. It wouldn't be the first time, would it?'

Jane chuckled. 'No, it wouldn't.'

Mrs May rolled her eyes and sighed with mock exasperation. 'You little devils, I've said my piece. But you never listen. You never have.' She turned back to the pot, shaking her head—but Abbie didn't miss the fond smile playing on her lips.

'And what about you?' Abbie asked, turning to Jane. 'You haven't visited me either.'

Jane wiped her hands on her apron and came around the table to embrace her. 'I didn't want to disturb you. How are you holding up?' she whispered in her ear.

'As well as I can be,' Abbie murmured back.

Jane pulled away and squeezed her shoulders. 'I am always here for you, you know that, right?'

'Of course I do.' Abbie smiled, grateful for her steadiness.

'Good, now come and help me.'

Abbie followed her to the table. 'I need something

sweet and comforting,' she admitted.

'Well, if you want some of this delicious dessert I'm making,' Jane replied with an exaggerated curtsy, 'you'll have to get your hands dirty, *Miss Abbie*.'

Abbie mimicked the gesture. 'It will be my pleasure, *Miss Jane*. What are we baking?'

Jane lifted the dough to throw it back onto the table, spreading more flour on top. 'Today, we are making *ratafia biscuits*,' Jane announced proudly. 'It's a new recipe from today's paper. I'm mixing the flour and almonds – you can start beating the egg whites. Remember, don't stop till they're good and fluffy.'

Abbie raised an eyebrow, and Jane gave her a knowing look. 'Don't look at me like that. You always get bored and leave them half-beaten.' Abbie threw her hands up in surrender – she had no defence, for Jane was right.

She took an apron from the hook by the door and tied it around her waist with a lace in the front. Taking the bowl from Jane, she began whisking the egg whites.

After a while, Jane glanced up and asked. 'Do you want to talk about it?' Abbie lifted her gaze to look at her friend.

'What do you mean?' Jane nodded towards the bowl Abbie was holding.

'You are ruining those egg whites. At this pace, they'll be ready by Michaelmas.'

Abbie looked down and saw how little progress she had made in fluffing the mixture.

'Oh... I'm sorry, Jane. I'm just a bit distracted.' She stopped whisking and rested her hands on the table.

'Does it have to do with a certain Lord that came to visit?' Jane asked with a raised eyebrow. Abbie blinked, surprised.

'What? No!' But Jane knew her too well. 'Well... maybe? Oh, I don't know Jane. There's just so much I don't understand.'

Jane reached over and squeezed her hand. 'Abbie, you can't make sense of something so senseless. No matter how hard you try, you won't find logic in what happened – not now, not ever. Your parents should never have died like that.'

Abbie rested her head on her friend's shoulder. She could feel tears rising, burning behind her eyes – but she inhaled deeply and pushed them back.

'I know,' she whispered.

She picked up the whisk again, this time pouring her full attention into it, determined to beat the egg whites into submission. When she was finally satisfied, she held the bowl up proudly.

'Et voilà!'

Jane peered over and nodded in approval. 'Well done!'

Abbie passed her the bowl so she could continue mixing the ingredients.

'So, why did he come, anyway?' Jane asked casually.

'Who?'

'Lord Crawford.'

Abbie hesitated. She wanted to confide in Jane – she always did – but something stopped her. If Lord Crawford was right, then sharing too much could endanger not only her friend but everyone in the house. No-one knew the truth about why he'd been there that night. She felt terrible about lying to her friend but knew it would be best for now.

'He heard what happened and came to pay his respects,' she said simply.

Jane looked surprised.

'Really? And how is he, then? I heard he's quite handsome.' She said, teasing her.

Abbie sputtered, 'What? No. He's insufferable, Jane. And it's astonishing how different he is from his ward.'

Jane's brow knitted together. 'Who?'

'Lord Everleigh's daughter. Do you remember him?' Jane nodded. 'After his passing, Lord Crawford became her guardian. A lovely little thing – she reminds me of us at that age. Adventurous, headstrong, always getting into trouble. I found her in the old mill this morning, and when I took her home, he was… less than pleased.' A smile tugged at the corner of her lips as she thought about the moment that he'd come rushing down the steps to meet them in the courtyard.

Jane caught it instantly. 'What's that smile?'

'Nothing,' Abbie said quickly, brushing flour off the table.

'You like him,' Jane accused, her eyes gleaming.

'Me? Don't be daft. I barely know the man. And his manners are dreadful. Do you know he didn't even introduce himself properly? That's hardly the mark of a gentleman.'

Jane just smiled, letting Abbie bury herself in her cleaning, choosing not to press the matter further. They both turned their attention to finishing the cakes, filling the kitchen with cheerful chatter that drifted away from dangerous topics.

When the ratafia biscuits finally came out of the oven, the sweet, nutty aroma filled the room.

'Oh, Jane, they smell divine!' Abbie leaned in to inhale the sweet scent of the biscuits.

'And they'll taste even better,' Jane said, full of pride.

Abbie laughed at her friend's self-assurance. 'You're so modest.'

'Well, I'm the best baker in the region, and everyone knows it,' Jane said with a dramatic toss of her flour-dusted hair.

Shaking her head with a smile, Abbie laughed along. 'Thank you, Jane.'

'For what?'
'For distracting me.'
Jane softened. 'Any time, Abbie. Any time.'

CHAPTER 6

With his gaze fixed on the horizon, Alexander stood by the lofty windows of the study at Everleigh Manor. His friend had chosen the location wisely where to set his place of work, for from there, one could see the sweeping garden and the path winding from the main gates up to the house. Lost in the greens of the land before him, Alexander replayed his most recent encounter with the compelling Abigail Clarkson.

He hadn't known what to expect from her reaction – but what surprised him more was his own. Seeing her seated on the floor, surrounded by mountains of papers and folders, entirely absorbed in her task, he had been caught off guard. She hadn't noticed who stood at the door; she was too lost in her own world, unconcerned with appearances or propriety. The sight had warmed something in him.

He'd felt a fleeting pang of guilt for intruding – but he didn't regret witnessing a moment that would remain etched in his mind forever. She had worn a simple black mourning dress, intended to convey solemnity and restraint, but on her, even the dark fabric seemed luminous. It only served to highlight the natural elegance of her figure.

Her hair, loosely braided, cascaded like golden water over her shoulder, and one rebellious curl had slipped to land on her chest, rising and falling with each breath. The memory of that image made his body tense once more.

Her expression had shifted from surprise at the butler's entrance to sheer annoyance when she spotted him behind Jacob. As recognition dawned, he could almost see how the pieces came together in her mind.

Her cheeks flushed as she fought to contain her temper – perhaps for the butler's sake – but her golden-brown eyes betrayed her rising anger. He could've sworn they sparked like amber fire.

He'd managed to provoke her not once, but twice in the space of a day – an unusual feat for him. Women were typically agreeable and obliging in his company, rarely showing their true natures. But Abigail Clarkson was a different creature entirely. She made no effort to hide her opinion of him. And he was beginning to wonder what might come of such a unique acquaintance.

'You've an intriguing look on your face,' The familiar voice behind him made him smile even before turning to see who the guest was.

The accent – a smooth American drawl, was easy to recognise. Captain Derek Colton watched him from the doorway, one brow arched. His blonde hair, brushing his shoulders, was streaked with dust – evidence of a long ride from whichever port he'd come from. It was rare to find Colton on dry land; the sea had long claimed his heart.

Alexander stepped forward, clasping his cousin's shoulder and giving him a once-over. Derek's brown coat was splatted with mud. 'I would offer you a hug, but you look like hell. When was the last time you bathed?'

Colton smirked. 'Charming as ever, cousin.'

Though Derek bore his American father's hair, his eyes belonged to his English mother – Alexander's aunt. The two men had often been mistaken for brothers, both tall and broad-shouldered, with an easy familiarity that came from years of shared trouble and loyalty. They were both so similar they could have easily been birthed by the same woman.

His half-humoured smile showed the tiredness he carried, and his expression darkened as he asked, 'I came as fast as I could. What happened, Alex?'

His seriousness sobered Alexander immediately. 'How did you find out?'

Stephen, Derek, and Alexander had forged a friendship when their families sent them to Eton at a young age. Together, they had grown into men – through mischief and mistakes, triumphs and heartbreak. Over the years, they had stood by one another through numerous adventures and mutually supporting each other in painful moments as they grew older. Now, only two remained, left to carry the memory of the third.

'Millie – Peter Dawley's wife – came to port when we docked yesterday, and she told us. She didn't have many details. Just that Stephen had… an accident. Is that right?'

'Yes, it is. But have a seat, Derek. A lot has happened since you left port a month ago.' Alexander motioned towards the dark green armchairs flanking the carved stone fireplace. The same chairs that the three of them had once occupied with brandy and idle conversation, never imagining one of them wouldn't live to see their next reunion.

Derek lowered himself into one of the chairs with a wince. 'You alright? Are you injured?' Alexander asked, pouring two glasses of port.

The captain dismissed his comment with a wave of his hand and a smile. 'Not injured,' Derek grunted, accepting the glass. 'But I borrowed a horse from an acquaintance down south. The beast was barely broken. Tried to throw me three times from the damn saddle before we'd even left town. A fine reminder of why I belong on a ship.' Alexander shook his head and sat opposite his cousin.

They sipped their amber liquid in silence until Alexander spoke again.

'It happened three weeks ago. Stephen was riding back from London to Everleigh Manor when – so they say – he fell from his horse and broke his neck.'

Derek's frown was immediate. 'That's impossible.' Derek shook his head and rested his elbows on his knees. 'Stephen was the best rider I've ever known. Do you remember the times he used to fall on purpose just to learn how to land safely? The man was a lunatic but he never lost control.'

'I know.' Alexander nodded grimly. 'That was my first thought too. Stephen's abilities were far beyond good'

'So, who told you?'

'Mr Fletcher – Stephen's manservant. He came to my house in London with the news. He said Stephen had fallen off the horse and died instantly.' Alexander drank from his glass, trying to palliate the pain. He looked at Derek, and his expression didn't give any doubt of his thoughts. 'But the man could barely speak for he kept shaking as he delivered his news, and I could tell he didn't believe a word of it. Neither did I.'

Derek sat back slowly; the glass cradled in his hands.

'I sent for Alan Clarkson.'

'Stephen's business partner?' Derek asked.

Alexander nodded. 'Yes. We rode here together to see for ourselves. I also spoke with the local constable, who told me the body had been found along the road leading to the manor. His horse was nearby, grazing calmly. They assumed something must've spooked it.'

Derek snorted.

'The constable just kept repeating, *These things happen, my Lord*. I wanted to shake the man until he came to his senses.'

'And that's all it took to close the investigation?'

Alexander nodded grimly. Derek's look was one of outrage for the lack of interest in his friend's death. 'So, they've stopped looking into it all together?'

'Yes. They claimed they had no reason to believe it was anything other than an accident. I tried to reason with the constable, but he dismissed me.'

Colton raised an eyebrow. 'He dismissed *you*?'

Alexander shook his head, still baffled. His title usually opened more doors than it closed, and he had been just as surprised as his cousin when a mere constable refused to heed his concerns.

'But why would they not investigate any further?' Derek asked. 'Surely they could've at least asked around – seen if anyone had witnessed anything?'

'I couldn't say for certain,' Alexander replied, swirling the port in his glass, 'but I suspect the constable was influenced – by someone with enough power or reach to make him ignore every reasonable doubt.'

'You really believe that to be possible?'

'Oh yes. His mannerisms were strange – uneasy. Like he was frightened of something… or someone. He's new to the area, and maybe I'm wrong. But it felt the dismissal of all my suggestions was done with the intention to shut down the case swiftly. As if someone behind the curtain had already decided that the matter was closed.'

'What was his name?'

'Constable Harrington.'

Derek frowned. 'Have you spoken with anyone at the state office?'

Alexander sighed. 'You know how little Nepean likes to get involved in personal matters – not without evidence, anyway. And right now, all I have is instinct to tell me it wasn't an accident. No witness, no motive, no suspect. Just a tangle of suspicion and the scent of conspiracy.'

Derek's brow furrowed further. Alexander's past work with the Home Office had given him connections with some important members of the British Government – discreet, powerful ones – but they came with conditions. Names like Nepean were not invoked lightly, and calling on favours from that realm risked exposure, or worse.

'And what about Georgina? Where was she?'

'Thankfully, she was with her grandmother in London.' The relief on Derek's face was instant; there was nothing they wouldn't do for that girl. They all loved her as if she was their own.

Alexander's voice softened. 'After our failed attempt to convince the constable of his mistake, we returned to London and agreed to reconvene in two days. I needed to see Georgina – to be the one to tell her.' He rubbed his eyes, voice heavy. 'It broke my heart, Derek. She cried so hard, and I had no way to soothe her. I was just as lost.'

That familiar tightness gripped his chest again, as if the grief refused to loosen its hold. Since Stephen's death, the anger and sorrow crushed him as if someone was pressing his chest with such force that it barely let him breathe. He fought to keep his composure, and pressed on.

'The days after are still a blur. Planning your friend's funeral is something no man is prepared for, Derek. Then came the letter from his lawyer – naming me Georgina's guardian. I still can't understand what he was thinking.'

Derek managed a faint smile. 'He was thinking there was no one better to protect his little girl. He knew that you'd do anything for Catherine's daughter.'

That name struck like a hammer. Catherine. The woman he had loved and lost – to Stephen. Georgina's smile and cheeky grin mirrored her mother's so closely, it pained him to look at her sometimes. But Derek was right. For Catherine's child, he would sacrifice anything, for what other thing could he do for the only woman that had ever captured his heart.

Alexander rose from the memory like surfacing from a deep wave.

'Two weeks ago, I went to Stephen's London house. I was hoping to find something – anything – that would help clarify what happened. But when I arrived, the place had been ransacked. Every drawer turned out. Papers missing. It looked like a storm had torn through. Someone had been in there looking for something, Derek.'

'Do you think this has anything to do with what I told Stephen about what I overheard in the tavern regarding the insurance and his dealings with Braxton?'

'I believe so. That's why I feared for Alan Clarkson. If they didn't find what they were looking for in Stephen's home, they'd look elsewhere. And I was right... But I arrived mere minutes too late. He and his wife were already dead.'

Derek's face turned ashen. 'God, Alex. And their daughter?'

Alexander shook his head, remembering Abbie's fierce actions. 'She fought back.' His voice darkened. He could still see her surprise after she pulled the trigger. 'There were two men in the house. She shot one. The other I hit in the shoulder, but he escaped, jumping through the window. John chased him through the garden but lost him a few blocks from the house. We gave the authorities a description, but I'm sure that will get us nowhere. You can find a dozen men like him in any tavern in London, so I do not have too much faith in finding the bastard any time soon.' He run a hand through his hair. 'She was badly hurt. Shot. Bruised. Her face was a mess when I found her.' His voice turned to steel. 'She still wears the marks on her face to remember that night. She is recovering, at least from the physical wounds. Seeing her parents die like that in front of her…I doubt that she will ever be able to forget what happened that night. That wound won't heal as easily.' He trailed off. He only knew too well how some wounds never faded.

Derek sat in stunned silence, his gaze one of disbelief and rage. 'How has this happened, Alex? Does she remember anything?'

'I'm trying to find out. I went to see her today, but she's not precisely happy with me.'

'And why is that?'

A young voice interrupted them from the doorway. 'Uncle Derek!' Georgina burst into the room and ran straight into Derek's arms. He greeted her with the same enthusiasm.

'Hello, cherry face!' She placed her hands on his chest and grinned up at him.

'It makes me laugh every time you call me that, Uncle Derek.' She said, giggling.

'Well, sweetie, you've the face of a cherry and the cheeks of a strawberry.'

That made her laugh again. 'Are you staying with us? I want to show you my new secret place!'

Colton chuckled. 'But if you show me, it won't be a secret anymore.'

She tapped her chin thoughtfully. 'You're right. But I know you can keep a secret, so I don't mind. And you know what else? I have a new friend! Her name is Abbie!'

Her wide smile made him laugh again, and then he looked at Alexander with curiosity.

'Abbie?' Alexander exchanged a glance with Derek, then turned to Georgina.

'Why don't you show Uncle Derek the new doll I bought you? Bring it so he can see her.'

Delighted, she nodded. 'Yes! Yes! Don't go anywhere – she's so beautiful!'

She ran from the room, and Derek turned to Alexander with a raised eyebrow.

'Georgina went exploring, as usual,' Alexander said, 'and ended up at the ruins of an old mill down on Alan's land. Ab– Miss Clarkson – found her and brought her home.'

'And that's the same Miss Clarkson who isn't too fond of you, right?'

'Well, Lord Fairfax was here recently. He was paying his respects. He mentioned the Clarkson's too and started talking about the daughter. He implied that she'd soon lose the house and estate, suggesting she was not capable of handling her father's business. I didn't contradict him.'

'You didn't?' Derek frowned.

'I couldn't. If I had, it would've exposed the fact I know more than I'm letting on – and we can't risk that. We don't know who's behind any of this yet.'

'So, what does that have to do with her being angry at you?'

'Georgina overheard the conversation. She told Miss Clarkson – in her own words of course – but the result was that Miss Clarkson believed I share Fairfax's opinion.' Alexander sighed and reached for his port.

Derek had to hide a smile, drinking from his glass.

'Do not laugh, Derek. You don't know how stubborn that woman can be.'

'I'd wager not more than you. Besides, I've every confidence you'll manage to convince her to trust you. You've always had a way with women.'

The captain only stated the truth; he never had a

problem in the past, but he wasn't too sure that his charms would work with her.

'Not this one.' He shook his head. 'I hope it will be that simple. If I were in her shoes, I wouldn't trust anyone either. She doesn't know who her allies are, and I've given her no reason to believe that I'm one of them. And I am not sure yet how I can convince her that I am to be trusted. She only knew about the first shipment. Alan kept her out of the rest – wisely, if you ask me.'

Georgina returned, clutching a doll to her chest. 'Look! Look at her beautiful dress!' she said, skipping into the room. Derek lifted her and perched her on the arm of his chair. 'It's green,' she beamed, 'and she has matching shoes!'

Everything was exciting under her young eyes. 'It's beautiful,' he agreed, 'but not as beautiful as you, Cherry Face.' She giggled. Derek gently pinched her chin. 'Uncle Alex told me you were a bit naughty the other day?'

Georgina dropped her gaze. 'I didn't mean to, Uncle Derek.' Alexander watched the little girl wrap the grown man around her finger without even trying. One look from her and he was defenceless.

'You're not going to do it again, right?' Derek asked, tickling her sides.

Giggling so hard she could hardly speak, she gasped, 'I promise, Uncle Derek! Oh, please stop!' It was clear she loved every second of it.

Derek hugged her and kissed her cheek. 'See, Alex? She won't do it again.'

'Not the first time I've heard that,' Alexander muttered with a smile. Georgina grinned up at him, feigning innocence. 'What are you up to now, Georgina?'

'I came to ask if I can go out. You said I should ask first, and I promised I would.'

Alexander hesitated. As much as he wanted to keep

her safe and close, he couldn't keep her locked in the house forever. 'You can go – only if John accompanies you.'

'Thank you, Uncle Alex!' She jumped from Derek's lap and ran to kiss Alexander's cheek and skipped out of the room.

John was waiting by the door. Alexander met him there and gave him a firm nod. 'Do not let her out of your sight.'

'I won't, my Lord.' John followed her out.

'She seems fine,' Derek said as Alexander returned to his seat.

'Yes, but she still has nightmares. And I worry, Derek. I know nothing about raising children, and I still don't understand why Stephen left Georgina in my care.'

'As far as I can see, you're doing just fine. She trusts you. She knows you're there for her.'

'Thank you, cousin.'

'So, explain why Miss Clarkson is still upset with you?'

'When she came by with Georgina, I sensed her hostility but didn't know why she behaved like that towards me until she left. She didn't give me the opportunity to introduce myself before she stormed off. Only afterwards did Georgina let slip what she'd overheard.'

Derek started to understand. 'So, when you saw her today, she discovered who you really were.'

'Precisely. You should've seen her face – she was furious. I swear I thought she was going to hit me there and then. I tried to explain everything but right when I was about to tell her what happened, Mr Williams, Alan's administrator, showed up and I had to leave before we could finish talking.'

'What was he doing there?'

'I've no idea. But Miss Clarkson was as surprised by

his arrival as I was. I'll go back tomorrow and hopefully finish the conversation. We need to talk, she deserves answers.'

'Well, cousin,' Derek said, lifting his glass with a grin. 'I wish you the best of luck in your quest.'

Alexander smirked. 'I'm sure you do.'

Derek was clearly enjoying the spectacle of a woman finally resisting Alexander's infamous charm. And he had no doubt that he would love to be there to see if he failed in his endeavours. But Alexander didn't mind. He relished the challenge. More than that – he needed to win Abbie's trust. Not just for the investigation, but because something deeper compelled him to protect her.

'Now,' he said, leaning forward, 'tell me where you have been. I expected you back weeks ago.'

'We hit a storm on the way back from Spain. It pushed us towards *La Rochelle*. The damage was worse than we thought. We docked, but it took days to find the right materials. That port is not what it used to be. It took us over a week to find what we needed to repair *The Isabella*.'

His voice softened on the ship's name. That vessel was one of his most treasured possessions. Anyone who didn't know better might have thought he was speaking of a lover, not a ship.

'Once she was fixed, we sailed to Dover. That's when I heard about Stephen – and rode straight here.' He leaned forward, resting on his knees. 'Now, what is your next move, Alex? How are you planning to uncover who is behind this?'

Alexander ran a hand through his hair and sat back with a sigh. 'Alan gave me some of the documents connected to the Braxton's transactions. I still need to go through them all and try to trace who's behind this and why. I can't believe that somebody would commit murder over a failed business deal.'

'You'd be surprised,' Derek said. 'People will do far worse for far less. Greed can drive a man to places even his nightmares wouldn't take him.' Alexander nodded, but his expression remained troubled. 'Still, I feel there's something else – something I'm missing. I believe Miss Clarkson holds part of the key to this, even if she doesn't know it yet.'

'Well, then, you need to make her trust you, Alexander.'

He let out a dry laugh. 'Easier said than done. But don't worry – I will. I intend to show her she's not alone in this. That she has someone on her side, whether she likes it not.'

He looked out toward the garden, his jaw tight with resolve. Alexander wasn't going to lose this battle. She could not be kept in the dark any longer. She needed to know the truth – not only for her safety, but for her peace. And he would be the one to see that happen. He had sworn to protect her, even if she had never asked for it.

Derek raised a brow, amused. 'I like your confidence, cousin.'

'I'll need it,' Alexander muttered, almost to himself.

'Well,' Derek said, setting his glass down, 'while you're charming the lady, I'll go back to London and do some digging of my own. If I uncover anything worth knowing, I'll make sure the message is delivered in person. We can't rely on letters. We can't trust anyone.'

Alexander nodded. 'Thank you, cousin.'

'You don't have to thank me. We protect each other.'

'Even so,' Alexander said quietly, 'it means something – having someone who's got your back.' He reached for the port decanter.

'Now, tell me something about your travels to Spain.'

Derek smirked, sinking back into his armchair. 'Oh,

cousin. You'll have to pour me a large glass for this one.'

CHAPTER 7

Brushing Hettie in the morning had always brought Abbie a moment of peace. She rested her head against the mare's neck and was rewarded by Hettie shifting her weight, leaning into her as if to return the hug.

'What am I going to do, girl?' Abbie murmured.

'Did you say something, miss?'

Abbie lifted her head to find Simon looking her, slightly puzzled. 'I was just talking to Hettie.'

The boy stepped closer and held out a juicy apple in front of the horse, which Hettie took eagerly from his hand, baring her teeth in delight. 'She likes it when you talk to her, miss,' he said.

Abbie stroked the mare's smooth flank. 'I know it's silly, but it feels like she could understand me.'

Simon shook his head in disagreement. 'I don't think that's silly at all, miss. Horses are clever creatures. Smarter than most people, if you ask me.'

They both laughed, and Abbie felt herself comforted by the boy's sincerity. She often felt the same – that the company of animals was far more rewarding than the company of certain humans. There were no false pretences or veiled expectations, nor judgement behind watchful eyes.

She didn't have many close friends beyond those within Redwood House. It wasn't that she was an introvert, but her eagerness to learn, to question, and to think deeply rarely went down well with the women she'd met over the years. Although sometimes it crossed her mind that it was not for lack of people who thought like her, but for the same reason that she remained silent, other women also did so. Perhaps there were more women like her, quietly observing, just as unwilling to speak out.

'Are you taking her out this morning, miss?'

'Yes,' Abbie said, running her hand along Hettie's glossy coat. 'I think we both need a bit of fresh air.'

Hettie gave a sharp snort and tossed her dark mane, as if agreeing with Abbie.

Simon caressed the mare's head. 'I'll fetch the saddle then.'

'Thank you, Simon.'

Soon after, he returned with a thick, dark brown leader saddle, worn but well-kept. Together, they finished preparing Hettie for the ride.

Just as Abbie was about to mount, Mrs White burst into the stables, almost out of breath. 'Oh, good – you haven't left yet!' She fished a small envelope from the pocket of her apron and handed it to Abbie. 'This just arrived for you, dear.'

Abbie took the missive from the woman's hands and broke the wax seal. Her pulse quickened when she saw the sender: Lord Crawford. He wished to call on her again – this afternoon.

She looked up. 'Could you send a message back accepting his request? I'll receive him at three.'

'Of course, dear. But first, if you're going out with that spirited beast, at least take something to eat!'

Abbie smiled as Mrs White offered a cloth-wrapped parcel. She tucked it into Hettie's satchel.

'You are relentless, Mrs White.'

The woman chuckled. 'Indeed, I am, child. My Patrick always said so. But only with those I care for. You wouldn't want to go and faint like a wilting flower, would you?'

Abbie placed a hand gently on the woman's shoulder. 'No, I wouldn't, Mrs White. I do appreciate everything you do for me. Truly.' She smiled and gave a kiss on the housekeeper's cheek.

The woman's face softened. 'You don't have to thank me, child. Now off you go – and please, be careful.'

With one foot in the stirrup and both hands on the saddle, Abbie swung herself up and took the reins. 'I will, Mrs White,' she called over her shoulder. The woman snorted playfully, clearly doubting her sincerity. Abbie responded with a teasing smile and flicked the reins, sending the mare into a gallop as soon as they left the yard.

The fresh morning breeze kissed her cheeks and tugged at her braid. She wished the wind could sweep away her worries as easily as it tangled her hair, but it carried no mercy – only the memory of Alexander Crawford and his troubling words. Unwilling to leave her a moment of peace.

His visit the day before had stirred more than just grief. It had deepened her unease, adding weight to the confusion that surrounded her parent's deaths. He had raised questions she hadn't dared ask herself. Doubts about her father, about the people he trusted. About whom, if anyone, she could trust now.

Abbie leaned forward spurring Hettie once again, and whispered something to her, a signal only the mare would understand. The horse responded in kind, picking up her pace. She galloped through the fields of Redwood House until she saw the old mill in the distance.

By the time they arrived, both were damp with sweat

and breathless. But luckily, her head was somehow clearer. Abbie dismounted and led Hettie to a tree by the river so that she could palliate her thirst.

'Here you go, girl. Drink and rest.' She stroked the mare's neck. 'While I let my mind betray me with thoughts of that insufferable Lord Crawford. Oh, Hettie. What am I going to do?'

Hettie responded with a gentle bump to Abbie's shoulder, followed by a huff, before lowering her head to the water.

'Oh, you're here!'

Abbie turned and saw Georgina beaming, Her rosy cheeks were flushed from exercise, making her face even more adorable. She stood atop a rock in a charming yellow dress that exposed her ankles, a blue trim around her waist and matching shoes.

Abbie stepped away from the horse and approached the girl by the rock she stood proudly on.

'You ran off again, Georgina? Your uncle won't be pleased – with you or with me. for that matter if he finds out you are back here.' She said, getting closer to the girl and helping her climb down the rock. Georgina reached for Abbie's hand and hopped down.

'Oh no, I didn't come alone. Look – Luke's here.' She pointed toward the mill. Abbie spotted the red-haired boy who had come to deliver the message for Lord Crawford the day before. He was by the mill door, resting his back against the crumbling wall.

'Good morning, miss!' Luke straightened and tugged off his hat. as soon as he realised who she was.

'Good morning, Luke,' she replied with a warm smile, before turning back to Georgina.

'My uncle said I couldn't come alone, so I asked – and he said yes.' She smiled, satisfied with herself. She cupped a hand to Abbie's ear, whispering far louder than necessary. 'But I had to bring someone... you know, like a nanny.' She said with her characteristic cheeky smile.

Luke, having heard every word, huffed in protest. 'I am not a nanny, Georgina.'

His voice cracked slightly, so he cleared his throat and repeated with exaggerated bass. 'I am not your nanny.'

Abbie bit her cheek to stifle a laugh. She could see why Alexander insisted that Georgina be accompanied – but Luke's slim build and youthful innocence didn't exactly inspire confidence.

'Are you sure you asked?' Abbie said, doubting the sincerity of the girl. Georgina looked the other way.

'I asked yesterday,' Georgina replied, too quickly. 'He said I could come – if someone came with me.' Abbie looked at her with her brows pinched.

'Yesterday? So, you haven't asked today?' Georgina's innocent smile widened. 'There wasn't time.'

'Georgina!' Luke exclaimed. 'You are going to get me in trouble! You told me he gave you permission!' The young man was clearly afraid of the repercussions of the adventure Georgina had concocted.

Georgina rolled her eyes and waved him off. 'I said there wasn't time, Luke. Don't worry.'

She leaned in and added with a dramatic whisper, 'He's just a little scared of Uncle Alex.' Giggling, she looked at Luke.

'I am *not* scared of him,' Luke said, straightening up and puffing out his chest.

'Whatever you say,' Georgina sang sweetly.

Abbie loved how cheeky she was, but stepped in. 'Stop teasing, Georgina. And Luke's right—you should have asked.'

Georgina's eyes dropped. 'Am I going to get in trouble?'

'Probably,' Abbie said. 'But I'll come with you and try

to calm your uncle down. Deal?'

Georgina brightened instantly. 'Sounds good, thank you.'

'Come, let's sit by the river. We need to let Hettie rest a little before we go. I brought some cakes – would you like to try them?'

Georgina opened her eyes wide. 'I *love* cakes!' She twirled, then skipped alongside Abbie while she retrieved a blanket and the parcel from Hettie's satchel.

Abbie offered the bundle to the girl, who unwrapped it with delight. She began laying a blanket on the grass, but paused to ask, 'What brings you back here, then?'

Georgina smiled with playful eyes. 'I love this place!' She declared; arms spread wide turning in circles. 'It's beautiful and peaceful.'

Abbie laughed. 'You and I are quite alike, you know?' I love this place, too. It is my favourite.'

Georgina opened her eyes widely. 'It's mine, too!' Georgina's face turned coy. She reached for Abbie's hand. 'Can I come every day?'

How could she negate anything to that little face? Abbie squeezed her fingers. 'Of course, I don't mind. You are more than welcome to come any time you want. As long you ask for permission.'

Her face lit up once more. 'Thank you!' she cried with joy.

Abbie looked toward the mill. 'Come, Luke! There is enough for all three of us.' Luke's eyes lit up. like Georgina's. 'You love cakes too?' she asked.

He nodded enthusiastically and descended the steps from the mill.

But Abbie's blood froze when suddenly two men appeared from around the side of the mill. They walked behind Luke with a dark intensity, one raising a wooden club.

'Luke!' Abbie shouted at him, but it was too late.

The club struck with brutal force. Luke collapsed, rolling down the steps like a rag doll, landing in the grass – unmoving.

Abbie shot to her feet, dragging Georgina behind her. to shield her with her body. 'Stay behind me. Don't speak,' she whispered.

'Well, well, look what we have here,' one of the men sneered. 'Two for the price of one.'

Abbie's eyes darted, searching for something – anything – to use as a weapon, but there was nothing around good enough to defend them. She glanced at the river and thought of jumping, but doubted they'd make it. Not with their skirts weighing them down. She didn't even know if Georgina could swim.

'Don't even think about runnin', pet.' The word *pet* made her stomach churn and she glared at the man defiantly.

'Let the girl go,' Abbie said. 'Take me but leave her be.'

She would not let the girl be hurt because of her. The man's crooked smile brought unpleasant memories to Abbie. His rotten teeth, framed by thin lips, made her stomach turn. 'Oh, pet. But that's why we're 'ere. *She's* the one we came fo'. You're just the extra loot.'

Abbie spun around to see Georgina clutching her skirt so tight her knuckles turned pale. She could see the fear in her eyes.

'Come on, Shaw,' he said to his partner. 'Grab 'em.'

The second man lunged for her and managed to grab her by the arm. She slapped him across the face, struggling to break free – but he retaliated with a savage fist to her jaw. Abbie felt the pain exploding across her skull before landing on the floor. Georgina's voice echoed in the distance.

'*Abbie!* No! Leave me alone! *Abbie!*'
And then everything went dark.

***

Alexander sat at the dining table, a newspaper open in front of him – but his eyes weren't moving. No matter how hard he tried, he couldn't concentrate. His mind was preoccupied with one thing: how to explain everything to Miss Clarkson.

How could he possibly tell her what had happened these past two months without sounding unhinged? And more importantly, how could he earn her trust? In her position, he wouldn't believe a word of it either. Even with the documents he had, evidence wasn't the same as trust. How did one prove themselves trustworthy to someone they'd only just met?

A soft knock interrupted his thoughts.

'A letter from Miss Clarkson has arrived, my lord.' He looked up as Thomas crossed the room, extending a folded piece of paper. Alexander took it and quickly broke the seal. 'She's agreed to see me this afternoon,' he said, folding the letter. Thomas was about to respond when the door to the dining room burst open making both turn.

'My lord! Please come at once!'

A maid stood in the doorway, breathless, her face white with panic. Alexander pushed back his chair so forcefully it toppled, clattering to the floor behind him. His stomach dropped – his first thought was that something awful had happened to Georgina. He ran from the room, Thomas close behind.

Outside, Marcus Finney – his horse master and Luke's father – was half-carrying his son towards the house. The boy's shirt was stained red, and he clutched his head, face twisted with pain.

Alexander rushed to meet them.

Before Alexander reached the boy, his knees gave out beneath him, but Marcus quickly grabbed his son and eased the boy onto the ground, resting the boy's back against his chest. When he lifted his head to look ahead, Alexander saw the fear in his young eyes.

Alexander dropped to his own knees beside him, lifting Luke's chin so their eyes met. 'What the hell happened? Who did this to you?'

Luke's voice trembled. 'I'm so sorry, my lord. I-I lost her. I lost her.' He repeated with tears in his eyes. Alexander's heart began to race.

'What are you talking about?' His voice sharpened. 'Where is Georgina, Luke?'

The boy looked at him, tears now uncontrolled running down his cheeks. 'They took her.'

Panic surged through Alexander's chest like a blade. '*Who*? Talk, boy – *now!*'

'I don't know,' Luke cried. 'I felt someone hit me. When I woke up, they were gone.'

Alexander clenched his jaw. *Please, no…* he prayed silently. But he couldn't afford to freeze now. 'Where were you?'

'By the old mill, my lord.'

'Damn it.'

'She told me you gave her permission,' Luke continued. 'And then Miss Clarkson said she would take her home, so I thought it was all right.'

Alexander's expression shifted. 'You said – Miss Clarkson?'

'Yes, my lord.'

'And where is she?'

'I don't know. She was gone too. I think… I think they took her as well.' His lip quivered. 'I failed you, my lord.'

Alexander gripped his shoulders. 'This is not your fault, Luke. I'll get them back.' He turned to Thomas. 'Send for the doctor. Make sure he's well-tended to.'

'Yes, my lord.'

The commotion had drawn the rest of the household, now gathered in a tight knot nearby. Alexander scanned the faces until he found the man he was looking for. 'John – ready our horses. We ride immediately.' Then, turning to Paige, Georgina's nursemaid. 'Prepare a room for Luke in the house.' She nodded at once and disappeared through the doorway to follow his instructions.

Alexander stormed to his study. He yanked open a drawer, pulled out both pistols, and began loading them. Every motion was sharp, practiced. There was no time to waste. He needed to find them, whatever it took. He stepped out, where Thomas was waiting with his coat. 'Your horse is ready, sir.'

Alexander let him help slip the coat over his shoulders. 'Where is Luke now?'

'Mrs Watson's taken him to a guest room. I've sent a maid to fetch the doctor.'

Alexander placed a firm hand on his shoulder. 'Send word to Jacob – tell him what happened, but not to breathe a word of it to anyone else. If we're not back by tomorrow, send a message to Captain Colton. He should be en-route to London by now.' Thomas nodded. But Alexander could see the worry in his eyes. 'I'll bring her back,' Alexander said quietly.

'I do not doubt it, my lord.' He made his way to the stables, where John already waited, mounted and ready.

'Where to?' John asked.

'The mill.'

With a hard flick of his reins, Alexander spurred his

horse into a gallop. John followed close behind, hooves pounding, dust rising in their wake – only one thought in Alexander's mind: *Bring them home. Whatever it takes.*

CHAPTER 8

The rough surface beneath her cheek felt like a bed of thorns. As consciousness slowly returned, Abbie stirred. Cold seeped into her skin. Little by little, the fog that prevented her from waking up dissipated. She placed a hand on the floor and sat up, blinking against the shadows. Disoriented, she looked around – where was she? And how had she ended up here? Then it all came back in a rush. The two men. The blow. And–

Georgina!

A soft moan behind her made her spin around. The little girl sat hunched over, cheeks streaked with dried tears. As she opened her eyes and saw Abbie, she threw herself into her arms.

'Abbie!' she cried. Georgina put her arms around her. 'You're alive!' Abbie hugged her tightly, exhaling a shudder of relief.

'Yes, sweetie, I'm alive,' she said, though pain shot through her jaw as she spoke. Her hand went to the aching spot. Still, she pushed it aside and focused on Georgina. 'Shh... It's alright.' She said, rubbing her tiny back to soothe her fears. 'Do you know where we are?'

Georgina loosened her grip and shook her head. 'No, we've been riding all day. I think we're in a cabin in the woods... but I have no idea where.'

Her small body trembled, and Abbie could see fear in her eyes. Rubbing her face with her thumb, she cleared the tears from her cheeks. 'It's alright. Can you tell me what you remember? What happened? Can you do that?'

The girl nodded, drawing a deep breath. 'They hit Luke. Then the man hit you, and you closed your eyes, and you didn't wake up. I was so scared. What if Luke is dead?' Her voice cracked as her lip trembled. Her breathing started to go faster as if she was going to start crying.

Abbie hugged her, resting the child's head against her shoulder. 'Shhh... Luke's strong. He'll be alright.'

He has to be, she thought, praying he was conscious, safe – and able to get help.

'I want to go home.'

The sadness in her eyes made her heart ache. 'Me too, Georgina. Me too. We are going to get out of here, I promise.'

Georgina straightened, wiping her face on her sleeve, and Abbie noticed that her lovely yellow dress was torn in several places.

'What happened to your skirt?'

Georgina's eyes lit with pride. 'Uncle Alex once told me a story about how he could rescue a friend because he left clues behind, so... I left pieces of my skirt on our way here.'

Abbie couldn't help but smile. 'Clever girl.'

Resting a hand on the wall, she looked around, her eyes adapting to the darkness surrounding them. Only a single ray of moonlight filtered through the cracks between the wooden boards of the cabin. The room was small, more like a storage pantry than a proper cabin room. It was mostly empty. A filthy sack lay in one corner. A bucket stood near it. Nothing else.

She turned to the door and tried the handle.

'It's locked,' Georgina whispered. 'I already tried.'

Abbie let go of the knob. Trying again will only bring the attention to them.

Voices murmured beyond the door. She crouched and peered through a narrow gap in the frame big enough to see through into the other room. Firelight flickering in the adjoining room, sufficiently for her to distinguish two men.

The despicable man that had struck Luke lounged in a chair next to the fire, his shirt stretched tight over his round gut, barely containing his large body, making his belly stick out on both sides of his body. As he drank from his cup, wine dribbled into his beard. He wiped it with a grimy sleeve, letting out a burp simultaneously, making Abbie wince in disgust.

The other, whom Abbie recognised as the one who hit her, Shaw, standing next to a big pot hanging over the hearth, tall and thin with dark, greasy hair, filled his plate with what Abbie assumed was stew, but it looked more like a lumpy pot of clay than food. His thin frame bent like a crow's, and he slurped loudly as he shovelled spoon after spoon into his mouth. Once he finished the disgusting-looking meal, he looked up to his partner.

'So…what now, Bill?' he spat.

Bill didn't even glance at him. 'We wait for the boss. He said he'd be 'ere in the mornin'… to get the brat.'

The skinny man dropped the empty plate, and his shoulders stiffened. 'That little rat. I want to smash 'er for bitin' me!'

Bill chuckled.

'It ain't funny! I'm still bleedin'!' He kicked his plate. 'Look!' He raised a bandaged hand, the cloth stained deep crimson.

The other man smirked. 'You better not tell anyone a little girl bit you, Shaw.'

He puffed, picked up a cup, poured what looked like wine, and drank the liquid in silence.

Abbie turned back to Georgina, startled. 'You bit

him?'

Georgina nodded proudly, the girl lifted her shoulders and straightened her back. 'He was hurting me.'

Abbie touched her cheek and grabbed her chin gently, a soft smile curving her lips. She loved her spirit and the fire inside her.

'Good girl. Did they hurt you?'

Georgina shook her head. 'No. The big man told him he couldn't touch me.' Relief washed over Abbie. They didn't harm her, but now more questions remained. Why did they want Georgina? And what were they planning to do with her? Who was this 'boss' they were waiting for? She turned again toward the door and looked through the gap.

'What do we do with the woman?' Shaw asked. 'I've got a few ideas of what I would do to her.'

Abbie's stomach turned. She clenched her teeth and promised herself she would not go down without a fight.

'We wait until he comes for the girl,' Bill muttered. 'Then we can enjoy the little pet.' His dirty smile made her shiver, and her stomach turned in disgust. She clenched her fists.

She wanted to vomit hearing those men talking about her like she was a piece of meat they could share. 'What did they say?' Georgina whispered behind her.

Abbie didn't want to share the conversation with her and quickly responded. 'Nothing I could make out clearly, darling,' Abbie lied quickly. They needed to get out of there as soon as possible.

She began pacing around the room, searching for anything – anything at all – that could help them escape. As she stepped across the floor, a soft creak stopped her.

She shifted her weight. There it was again. One of the boards beneath her was loose.

Looking down, she placed one foot on the board and

stepped on it, glad to listen to the squeaky noise again. One side of the board was slightly loose, and as she got closer, she noticed she could see the ground through the gap.

'Georgina… is the cabin on a hill?'

The girl furrowed her brows. 'Yes,' she whispered, nodding effusively, satisfied with herself for remembering.

Abbie sat on the floor next to the board. 'Go to the door and let me know if anyone comes,' Abbie said with a jerk of her head. The girl obediently walked over to the door, proud to have been given the responsibility. She crouched down and peeked through the gap, just as Abbie had done before.

Abbie examined the loose plank, then looked around for something to pry it up. There was nothing, just the bucket and the sack. Then, she remembered the ribbon holding her hair in place. She pulled it free, wound it around the nail head, and yanked until there was enough space for her fingers to go underneath the board. Slowly, the board lifted with a quiet crack. She froze, looking at Georgina and hoping they didn't hear the noise. Georgina turned from the door and shook her head – *they hadn't heard.*

Letting out a sigh of relief, she looked back at the hole. Tilting her head, she could see the edge of the cabin. As she expected, the cabin was built on a slope, leaving a gap between the floor and the ground. The space was ample enough for a small body to slip through. *Not me*, she thought. *But Georgina might fit.*

Suddenly, a sound outside the cabin made both of them freeze. A knock followed. Georgina darted back from the door. Abbie quickly lowered the board, covered it with the sack, and crouched down beside the girl. She saw how the two men tense at the unexpected arrival.

Bill rose, grabbing a knife from his boot. His eyes narrowed, tightening the grip around the handle. He looked at Shaw, fiercely staring, as if he was ready to kill anyone who came through the door uninvited.

'Get your pistol,' he ordered. Shaw obeyed, leaving his cup on the floor and taking a pistol from the table next to the door. As Bill approached the door, knife in hand, Abbie could see a pistol sticking out of the waistband of his pants.

'Who is it?' he barked.

'It's me, you idiot! Open the bloody door!' The voice struck a note of familiarity in Abbie's ears. Bill growled and cracked the door open. The stranger didn't give his name, but they must have recognised his voice, for Bill swore before opening the door, but he stood in front of the man, cutting him off so he wouldn't enter. 'What the 'ell are *you* doin' here?'

'What do you think? You really thought the boss would come out here himself and dirty his precious hands? Don't be daft!' The man shoved his way inside.

Abbie's breath caught in her lungs. *I know that voice.* She crept back to have a look through the gap in the door. The firelight didn't quite reach his face, but something about the way he moved, spoke and commanded attention sent a warning deep through her bones.

Her heart pounded so loudly she was sure they'd hear it. She watched the man pace across the room. *Please no…* she thought. He was here for Georgina, she could feel it. The man turned to Shaw.

'Put the gun down, you fool,' he said, the contempt in his voice unmistakeable. Shaw obeyed, setting the gun back down on the table.

'You have the girl?' the man asked.

'Of course we do,' Bill replied, slamming the door

shut. 'What are you doin' here?' His tone was cold.

The stranger didn't answer right away. Instead, he began removing his gloves, slowly peeling the leather from his fingers one by one before finally looking up at Bill. His movements carried authority, and Abbie could tell both men were wary of him. His face still hidden to Abbie's eyes.

Bill's shoulders were tense. He looked uneasy – waiting until the man spoke again.

'I am here to make sure you have the girl,' the stranger said. 'It's not the first time you've been sent on an errand and failed to finish it.' He paused. 'Now, I don't have all night. Where is she?'

Bill jerked his head toward the back room. 'Shaw, bring the girl.' As Shaw passed him, he muttered something under his breath. Shaw nodded.

Bill offered the man a glass of wine, which he declined. He stood by the door, never removing his coat.

Abbie backed away from the door, taking Georgina's hand and pulling her in close, shielding her with her body. The door opened slightly, and Shaw slipped in.

His eyes scanned the room before he pressed a finger to his lips. 'Make a noise, and y'll regret it. Girl – come with me.' He stared at Abbie with narrowed eyes and she opened her mouth to object, but he lifted a hand to silence her. 'I'll bring her back, he just wants to see her.'

Georgina clutched Abbie's skirt. 'I don't want to go,' she whispered.

'She comes, you both live. You fight, you both die,' Shaw growled. His smile sent a shiver down Abbie's spine. Squaring her back, Georgina stepped forward, but Abbie instinctively reached out and grabbed her arm.

'No,' she whispered.

Georgina met her eyes. 'I'll be right back.'

Shaw seized her by the wrist and yanked her forward.

He gave Abbie a final warning. 'Don't move, or you will regret it.'

Her eyes blazed with fury. 'If you don't bring her back,' she said, '*you* will regret it.' He pulled Georgina out the door and slammed it shut behind him. Abbie didn't wait.

She rushed to the crack in the doorway, unwilling to lose sight of Georgina.

Shaw dragged the little girl to the other side of the room, pushing her to stand before the stranger. Her head was bowed, hands clenched together, small frame trembling. With his back to her, the man bent and took her chin, lifting her face to look him right in the eyes. Abbie watched, her stomach twisting in rage.

You bastard, she thought. *You will pay for this.*

He finally released her and turned to Bill. 'I'm impressed. Honestly, I didn't think you were smart enough to pull this off.'

Shaw flushed with anger but he kept quiet. 'You've seen her now,' Bill said flatly. 'You can tell the boss. Make sure we get our money.' He gave a sharp jab with his finger, signalling Shaw to take the girl back to the back room. Obedient, he grabbed her arm again.

The stranger gave a humourless groan. 'Be careful, Bill. Greed's a dangerous vice. There are always consequences. But don't worry – he'll pay. Just make sure the girl is in one piece when we come for her. If anything happens, we won't get what we need from Crawford. And we do not like wasting our time. Are we clear?' Bill nodded.

Crawford? Abbie's heart skipped. *This is about him?* None of it made sense.

The stranger put back his gloves and walked to the door. 'I'll keep in touch,' the man continued, with his hand on the doorknob. 'If this doesn't work, you'll have to go and get someone else.'

'Who?' Shaw asked.

'You don't need to know yet,' the stranger replied with a sneer. He turned and walked out, leaving the door to slam behind him.

Abbie's stomach churned. This wasn't just some thug – this man was important, not just a puppet in the hands of whoever was moving the strings. He was a decision maker.

Still gripping Georgina, Shaw grunted, 'More money for us, Bill. Hopefully the next one's as easy to catch as this little rat.' He flung open the door and shoved Georgina through so hard that she landed on her knees. Then he turned and left without a backwards glance.

Abbie ran to her side. 'Are you alright?'

Georgina dusted off her dress. 'Yes… but did you hear them? They want Uncle Alex to do something!'

'I heard,' Abbie said, hugging her close.

'Who was that man?' Georgina asked concerned, 'he scares me very much.'

'He scares me too, Georgina. But you did very well. You are a brave little girl.' She stroked her hair gently.

The girl gave a small, quivering smile. 'What do we do now?'

'Now,' Abbie said, moving quickly. 'It's time to escape.'

She pulled the sack aside and lifted the loose floorboard again and offered her hand to Georgina. 'Come here.' Georgina crouched beside her, and they both stared at the opening. A soft breeze drifted through the gap, carrying the earthy smell of the forest. Abbie leaned in and spotted the base of a tree just a few feet from the cabin's side. Lifting her head to look at Georgina, she asked.

'Did you see trees behind the cabin?' she asked.

'Yes,' Georgina whispered. 'Many. It was so thick I could not see anything past the trees. Is that good?'

Abbie smiled. 'It's perfect for what you need to do.'

Georgina's eyebrows drew together in confusion. 'Perfect for what?'

Abbie turned to her, resting her hands on the girl's shoulders. 'For you to run. I need you to crawl through this hole, get into the woods, and hide.'

Georgina's eyes widened. 'Me?'

It didn't take long for the girl to realise what she was asking her to do. Abbie forced a smile, but the girl was too clever. 'I can't fit through the gap, sweetie. But you can.'

Georgina's lip trembled. 'No.' Her voice was almost a whisper.

Abbie rubbed her arms to comfort her. 'Georgina, this is our only chance to escape.'

'But what about you?'

'I will work on lifting the other board so I can follow you.'

'By myself? I don't want to leave you. I cannot do this, Abbie.' She whispered and put her arms around Abbie's neck.

'Yes, you can. You're strong, you're smart. You'll find a tree, climb it and stay hidden until I come. I promise, I'll follow you as fast as I can.'

Georgina looked at her frightened, shaking her head. 'What if they hurt you?'

'They won't.' Abbie's voice shook, but she forced a smile. 'We don't have too much time, Georgina. I promise I will follow you.' Abbie cleaned the tears that started running in silence through her cheeks. 'Besides, I have no doubt your uncle will come after you; we need to buy time for him to come. You understand?'

At least, that was what she hoped. She was sure that

Alexander would move heaven and earth to find his niece.

Georgina finally nodded and looked at the hole. 'But what if they try to hurt you?'

'They need both of us, Georgina; they won't hurt me if they need me.' She smiled, trying not to let it be obvious that what she was saying was not entirely true, since in reality the only one they needed was Georgina. But what happened to her mattered little if she could save the little girl. This would give Alexander time to find her, to take her home safely.

'You have to promise me something, Georgina,' she said, wiping the girl's face with her sleeve.

'What?'

'No matter what, do not come back. You promise?'

The girl hesitated. 'But…'

'Promise me, Georgina.' Her face fell. She nodded.

'I will be with you as soon as I can.' Georgina took a deep breath. 'That's my brave girl.' Abbie kissed her cheek. 'Come on, then. Step in.'

Abbie helped her down the hole and kissed her before she began to crawl out from under the cabin. Once Georgina was outside, she stood, and before running into the woods, she looked back. Abbie gave her an encouraging smile and a nod. Georgina ran the short distance toward the thick woods and vanished into the leafy trees. Abbie pressed a hand to her chest and prayed that she would be safe, that she would find a tree to climb and hide. And she also prayed that Alexander would come for her. Soon.

***

Alexander and John picked up the trail from the mill. They found a blanket laid out on the grass by the river, a few scattered crumbs of food, and the hoof prints of three horses. The ground was soft enough for Alexander to follow the direction they had taken – north, into the forest. They had at least a four hour head start, but nothing would stop him from finding Georgina.

As they pressed on, a scrap of yellow fabric caught his eye. He dismounted immediately, heart pounding, and snatched it from a thorny bush. The tear was clean. Not an accident, a message.

Ahead, where the path forked, he saw another piece of yellow fabric fluttered on the right-hand trail. Georgina was telling him where to go.

He thanked the heavens for that. For once, she'd listened to his stories.

'This way, John.' He mounted again and galloped along the narrowing path, eyes sharp for further signs. As the sun dipped below the trees, twilight settled over the forest – but fortune was on their side. The moon was full, and the sky was clear, lighting their way with its cold silver glow.

At last, through the dense woodland, they spotted a cabin. Three horses were tied out front – one of them unmistakably Abbie's mare.

Alexander signalled John to halt.

They dismounted silently, securing their own horses to a nearby tree. Crouched low, they crept closer.

'That's Miss Clarkson's horse,' Alexander whispered. They scanned the clearing for signs of movement.

Suddenly, John tapped Alexander's arm to claim his attention and pointed to the far side of the cabin. A small figure in a bright yellow dress emerged from beneath the structure. She paused, glanced behind her, then bolted toward the woods. Alexander's heart surged in relief when he recognised Georgina.

They rose and sprinted after her. She had reached a

tree and was trying to climb it when Alexander caught up, grabbing her gently from behind and placing a hand over her mouth.

She began to struggle, but he whispered in her ear, 'Georgina, it's me. Uncle Alex.'

She froze. Then slowly turned. Georgina's face lightened up, tears forming in her eyes. 'Uncle Alex!' she cried, throwing her arms around his neck. Her little body trembled, whether from cold or fear he couldn't say.

'Shhh, I'm here now. You are safe.' He wrapped his coat around her, cradling her as though she might vanish again if he let her go. 'Are you hurt?' he asked, cupping her cheeks.

She shook her head. 'You found my clues?' Georgina asked.

'I did. And I'm so proud of you, Georgina.' He hugged her tightly again. 'What happened?' His voice was low, controlled.

'Two men took us from the old mill. Abbie's still there, Uncle. You have to help her.' The little girl couldn't hold back the tears from the relief at seeing her uncle.

'I will,' he promised. 'But first, tell me – who's inside?'

'The two men that took us. Abbie's locked in a room at the back. She pulled up a floorboard and made me crawl out. She told me to run and hide in a tree and wait for you. I didn't want to leave her. I promise.' Alexander cleared her tears, wishing he could erase the experience altogether.

'I know, darling. You're brave, and Abbie knows that. But now, you're going to stay here with John, alright?' He looked at John, who nodded. The man extended a hand, and Georgina took it.

'Stay with her.'. Alexander got closer to him, lowering his voice so Georgina couldn't hear it, he said. 'Don't let her out of your sight.'

John nodded. 'I'll protect her with my life.'

'I know, my friend. I'll signal you when it's safe.'

He caressed Georgina's cheek one last time. 'I'll come back soon.'

'With Abbie?' Her voice was small, hopeful.

'Yes. With Abbie.' He said, hugging her.

Alexander's heart ached to see how worried she was for Abbie. He couldn't let her lose anyone else close to her; she had already lost too much in a short time.

He turned and ran silently back toward the cabin, skirting the tree line and crouching low as he neared the clearing. He paused, watching for any sign of movement, then crept slowly along the outer wall. Leaning his back against the timber, he inched towards the nearest window.

The pane was too grimy to see through. He lifted his sleeve to wipe it when a scream erupted from inside.

A moment later, the front door flew open. A man burst out, fury etched into his face and a pistol gripped tightly in his hand.

Without wasting time, Alexander flattened himself against the wall and waited for the man to approach him to wrap an arm around his throat, yanking him backwards, to prevent him from raising the alarm to whoever was inside.

The pistol dropped with a muffled thud onto the earth. The man flailed, clawing at Alexander's grip, but it was no use. Alexander held him until his body went slack. Lowering him to the ground, he removed the belt from the man's filthy trousers, using it to bind his wrists behind his back. He tore the man's scarf free and gagged him, leaving his unconscious body against the cabin wall.

Then, picking up his pistol, he turned back towards the door.

And knocked.

***

Abbie tried to pry up the board next to the one she had already loosened, but this one had more nails – some so deeply embedded in the wood she couldn't even reach them. Her fragile ribbon would not suffice to pull them out. She needed something sturdier to make the board give way. But she didn't dare make noise; drawing attention now would be dangerous.

She carefully replaced the board, laid the sack back over it, and crept to the door to peer through the gap in the next room.

The men were still seated near the fireplace without speaking. Bill was carving at a block of wood with his knife. Shaw sipped slowly from his cup, his body slouched, his mind clearly dulled by drink.

Eventually, Shaw broke the silence. 'Should we feed 'em, Bill?'

'Yeah,' Bill muttered without looking up. Shaw reached for two plates from the floor and bent to retrieve a wooden spoon. He began spooning stew into the first dish.

'Eh! What you doin'?!' Bill's bark was so loud it even made Abbie jump.

Shaw froze, confused. 'Ye said to feed 'em…' Realising immediately that he responded more effusively than he obviously intended, his gaze lowered to avoid facing Bill's wrath.

'I said let's feed 'em, not give 'em all our bloody food. They eat more in a day than we do in a week! One spoon each, let 'em know what hunger feels like.'

Shaw grumbled, 'Alright, alright. No need to yell.' He dumped the contents back into the pot, and re-filled each plate with a single measly spoonful.

When he came to unlock the door, Abbie moved back to the far wall, bracing herself. The key rattled in the lock, and then the door slammed open so violently that it rebounded off the wall. Abbie held her breath.

'Here!' He said as he put the plates on the floor. 'Eat your– ' Shaw stopped short, eyes scanning the room, his expression turned thunderous. 'Where's the rat?' he snarled.

With a single stride, he grabbed Abbie's arm and wrenched her forward, peering behind her skirts, as if he expected Georgina to be hiding there.

Rage and desperation twisted his face. He slammed her back and anger lifted to his face, he pushed her up and against the wall, pinning her shoulders tight to the wall. Abbie met his gaze, head high, jaw clenched, defiant.

'Where is she?' She said nothing. 'Yo' fuckin' whore!' he bellowed, shaking her hard enough to knock the breath from her lungs.

Attracted by Shaw's screams, Bill burst in, face dark with fury. 'What's goin' on?!'

'The rat's gone!'

Anger crossed through Bill's expression and pushed Shaw to the side to jolt her, pressing her back against the dirty walls. 'Where is she, bitch?' Abbie stared at him and smiled. 'Stop smiling and tell me where she is!'

With a mocking grin, she said. 'You'll never find her.'

His face contorted with rage. Lifting his hand he struck her hard across the face. She hit the floor, clutching her cheek as her vision blurred with the force of it.

'Make sure this one doesn't go anywhere,' Bill growled, grabbing his pistol. 'I'll find the brat.'

'But where?'

Bill looked at Abbie with disgust. 'She can't be far.'

He handed the weapon to Shaw. 'If I don't find her, you will suffer. Shoot her if she moves. I'll take yours.'

As he stormed out, Shaw turned to Abbie, eyes full of malice. He grabbed her by the throat and began to squeeze. Abbie struggled and tried to get his hands off her, her vision becoming blurrier by the second. Abbie clawed at his hands, her feet barely touching the floor.

'I was gonna wait for the boss to come for the brat, but you? You need to be taught a lesson. No one messes with my coin, pet, and you will cost me lots of coin if we don't find the girl.'

He pinned her to the wall, fingers tightening. He put the gun in his belt behind his back and moved his sight from her face to her breasts and, grabbing one with his filthy hands, he squeezed violently. Abbie's senses flared back from the stupor she was fading into with a surge of fury.

She pushed his hands with all the strength she had left. 'Take your filthy hands off me!' she rasped.

He laughed, pressing harder. With the other hand, he tore the top of her dress, revealing her thin white chemise beneath. 'I'm gonna have some fun with you.' She couldn't breathe. Her vision narrowed. Her limbs grew weak.

A knock on the door made Shaw halt, distracting him enough to ease the pressure on her throat, air finally flowing into her lungs. He looked towards the door, and Abbie took the opportunity, with the little strength she had left, and kicked him between his legs.

He let out a strangled cry grabbing his parts with both hands and stumbled back. Abbie dropped to the ground, coughing, dragging air into her burning lungs.

'Fucking whore!' he growled, grabbing her ankle.

She kicked him with her free leg and caught him in the face. 'Get away from me!'

Then, the door burst open, and the sound filled the whole cabin with a thunderous crack. A figure stood in the doorway, framed by the moonlight, a pistol in each hand.

Shaw whirled, pulling the gun from his belt.

'Who the fuck are *you*?!' he said as he walked out of the room, taking his gun out of his belt and pointing at Alexander.

Abbie crawled through the floor to get a better view. The familiar silhouette almost made her cry with happiness. She would never have thought she would feel so glad to see him.

***

Alexander stepped inside, eyes locking onto Abbie. Her torn dress. Her bruised face.

Rage unlike any he had ever known boiled beneath his skin – but he kept it under control.

'Step away from her,' he said.

Shaw looked from Abbie to Alexander, assessing. 'Sorry mate, but this one's mine.'

Both men stared at each other, waiting to see who would make the first move.

'I must insist. If you don't, I'll be forced to shoot you.' Abbie slowly crawled out of Shaw's reach.

Shaw sneered. 'You won't have 'er. How can you shoot me... if you're dead?' He raised the pistol.

'No!' Abbie cried. Shaw fired but Alexander shifted, just enough. The bullet sang through the air, missing him by a mere inch.

He returned fire. The shot struck Shaw square in the chest. The man staggered, eyes wide, and collapsed to the floor. Blood pouring through the wound, tinting his dirty shirt and his eyes wide open. A pool of blood surrounded him in seconds.

Alexander rushed to Abbie's side and gently pulled her into his arms. 'Are you alright?' She tried to speak, but no sound came. Her hands flew to her throat, bruises already forming around her soft neck. 'Careful.' he whispered, guiding her close.

She leaned into him, trembling, and finally managed to whisper hoarsely, 'Georgina?'

'She's safe. John is with her. They're hidden in the woods.' Abbie nodded, eyes brimming. Alexander helped her to a chair and found a basin of water nearby. As she sipped from the cup he filled, he wrapped a blanket around her shoulders, hiding the torn fabric of her gown.

She cleared her throat again. 'There was a second man.'

'I know, he's outside. I tied him up. Can you walk?'

'Yes.' Her voice was nearly gone, but her resolve was intact.

He supported her as she stood, surprised again by her strength. She leaned on him as they left the cabin, leaving Shaw's lifeless body behind.

They reached the clearing where the horses waited. 'Can you ride?'

'I don't know.' He guided her hand to Hettie's saddle, caressing her fingers. The loyal horse shifted gently beneath her touch, and Abbie rested her head on the horse's neck, closing her eyes as the sense of relief washed over her.

'Wait here,' he said.

He circled back to the cabin. But his heart sank – his prisoner was gone. One of the horses was missing too. They couldn't afford to stay. He turned and whistled – a sharp, low sound that cut through the quiet night. Moments later, John emerged with Georgina by his side.

'You're back!' she cried, running to him jumping into his arms. 'Where is Abbie?' He gestured toward her, pale and leaning against her horse. Placing Georgina on the ground, the girl ran to her, throwing her arms around her waist. Alexander steadied them both.

'Abbie! I'm so sorry – look at your face! They hurt you!' She touched her face with her little hands and looked at her, tears falling uncontrollably down her cheeks.

Abbie washed the tears away. 'I'll be alright sweetie. Don't cry, or you'll make me cry.' She hugged her tiny body, and Georgina let out a big sigh of relief.

'I should've done something.'

'No, darling. You did everything right. If you hadn't escaped, your uncle wouldn't have found me.' Georgina nodded, hugging her tight again.

'We need to leave,' Alexander said. He looked at John, who was guiding both of their horses. 'Georgina will ride with you.' John mounted, and Alexander handed her up, settling her in front of him.

Then he turned to Abbie. She raised an eyebrow as he tied her horse to his own. 'You're riding with me.' His tone left no room for argument. She didn't even open her mouth in protest. That alone told him how much pain she was in.

He lifted her onto his saddle and climbed up behind her, wrapping the blanket tighter around her shoulders and drawing her against his chest.

'Where are we?' she whispered.

'A few miles north of Woolhampton. Are you ready?'

She nodded. 'As ready as I can be.'

He flicked the reins, setting the horse to a steady trot. He couldn't push the horses as hard as he wished – not with Georgina and Abbie in this condition. But every part of him prayed it was fast enough. Fast enough to get them all home – before anyone else came looking.

CHAPTER 9

They rode for hours through the thick forest. Thanks to the moonlight filtering through the trees, the path was just visible enough to guide the horses. Abbie let herself relax against Alexander's firm chest. The steady rhythm of the ride lulled her into a state of drowsiness. After all they had endured – the bruises, the fear and the constant strain – exhaustion had seeped into every part of her body. In that moment, the only thing she wanted was to lose herself in the arms of the man holding her.

'John, how is Georgina?' Alexander's whisper brushed her ear.

'She's half-asleep,' came the reply, 'but I can tell she's restless.'

'I'm tired,' said Georgina through a yawn, her voice drowsy. She blinked up at her uncle with heavy eyes.

'We'll stop now so you can rest, darling.' Abbie felt Alexander shift slightly as he looked around. He guided his horse left toward a clearing where the trees thinned. 'John, this way,' he called, motioning toward the wide patch of grass ahead.

Abbie raised her head over Alexander's shoulder. She spotted Georgina struggling to stay upright in the saddle. As they slowed, Alexander's gaze shifted to her. When their eyes met, a flicker of heat sparked low in her belly, spreading fast like a flame quickly spreading in a fire.

He didn't look away as he reined in and brought the horse to a halt. And neither did she. The moment felt suspended in time – just the two of them, the silent forest surrounding them. Part of her didn't want it to end. But how could she let herself get lost in those piercing blue eyes, when she didn't even know if she could truly trust him?

She turned her gaze forward, willing her heart to slow.

'We'll rest here,' he said. His voice was deeper than before, the low timbre resonating against her back.

'Is it safe?' she asked, keeping her eyes fixed ahead.

'Aye.' His reply was quiet, close. 'They won't be coming after us just yet. A short rest won't hurt.'

They reached the clearing, and Alexander dismounted first. Raising his arms to help her down, he gripped her waist and lowered her gently to the ground. His hands, though large and calloused, were startlingly tender as they touched her skin.

'How are you feeling?' he asked, examining the bruises on her cheek and neck.

'I'll be alright. I just need a moment to rest.'

'Can you stand?'

She nodded and he helped her to a fallen tree trunk, guiding her down to sit before turning to retrieve Georgina from the saddle.

The girl curled her head against his shoulder, eyes barely open as he carried her over. He set her beside Abbie, where she promptly laid her head on her lap. With the tenderness of a mother, Abbie stroked her hair, feeling the little girl's breathing steady under her touch.

'How are you, sweetie?' she murmured.

'I'm fine,' Georgina whispered. 'I'm so glad Uncle Alex found us.'

'Me too, Georgina. Me too.' Abbie agreed softly.

She looked over at the two men tending the horses. This was now the second time that this man had rescued her. She didn't even want to imagine what might have happened if he hadn't found them. She didn't yet know what to make of him – but deep down, she felt she could trust him. With him, she felt safe.

Alexander and John secured the horses, and he opened his saddlebag, taking a blanket. He draped it around Abbie and Georgina's shoulders.

'Thank you, Lord–'

'Alexander,' he interrupted gently. 'Please. After all we've been through, I think we can dispense with formalities. Don't you agree?'

Abbie smiled. 'Thank you, Alexander.' He inclined his head, a faint smile touching his lips.

'Are you hungry, Miss?' John asked.

'Yes, famished. What about you, Georgina?'

The girl didn't lift her head. 'Me too,' she replied, with a sleepy voice.

John handed them some bread and cheese, which tasted heavenly after they had gone almost a day without food. Georgina perked up quickly, and moved to sit beside John, who was, according to her, the best storyteller in the world. He didn't disappoint, launching into a tale about mischievous forest fairies with such gusto that Abbie couldn't help but smile.

Alexander sat beside her; his voice low so only she could listen. 'Are you feeling better?'

'Yes. Thank you.'

'I'm glad to hear it.' They remained silent, listening to John's tale for a while, until Alexander touched her arm, drawing her attention. 'Abbie… what happened?'

She took a slow breath, gathering her thoughts. 'I went to the mill in the morning and found Georgina with Luke. We were setting up to eat something when two men appeared behind him and struck him in the head.' She turned to him. 'How is he?' Alexander touched her hand.

'He's alright. Nasty cut on his head, but he'll survive.' Abbie sighed, relieved.

'What did they want from you?' He asked.

Abbie shook her head. 'It wasn't me they wanted, Alexander; they wanted Georgina. I was only taken because I was there with her.' He looked at her sharply.

'Georgina? Why?' He turned to Georgina, worry building up in his eyes.

'They were using her to get to you. They had instructions from someone to kidnap her and not to harm her. Someone was supposed to come for her in the morning.' Alexander's expression didn't shift much – but she saw something tighten behind his eyes. 'You know who did this?'

'Not for certain,' he admitted, then shook his head. 'Please, continue. What happened next?' Abbie could hear the tension in his voice.

'I tried to stop them, but one of them hit me, and after that, I don't remember anything else until I woke up in the room with Georgina crying over me. They didn't hurt her, but she was terrified.' Abbie told him about the loose board on the floor and how someone came to the cabin demanding to see Georgina.

'Did you recognise him?'

'No. But something about his voice felt very familiar.'

'Was he the one who ordered the kidnapping?'

'No, he was just there to verify it had been done.'

'Did he see you?'

'No. They hid me in the room and didn't tell the man I was there.'

Alexander looked at her, his eyes betraying the calm of his voice. 'Did they say why?'

Her fingers tightened in her lap. 'No, and they didn't even know who I was. They just took me to…to…'

He gently grabbed her arm. 'To what, Abbie?'

Abbie took a deep breath. 'They said they were going to 'have fun' with me. That's what they said.' She closed her eyes, fighting the wave of nausea that rose in her stomach as she remembered what Shaw tried to do to her, instinctively placing her hand on her bruised neck.

Alexander was silent. But she felt his whole body tense. 'You're safe now,' he said. His voice was low and steady. He put a hand on her back, calming her with the strength of his body.

'I know.' She swallowed. 'I am just struggling to understand what is happening. All this… violence. For what? The thought of what could have happened. And Georgina… I hate that she had to endure all this; she's too young.' Her voice cracked.

He cupped her chin gently, coaxing her to meet his penetrating gaze. 'I am not sure what is happening either,' he said. 'But I swear, we will find out. I won't let anything happen to either one of you again.' Somehow, she believed him. Maybe it was the exhaustion or the aching loneliness she'd carried since her parents died, but for the first time in weeks, she felt like she could breathe. She let her head rest on his shoulder.

'I helped Georgina escape,' she whispered. 'After the man left, I pried up a floorboard and sent her through it. She ran for the woods. When the man you shot, Shaw, came to bring us food, he realised Georgina wasn't there and the other man, Bill, went out looking for her. You know what happened next.' Alexander took a deep breath. She could feel he was afraid to formulate the question.

'Abbie, did he hurt you?'

She looked down at her skirt, fingers twisting the fabric. 'No. You stopped him before he could.' Alexander closed his eyes for a long moment, then relaxed slightly beside her.

They sat like that for a while, until his voice came soft against her ear. 'Abbie?'

'Hm?'

'We need to keep going.'

She blinked, realising her head was still on his shoulder. She straightened up at once.

'Yes, of course.'

He smoothed a hand across her back as she rose, leaving a trail of heat on her skin. Her cheeks flushed. If this kept up, she would throw herself into his arms, and then there would be no turning back. The man could make her lose her senses just with a simple look.

'John, let's ready the horses,' he called. They put away the provisions that John had taken out of his saddlebag.

Georgina skipped over to Abbie, who took her arm and wrapped it around her little body. 'How are you feeling?'

'Good. I was really tired. Were you really tired, too?'

'Yes,' Abbie said with a smile, 'but I feel better now. Are you ready to go?'

She jumped and said excitedly as if nothing had happened. 'Yes, I am!' Georgina grinned and ran to her uncle, flinging her arms around him. 'I'm ready to go home, Uncle Alex.'

He scooped her up. 'Very well then. Let's go home.'

Abbie joined them and noticed her reins had been tied to Alexander's saddle. 'I can ride on my own,' she said more effusively than intended. Quickly – too quickly. 'I *will* ride on my own.'

He raised an eyebrow. 'You're still–'

'I'm fine,' she cut in. 'Besides, I am sure Georgina would love to ride with you. Wouldn't you, darling?'

Georgina's face lit up. 'Yes, Uncle Alex!' she chirped. 'Can I ride with you now?'

'It's settled then,' Abbie said firmly, not waiting for

further objection. She untied Hettie and began mounting. Just as she lifted her foot in the stirrup, she felt Alexander behind her.

His hands circled her waist. 'Are you trying to avoid me?' he murmured. His hands were burning against her waist.

'Do not flatter yourself, Lord Crawford.'

'I thought we agreed you'd call me Alexander.'

She didn't reply. But as he lifted her easily into the saddle, she kept her eyes fixed ahead. He was right. She was avoiding him – his voice, his hands, his eyes… and everything they made her feel.

'Come on, Uncle Alex! I want to go home.' Georgina called, already seated on Alexander's horse. Once he mounted behind her, they all returned to the path that would lead them home.

***

Exhausted and covered in a fine veil of dust and grime from the long ride, they finally reached Everleigh Manor just as the sky began to blush with the first hues of dawn. A hush hung over the estate, broken only by the sound of hooves on the gravel and the soft rustle of the wind through the trees.

Abbie, bone-weary and aching in every limb, followed Alexander through the wrought-iron gates.

They dismounted, while John took the horses, Abbie followed Alexander into the house, carrying a sleepy Georgina in his arms.

She hadn't noticed the splendour of Everleigh Manor when she brought Georgina back only two days ago. But now, as they climbed the steps of the grand house, she admired the white carved stone with a floral theme as they walked up the covered stairs leading to the main door. In the delicate pre-dawn stillness, the high-arched windows reflected the first sun lights shining like gemstones.

Alexander pulled the bell cord, its tone echoing faintly through the corridors within. In his arms, Georgina stirred, her tiny fingers clinging to his coat. He brushed a wisp of hair from her cheek, whispering soothing words into her ear that seemed to lull her back into a slumber.

The door opened with a quiet creak, revealing the family butler. Though impeccably dressed, his cravat was slightly askew, and his eyes bore the red-rimmed mark of a sleepless night. His face lit up with joy as soon as he recognised who was standing by the doorstep. His eyes became two glassy orbs filled with excitement; his relief unmistakable. There was no doubt that everyone loved Georgina very much.

'My lord! You found them!'

Alexander shifted his weight and inclined his head. 'Yes, we did, Thomas.'

The butler's eyes flicked from Alexander to Abbie, his smile warm and earnest as he gave her a respectful bow. 'Miss Clarkson. Thank heavens.'

They stepped into the entrance hall. The floor gleamed in marble, showing the status of the house's inhabitants. The walls were adorned with countryside landscapes that lent the grand space an inviting warmth.

'We were so worried,' Thomas murmured, leading them through a corridor.

'Georgina is exhausted. Where's Paige?'

But before the butler could respond, a young woman, no more than twenty years old, hurried down the spiral staircase at a near run. Her apron was wrinkled, her eyes wide with relief. 'Oh, thank God! You found her!' She reached for Georgina's hand, brushing the curls from her forehead with the soft reverence of one who loved the girl deeply. Seeing her sleeping so profoundly, she lowered her voice. 'Is she hurt?'

Alexander shook his head. 'She's only tired. Would you stay with her? I don't want her to be by herself in case she wakes up.'

'But of course, My Lord.'

He turned to Abbie then. 'I'll take her upstairs. Will you wait for me in the study? Thomas will bring you some refreshment.' Abbie nodded, too tired to argue.

Alexander started to ascend the staircase with Paige close behind, when he paused once more. 'Oh– Thomas, how is Luke?'

The butler's expression softened. 'He's resting, my lord. The doctor stitched the wound cleanly. Said the boy will recover without trouble. He will be happy to know that little Georgina has returned safely. The poor boy was so worried that the doctor had to give him laudanum to help him sleep.'

'Good. Let him rest as long as he needs.' And with that, Alexander disappeared up the stairs, Paige trailing closely behind. Abbie watched until he vanished from view, her mind heavy with all she had seen and endured. Only Thomas' gentle voice recalled her to herself.

'Miss Clarkson?' he prompted softly.

She startled, realising she had been staring at Alexander's figure as he ascended the last steps of the staircase. She quickly shifted her attention to the butler. 'My apologies, Mr...?'

'Thomas, please.' He gestured politely down the corridor toward a set of panelled doors. 'If you'd follow me, miss. I believe you'll find the study more comfortable.'

The door swung open on creaking hinges to reveal a masculine sanctuary – dark walls, green velvet drapes

'Would you like anything to drink?'

'No, Thomas. Thank you.'

'Please let me know if you change your mind, miss.' With a polite nod, he withdrew, leaving her alone in the room.

The richly polished wood furniture glinted faintly in the firelight. The scent of aged leather and tobacco lingered in the air. Dominating the room was a wide oak desk by the window, its frame intricately carved with vine and leaf motifs that seemed to be almost alive in the flickering light.

Abbie ran her fingers lightly over the surface, grounding herself in its cool smoothness.

Her gaze moved to the pair of crimson damask armchairs flanking the fireplace. Aware of her dirty state, she hesitated to sit down but was so tired that the temptation was too great. She found a folded blanket, draped it over the armchair, and carefully lowered herself down. The cushions welcomed her. Her limbs relaxed, her head resting back. She could feel the tension ease as she sat, and resting her head, she closed her eyes.

She wasn't sure how long she remained like that, the warmth of the fire lulling her into a soft doze, when a soft touch to her cheek made her stir. His delicate caress made her lean in to feel his touch against her skin, and when she opened her eyes slowly, she found Alexander looking at her with quiet concern, his sapphire gaze softened by something she dared not name.

'How are you feeling?' he asked, his voice low.

She straightened, smoothing her hair with nervous fingers, knowing there was little she could do to improve her appearance.

'I'm fine. Just... tired. I need to go home and rest — that's all.' He turned to the liquor cabinet and poured two fingers of amber liquid into a pair of crystal glasses.

'Here. This will help.' She took the drink and sipped.

The warmth of the whisky slid down her throat and began to unknot something inside her chest.

They sat in silence for a time, the fire crackling between them, letting the tension caused by the trip fade away. Abbie watched Alexander rock his glass, swirling the liquid in rhythm back and forth like the tide rising and falling.

Then, softly, Alexander said, staring at his drink, 'I can't let you go home. Not tonight.'

Abbie's eyebrows drew together, feeling the anger rising within her. 'I beg your pardon?'

Alexander took a deep breath. He exhaled and glanced at her, the flicker of conflict in his eyes warning her that what he was about to say would not be to her liking.

'They are not looking for you yet,' He looked at her with determination in his eyes. 'But they will. It won't be long until they realise who you are and what you may know. I can't leave you alone in your house with no one to protect you.' Abbie straightened back in her seat.

'I appreciate everything that you have done for me, Lord Crawford – truly – but my safety is not your responsibility. You should focus on your family. I have staff at the house; they'll protect me.' She remained calm, wanting to believe her own words.

'You mean an elderly butler and a housekeeper in her twilight years?' His tone was gentle but firm. She winced inwardly. He wasn't wrong. Poor Jacob; she doubted he even knew how to shoot a gun.

'I can hire men to protect me.' She said stubbornly.

He shook his head. 'Men, you don't know. Who might sell you out for a coin?' He leaned forward. 'Would you bet your life on a stranger's honour?' She fell silent, not knowing what to respond.

She drew a breath. 'So, what do you suggest? And why should you be burdened with my protection?

Alexander looked at her over the rim of his glass, gaze steady.

'Because I made a promise to your father. And my suggestion is that you stay here with me.' That stunned her into stillness.

Abbie's eyes widened. Slowly, she set her glass aside and stood. 'Here with you? Have you lost your mind? Not that I care much about how inappropriate that suggestion is, but I am not prepared to be the centre of the gossip in the region. I have been the centre for no reason, and I'm not planning on giving them one now!'

'Right now, that is the last of my concerns.' Unable to stand still, Abbie started pacing the room and was going to reply when she suddenly realised what he said.

'Wait. What did you mean when you said you promised my father?' Alexander let a sigh go.

'Sit down, and I'll explain everything.'

'But...' He lifted his hand to prevent her from talking and pointed her to the armchair.

'Please, Miss Clarkson, have a seat.' With all the strength she could muster not to start asking a thousand questions to explain himself. Reluctantly, Abbie sat back down, arms crossed tightly in the middle of her chest.

'Explain,' she pressed, her throat dry. Her heart began to pound.

Alexander leaned back in his own chair, his eyes distant as memory took hold. 'As I mentioned yesterday, your father and my friend Stephen, Lord Everleigh, were business partners. I didn't meet your father until after they started working together. Stephen and I hadn't spoken in years, but when he got into trouble, he called me for help. There was... a shipment,' he began, his tone quiet, deliberate. 'The first shipment, everything went to plan. The venture was a promising opportunity. So, they proceeded with a second shipment. And when it set sail, they found the insurance made by his partner's agent was a fraud. That's when they contacted me to make emergency insurance.'

Abbie's throat went dry, her hands curling into the folds of her gown. 'Why you?' she asked warily.

Alexander's lips pressed together for a moment before he spoke. 'Stephen and I were at Eton together. We drifted apart over the years.' A fleeting shadow crossed his features; sorrow etched faintly at the corners of his eyes. 'But when this all started to happen, he knew I had contacts at the Admiralty. I was able to push through an emergency policy to safeguard the venture. Only days later, we received word – the ship had been attacked. The cargo lost at sea, or so they claimed.'

Abbie swallowed past the lump that was forming in her throat. 'So that was their plan all along?' she whispered.

'We believe so,' he answered grimly. 'I'm convinced the cargo was stolen... and the vessel deliberately scuttled. That's why your father and Stephen entrusted the transaction documents to me. They suspected betrayal.'

Abbie's fingers dug into the upholstery beneath her. 'And where is this new insurance?' she pressed.

'Your father kept that in his possession,' Alexander said, his tone sombre.

'And you don't have any idea of where it could be?' Her question was filled with suspicion. *Was Alexander intending to claim the insurance? Was that the only reason he was involved?*

He shook his head, reclining back in his chair. 'I've no idea, Abbie. You?'

'I truly wish I did,' she admitted with a sigh. 'My father told the men who came to our home that it was in Redwood House, but I don't know if that was just a distraction to buy us time, or if it was the truth. I've searched every inch but found nothing.' A long silence settled between them, broken only by the gentle crackle of the hearth. Abbie stared into the flames, their glow reflecting in her weary eyes. Finally, she spoke, her voice hollow. 'Is that why Williams said I will lose Redwood House?'

Alexander looked puzzled. 'What do you mean?'

She looked up, her tone sharper now. 'When he came to me yesterday, he told me I'd have to sell Redwood House if I wanted to clear my father's debts. According to him, the house was put up as collateral against a loan.'

Alexander's jaw clenched, but his voice remained calm. 'That may well be possible, but with the insurance policy we took out, the debt would have been repaid. I didn't know your father long, but he was a cautious man, methodical. He never took a step without knowing where it would lead next.' Abbie nodded in agreement; he would never have jeopardised leaving her and her mother without a roof over their heads.

'So,' she continued, 'you think Williams knew the insurance was false?'

'I wouldn't be surprised,' Alexander replied. 'I don't know who else is involved in all of this, but he could be working for whoever is pulling the strings. Why else would he tell you that your father was in debt if he weren't aware of the insurance being a fraud?'

Her fingers closed tightly around the armrest. 'Then I must find that document, or I'm going to lose everything.'

'Yes,' he said quietly. 'You must.'

Abbie pinched the bridge of her nose; a headache was beginning to build. 'And who is the man my father and Everleigh were in business with?'

'Braxton.' Her head shot up, eyes flashing.

'Phillip Braxton?' she asked incredulously.

Alexander gave a slow nod. 'You know him?'

Her stomach turned. 'He attended my parent's funeral.' Anger consumed her. How dare that man come to her offering his help, when he was the very person who had put them in the ground! It was all his fault that her parents were dead. Her throat closed up, and she grabbed her glass, draining it in a single, determined swallow.

'Braxton was the one who approached them and convinced them to start working with him,' Alexander explained. 'On paper, he was an honest businessman. He owns a well-established shipbuilding company, carried the right contacts. With Everleigh's capital and your father's knowledge in the trading business, it seemed like the perfect business deal. And since the ship's value exceeded that of the cargo, Braxton stood to gain a hefty share of the returns.'

Abbie's mouth twisted into a sneer. 'So, you're telling me that he orchestrated the whole thing? For what purpose? If the insurance was a sham, what could he have gained?'

'My guess?' Alexander's gaze darkened. 'He arranged his own insurance and stole the cargo. Profited from both ends. But... we've got no proof of that.'

Abbie's voice grew tighter. 'Then how did Braxton learn of the emergency policy?'

'I wasn't sure until now,' Alexander admitted. 'But with what you just told me about Williams... it makes sense, the information could've come from him. He had access to your father's accounts, so he might have been the one who let it slip to Braxton about the insurance in the first place.'

Her jaw clenched. 'And how did you find out about the fake insurance.'

Alexander's smile was grim. 'My cousin Derek – who

was also a friend of Stephen's – overheard some drunkard bragging about it at a tavern. The man who had posed as the insurer couldn't keep his mouth shut.'

'So, my father and Lord Everleigh were both killed... for money,' Abbie whispered, devastation washing over her.

Alexander's jaw tightened, his knuckles whitening around his glass. 'It wasn't just for the money, Abbie. Braxton has so many operations with the same modus operandi and a lot of people are involved. He would be taken to Newgate or even killed if this ever came to light. That man will do whatever is necessary to protect himself. And right now, we are the ones standing between him and his success.'

Abbie's voice trembled. 'We? Why me? I didn't know anything until now.'

'Maybe,' Alexander said softly. 'But they'll believe you do. You're your father's daughter, and he might think you know more than you're letting on. And someone found I was in your house that night, which is why they assume I'm involved too.' His voice darkened. 'That must be why they took Georgina. To–'

'To force you to give them the documents,' she said numbly, finishing his sentence.

He inclined his head. 'Precisely.'

Abbie sat back in the chair, placing her head between her hands. Exhaustion was too small a word to describe how she was feeling. She stared into the fire, taking a long, slow breath as her thoughts swirled chaotically. Her head spun with all the new layers of information she had just learnt.

'After everything you've told me,' She said quietly, 'how can I trust anyone? For all I know, you could be involved in all this as much as anyone else, and you just want to trick me into telling you where the insurance document is.' Everything he said seemed to make sense, but if she had learned anything in these last few weeks, it was that trust had to be earned – especially now. Alexander was no exception. She had to keep her guard up and resist being swayed by those unsettlingly beautiful blue eyes.

'I understand your doubts,' he said evenly, 'and I will get you the proof you need. I want you to trust me, Abbie.' She looked at him and gave a slight nod. She wanted to believe him. Yet her eyelids grew heavier by the second, the weight of exhaustion pressing down on her limbs. All she wanted was to go home to her bed. As if reading her thoughts, Alexander said. 'You must rest. We can speak further in the morning and devise a plan. Thomas has prepared the guest room for you.'

Abbie's eyes narrowed. 'I can't stay the night here. I told you – I have enough attention on me without adding to it.'

'Yes, you will.' He spoke with a low, serious tone, fitting of a man who was used to being obeyed. 'If I take you home now, we could be seen. And you know that that would only make matters worse. An even bigger scandal is the last thing you need. Besides, we don't know if anyone in your household is involved with Braxton. I will not take that risk. Here, we can keep things quiet.'

She folded her arms. 'And what if someone comes looking for me?'

'You don't have to worry about that. I sent word to Jacob. He will be discreet, as always.'

Abbie huffed, frustration prickling under her skin. 'Fantastic. So now you've taken charge of my household too.'

'I'm merely doing what is best for you.' All the frustration and anger coursed through her body, propelling her to her feet to confront him. Standing, she felt marginally more in control, but Alexander immediately rose as well, towering over her with his broad shoulders and a calm, commanding presence.

She tilted her chin defiantly. Being almost a head taller, she had to look up at him, not letting herself be intimidated by his height or massive bearing.

'You don't know what's best for me,' she snapped. Yet the words rang hollow. He was too close. His warmth enveloped her like a cloak, making her senses unsteady. She had to get some distance between them, but her body betrayed her. It was as if the attraction she felt for him had stolen her will.

He lowered his head slightly, and she felt a tremor ripple through her in anticipation. Was he about to kiss her? In a low, velvety voice, he murmured,

'Yes, Abbie, I do.'

Then, just as suddenly, and to her disappointment, he stepped away. The air that had previously felt warm now turned cold as ice in his absence. *Abbie, compose yourself!* She scolded herself silently.

Alexander walked to the door and called for the butler. 'Thomas, could you accompany Miss Clarkson to the guest room, please?'

'Of course, my lord,' came the butler's reply, as he appeared in the doorway. Irritation quickly replaced the fluttering disappointment in Abbie's chest.

'Wonderful,' she muttered, 'I don't even have a say in my own life anymore. What's next? Are you going to lock me up in my room?' Alexander smiled warmly. 'Only if it's necessary.'

Abbie huffed and spun around, stalking towards the door. Yet before crossing the threshold, she cast one last searing glare over her shoulder, her eyes sharp enough to cut glass.

Following Thomas up the stairs, Abbie's mind raced.

How had she lost control so quickly around him? She was not a girl easily impressed. In fact, she had never lost composure like this – not with anyone. She had always found the men who tried to court her rather tedious and uninspiring. But Alexander… he was different.

Her thoughts churned with the revelations of the night, each twist of deceit and betrayal making her head spin. The crush of emotions was starting to overwhelm her, and she started to feel slightly dizzy.

Thomas' voice cut through her reverie. 'If I may, miss?' She blinked back to the present.

'Of course, Thomas.' He glanced back at her, his expression warm but honest. 'Lord Crawford only wishes to see you safe.'

Abbie frowned slightly. 'What do you mean?'

'I've known all of them since they were boys. Lord Crawford and his cousin, Captain Colton, used to come here every summer. They are good men, miss. Your father trusted Lord Everleigh and Lord Crawford enough to ask them to protect you if anything ever happened. After Lord Everleigh's death – God rest his soul – they knew they would have to rely on one another. I hope, in time, you'll allow yourself to trust him.'

Abbie pressed her lips together, torn between caution and the quiet hope kindling inside her. She wanted to trust Alexander, but she needed more than his word.

'I hope so, too, Thomas.'

They walked along a wide corridor, the soft cream and blue carpet cushioning their steps. Doors lined the hall, each leading to well-appointed guest rooms.

Thomas paused at one and opened it for her. 'I trust this chamber will be to your liking, Miss Clarkson. If you need anything, don't hesitate to call.'

'Thank you, Thomas.' As he turned to go, she hesitated. 'Where is Georgina?'

'In the room beside yours, miss.' Her shoulders loosened at that.

'Thank you again, Thomas.'

'Rest well, miss.'

With the door closed behind her, Abbie surveyed the room. The soft glow of early morning streamed through the windows, casting a golden hue over the pale blue walls and elegant furnishings. Despite the large four-poster bed commanding the space, the room felt cosy and welcoming. A basin of fresh water awaited her on the dresser, and the sight of it made her realise how grimy she felt, and she couldn't wait to clean the dirt on her body.

Approaching the mirror, she gasped aloud, covering her hand in dismay. Her hair was a wild, tangled mess, stray twigs and leaves poking out from beneath her curls, loosely falling over her shoulders after she had to remove the lace that kept the braid together. No doubt a result of the ride, the scuffle, and everything that had happened since. Thankfully, someone had thoughtfully left out a hairbrush and fresh towels. She set to work, wincing as she tugged twigs from her hair. Her dress, when she unfastened it, was beyond repair – torn, soiled, ruined beyond salvation. She let it fall to the floor and slipped into the soft white nightgown that laid atop the bed and started with the arduous task of untangling her wild blonde curls.

The stress of the day was catching up to her. At last, clean and dressed for bed, she slid between the crisp linens, sinking into the plush mattress. Her limbs felt heavy, her eyelids drooping at last.

Safe. Warm, she allowed herself to relax.

Within moments, Abbie drifted off into a deep sleep.

CHAPTER 10

'Pardon me?!' Alexander watched Abbie stand from her chair in the dining room when she heard his proposal.

How could he provoke her so easily? he wondered, seeing her anger increase by the second.

He hadn't expected her to jump for joy upon hearing his thoughts on the situation, but her reaction felt oddly unflattering.

She stood there in a beautiful green dress that had belonged to Georgina's mother. He had never seen Catherine in that dress; in fact, he had never seen her again since the day she chose Everleigh over him. Catherine had been smaller than Abbie in both height and size, so the dress, instead of covering her feet as intended, revealed Abbie's riding boots, visible up to her ankles. The bodice strained across her bust, hugging her figure like a second skin, and Alexander's senses faltered.

The neckline left her throat exposed, though she had tied a scarf to conceal the bruises the bastards had inflicted. Although he knew it would be of little use, his instinct made him want to rise, to run his fingers gently over her injuries, to erase the pain she had endured. Knowing all she had suffered – not once, but twice – made his blood boil, fuelling a fierce desire to shield her from harm. He would not allow anyone to lay a finger on her again.

Since finding her in that wretched cabin, he had

turned over every possible means of keeping her safe – of keeping both Abbie and Georgina safe – and his mind always returned to the same solution.

'I have been thinking about our predicament and have concluded that you and I should marry as soon as possible.' Alexander leaned back in his chair, crossing his arms, his gaze fixed on Abbie with quiet determination.

'Are you out of your mind?' She began pacing the room. 'Yes, that must be it, because otherwise you wouldn't suggest something so absurd!' she exclaimed, fury sparking in her amber eyes. He raised an eyebrow in amusement.

'No, I am not, Abbie. Our best option is to marry.' His tone remained even, though he could feel irritation mounting. She made it sound as though marrying him would be as disagreeable as marrying a pig.

'I heard you the first time,' she retorted, 'but I still don't understand why you think we should marry.'

'It is not safe for you to be alone,' he replied, exasperation creeping into his voice as his patience began to fray.

'If you are worried about my safety, I can hire more men to protect me! There is no need to resort to something as drastic as marriage!' She planted her hands on the table, leaning forward to emphasise her point.

'Do you prefer to live here with us, as an unmarried woman? Or us with you?' His voice sharpened. 'Because I will not let you out of my sight, Abbie. I will not fail your father again. This is the only way I can keep you and Georgina safe – under the same roof.' His frustration was starting to show. How could she not understand that this was for her own benefit?

'I don't like either of those options!' she snapped.

'We are in extraordinary circumstances, Abbie. We did not choose them, but we have to face them. What do you suggest we do until this is all resolved?'

Abbie sank into the chair beside him and buried her face in her hands. 'I don't know.' She lifted her head and looked at him, and his anger softened as he caught the despair in her eyes. She wasn't rejecting him – she simply wanted the freedom to choose her own path.

'You would give up the chance to marry someone of your choosing?' she asked quietly, surprising him.

Her words stirred an old ache, one he thought long buried. He could not help but think of Catherine – the only woman he had ever loved – and how he had lost her before he could declare his feelings to her. But this was different. Abbie was nothing like Catherine. Her wild, fierce spirit stood in stark contrast with Catherine's gentle composure – and to his surprise, he liked it. Perhaps too much. But this was not the time to reveal it. He was afraid that if he showed it to her, it would make her refuse his proposal even more. No, it wasn't time yet. Instead, he continued to defend the practicality of his proposal.

He forced himself to keep a steady voice. 'My word means a great deal to me.' For a fleeting moment, but he could have sworn he saw disappointment flash in her eyes.

'You didn't promise my father you would marry me,' she said softly.

'No, I didn't.'

'Then why? Why would you sacrifice everything for someone you barely know?'

Alexander smiled faintly. 'Would it be such a sacrifice to marry me?' Abbie blushed, and though her lips parted, no sound came out.

For him, marriage would not be a sacrifice – not today, not ever. Yet it would be an ordeal to have her so close, while denying himself something that he could not yet claim. Still, he would not abandon her to face danger alone.

'I simply don't understand why everyone thinks marriage is the answer to every problem,' she said, her voice weary, as if the strength she once had was fading.

'Everyone?'

'My uncle also thought it was my only option.'

'And what do you think?'

'I think I can take care of myself. My problems are mine and no one else's.' There was something admirable in her strength, in her refusal to burden others, her determination to face hardship unaided. But she didn't have to endure it all, not when there was another way.

'I have seen for myself how capable you are of taking care of yourself, Abbie, but that's not what this is about. There is far more at stake. They will not stop until they have what they want – one way or another. You are in a dangerous position: a single woman with a legacy to protect, facing enemies that we haven't been able to uncover in months and that now threatens our families again. I am your best chance to protect everything you hold dear, and you are mine to finally end this threat once and for all.'

'And after we marry, what would stop you from taking everything from me? You're asking me to place all my trust in you, and I barely know you.'

'I am willing to sign a marriage settlement,' he said simply, 'guaranteeing you full autonomy over your fortune and your properties. You will remain in control of all that rightfully belongs to you.'

'You would do that?' Abbie's eyes widened, a mixture of surprise and lingering doubt.

'Believe it or not, I have no need of your money, Abbie. It would be wrong to claim anything your father worked so hard to build. Your fortune is not mine to take. When Braxton is dealt with and you are safe, you may do as you please. Seek an annulment, live separately, do whatever you wish – I will not stand in your way. Think of this as a business arrangement, one that will benefit us both. I will keep my word to your father, and you will safeguard your freedom and your estate. I doubt you'll find a better bargain.'

'A business arrangement…' she whispered. Maybe he imagined it, but he thought he saw a flicker of disappointment cross her face.

'Marriage often is little more than a business contract dressed in the guise of romance.'

'My parents married for love.'

'Then they were among the fortunate few.'

'You may be right… I just didn't think…' Her words faltered, so he completed her sentence for her.

'…that you would not marry without love?'

'It's not that. I never really thought about marriage at all. Or maybe I did, I don't know… But I certainly never imagined marrying because it was my only option. I thought… at least I would have the freedom to choose who to marry. With or without love.'

Her inner conflict was written plainly across her features. It wasn't flattering to a man's pride, having to convince a woman to marry him. And it was something he never thought he would have to do. But how could it be otherwise? This was not a proposal made in leisurely courtship; it was born from necessity.

'I need time to think,' she said.

'We don't have much time, Abbie.'

'I know,' she replied firmly. 'But this is my life. If we fail to catch Braxton soon, we could be married for a very long time. I need to be certain it's the only path I've got left. So, I hope you can understand that I won't rush into a decision that will alter the rest of my days. I need time to process everything.'

He inclined his head. 'Fair enough. But Abbie... this does not have to be an unhappy arrangement.' He reached out, taking her hand, tracing her palm with his thumb. Their eyes met, and for a brief, suspended moment, he felt she understood. That she wouldn't be a burden to him, that she could be cherished. He realised then how much he wanted her to accept his proposal.

Before she could speak, the door burst open and Georgina skipped inside, with Paige following behind. Abbie withdrew her hand, and the loss of her warmth settled heavily in Alexander's chest as she turned to the child.

Georgina bounced towards him, full of energy, her hardships forgotten in childish resilience. He was struck by how much the little girl had suffered in such a short time, yet she showed a unique and endless strength. Either that or that she hid her pain very well, which worried him greatly.

She climbed onto Alexander's lap, wrapping her small arms around his neck before planting a kiss on his cheek. He hugged her tightly, her laugh ringing out. 'How did you sleep, darling?' he asked.

'Good! But now I'm very, very hungry, Uncle Alex. My belly is making noises.'

Alexander smiled, glancing towards Paige. 'Would you ask Thomas to bring something to eat?'

'Of course, my lord.'

Georgina slid into the chair across from Abbie, and only then did she seem to notice her presence. 'Abbie! You're here! Did you sleep well, too?' She seemed even smaller in the high-backed chair.

'Yes, I did, Georgina.'

'I really needed to sleep – I was so tired! But now I'm hungry. Are you hungry too?' Her infectious enthusiasm was contagious, and Alexander could not but smile.

'Yes,' Abbie responded, matching the girl's bright tone.

'Are you staying with us?'

'I don't know yet.' Her glance shifted to Alexander, her unspoken questions hanging in the air.

'I would like you to stay. I can show you my dolls! I have two – very, very pretty – and a wooden horse too! Want me to show you?'

'You must eat something first, don't you think?'

'Oh, yes! I'm hungry!' As if she had forgotten that just a few moments earlier, she had declared how hungry she was.

Thomas soon arrived with a tray of fresh fruit, cakes and tea for everyone. Georgina chatted without pause while she ate, regaling Abbie with news of her toys and her room, barely giving her a chance to reply. It was as if she had so much information in her little head and needed to get it out before she forgot it. Alexander watched the easy smiles passing between them, and something warm settled in his chest. Whatever happened – marriage or not – he wanted Abbie in Georgina's life. And if he admitted it, he wanted her in his own life, too.

After the meal, Georgina asked eagerly. 'Do you want to see my toys?'

'I would love to, Georgina, but I must go home,' Abbie said gently. Georgina's little face fell, until Abbie added, 'I could come back tomorrow?'

'That would be wonderful!' she cheered. Then, true to her quicksilver moods, she turned to Alexander. 'Uncle Alex, may I go and play now?'

'Yes, darling.'

With a cheerful wave, Georgina skipped from the room, leaving a contented silence in her wake. When Alexander's eyes met Abbie's, they let it envelop them as if nothing else existed. He wanted to hold her hand again, to return to that shared moment where he could feel her reaction to his touch.

Before he could speak, a discreet cough drew his attention. Thomas stood at the door, waiting patiently but with an inquisitive look on his face. Alexander deduced that he must have been trying to get his attention for some time before coughing.

'Yes, Thomas?'

'Lady Charlotte has arrived, my lord. She requests to see you in the drawing room.'

'We shall be there shortly. Offer Lady Charlotte some refreshment, please.'

'Yes, my lord.'

'Thank you.'

'Who is Lady Charlotte?' Abbie asked.

'Georgina's grandmother. Stephen's mother.' Alexander stood up, pulling out Abbie's chair with quiet gallantry. 'Come, I'll introduce you.'

She hesitated a moment before standing, declining the hand he extended. He smiled slightly at her stubbornness before turning towards the door, waiting for her to follow.

***

Abbie felt the tension between them, beginning to doubt whether she should have accepted his hand and allowed herself to enjoy his touch again. She had never felt a spark like this with anyone before. His strong hand caressing hers ignited something deep within her whenever he touched her.

If this continues, I am going to burst into flames. She thought.

The two walked silently down the hallway until they

reached the drawing room. This room was unlike the others. There was a gentleness to it, a sense of peace produced by the soft combination of pastel colours and the light that poured through the magnificent skylight.

In the centre, an elegant lady with white hair sat on a cream-coloured sofa. Despite her years, the woman retained a beauty Abbie had rarely seen. Her emerald-green eyes shone with remarkable intensity. At once, Abbie felt herself relax, recognising the same sharp wit in Lady Charlotte's expression that she had often noticed in Georgina. It was clear the young girl had inherited her looks from her paternal family.

With a cane in her hands, the lady regarded them with a raised brow, likely because she had not expected Alexander to be accompanied.

When they reached her, Alexander stepped away from Abbie and approached the lady, bending to kiss her on the cheek.

'It's nice to see you, Lady Charlotte.'

She patted his cheek affectionately, as if he were a little boy, and the sight made Abbie smile. 'How many times must I remind you? Leave the formalities for the ton. You will call me Grandma Charlotte. The family calls me that, and you, Alexander, are family,' she scolded, though her eyes were warm with affection.

Then, leaning slightly to the side, she looked past him. 'And where are your manners, young man? Are you not planning on introducing me to this beauty?' she chided, though the spark in her eyes suggested only good humour, making Alexander smile in return.

'My apologies, Grandma Charlotte. Allow me to introduce Miss Abigail Clarkson.' Abbie gave a short curtsy, offering a polite smile.

'Pleased to meet you, my lady.'

'Come closer, child. My eyesight is not what it once

was, and I wish to look at you properly. Don't be frightened, I don't bite – regardless of what others may say.'

Abbie thought it amusing that anyone would accuse Grandma Charlotte of such a thing. There was something about the older woman that immediately put her at ease, and so she moved closer and seated herself beside her.

'Abigail Clarkson,' the lady murmured, her voice gentle. 'I am so sorry for your loss, child. Your parents were beautiful people.'

Abbie looked at her, shocked. 'You knew my parents?'

The older woman nodded. 'Yes, child, I met them once in this very room. Your Aunt Agatha and I were friends in our youth, though regrettably, we lost contact after she married.' Her tone was laced with sadness. She reached for Abbie's hand, giving it a gentle, motherly squeeze.

Then, as her eyes travelled to the bruises on Abigail's face, her expression changed. 'Oh, my dear!'

She pulled Abbie's hand closer, the other hand rising to rest lightly against Abbie's cheek, inspecting the injuries. Abbie winced, the skin still tender, despite Lady Charlotte's care, and at once the older woman withdrew her hand to avoid causing further pain.

'What happened to you, child?' Lady Charlotte asked, concern evident in her voice. Her eyes darted briefly to Alexander before settling back on Abbie.

Not wishing to trouble her further, Abbie forced a smile and shrugged lightly.

'Do not worry, my lady. It was only an accident. I can be rather clumsy at times.' Lady Charlotte raised her hand, halting her.

'Please, child, do not take me for naïve. Anyone can see that those marks are not from a simple accident. Someone has done this to you, and I demand to know who.' Her gaze shifted between Abbie and Alexander.

'Alexander,' she continued, her voice dipping with unease, 'is this related to my son's death?' The tremor in her voice sent a shiver through Abbie. Slowly, she began to understand the deeper meaning of her words.

'You know?' Abbie asked quietly.

Lady Charlotte nodded solemnly. 'Yes, child. I know that someone took the life of my beloved son... and your parents as well. Alexander attempted to shield me from the truth, to spare me further headache, but I have lived too long to be fooled by comforting lies.' Turning to Alexander, she said, 'Now, tell me everything, and I beg you, do not sugar-coat it. I am not made of glass.'

Alexander nodded, resigned, and recounted the events of the past two days. Abbie was quietly grateful that he omitted the worst details. The older woman had asked for honesty, but some truths were too brutal to be of any use.

'We finally arrived at sunrise today,' Alexander finished.

'Oh, heavens.' Lady Charlotte placed a hand against her chest. 'And Georgina?' Her voice trembled.

'She is well, my lady. Only shaken and tired, nothing more.'

The older woman breathed a sigh of relief. 'Thank God.'

Her emerald gaze returned to Abbie. 'Did they harm you?' Her meaning was clear – Lady Charlotte was a woman who understood the risks of being alone in a cabin with two thugs; she did her best not to worry her further.

'Only the bruises on my face, my lady. Nothing else.'

Lady Charlotte pressed Abbie's hands between her own in silent comfort, then turned to Alexander.

'Now, Alexander... do you have a date in mind?' He

blinked, surprised.

'To what date will you be referring exactly?' he asked, but they both knew what she was referring to.

'For your wedding, of course.'

Abbie felt her stomach twist. *Why was everyone in such a rush to march her to the altar?* She wanted to get out of there.

'I have already made the suggestion, Grandma Charlotte,' Alexander said stiffly, 'but Miss Clarkson is yet to give me her answer.' His exasperated look only served to irritate Abbie further.

'Darling,' Lady Charlotte interjected smoothly, 'would you be so kind as to ask Thomas to bring us some tea?'

'I have alre–' Alexander began, but she silenced him with a pointed look. Abbie, too, quickly recognised the older woman's intent. She wished to speak with her alone, and Alexander seemed to grasp it as well, for he inclined his head and said,

'Of course, Grandma Charlotte.'

Once Alexander left, Lady Charlotte turned back to Abbie. 'So then, when is the date?'

Abbie's throat tightened. She didn't know how to answer since she had not decided herself, nor did she wish to be pressed. She knew it was the most reasonable thing to do, but she refused to believe it was the only solution.

'Why must marriage be my only option?' she asked quietly.

Lady Charlotte's expression softened. 'From what your father said, you are an intelligent woman, Abigail. And I presume Alexander has explained the circumstances to you by now. I always said they ought to have told you everything sooner – keeping you in ignorance has only placed you in greater danger.'

Abbie frowned. 'What do you mean by that?'

'When my son and your father suspected Braxton of

deceit, they chose to remain silent, believing it would be safer for their families. In my opinion, it was a grave mistake. If our suspicions are correct, it means that Philip Braxton is a dangerous man. He has already taken too much from us – my dear son, your parents… it must end, child. And until it does, we must protect each other. The best way Alexander can protect you is by marrying you. Surely you can see the sense in that.'

'I understand the danger I am in, Lady Charlotte, and I agree that we must get to the bottom of this situation. But surely I could remain here, safely, without having to marry him.'

Lady Charlotte shook her head from side to side, scandalised. 'No, no, that would never do. Your father would rise from his grave to haunt me, and I shudder to think what your aunt would do! No, child. You must marry.'

Abbie felt deflated. She could not deny it; her father would never have allowed such impropriety. Yet she hesitated – she didn't want to rush into making a decision. 'I need to think about it.' It was the only thing she could respond.

Lady Charlotte patted her hand gently. 'I understand.'

'Then, if you'll excuse me, my lady, I would like to return home and change.'

'If you are going home, I will accompany you,' Alexander said, re-entering the room, followed by Thomas, who was carrying a tea tray.

'That's not ne–' Abbie began, but he cut her off.

'Abbie,' he said firmly, his intense gaze daring her to argue, showing that this was a disagreement she would definitely not win.

She sighed in frustration. 'Fine. I'll fetch my coat.' She got up to leave, but remembering her manners, she curtsied to Lady Charlotte. She swept from the room in apparent irritation.

Alexander exhaled slowly, leaning against the door frame, his eyes following her departure. *This woman will be the death of me,* he thought grimly, watching her retreat up the stairs.

'Thomas, can you see that the horses are prepared?' he ordered.

'Yes, my lord.'

Lady Charlotte watched him with a knowing smile, 'Love and cough, darling – neither can be hidden.'

Alexander arched his brow but gave no reply. He was unsure if she was talking about him or Abbie. So he chose to remain in the dark. He wasn't about to confess anything to the sharp-eyed older woman.

***

How dare he! Her frustration at his authoritarianism set her nerves on edge. She was no longer a child. How could he possibly believe he had the right to dictate her actions? Yes, she was well aware of the danger, but it was not his place to control her life as he pleased, as though she had no will or judgement of her own. Now that she understood the risks, she would not allow herself to be caught unaware so easily. Her house was only a few minutes away, and there was still enough daylight to make the journey without difficulty.

Once back in her room, she wrapped yesterday's clothes in one of the blankets. Alexander had not noticed that she did not have a coat; she had only mentioned it as an excuse to slip away. She had seen one of the maids disappear through a door at the end of the corridor, and so she made her way in that direction. The spiral staircase brought her to a small hallway with a door that, fortunately, led straight out to the stables.

As she had anticipated, Alexander had already ordered the horses to be saddled, and finding the area momentarily unattended, she made her way towards Hettie. She had just reached for the reins when a middle-aged man stepped out from one of the stalls.

'Can I help you, miss?' he asked. Startled, Abbie turned towards him. 'Pardon me, miss, I didn't mean to frighten you.' She waved a hand dismissively, brushing off the moment.

'It's quite all right… Mr…?'

'Finney, miss. I'm the horse master – Luke's father.'

'Oh! How is Luke?' she asked warmly.

'He's doing well, miss. Resting and recovering.'

'He is a courageous boy. I do not like to think what might have happened had he not returned to warn Lord Crawford.'

'We were all worried,' Finney replied, his face earnest. 'I'm glad to see you all home safe, miss.'

'As am I, Mr Finney,' she said sincerely.

'Is there something I can help you with?' he asked again. Abbie glanced around briefly, searching for an excuse to have him leave so she could make her escape. She felt a brief pang of guilt for deceiving the man – he had such a sweet and kindly expression. But then inspiration struck. *That's it! Sweets!* she thought.

'Yes, Mr Finney,' she replied, adopting a pleasant smile. 'Would you be so good as to fetch a little treat for Hettie? I always give her something before we ride.'

Finney nodded obligingly. 'Of course, miss. I'll see what I can find.'

'Thank you,' she said, her smile widening.

No sooner had he disappeared through the rear door than she swung herself up onto Hettie's back and set off at a gallop, wasting no time in making her escape.

***

Returning to the house was no easy task. Her entire body ached from the day before, and a headache had begun to form above her temple.

Luckily, she didn't meet anyone along the way. She left Hettie in the stables with Simon and went straight into the house.

Jacob was already opening the door before she could even knock.

'Miss! You are back!' he said, his voice trembling. Dispensing with protocol, the older man embraced her. His affectionate gesture made her hug him back, and she was surprised to realise just how much she needed that simple display of affection.

'Lord Crawford told us what happened,' he said, lowering his voice. She did not understand why until she heard raised voices – an argument between the housekeeper and an unpleasant, grating male voice. Her uncle. The absolute last person she wished to see. Her headache throbbed worse by the minute.

'We told him you went for a ride, miss,' Jacob whispered again.

'Thank you, Jacob,' she replied quietly, and, taking a deep breath, she walked towards the drawing room.

'She just went for a ride, sir. She'll be back in a few hours,' she heard Mrs White say, attempting to pacify Uncle Harper.

'She shouldn't be riding alone. That girl must learn to behave like a lady, not like a common maid. I always told my brother-in-law that he gave her too much freedom. He should've—'

'And still, he did, Uncle. Alas, I do not understand what you are doing here after I told you never to set foot in this house again.' Abbie's voice cut through the conversation, sharp and angry. She had suffered more than enough insolence from this man.

Ignoring her, he arrogantly lifted his chin and pressed on. 'Where have you been, Abigail?' His gaze swept over her, then his expression turned to shock. 'Dear Lord, what happened to you, child?'

It was only then that she realised how she must appear. The dress Alexander had provided helped her look somewhat presentable, but the bruises on her face and neck remained starkly visible. Mrs White, too, seemed to register this, though the housekeeper kept her expression carefully neutral.

Casually, Abbie replied, 'I had a small accident while riding, that's all. And now, if you will excuse me, I would like to change.'

Her uncle blinked in stunned silence. Turning to Mrs White, she said, 'Would you kindly see that a bath is brought to my chambers, please, Mrs White?'

'But of course, darling. I'll have Suzie bring everything up shortly.' Mrs White rested a reassuring hand on hers, giving it a soft squeeze. Abbie knew the housekeeper would want all the details later. Leaning in, she whispered, 'Do not let my aunt leave her room.' Mrs White gave a knowing nod.

Abbie turned on her heel, intending to head upstairs, but her uncle's voice followed her. 'I'll wait for you in your father's study,' he called after her.

Abbie paused, casting a look over her shoulder. 'No, you will wait in the drawing room,' she said firmly. Her cold gaze left no room for her uncle to contradict her. She glanced at Jacob, who stood silently behind her uncle, and he gave a subtle nod of understanding. Without another word, she continued her way up the stairs, ignoring whatever protests her uncle might have made. She was simply too exhausted to deal with him at the moment.

Her body felt impossibly heavy, as though she were carrying a sack of stones on her back. She dragged her feet into her room and collapsed onto the bed, arms spread wide. Closing her eyes, she allowed herself to sink into the feather mattress, feeling the accumulated weight of the past two days pressing down on her. She wanted nothing more than to drift off to sleep and wake up in a world where none of the pain or misery of the past month existed. She was strong – but everyone had their limits.

'Miss Abbie?' came Suzie's gentle voice behind her. Forcing herself to lift her head, she managed to sit up with great effort. Suzie quickly came to her side, offering her hand to help. 'Come, miss. Let me help you undress.' Abbie gratefully accepted her help.

She heard Suzie's sharp intake of breath as her bruises were revealed. Her maid's face crumpled, eyes glistening with unshed tears as she took in the marks on her neck. 'Oh, miss…'

Abbie squeezed her hand lightly, managing a small, reassuring smile. 'I'm fine, Suzie. Just a few bruises. But I'll be recovered in no time.' But Suzie's expression remained troubled.

'But, miss… you've endured so much. I'm so sorry…' Her voice caught on a lump of emotion.

'It will be fine. Come, fetch my robe, please.'

Suzie nodded and wrapped her in soft, silken fabric. Abbie sank into a chair while Suzie gently worked through the tangles in her curls, her fingers careful not to tug.

Two other maids arrived with the bathwater, and when everything was ready, they departed, leaving Suzie to help her lower herself into the bathtub. As soon as she slipped into the hot water, a wave of relief swept over her. Her muscles slowly unclenched, soothed by the warmth. She leaned back, allowing the heat to work its magic on her weary limbs. Suzie pulled over a chair and sat beside her, washing her hair with quiet tenderness. Abbie rested her head on a towel that the maid had placed on the edge of the tub; all she wanted was to relax and just let her mind go blank.

Abbie lost track of time, slipping into a near trance, until a gentle shake of her shoulder brought her back.

'Miss, you'll catch a chill. The water's gone cold,' Suzie said softly.

With a tired nod, Abbie let herself be helped out of the tub. Sitting in front of the dressing mirror, she could not help but frown at her reflection. The purpling bruises stood out starkly on her face and neck, and she could even make out the cruel imprint of fingers tinting her skin. Her heart clenched. *I'm tired of getting hurt*, she thought grimly. *I need to be able to defend myself... I need a pistol.*

Once she was dressed in fresh clothes, Mrs White arrived with a steaming cup of tea and some biscuits.

'How are you feeling, darling?'

'I've been better, but I'll be alright,' Abbie replied, forcing a smile as she sipped the warm tea. Suzie excused herself, gathering the soiled garments, leaving the two women alone. Abbie could no longer hold back her curiosity. 'How did you know where I was, Mrs White?'

'Lord Alexander sent a message saying there had been an incident. We were so worried, but Thomas said not to tell anyone. Then he sent another message saying you were safe and would be staying with him.' The housekeeper said no more, but there was no need – Abbie knew precisely what the woman was thinking by the way she glanced downward. That something had happened between her and Lord Crawford – precisely what Abbie feared others would assume. She didn't want to share too many details for Mrs White's safety, but she needed her to understand that she hadn't done anything improper. After all, Mrs White had always been like a mother to her.

'I was kidnapped, Mrs White.'

The woman's eyes widened, her hand flying to her mouth. 'Oh, dear child.' She dropped to her knees before her, taking her hands in hers. 'What happened?'

'I am not entirely sure yet. I was with Georgina Everleigh – Lord Everleigh's child – and two men came and took us. Lord Crawford found us and brought us home.'

Mrs White closed her eyes, exhaling a prayer. 'Thank God he found you.' How was it that everyone trusted him? Everyone in her household seemed to follow his instructions without hesitation.

'How long have you known Lord Crawford, Mrs White?'

'Not long, darling. He came to see your father after Lord Everleigh's death, and I had the impression they knew each other from before.'

'Why did you think that?'

'Because when he came to the house, they shook hands like men who had met before – there was familiarity in it. Jacob said they met in London before.'

'And why didn't you mention this before?'

Mrs White shook her head. 'I didn't think it was relevant, darling. Is it?'

Abbie realised then that the housekeeper knew nothing about the true events surrounding their deaths – and it was safer if she remained ignorant. She forced herself to take a deep breath, willing herself to calm down. It wasn't fair to heap her frustration onto Mrs White.

'I don't know, Mrs White. My apologies. I suppose I'm just a bit on edge after… everything.'

'Completely understandable, darling.' Mrs White gave her hand a comforting squeeze. 'Now, your uncle is still waiting.'

Abbie rolled her eyes and groaned. 'Can't you just tell him to leave?'

'I wish I could, but you know if you don't face him, he'll raise his voice and make your aunt aware he is here.'

She was right, of course. And the last thing she wanted was for her aunt to have to face that rat of a husband she had.

'Fine,' she sighed, 'I'll be down in a minute.' Mrs White patted her hand and left her in peace.

Abbie grabbed a shawl to cover the bruises on her neck and headed downstairs to meet the insufferable man.

When she entered the drawing room, she found her uncle rifling through the drawers of one of the drawing room desks. Fury tightened in her chest.

'Can I help you, Uncle?' she asked, keeping her tone controlled with as much restraint as she could. He jumped slightly, startled, then quickly stepped away from the desk, pretending he hadn't been caught snooping.

'Where are your manners, child? You left me waiting almost an hour!'

She ignored his complaint. 'Why are you here, Uncle? I've told you before – you are not welcome in this house. So you better have a very good reason to bother me with your presence.' She wanted him gone and fast.

His face darkened. 'Do not speak to me in that tone, child!'

'I am not a child, so do not treat me like one.' She braced herself. This was going to be an exhausting conversation.

'No, you are not. Which is exactly why I am here. As I told you a few days ago, you need to marry.'

Abbie looked at him, puzzled. 'I thought I made myself perfectly clear on my feelings towards marriage.'

He raised his pudgy chin in defiance. 'What you want is irrelevant. You will marry, and you will marry soon.'

Abbie's jaw tightened. 'I do not need to marry.'

'Yes, you do. And as your legal guardian, you will do as I say.'

He straightened as much as his squat figure allowed, trying to appear taller, but even so, the man was still a head shorter than Abbie. The effort might have been laughable had she not been so irritated.

'Let me remind you, Uncle, I am of an age where I require no guardian.'

'I have a document signed by your father!' he barked, waving a paper at her. She snatched it from his hand and read it over. 'This was redacted ten years ago. And it doesn't place you as my guardian, but my aunt.'

'That doesn't matter, and it remains valid! And besides, I have already selected a suitor for you.'

Her temper flared. 'No, it is not valid. I am over twenty-one – I require no legal guardian.'

His mouth opened, but no sound came out. Abbie could barely contain her fury. 'I will never marry any man chosen by you,' she said, ensuring the disgust dripped not just from her tone but also showed in her face.

'Yes, you will! You insolent–' He cut off abruptly as shouts echoed from the corridor.

'Where is she?'

'What's all this commotion?!' her uncle sputtered. Before she could respond, Alexander stormed into the drawing room with rage in his eyes.

'Why in God's name did you leave? I told you I would accompany you!'

Abbie met his glower with pride. 'As I told you – I do not need someone following me everywhere! As you can see, I managed to arrive all by myself!'

'You are–' He stopped, noticing her uncle for the first time, standing awkwardly with his arms crossed and an impatient look on his face.

In that instant, a plan formed in Abbie's mind. She slid her arm through Alexander's. He looked down at her, surprised, but she tilted her chin and looked at her uncle straight in the eye.

'I cannot marry whomever you have chosen, Uncle, because I am marrying Lord Crawford.'

She shot Alexander a pleading look, hoping he would understand what she wanted without the need for words. To her relief, he did.

'You will not!' her uncle bellowed, his face turning an unhealthy shade of red. 'I have already given my word to Mr Braxton!'

At the sound of that cursed name, she noted how they both tensed up, the air becoming trapped in their lungs. As if he read her body, his arm tightened around her waist without hesitation, pulling her closer to him.

'I am sorry to disappoint you, sir, but you'll have to retract that offer. Your niece and I are to be wed next week.'

'I gave my word!' her uncle seethed, his hands clenched tightly into fists.

'Then break it – unless you want to see your niece's reputation ruined beyond repair.'

Abbie glanced up at Alexander, startled. He looked back at her, and that's when she realised his intention. This was the only way. If her uncle had already promised her hand in marriage, the only way he would be forced to relinquish that control was if he thought her honour had already been compromised. This was not what she had in mind – she had merely wanted to buy some time to decide what to do. But there was no turning back.

'You bastard,' her uncle snarled. 'How dare you dishonour her? And you,' he spat, turning to Abbie, looking at her up and down. 'You are as loose as your mother!'

'How dare you!' Abbie stepped forward, trembling with rage. 'You will never speak of my parents again, do you hear me? Ever! You are a pitiful excuse of a man, forever after Papa's money, because you squandered your own fortune gambling. You disgust me.'

He raised a hand to strike her, but before the blow could land, Alexander's hand shot out, seizing him by the wrist. In one smooth motion, he hauled the smaller man up by the lapels with such force that the little man's toes were barely scraping the ground.

'Try to lay a hand on her again,' Alexander growled, 'and you won't live to regret it. Have I made myself clear?' Her uncle nodded, his bravado dissolving into fear. 'Good. Now get out before I change my mind.'

When the door slammed behind him, Abbie turned to Alexander.

'Do you realise what you've done? Now we will have to marry!'

'I simply followed your lead, darling. You said it to him first, not me,' he replied mildly.

'Do not call me darling! I was trying to buy time! I didn't think you would be so indecent as to suggest that we…' She trailed off, cheeks burning. She closed her eyes and tried to control her embarrassment. 'What are you doing here anyway?' she snapped, desperate to redirect the conversation.

Alexander's patience finally snapped. 'What am I–? You left my house without a word! I told you to stay in the house, damn it! After what happened yesterday, I thought you would have the common sense to stay where you were safe.'

'They weren't after me; they wanted you. I will say I'm safer in my house than in yours,' she retorted, though she knew it was a poor excuse. Why did this man infuriate her to the point of saying things she wouldn't do otherwise?

'You are insufferable,' he bit out, stepping closer. Their bodies were so close she could feel his heart beating as fast as hers.

'Likewise,' she shot back. But her intention to say it out of spite vanished when she saw the intensity in his eyes. This was the second time they had been in this position. Their bodies were only inches apart, almost touching, their breaths synchronised and the air suddenly thick with something she couldn't quite name.

'So?' he asked quietly.

'So…?' she echoed, her eyes flicking to his lips as they inched closer.

'So, we are getting married,' he murmured. And in that same instant, the spell broke.

She stepped aside and started fussing with her skirt. 'Fine.'

'Fine?' His brows shot up.

'Yes, fine! Thanks to you, it's now the only option.'

'Fine!' he thundered. 'We will wed the day after tomorrow.' And with that, he stormed out.

'Argh!' Abbie let out a growl of frustration, louder than she intended. Glancing at the door, she spotted Mrs White standing there, looking at her with a bemused smile.

'Everything all right, darling?' Mrs White asked innocently.

'Yes... No! That man is utterly insufferable!' Abbie huffed, storming past her, leaving a bewildered Mrs

White in her wake.

CHAPTER 11

When you don't want something to happen, somehow, despite however much you pray to delay the inevitable, it happens even sooner than you had anticipated. Abbie thought, staring at her reflection in the mirror.

The dress Lady Charlotte and Aunt Agatha had chosen for her was made of pale blue fabric, and under the skilful hands of the dressmaker – whom Lady Charlotte had insisted on bringing from Oxford – they had the poor woman working through the night to finish it in time. Tiny white flowers had been embroidered along the flowing chiffon skirt, while the shoes, lined with the same blue fabric, were a gift from her father for her first ball.

The bodice of the gown had a square neckline, trimmed with white muslin that swept from the centre of her chest to her shoulders and met delicately at the nape of her neck. A matching muslin scarf had been added to conceal the fading bruises around her throat.

Aunt Agatha had gifted her a beautiful pair of pearl earrings that complemented the intricate hairstyle Suzie had created. As a final touch, they had woven in a few white wildflowers Georgina had picked herself that morning.

And just like that, she was ready – ready to walk down the aisle, ready to become a wife. Well… she was prepared on the outside. Inside, she was a storm of nerves and doubts, uneasy about the step she was about to take.

She didn't even know what was going to happen next. Lady Charlotte had overseen all the arrangements – the wedding, the banquet, the flowers... Abbie hadn't had the energy nor the will to involve herself in any of it. She had even allowed Lady Charlotte to concoct a suitable story about why the marriage was so rushed, to satisfy any gossiping tongues.

According to their agreed tale, her father had arranged their wedding a few months before his death, and now, since she was alone, she and Alexander had decided to wed before travelling to London.

Of course, there was also some romantic nonsense thrown in – something about love at first sight, if she recalled correctly. How foolish people could be, to believe they were so besotted they couldn't live without each other. The truth was, they could barely tolerate each other.

Informing Aunt Agatha had been easier than expected. Though surprised by the sudden wedding announcement when Lady Charlotte arrived at Redwood House, she wasn't difficult to convince, for she seemed to trust Lady Charlotte implicitly. After warm embraces, the three of them had settled in the drawing room, reminiscing about their childhood and regretting the lost years of friendship.

From there, they moved on to the tedious topic of the wedding. Tedious, at least to Abbie, as the two older women sitting next to her seemed positively delighted at the prospect of overseeing every detail.

But Abbie couldn't care less and simply sat there, answering the questions without much thought, feeling like a bystander in her own life, watching others shape her future. Yet she knew they only sought what was best for her.

She had already considered every possible alternative, and this remained the least catastrophic. Well – assuming that she and Alexander didn't kill each other first.

When Aunt Agatha asked her what she intended to wear, Abbie could only answer, 'I don't know.'

Within minutes, they were in her room, rummaging through gowns until they found one they liked. Abbie let them decide for her; what did it matter anyway? This was no true wedding. They didn't love each other. He didn't love her, and she certainly didn't love him. It was all an arrangement – him honouring his word to her father, her escaping having to marry her uncle's poor choice of groom. She kept telling herself there was no other reason. And she almost believed it.

Only the legal formalities remained. She learned from Lady Charlotte that the vicar at Everleigh Chapel had agreed to officiate without asking too many questions, as Alexander had secured a special license directly from the Archbishop of Canterbury.

And so, the morning of the wedding arrived. She travelled with Aunt Agatha to Everleigh Manor, recalling the chaos of preparation upon their arrival – maids rushing about with flowers, servants setting the tables, everyone bustling around as if it were the happiest day of her life. It made her want to turn and run.

But there was no running. To refuse this marriage would mean to risk losing everything: her home, her fortune, and most importantly, her freedom. At least Alexander had kept his word. That very morning, as she arrived at Everleigh Manor, he had given her the marriage settlement, signed and sealed. It stated that he would not touch a penny of the fortune her parents had left her, and he would give her complete autonomy to manage it at her own convenience. Like he said, she wouldn't find a better offer anywhere else. And he was right.

Now here she stood – a bride-to-be.

'You look beautiful, dear.' Aunt Agatha said softly, tears threatening to flow down her cheeks. 'You remind me so much of your mother on her wedding day. She was as radiant as you are now. She would be so proud of you, my sweet girl.' Standing behind her, Abbie could see her aunt's reflection in the mirror, a loving hand resting tenderly on her shoulder. Abbie covered it with her own, offering a small, grateful smile.

'Thank you, Aunt Agatha.'

Pride might not have been exactly what her mother would have felt in this unusual situation. This wasn't the future any mother would have envisioned for her daughter: a marriage made not out of love, but out of protection – born from fear. Her mother had likely dreamed of her marrying a man she loved, and in an ideal world, Abbie knew she would have done just that.

The door opened, and Lady Charlotte entered, followed by a bouncing Georgina.

'Oh, Georgina, you look so lovely,' she said, hand on her chest and eyes soft with affection.

'Abbie! You look so pretty!' Georgina ran towards her, wrapping her little arms around her waist and hugging her tightly. She wore a charming turquoise gown that brought out the green in her eyes, making them shine like tiny emeralds.

'Georgina, careful! You'll ruin Abbie's dress!' Lady Charlotte scolded.

Georgina instantly released her hold and looked up at her, blushing. 'I'm sorry.'

'Don't worry, Georgina.' Abbie smiled and caressed her cheek affectionately.

The girl beamed, her smile lighting up the whole room. 'When you marry Uncle Alexander, does that mean you'll be my aunt?'

Abbie crouched down, taking her small hands in hers. 'I suppose it does. Would you like that?'

'I'd like that very much,' Georgina whispered and threw her arms around Abbie's neck again, ignoring her grandmother's exaggerated huffs about the dress.

Abbie hugged her back, her heart unexpectedly full. 'Me too, Georgina. Me too.'

Lady Charlotte and Aunt Agatha exchanged glances, their eyes misty with emotion.

'Come, child. It's time,' Lady Charlotte announced gently.

Abbie rose, accepted the bouquet from Aunt Agatha, and took a deep breath. 'Yes,' she said, though not with much conviction.

'Oh, come on, child, change that face – it looks like you're going to the slaughterhouse instead of your wedding', Lady Charlotte chided. 'He doesn't bite, you know. Alexander is a good man. He'll make a fine husband. Or he will have to deal with this old lady, I can assure you that.' Lady Charlotte emphasised her last words. Abbie almost smiled. She didn't doubt Lady Charlotte's threat for a second.

And what would happen after the ceremony? After everyone left, they would have to... oh God, no, she didn't even want to think about it.

'I'll do my best, Lady Charlotte,' Abbie said politely, but the woman raised a hand.

'Not Lady Charlotte, please. You'll call me Grandma Charlotte, child. You're family now, same as Alexander.' Abbie's lips curved into a proper smile.

'Grandma Charlotte.' She murmured.

'Very good.' Lady Charlotte nodded approvingly. 'Now, we should go, or we'll be late.'

Drawing on every ounce of willpower, Abbie took her first step, her gown sweeping around her feet as she moved towards the door. She had no choice but to follow through, though in the back of her mind, she could not help but wonder – what would become of her as she walked through that door and toward the altar.

***

Alexander's mixed feelings were reflected on his face, for he didn't know what to make of his impending wedding. He had barely exchanged two words with his future wife since she had, reluctantly and without emotion, agreed to marry him. Well – not without any emotion. What she had shown him was frustration. She had made it very clear that she would not have chosen him if she had been given any other option.

This had stirred in him a sense of apprehension he had never experienced before. To him, this was meant to be a simple arrangement, a mere financial transaction, a means of fulfilling the promise he made to her father. Yet, somehow, it no longer felt like that – perhaps because whenever she was near, the steady rationality that had always characterised him seemed to vanish. The greatest question that now lingered in his mind was whether he could truly keep his word – that this marriage would remain only a formality.

The chapel stood on the road near the main house. Though modest in size, it was perfectly sufficient for the estate's needs. Standing before the priest, Alexander could feel the shorter man studying him with a critical eye. The vicar was clearly displeased at being asked to officiate a wedding with such haste, most likely presuming that the cause of the urgency was a child on the way. Alexander would not have been surprised if the man's first glance fell upon Abbie's waist rather than her face.

But Alexander's thoughts were far removed from the vicar's scrutiny. He kept telling himself that he was the one doing her a favour – Abbie needed him, not the other way around. How many times had he repeated that same thought to himself? Yet, little by little, he came to realise that he was only denying the truth. Somehow, the need to protect her had become something… more.

The mere thought of her ending up with another man was enough to tighten his jaw in anger. How could this be, when they barely knew one another? There was something about her – something powerful and unexplainable – that drew him in, and no matter how hard he tried, there was nothing he could do to fight it.

'Everything all right, my lord?' John asked quietly, standing at his left side. In the absence of his cousin and closest friend, Derek Colton, Alexander had needed a witness – and there was no man he trusted more than John.

'Yes, John. Everything is fine,' Alexander replied, though it was a lie. How could everything be fine when he was about to marry a woman who drove him to madness – and when, in truth, he could not even be sure she would show?

But he did not have to wait much longer to find out. The chapel door creaked open, the sound echoing softly against the aged stone walls. Georgina was the first to enter, beaming brightly as she concentrated on keeping step with her little feet, looking down to count – one, two, three, and so on. – her small hands clutching the ring box with great care. As she grew more confident in her pace, she lifted her head and whispered loudly, 'We are here, Uncle Alex.'

Alexander smiled at the girl, but his attention shifted the moment Abbie appeared at the doorway, filling the space with her light.

She looked like a vision, an ethereal presence who had come to unsettle his existence. She walked towards him with effortless grace and elegance that took his breath away. Each step she took caused the soft blue fabric of her gown to sway gently about her hips. Her eyes remained fixed on his the entire way to the altar. They were filled with the determination of a woman who wished to display her strength – yet he could see there was also uncertainty about what she was about to do. Still, the quiet confidence in her stride was enough to release some of the tension coiled inside him.

When she reached his side, Alexander took her hand delicately, lowering his head to murmur in her ear, 'You look beautiful, Abbie.'

'Thank you,' she said timidly.

They both turned to face the priest, who began the ceremony. From that point on, Alexander's recollection of the event blurred. He remembered glancing at Abbie from the corner of his eye and sensing when she looked back at him, as though she could feel the weight of his gaze.

He repeated the vows as instructed, his voice sounding distant from his own ears. Then it was her turn – he heard her say, 'I do,' and soon followed with his own, 'Yes, I do.' He slipped the ring onto her delicate finger, taking the opportunity to let his thumb brush lightly against her skin. Then it was done – the priest's words confirmed it: man and wife.

As the small congregation gathered to offer their congratulations to the happy couple, Lady Charlotte's voice rang out,

'Aren't you going to kiss your wife?' She stood tall, an eyebrow raised, and her cane held in both hands. Alexander did not hesitate. Turning to Abbie – determined not to give her a chance to reconsider – he placed a hand at the back of her head, drawing her gently towards him. His lips pressed against hers in a lingering kiss, longer than tradition dictated, and he was caught off guard when she placed a hand on his arm, responding with a soft pull, drawing him closer still. When they finally parted, their eyes remained locked, and to his astonishment, he saw reflected in hers the very same desire that burned within him.

***

Abbie's next hours were filled with turbulent thoughts, dreading the moment when she would have to go upstairs with him. Even more so now, after the kiss they had shared. Afraid she would beg for more if left alone with him – how could anyone resist those perfect lips?

She had to avoid being alone with him at all costs, and she took the opportunity to tell him as they shared the first dance.

'I don't think we should sleep in the same room.' She tried to avoid his beautiful eyes, but he took her chin gently between his fingers, forcing her to look at him, piercing her with the intensity of those cobalt-blue depths.

'And why is that?' His voice dropped to a deep, sensual tone.

'Because there is no need. Since you already told my uncle that you and I... that we have already...' She faltered, unable to finish the sentence, too mortified to speak the words aloud. Her cheeks flushed, burning with the fire she could already feel rising inside her. His lips curled into a smile when he saw her blush, but before he could say more, the dance ended and Lady Charlotte approached to request a turn with the groom.

Abbie returned to the table and sat, still watching Alexander's graceful movements across the floor. *Oh, Abbie, please stop,* she reprimanded herself, then reached for her glass and finished the remaining wine in a single gulp. Behind her, a hand rested on her shoulder.

'Darling, it's time,' Aunt Agatha said softly in her ear.

'Time?'

'Come, we have everything ready.'

Oh Lord, here we go. Guided by her aunt, Abbie followed her upstairs, each step feeling heavier than the last.

As Aunt Agatha had said, everything was ready. Suzie was waiting to help her change into a beautiful nightgown that left little to the imagination, along with a robe that offered minimal additional protection. Still, with both garments on, at least her modesty remained somewhat intact.

Lady Charlotte joined them shortly after, and together the two women launched into a discussion about what she should expect that night – as though Abbie were some naïve child, as though she did not understand, at least in theory, what happened between a man and a woman. Well, she had read about it. But it hardly mattered, because nothing was going to happen between them. Nothing at all. She simply wanted them to leave so she could lock the door and avoid anyone entering. Especially him.

She sighed in relief when they kissed her cheeks and turned to go, but of course, the moment they opened the door, there stood Alexander, hand raised as if about to knock. Like a solid wall of muscle, he blocked any hope of escape, and all her plans to avoid him crumbled to pieces.

The women hurried out, giggling as they went, without so much as a backwards glance. Abbie could have shouted *Don't leave!* But swallowed the impulse, standing silently as he closed the door behind him. Resting his back against it, Alexander's gaze swept over her from head to toe, making her cross her arms instinctively over her chest.

After what seemed like an eternity, he pushed himself away from the door and walked towards her. She took a step backwards to maintain some distance between their bodies.

'You can leave now.'

'And why would I do that?'

'I told you – there is no need for us to spend the night... together. I'll tell everyone we shared a bed; they'll believe it. So, you can leave.' Her voice wavered slightly, betraying her nerves. But Alexander continued forward, steadily reducing the distance between them. She could feel the air grow warmer with every step, as though the very heat from their bodies was raising the temperature in the room.

'No one will believe it if I leave after two minutes, Abbie.'

She pressed her lips together. He had a point.

'Fine! You can stay ten minutes,' she snapped. He arched an eyebrow.

'That won't do much for my reputation,' he murmured.

'What did you say?' she asked, though she had heard him perfectly well.

'Nothing, Abbie. Nothing'

The way her name sounded on his lips gave her shivers; it sounded far too good, far too intimate, and she wanted him to repeat it over and over again. He looked devastatingly handsome in his dark suit – how was she supposed to avoid succumbing to his charms? Before she realised, he was only an arm's length away from her. How did he get so close?

Abbie forced herself to meet his gaze and, in that instant, realised she was doomed. Those piercing blue eyes had her completely ensnared. She wanted to step back, away from him and the heat emanating from his body. She needed to put distance between them, but her legs refused to follow her instructions.

'This is not a real marriage,' she said firmly.

'But it could be.'

Why didn't her body obey? *Step away from him now, Abbie,* she commanded herself. *Or you'll regret it.* She tried, but without success; it felt like her feet had been nailed to the ground.

'No, it can't,' she said, but the words that came out of her mouth were barely a whisper that faded gradually the closer he got to her.

He was so close that she could feel the heat emanating from his body. Desperate to stop him from advancing, she pressed her palm to his chest – but instantly regretted it. He looked down at her hand and, without hesitation, took it in his own, trapping it against his strong, muscular torso, letting her feel the wild rhythm of his heart. Their gazes locked again, and all she could see now was desire.

His lips hovered just a breath from hers, waiting – waiting for her to… to what? To say no? To stop this madness? But how could she resist him if her voice had practically abandoned her? It was like he had left her speechless and without the will to reject his advances. Unable to find the strength to stop him, instinct took over, and she let herself be carried away by the feeling that ran through her entire being. She tilted forward, her lips closing the last sliver of distance.

She didn't know who moved first, but the moment they kissed, all reason vanished. Her hands flew to his neck, and he responded with just as much passion, pulling her to him. His strong arms circled her waist, lifting her up to bring her mouth closer to his. She found herself opening to him, and when his tongue touched hers, she couldn't help but let out a sigh of pleasure, making him kiss her even deeper.

His mouth travelled to her ear, his teeth nipping gently, causing a tingle to run through every fibre of her body. The wetness of his tongue left a trail down her neck, and instinctively, she tilted her head back to expose it further and give him access to her body, her hands clutching at his shoulders.

Then, without warning, his kisses slowed. His fingers tracing the tender skin of her neck, caressing her softly while unbuttoning the buttons one by one until he noticed how his touch was making her shudder. But contrary to what Abbie wanted, his hand stopped advancing, stopping at the visible bruises that still remained from the attack she had suffered. She blinked, startled out of her haze, to see pain and fury reflected in his eyes, bringing them both back to the reality of the present moment.

'I'm sorry,' he whispered, stepping back.

The sudden coldness she felt in his absence brought her out of her trance, and the idea of what this would lead to flashed into her head. If they consummated the marriage, there would be no turning back, and no annulment would be possible. They would be bound forever, trapped in a marriage neither of them had wanted. Seeing how little they could tolerate each other, it was not a future she could truly consider. When the Braxton issue was all over, they could still go their separate ways. *The fact that you want to continue kissing him doesn't mean that you like him,* she lied to herself. *This is only lust and nothing more.* Deep in thought, it took her a second to realise he was talking, so she forced herself to pay attention.

'Abbie, I didn't mean to...' She noticed the regret in his voice, and it pierced her unexpectedly, as if what they had just shared was a huge mistake. But how could something so wrong awaken so many feelings in her?

Her cheeks flushed with shame, and with trembling hands, she buttoned the top of her gown and pulled the robe tighter around her body, using her arms as an extra layer of protection.

'There's nothing to apologise for,' she said quickly, so ashamed of herself that she couldn't even look at him. To hide her feelings, she launched into a tirade of words. 'This marriage is an agreement, a commercial contract – nothing more. If we continue like this, it will only complicate matters, tying us together forever. Something that neither of us wants. Would you really like to be tied down for life to someone you didn't choose?'

He opened his mouth to respond, but the question was rhetorical, and she cut him off before he could speak. 'We already have enough to deal with. This is just... a distraction. I think you'll at least agree with me on that.'

He inhaled deeply and straightened his clothes, looking at her stoically. 'You are right. This should not have happened. It won't happen again.'

'Perfect,' she replied briskly, nodding and pointing to the door. 'Now, please leave.' But instead of heading for the door, Alexander strode to a side wall – where, she only now noticed another door.

'Where are you going?' she demanded.

'To my room.'

'You mean, you could have left... without anyone seeing?' he shrugged, a mischievous smile tugging at the sides of his mouth. 'You–' she surged towards him, but he was already through the door, closing it behind him.

Fuming, she rushed over and locked it with a satisfying click. 'Unbelievable!'

CHAPTER 12

After tossing and turning all night, Abbie finally fell asleep just as the morning sun bathed her new room in the warm light. Unfortunately, the rest did not last long. Only a few hours later, a cheerful Suzie entered the room, letting out a surprised cry that jolted Abbie from her restless sleep.

Still half lost in Morpheus's kingdom, Abbie didn't immediately understand the maid's exaggerated reaction. But when she saw Suzie glancing around the room as if searching for something, she realised what it was. Suzie wasn't looking for something but for someone –her husband. Because Abbie was now married, and this had been her wedding night. Or at least, it was supposed to have been.

'Oh, my lady! Sorry for waking you up. I didn't know you were inside. Since no one answered, I thought...' Suzie's cheeks turned red as she tried to hide a smile.

Feigning innocence, unwilling to explain why she wasn't with her husband, Abbie waved her hand lightly. 'Don't fret, Suzie. What time is it?' she asked, sitting up in bed.

'Nine in the morning. I just came to change the sheets,' Suzie replied, tilting her head.

And again, Abbie was reminded – this had been her wedding night, and certain… expectations came with that. The poor maid would be in for a surprise when, upon pulling back the sheets, she would find them as pristine as the day before, instead of marked by a night of passion.

Quickly, Abbie yawned. 'Would you mind if I stay in bed a bit longer? I am still a little tired.'

'Of course, Lady Crawford.' The sound of her new title made Abbie cringe. She doubted she would ever grow used to it. 'I'll bring you some water. Shall I come back in an hour?' Suzie asked, and Abbie nodded, pretending to settle back to sleep.

As soon as Suzie left, Abbie reached for a knife. She wasn't sure how much blood was needed to stain the sheets, but she pricked her finger with the sharp object and let two drops of blood fall in the centre of the bed, spreading them lightly and hoping it would suffice. With that problem solved, she lay back down and closed her eyes. It wasn't a lie – she was utterly exhausted, and before long, she drifted back to sleep.

Suzie returned as promised an hour later with a basin of warm water, placing it behind the folding screen. The water quickly turned pink from the small wound on Abbie's finger. Suzie looked at her sympathetically when she finished.

'Are you alright, Lady…' Suzie began, but Abbie raised her hand.

'Please, Suzie, don't call me Lady Crawford. Just Abbie.'

'But…'

'At least when we are alone. I beg you.'

Suzie hesitated, then nodded. 'Fine, but only when no one is around. I would not like Mrs White to reprimand me.'

'I wouldn't like that either.'

Suzie turned to the wardrobe and asked, 'Now, what dress would you like to wear today?' She opened the wooden doors, and Abbie was surprised to see all her dresses hanging neatly.

'Everything is here?'

'Your aunt told us to pack everything and bring it to Everleigh Manor.'

Of course, Aunt Agatha was always a step ahead. She hadn't even thought about it.

'There are still a few things to bring, but I'll make sure it's all ready for your trip to London.'

'Trip?'

'Yes. The whole household is preparing for your departure.'

Great, Abbie thought. Where had she been the last few days, not to know she was going to London?

'Right… and remind me, when will this be?' Suzie raised an eyebrow.

'Tomorrow. Lady Charlotte said…'

Abbie vaguely recalled a conversation between her aunt and Lady Charlotte.

'Yes, yes. Sorry, Suzie. I must still be a bit tired and confused. Everything has happened so fast.'

'Don't worry, it will be fine. Lord Crawford is a nice man. And handsome!' Suzie giggled. Abbie couldn't deny that. He was the most attractive man she had ever seen. And his kisses…

'Miss Abbie?' Suzie's voice broke her thoughts. She was still standing by the wardrobe, pointing at the dresses.

'Yes, right. The dress… Can you bring my riding dress, please? I want to go to Redwood House and collect a few things.'

'But I can do that.'

'I need some things from my father's study, Suzie. But thank you for offering.'

'Alright, then.' Suzie selected the blue riding dress and helped her into it.

Once dressed, Abbie headed straight for the stables. She slipped down the service staircase, unwilling to run into Alexander. She knew she couldn't avoid him forever, but she could at least delay it as long as she could. Her cheeks still burned from the events of the previous night, and she wasn't ready to face him – at least not until she had cleared her head.

As she arrived, she saw Luke stacking hay near the stalls. Sensing her presence, he turned, stopped what he was doing, and bowed politely with a smile.

'Good morning, m'lady.'

There it was again – *my lady*. She wanted to correct him, but what was the point? Was she going to correct everyone from now on? *Leave it, Abbie,* she told herself and smiled back.

'Good morning, Luke. I'm glad you're feeling better, though I still think you should be resting.'

He shook his head, dismissing her concern. 'I'm completely recovered, m'lady. The doctor said I was fit to work again, and my Pa needed help, you see? There's much to be done.'

'Your father has raised a good boy,' she said, smiling warmly.

'Thank you, m'lady. May I be of service?'

'Yes, please. I'd like to go to Redwood House. Where's Hettie?' Luke hesitated.

'I'm sorry, m'lady, but Lord Crawford gave orders not to let you leave without his consent.'

'He did what?'

'I am sorry, m'lady. I can go and ask.'

Abbie noticed the nervousness in the boy's face, a reaction to her rising anger. But she knew Luke was not to blame – it was her arrogant husband. This would not stand. Did Alexander truly believe that he could hold her captive?

'Don't worry, Luke. I'll ask him myself.'

She turned on her heel and stormed back towards the house, throwing open the doors with force. When she reached his study, she flung the door open so violently that it slammed against the wall, startling Alexander from his seat. He looked at her, eyebrows raised, but she didn't give him a chance to speak.

'How dare you tell the household I'm not allowed to leave the house!'

'Nice to see you, dear wife. I hope you slept well,' he said dryly. Her anger boiled at his insolence.

'I asked you a question. Am I your prisoner now?'

'You are not a prisoner, Abbie. This is for your own safety.'

'My own safe–' she choked on the word. 'There are many ways to keep me safe without making me obey your orders like a child. Do I have to report my every move to you now?'

'You're overreacting, Abbie.'

'Oh, *this* is not overreacting.' Her eyes landed on a crystal bird figurine sitting on the side table. She seized it and threw it straight at Alexander. He ducked, and the glass shattered behind him. 'That was overreacting!' she shouted, looking around for something else to throw, but Alexander reached her in two strides and grabbed her wrist.

'I'd appreciate it if you stopped breaking everything in the house.'

She glared up at him defiantly. 'And I would appreciate it if you'd stop trying to control me, Lord Crawford.' They stood there, neither backing down, for what felt like an eternity. It was distracting how much it felt like time just stopped around them. His hand was strong around her wrist, his nearness unnerving, the heat of his touch sending an involuntary shiver through her.

She yanked her hand free, determined to hide how much he affected her. She could still feel the warmth of his touch.

Alexander lifted both hands in a peace offering. 'I'm not trying to control you, Abbie. And perhaps I shouldn't have given that order, but after what happened last time... what did you expect?'

'Was that a question?' she snapped. 'Because I expected many things from you, but locking me up in your house was not one of them!'

'No, it wasn't a question. And I'm not locking you up.'

'Then what do you call this?'

He ran a hand through his hair, visibly frustrated. 'I can't risk you being harmed again, Abbie. So, we need to come to an agreement. Just promise me you'll always be accompanied by one of my men when you go out.' The rage she felt inside began to ebb; reaching an agreement would be the best for them both.

'Fine. That's a reasonable request.'

'And that you will inform me when you leave.'

'Fine.' She nodded. 'I'm going to Redwood House. Which of your men is available?'

'No one is free at the moment. I'll take you myself. Just let me know when you're ready.'

'I'm leaving now.' She turned to go, but his voice stopped her.

'One more thing, Abbie. You'll call me Alexander, not Lord Crawford. We're married now, and we should get used to speaking more familiarly. No one in this house would mention it, but we need to make it a habit so we don't make a mistake in public.'

She nodded with a curtsy. 'Get ready, my dear *husband, Alexander*,' she said sweetly, drawing his name out in a way that made his jaw tighten.

'God give me strength,' she heard him mutter. *Good,*

she thought. Now *he* was as irritated as she was. Oddly, she found it… entertaining. Annoying Alexander might prove to be more enjoyable than she'd anticipated. She turned around and made her way back to the stables.

***

The arrival at Redwood House caused quite the commotion among the household staff. Jacob opened the door with effusive congratulations on their recent wedding, quickly alerting the rest of the servants to the presence of the newlyweds. Mrs White hugged her warmly, and Jane appeared on the stairs leading to the kitchens, almost out of breath.

'Abbie!' The two friends embraced.

'I was so worried about you. Jacob told us what happened – Ma and I were so scared.' Stepping back, Jane cupped Abbie's face, gently touching the fading bruise under her eye. 'Oh, Abbie.' Tears welled in her eyes. 'Are you alright?'

'Don't worry, Jane, I'm fine. Where have you been?' Abbie asked, changing the subject.

'I went to see my aunt in London, but that's not important. What happened? You were kidnapped? And what about the wedding? You didn't even like the man, and now you are suddenly married to him?' In her usual rambling manner, Jane fired questions at her, making Abbie smile, for Jane hadn't realised that Alexander was standing right behind her.

She leaned in and whispered in Jane's ear, 'He's right here.'

Jane peeked over Abbie's shoulder to find the tall man standing there, his brow slightly raised in question. Jane offered a shy smile before turning back to Abbie and whispering.

'You could have told me.'

'You didn't give me time,' Abbie whispered back. Stepping aside, Abbie made the introductions properly.

'Jane, this is Lord Crawford. Lord Crawford, may I present Miss Jane May, the best baker in England.' Jane gave a small curtsy.

'A pleasure to meet you, my lord.' Then, with a playful glance at Abbie, she added. 'Do I have to call you Lady now?'

'Don't you dare, Jane,' Abbie replied with mock sternness, making Jane laugh.

Alexander cleared his throat politely. 'A pleasure to meet you, Miss May.'

'He's handsome,' Jane murmured.

'He can hear you,' Abbie replied in the same low tone.

'I can hear you both,' Alexander said, unable to hide a smile at their exchange. 'I'll have Jacob bring up a trunk for the rest of your belongings.' With that, he turned to look for the butler, leaving the two women alone.

'So, you're moving to Everleigh Manor, then?' Jane asked, her voice tinged with concern.

'Yes… and no.'

Jane grasped her hands. 'What do you mean?'

'My dear husband,' Abbie said sarcastically, making her feelings clear, 'wants to leave for London tomorrow.'

'For how long?'

'I don't know.' Abbie squeezed Jane's hands gently. 'But it won't be forever, Jane.'

'Are you going to close Redwood House?'

'Close it? God, no! This is my home, and I will come back.'

'But… you're married now, Abbie.'

'It's complicated.' And it was. The realisation struck her of how much all this could change for Redwood House. She would need to speak to Alexander. Perhaps he lacked sufficient staff in his London home and would allow her to bring her own. She would feel far more comfortable with familiar faces around her.

Jane was looking at her, expecting an explanation. 'It's a long story,' Abbie said at last. 'One, I promise to tell you – but it will take more than a few minutes.' How could she possibly explain everything that had happened over the past few weeks? The truth was, she couldn't. The more Jane knew, the more danger she would be in. Abbie couldn't bear the thought of her dear friend suffering because of her.

Jane gave her a soft smile and tapped her hand. 'That's alright, Abbie. Have you eaten?' Abbie shook her head and instinctively pressed a hand to her empty stomach, which growled in response. Jane smiled knowingly. 'I'll bring you tea and biscuits to your room. Shall I bring some for your fancy husband, too?' she teased.

Abbie rolled her eyes. 'I suppose…' Jane giggled as she disappeared through the service door.

As Abbie walked up to her room, a wave of nostalgia washed over her. She glanced around, feeling as though she hadn't been there for years rather than just a day. For some reason, everything felt different. The room was practically bare – Suzie had done a remarkably thorough job packing her things – and it suddenly struck Abbie that all her good memories in this house were now part of the past.

She walked inside, remembering how happy she had been here. Memories of her mother brushing her hair, singing softly before tucking her into bed as a little girl. It brought tears to her eyes, but she stopped them with a shake of her head. No. She wouldn't cry again.

Moments later, Alexander appeared in the doorway, carrying a trunk on each shoulder.

'Where do you want these?'

'Just over there,' Abbie said, pointing. He set the trunks down with ease.

'Do you need help packing?'

'Why? Are you volunteering?' she replied dryly.

'No, I meant you could ask a maid.'

'I don't need help. There is not much left...' She looked around the room and her eyes fell on a small silver box. She picked it up like a precious treasure and showed it to him.. 'Found it!' she said, feigning triumph.

'You could've told me that before I hauled these trunks upstairs.'

'What? And miss your grand display of strength?'

Alexander's jaw tightened. 'Then why are we here?'

'I need something from the study, not here.'

He sighed in exasperation, bending to pick up the trunks, piercing her with his gaze. *This is not going to end well,* Abbie thought as she followed him to the corridor. He paused by the stairwell, his brow furrowing as a distant commotion reached them.

Abbie followed his gaze, then heard it – raised voices downstairs. Alexander set the trunks down and headed for the stairs, Abbie close behind. But before he could descend, she grabbed his arm, her body flooding with fear as she recognised a voice that had haunted her dreams. Alexander looked at her and immediately grabbed her arm.

'Abbie, are you alright?' Alexander asked, pulling her close, concern etched on his face.

'That voice,' she whispered, panic tightening her chest. 'I've heard that voice before... It's him. The man who came to the cabin to look for Georgina.'

'Are you certain?' She nodded, her expression fierce.

'Yes, I'm certain. I'll never forget that voice.' Alexander's jaw clenched. Downstairs, Jacob's voice rose above all the others.

'Mr. Williams! The lady already warned you not to come without an invitation. Leave now, and only return when you properly request an audience!'

'Williams?' Abbie breathed in disbelief, clutching his jacket.

'Your administrator?' They peered over the railing and saw Williams – face red, fists clenched – looming threateningly over Jacob. He was getting closer and closer to the butler with his eyes full of fury, gesticulating maniacally. Although she knew this was the same man, she had difficulty believing it. This wasn't the mild, bumbling administrator who had always visited their house to speak with her father. This was a man full of menace and fury – so terrifying that just the sound of his voice made her blood run cold.

'You will let me in!' Williams roared.

Alexander turned her away from the railing. 'Are you sure he didn't see you?'

'Yes. He never knew I was there, and the two men who kidnapped us didn't want him to know.'

'Then I doubt the man who escaped told him, out of fear. We'll go down, but remember – act as though you know nothing about Braxton, about the kidnapping… or your parents.'

Abbie bit down her fury, her whole body trembling. 'He was probably involved in the attack on my parents.' She wanted to scream and shout, but managed to control herself enough to keep her voice low.

'I know,' Alexander replied, steady and grim. 'But if we reveal that now, we'll never uncover the truth.' He was right. It wasn't the time to reveal their cards just yet; there were so many missing pieces of the puzzle. Abbie was shaking from head to toe from not being able to tell Williams to his ugly face just exactly what she thought of him in that moment, but she nodded and took a deep breath, forcing herself to calm down.

'I won't say anything,' she said firmly, straightening her back and squaring her shoulders as if she were preparing herself for battle.

Alexander's hand brushed her arm. 'He can't harm you, Abbie.' A slight grin tugged at the corners of his mouth. 'Although, frankly, I don't know whether it's you or him who should be afraid. I have seen firsthand your good aim.' She smirked. It would please her greatly if she could throw something at the fat-headed pig below, she thought.

'Not that good. I was aiming for your head.' His eyes lit with amusement, and he squeezed her hand.

'Come on.'

Hand in hand, they descended the stairs, and when they reached the hall, they could see Jacob struggling to stop the undesirable administrator. But when Williams caught sight of Abbie and Alexander at the bottom of the stairs, his stance shifted. The fury melted away, replaced by the snivelling façade she'd always known. He bowed; eyes averted.

'M-my apologies for the intrusion… I only came for some d-documents, Miss Clarkson.' He looked down at the floor like a frightened dog begging for pity, but now Abbie could see him for what he was – a snake who had betrayed her father, and then been responsible for the death of the two people she had loved most in this world. Rage overtook fear quickly, tensing up her entire body. She felt Alexander's hand resting gently on her back, a simple gesture that conveyed so much meaning. It was as though, without words, he had whispered in her ear, *You are not alone in this*. Grateful for the gesture, she took a deep breath and remained calm.

'You intended to enter my home without an invitation again, Mr. Williams?'

'N-no, Miss Clarkson. I was s-simply asking if you were home.' He trembled; eyes glued to the rug beneath her feet. If Abbie hadn't known the truth, she would have believed his nervousness was sincere.

Jacob looked at him indignantly and immediately opened his mouth in protest. Abbie tilted her head, indicating to him that he didn't need to worry. The faithful butler understood immediately and lowered his head, placing his hands behind his back, curious to see what was about to unfold.

'It's Lady Crawford,' Alexander said flatly. Williams looked up in surprise at the words from the tall man standing beside Abbie, his hand resting protectively on her back.

He blinked. 'I beg your pardon?'

'Lady Crawford. My wife.' Alexander's tone left no doubt that there was an implicit threat in his words. She was his wife and was under his protection.

'M-my apologies, I wasn't aware you had married.' He gave them a tense bow.

'You didn't need to know,' Abbie said coldly. 'Now, to the matter at hand. There are no documents of yours in this house, so forgive me if I am confused by your request.'

'Well, yes. I think I left–' Abbie lifted her hand to stop him from talking.

'No, you didn't. I have looked everywhere in my father's study, and I haven't seen anything that belonged to you, Mr Williams.'

'If you let me look–' Again, she interrupted him.

'Absolutely not.'

It took all her strength to restrain the urge to command Jacob to remove him from her presence, but she reminded herself to keep her composure and not give away what she knew.

'I was going to write you a letter, Mr. Williams, but since you are here, I would like to inform you that you are no longer my administrator. My husband will take care of my affairs from now on. I don't know very well what I'm doing, you see? He will be better at managing everything. Is that not right, dear husband?' She looked at Alexander with a smile.

He returned the smile and nodded.

'I am sorry you wasted your time coming here. As I mentioned the last time, you should have made an appointment. It is not proper to come unannounced.'

For a moment, she saw his frustration reflected on his face and felt a flicker of satisfaction knowing that she had at least infuriated him. But it was a fleeting moment, for he disguised his expression quickly with a forced smile and cleared his throat.

'I am s-sorry you made that decision, Lady C-Crawford. I would have been happy to c-continue managing your affairs. Please let me know if you need anything in the f-future.'

'I will,' she said sharply. But what she wanted to say was, *'I won't.'* She wanted to say many more things, but forced herself to refrain, not even allowing herself to think about them.

'Please, Jacob, escort Mr. Williams to the door,' Alexander said. Jacob looked more than happy to follow the command and promptly urged Williams to leave the house. Once the front door closed behind him, Abbie finally felt able to breathe again.

Alexander encouraged her to follow him into the study, and once inside, he closed the door behind them.

'Abbie?' he said, following her as she walked to the window.

'I am raging, Alexander.' He placed his hands on her shoulders. His familiar gesture should have surprised her, but instead of rejecting it, she welcomed his touch, relaxing under the warmth it stirred within her.

'I know, but you did well, Abbie. You did very well.' Abbie lifted her head to look back at him.

'That little weasel had everyone fooled! His stutter is gone, and he's nothing like the simpleton he pretended to be!' She hit the windowsill with her fist.

The memories of him at the cabin made her stomach churn. She couldn't believe the same man had tried to intimidate Georgina. What kind of monster was one who rejoiced in a little girl's suffering? The person she had just seen was nothing like the man in that filthy old cabin. All this time, he had been playing everyone, pretending to be a sheep, when in reality, he was the wolf. Who would have thought he could be such a despicable being?

'Don't worry, Abbie. He's a man who's hidden his true nature well. Not even your father noticed.'

'I think he did get his suspicions eventually. But I don't think he ever imagined he'd be capable of something as vile as kidnapping a child.' Abbie shook her head. 'How are we going to find out everything he's done? Maybe I shouldn't have fired him.'

'I think it's best not to keep him too close. Once we're in London, we can lure them to us. We'll draw their attention and wait.'

'Wait for what?' she asked.

'We'll wait for them to make a mistake.'

CHAPTER 13

Their departure to London early the following day, with what looked like a royal conclave, was not as prompt as Alexander had hoped it would be. They had to hire two additional coaches, for apart from all of their belongings, the party included half of Abbie's household staff, Aunt Agatha and Grandma Charlotte. Abbie had refused to leave her aunt behind, and there was no need for her to explain her reasons; from what Alexander had witnessed of her uncle's character, the woman would have been in grave danger if left in the hands of that fiend.

As they prepared to leave, Abbie turned toward the older women's carriage, but anticipating her intentions, Alexander stepped in front of her, blocking her advance.

'Where are you going?' Lifting her gaze to his, she raised her eyebrows questioningly.

'Why, to the carriage, of course.'

He shook his head, a smile playing on his lips, accompanied by a clicking of his tongue. 'Tsk-tsk-tsk. That is not your carriage, my lady.' She rolled her eyes and lowered her voice so no one else could hear.

'I would prefer to ride with my aunt if you wouldn't mind.'

'I do mind.'

'Why does everything have to be so difficult with you? You cannot dictate my every move, Alexander.'

'Nice to hear you saying my name,' he whispered, stepping closer and lowering his tone, making his voice vibrate in her ear. Feeling the heat radiating from her body as she reacted to his voice, he dared to place a finger softly under her chin, tilting her face so she had to look him in the eyes when he said, 'You cannot avoid me forever, Abbie. Besides, the only thing you will achieve is to make people wonder why my wife would not ride with me, which is the last thing we need. Anyone in their right mind would question the veracity of our marriage.'

Seeing how she wanted to refuse again, he couldn't help but smile when she closed her eyes and replied stoically, finally surrendering to his logic.

'I am not avoiding you.' Stepping away from him, she jumped inside the carriage where they would travel together with Georgina, giving him no time to help her up.

Talking with his men, Alexander marked their positions – at both flanks of the caravan and one at each end – ensuring their journey to London would be as safe as he could make it.

Once everyone was ready to leave, he entered the carriage, sitting opposite Abbie and Georgina, who, even before the horses began to move, proceeded to list all the dolls she had packed in her trunk and explained the reasoning behind the names she had given each one.

That kept them entertained for at least an hour, and the little girl did not miss the opportunity to tell him he should buy her a doll with a yellow dress and blue ribbons, since she knew her other dolls needed company.

'Is that so?' he asked.

'Yes! They have told me,' she exclaimed, sitting straighter in her seat. He laughed and looked at Abbie, who could not hide her smile either.

'Well, if the other dolls have said so, we must find that doll with the yellow dress.'

'And the blue ribbons, Uncle Alex. Don't forget the

blue ribbons.'

'I won't. Don't worry.'

With Georgina leading the conversation, they barely exchanged more than a few glances, and no matter how much he tried to address her directly, Abbie responded only with brief words, returning her attention to the girl as if he wasn't even in the carriage. The tension between them was palpable, and he couldn't help but wonder why. He had thought they had made some progress after they went to her house, but whenever they were even remotely close, she made sure to put distance between them in any way she could, and since they were now in the confined space of the carriage, her only option was to ignore him.

When they stopped to change horses, Alexander helped Aunt Agatha and Grandma Charlotte descend from the carriage to stretch their legs, while Abbie looked after an excited Georgina, who had discovered some kittens next to the stables and didn't hesitate to kneel to pet them.

'Can we take them with us?' she asked, her face imploring.

'No, we can't.'

'But Uncle Alex...' She looked up at him with her innocent emerald gaze, hoping to cajole him.

He bent down, pinched her little nose, and said, 'Georgina, we can't take them with us. They need to stay here with their mother.' She looked back at the kittens and nodded, picking one of them up in her arms.

'I'm sorry, kitten, but I cannot take you with me. Uncle Alex is right; you need to stay with your mother. She will take care of you. I promise.' Abbie stood behind them, watching, her head tilted to one side, a smile curving her lips.

'You almost conceded, my lord,' she said as he stood beside her, both watching Georgina play with the kittens.

'If she had asked once more, I probably wouldn't have been able to refuse her.'

Alexander's thoughts drifted to Georgina's mother as he remembered how impossible it had been for him to refuse her. No matter what she wished for, he would have granted it with just a glance, and her daughter had inherited the same charming smile that could bend him to her will. Shaking those thoughts from his mind, he said.

'I will see that the horses are changed and fetch something for us to eat. It will take us another two hours until we reach the inn at Beaconsfield.'

Abbie nodded in his direction before kneeling beside Georgina and petting the kittens that were beginning to climb up her dress, demanding the little girl's attention.

Alexander paused, wishing to preserve that image in his memory – the two people who mattered most in his life sharing a tender moment, oblivious to anyone around them. In a short time, they had bonded in a way that fascinated him, and sharing a dangerous experience such as the one they had endured only a few days before had created a link between them that would last forever.

It had been a long time since he had felt so at ease, and knowing that it would not last long, he wanted to freeze time, to hold them safe in this moment, for as soon as they arrived in London, everything would become complicated again. The danger that was now distant would soon be very real once more.

After arranging the change of horses and buying some food, he returned to the carriages, handing out a few pieces of cheese and a loaf of bread among the retinue members, and soon they resumed their journey.

The uneven terrain made the carriage bounce, but as if she barely noticed, Georgina slid down slowly until her head rested on Abbie's lap. Abbie placed an arm protectively over her to ensure the little girl wouldn't slip off with the rattle of the carriage. For the remainder of the journey, Abbie avoided Alexander's gaze, focusing on the green pastures visible from the small carriage window. Alexander, on the other hand, allowed his gaze to linger on Abbie's beautiful features, softened by Georgina's head resting on her lap, admiring the gentle way she protected the child.

Georgina needed a mother, for there would be many things a man would never suffice to guide her through womanhood, and Alexander couldn't think of anyone better suited for that role than Abbie – at least until she decided to leave them. And the truth was, he didn't know how to prevent that moment from coming. In the end, he pretended to fall asleep to make the silence less uncomfortable, not only for her sake but for his own.

When the carriage stopped, Georgina opened her eyes, still half-asleep. 'Have we arrived home?' she asked, rubbing her eyes with her tiny hands.

'Not to London, darling,' Alexander said, extending his hand to caress her cheek. 'Come, you must be hungry. We're going to stop at this inn for the night so you can rest in a proper bed.'

Abbie looked down at the sleepy girl in her lap and brushed her hair out of her face with her fingers. 'I am sure Aunt Agatha and Grandma Charlotte will also need some rest.'

Alexander opened the door and stepped outside, turning to take Georgina into his arms. Shifting the weight to one arm, he offered his hand to Abbie.

'Thank you,' she said with a soft smile.

They waited for the women in the carriage behind them to join.

'I am pleased we stopped, boy. These old bones are not what they used to be, and I'll need a fortnight to recover from this long journey!' said Grandma Charlotte, running a hand along her back to emphasise her words, expecting a reaction from Alexander, who smiled at her.

'I will procure you the most comfortable bed in this prestigious inn, Lady Charlotte.'

She looked at the inn dubiously, for the building seemed a tad disregarded by the looks of it. 'I would not call this inn prestigious, darling. But as tired as I am, I will accept anything they could offer.'

Leaving his men to take the horses to the safety of the stables, Alexander asked Thomas to accompany them. They all went inside and, to their surprise, found the inn in much better condition than they had expected. Though not luxurious, the dining room was clean and simply decorated, but with tasteful touches. Only a few tables were occupied by other travellers, and selecting one by the hearth at the end of the room, Alexander led the ladies to sit, accommodating Georgina on Abbie's lap before seeking out the innkeeper to arrange rooms for everyone.

The innkeeper, a man in his fifties, assigned rooms for the servants and the ladies.

'Please, good sir,' Alexander said to the man, 'see that everyone has a good portion of your fine food; it has been a long journey for everyone.' Alexander handed the keys to Thomas. 'See that everyone eats before bed, and once they've finished, send Suzie to tend to Lady Agatha and Lady Charlotte.'

The man nodded. 'Yes, my lord.'

When he returned to the ladies' table, Georgina was fully awake, sniffing the air and peering behind him as if she was expecting something.

'I'm hungry, Uncle Alex. Have you ordered food?'

Sitting beside Abbie, she nearly jumped out of her chair when a maid appeared with a tray of steaming dishes, their aroma filling the room. As soon as they were placed before Georgina, she began devouring the food eagerly.

'Georgina, you are going to choke, girl! Eat slowly and with elegance; never forget you are a lady,' scolded Grandma Charlotte, though her tone was warm. Georgina slowed, and the others followed her lead, everyone murmuring their approval, for the stew was unexpectedly delicious. Alexander was pleased to see everyone enjoying the same meal.

Afterwards, he called John and Reece to make sure that between the three of them, they took turns guarding the inn, ever cautious that Braxton might concoct another plan to attack them when they were most vulnerable.

'John, you take the first round and then swap with Reece. I'll take his position early in the morning. That way, we can all have some rest.'

***

Abbie looked over at Alexander's face in concentration as he talked with his men, probably assuring they would all be safe.

'Dear?' Her aunt rested a wrinkled hand over hers. 'We are tired, darling. Lady Charlotte and I will retire now.' Abbie covered her hand and smiled. 'Of course, Aunt.'

As if he had been there all along, Alexander called for the innkeeper to show them to their rooms, startling her as he spoke just inches behind her. He bent to take a sleepy Georgina from her arms just as the innkeeper's wife approached them.

'Please, follow me, m'lord. Yer room is on the second floor.' They both followed the woman up the narrow stairs to the inn's top floor. When they finally arrived, she opened the door to let them in, and seeing the questioning look on Abbie's face, the woman asked, concerned.

'It is no' of yer liking, m'lady?'

Before she could answer, Alexander stepped in. 'It is perfect, Mrs…'

'Fields, m'lord. Mrs Fields,' she said with a timid smile.

'Mrs Fields. My wife is just tired, that is all.'

She smiled, showing sympathy and looking at the sleepy Georgina in Alexander's arms, she exclaimed, 'But, of course! You must be exhausted from your travels. Do not hesitate to tell me if ye need anything, m'lord.' She curtsied and left the room, closing the door behind her.

Abbie stepped into his view with her arms on her hips. 'Where are *you* sleeping?'

Taking Georgina to the bed, the girl rolled to lie in the centre. 'Here.'

'Alexander…' There was a warning tone in her voice.

'There was only one room left, Abbie. You're always welcome to go and complain to the lovely Mrs Fields – I would definitely enjoy your face when she asks why you would like to have a room separate from your husband.'

'You are insufferable.'

'That may be true, but I am also right.'

Abbie looked at him, wanting to argue with the man, but what could she do? Force him to sleep in the stables? The idea was tempting, but it would only spread rumours they didn't need. Resigned to the sleeping arrangements, she looked around the room.

Being the only room on the second floor, the space was quite ample. The fireplace spread its brilliant glow throughout the room, shimmering crimson and gold, painting the walls with a homely warmth. The crackling of the flames evoked a welcoming sensation that encouraged her to get closer to absorb the warmth it radiated. The four-poster bed crowned the room elegantly, and on a table, the woman had left a jug of wine with two glasses for her guests to enjoy. Little did she know that there was not much to celebrate between the two of them since they were not a newlywed couple in love, but rather two strangers whose lives had forced them to make a decision she hoped would not be regretted.

Abbie looked at the travel bag she had prepared for her and Georgina, imagining that the two of them would be alone; what she did not expect was to have to share the room with the man who invaded her dreams at night, causing her to wake up agitated and covered in sweat. How could she sleep with him in the same room?

She could feel Alexander's gaze on her as she walked to the bag and took Georgina's nightgown.

'Georgina, darling. Let me help you change your dress. You don't want to ruin it by sleeping on it, would you?'

'No,' she said, more asleep than awake.

Abbie turned to look at Alexander, but he had turned to look at the hearth to give them some privacy. She took Georgina's dress off, gently sliding her nightgown over her head. Once the girl was tucked inside the bed, she called for Alexander.

'Uncle Alex, can you tell me a story?'

Smiling, he happily complied with the girl's wishes, he sat on the bed beside her and commenced telling her a story about a rabbit who found a fairy in the woods, while soothingly stroking her hair. She could see how Alexander's deep voice caused an undoubted peace in the girl, making her eyes close further with each word he said. But for Abbie, that manly voice had the opposite effect, for just hearing it made her skin shiver.

Not wanting him to see how he affected her, she looked for somewhere to change. Feeling relieved to find a folding screen laid against the wardrobe in the corner of the room, she unfolded it as quietly as possible, partly not to disturb Georgina but mostly not to draw Alexander's attention to her. She didn't dare look at them to find out, and sliding behind the protection of the screen, she started untying her dress. Still, the task proved more complicated than she expected, for even though Suzie had tied the laces in a simple knot, without the help of a mirror, she had pulled the wrong side, making the knot tighter instead of looser.

He must have heard her struggle, for he said, dangerously close to her from the other side of the screen. 'Do you need any help?'

'No,' she blurted out, exasperated.

But if she kept pulling on the ties, she would eventually have to cut the dress to get out of it. Hearing him turn, she said, 'Wait.' She came out from behind the screen, turning her back to him and shifting her hair to one side to give him access to the knot in question. 'I cannot untie the lace.' Without a word, she heard him take a step closer. She stood completely still, holding her breath until she felt the heat of his body behind her, and unable to stop herself, she sneaked a look over her shoulder. Seeing his lips lifted in half a smile, she snapped,

'Are you enjoying my misfortune?'

Although he erased the smirk from his lips, his eyes continued to reflect amusement.

'Me? Not at all, my lady. I am only here to serve you.'

She rolled her eyes and spoke with a more authoritative tone. 'Undo my laces and take that smile off your face,' she said, whispering over her shoulder.

'I am not smiling.'

'Your eyes are. So stop it at once.'

He rested his masculine hands over her shoulders and leaned closer to her ear. 'I will do my best.'

Feeling the warmth of his breath on her skin, the man's closeness gave her goosebumps. Though her mind screamed for her to get away from him, her body refused to respond, and she remained still, closing her eyes to only feel the power he emanated.

His skilled hands moved along her shoulders, meeting at her nape, slowly stroking her neck with his fingers, delaying the moment of starting the task he was asked to do. She felt how he loosened the silky strings until he managed to undo the mess she had caused. Still, instead of letting her continue undressing once he had finished what she had asked him to do, Alexander continued pulling at the cords, making them slide one by one through the holes of the dress –forcing her to hold the front of the dress as to stop it from sliding forward and leaving her exposed to him.

Alexander didn't miss the opportunity to caress her back each time he pulled the delicate fabric, making her body tremble each time his fingers touched her skin, and the sound of the strings sliding did nothing but make her breath hitch as if there wasn't enough air in the room.

She felt a sense of despair when she realised he had run out of lace to unthread, as, without knowing why, she had wished it would never end, since that would mean that he would walk away from her, leaving her not knowing what to do with all the sensations running through her body.

But when Alexander slid his hand inside her dress, the warm touch made her close her eyes, and contrary to what she had promised herself, she enjoyed the touch of this man who stirred things in her that she would never have discovered if it wasn't for him. His unrelenting advance provoked her hair to bristle in anticipation. The closer he was to her, the closer she was to losing all her will, for as soon as his skilled hands touched her skin, the world ceased to exist, and it was only them in the world.

He leaned over her shoulder, whispering hoarsely against her ear, 'Anything else I can assist you with?'

As if a bucket of cold water had been thrown over her, Abbie emerged from the delicious trance in which she was immersed and stepped forward, putting distance between their bodies and securing the dress with her arms around her waist. In an instant, she was behind the safety of the screen. Relieved, she haughtily answered him to hide what she was really feeling.

'That will be all. Thank you.'

'It was *my* pleasure.' The emphasis he placed on the word *my* showed how much he enjoyed undressing her. She couldn't see it now, but she was sure that his smile of satisfaction at having provoked her to the point that she had let him caress her so freely would be plastered all over his attractive face.

***

Alexander stood still where Abbie had left him, feeling as if he was about to burst into flames. He didn't know where he had found the strength to walk away from her.

But she had reacted to him, there was no doubt about it; he could feel her skin warming under his touch. So why was she resisting the inevitable? Her rejection certainly wasn't flattering, but he would not cease in his quest to win her over, and her reaction had proven to him that she was just as affected as he was by their close proximity.

He blew the candles out, leaving only the tenuous light

of the crackling fire. Taking his jacket off, he lay on top of the covers next to Georgina, who turned towards him, resting her hand on his chest. He could not help but smile at the little girl. He kissed her forehead and closed his eyes, trying to concentrate on the goal of sleeping.

When he heard Abbie's footsteps approaching the bed, he couldn't help but steal a glance. Her nightgown floated around her body and made it seem like she was straight out of a fairy tale. The thin fabric didn't leave much to the imagination, thanks to the firelight that served to highlight her delicate curves. But she got into bed hurriedly, pulling the blankets up to her neck. He closed his eyes again and wished her goodnight with a crooked smile, to which Abbie responded by turning her back to him.

He took a deep breath, concentrating on the arduous task of not thinking about Abbie and forced himself to fall asleep before taking over his turn to guard the inn.

The sun had not yet gifted them with its warmth when Alexander roused with an unfamiliar sensation. To his surprise, his hand had curled around not just Georgina but Abbie as well. During the long night, she must have sought the warmth of the little girl, and now they were embraced like mother and daughter in each other's arms, with him sealing the bond and protectively enveloping them both.

A smile curved his lips as he took one of Abbie's silken locks between his fingers, curling the soft hair around his finger. Her golden mane ran loose over her shoulders, where the satin fabric of her gown had slid down, revealing a glimpse of her naked skin. The thought of having her in his bed every morning made his smile widen. He found himself daydreaming about the joys of having a family of his own. What he had in his arms right now could be his future, and he wouldn't let it slip away easily; he would have to find a way to convince Abbie to stay with them. He wasn't sure how just yet, but he was determined to find out how to win her trust and, hopefully, something more.

Careful not to disturb the two sleeping angels, he rose from bed, dressed in a clean shirt, and seized his belongings. Slipping on his boots, he quietly left the room and went downstairs to make the necessary arrangements for their departure. But at no moment did the image of Abbie sleeping peacefully in his arms, or his fervent desire to wake up beside her every morning, leave his mind.

***

Abbie woke to the first light of dawn. When she looked at where Alexander had slept, the only proof of his presence was the sunken marks his body had left on the mattress. Instinctively, she pushed a palm to the space, wishing he was still there, but then she shook her head, banishing those thoughts from her mind. *Abigail, stop fantasising about the man! This is only a temporary arrangement,* she reminded herself, reprimanding her treacherous thoughts. But as she remembered his strong fingers sliding gently down her back, a shiver ran through her, right where those ready hands had left a feverish trail on her skin.

Georgina rolled onto her side and stretched her arms over her head, exaggerating a yawn.

'Ahhhh! Good morning, Abbie! How did you sleep? I slept very well. Where is Uncle Alex?' Abbie pinched her cheek tenderly, smiling at the battery of questions the little girl fired off in her typically exuberant way.

'Good morning. I did sleep well. And I don't know where your uncle is. What do you say we dress and go find him? Are you hungry?'

The girl sat up straight in bed. 'Yes! I am staaaaarving!'

'Up you get then. There is no time to waste.' A gentle knock made them both turn to the door. Fearing it could be Alexander, Abbie lifted the sheets to her neck before answering. 'Who is it?'

'It's me, Lady Abbie, Suzie.' Abbie's sigh of relief had Georgina turning to look at her, but she smiled and kissed the little girl's forehead to distract her from asking any more questions.

'Come in, Suzie.' The maid entered the room with a basin of water for Abbie and Georgina.

'Lord Crawford sent me, my lady.' Abbie lifted the covers and helped Georgina climb out of bed. 'He is so thoughtful, Lady Abbie.' Abbie rolled her eyes; all the servants praised him like he was some kind of saint. If only they knew how much of a devil he could be.

The thought of the night before brought a too-familiar flush to her cheeks. *Not again, Abbie.* Her reaction to him was becoming a problem, and fearing the maid would notice how much he disturbed her, she turned to Georgina's bag and started looking for a fresh chemise for the girl.

Suzie placed the basin on the table. 'Let me, Lady Abbie.' Turning to Georgina, she coaxed, 'Come here, little one. Do you want me to put a nice bow in your hair, Georgina?' The girl jumped with enthusiasm.

'Oh yes, please! I love bows.' Suzie, enjoying her excitement, gifted her a cheerful smile.

Seeing Suzie had everything well in hand, Abbie took a cloth and dipped it in the water before slipping behind the safety of the folding screen to wash. She sighed as the soft fabric touched her skin. After being unable to clean herself the night before, she closed her eyes, relishing the feeling of finally being refreshed.

'Are you alright, my lady?' she heard Suzie say.

'Oh yes, Suzie. More than alright. I needed to clean myself after yesterday's long trip.'

'You should have called for me, my lady. I would've brought you water last night!' Abbie knew she could have called for the maid, but she had been too preoccupied, her attention consumed by her exasperating yet dashing husband.

'I was too tired yesterday,' she lied.

'Me too,' said Georgina. 'But Uncle Alex read me a story, and I fell asleep really quickly. I don't even remember!'

'You are a lucky girl.' She heard Georgina giggling. *A lucky girl,* Abbie thought. Suzie was right about that; he was a great uncle. Caring, sweet, always there for the girl.

A knock sounded at the door, and Suzie went to open it, welcoming the innkeeper's wife.

'Good mornin',' she said from the doorway.' I've brought somethin' to eat for Lady Crawford and the little girl.'

'Thank you, Mrs Fields. That is very kind.' Abbie called from behind the screen.

'Lord Crawford said to bring it, m'lady. You'll be leavin' soon, and he didn't want either of ye to starve. How thoughtful of him!'

Thoughtful? It is a basic need! Food! That is not being thoughtful, that's just being a normal person, she grumbled under her breath in frustration.

'Did ye say something, m'lady?'

'Nothing at all,' she replied, continuing to dress.

The woman left the food on the table, but lingered, chatting away to Suzie. 'I don't know what we would've done if ye hadn't come yesterday. It has been a difficult month for my Henry and me. They opened another inn just a few miles from here, and business hasn't been as good.'

'Why is that, Mrs Fields?' Suzie asked.

'Their prices are lower, but I can assure you they do not have the standards we keep here – not in wine, nor in food! If not for the lot of you, we wouldn't have filled most of the rooms!'

That last comment caught Abbie's attention. 'Did you say 'most', Mrs Fields?' she asked, poking her head out from behind the screen. The woman's chest puffed with pride.

'Yes, m'lady. This is a big inn, but even with all of you lot here, we still have two rooms unoccupied.'

Abbie smiled politely, but inside, she wanted to scream. He had tricked her! Emerging from the screen, she asked Suzie to help tie her gown, and after doing her hair, she practically stormed off in search of her *thoughtful* husband, prepared to call him every epithet she could think of until he understood just how angry she was.

She found him talking with John next to the carriages. When John spotted her, he wisely made himself scarce, leaving Alexander to deal with the storm heading his way. At his prompt scape, Alexander turned to see what had sent John fleeing like a scared child, and the moment he caught sight of Abbie marching across the courtyard with fury blazing in her eyes, he understood.

He instinctively stepped backwards as she stopped in front of him, dangerously close, her voice low but trembling with rage.

'No more rooms, you said!'

'Did I say that?' He pressed a hand innocently to his chest.

'Yes, you did. Don't pretend to be a saint with me, Alexander. You may have fooled everyone else, but not me!'

'Everyone thinks I'm a saint?'

'Do not change the subject! And stop replying with a question!'

She could see how her proximity did strange things to him, and he finally let the truth slip out before he could stop it.

'Fine. Yes, there were more rooms available. But I didn't want you in any of them.'

'And why not?' Abbie raised her chin defiantly, her suspicions confirmed.

Alexander took a step forward, closing the distance between them like a lion stalking its prey, his head lowering as though it was unbearable to be separated from her. Fixing her with a heated stare, his voice dropped low and rough.

'Because I didn't want to lose sight of you.'

For a moment, she faltered, unsure how to respond to his brazen admission, but she quickly recovered her composure, meeting his gaze head-on.

'And what do you plan to do? Sleep every night in my room?'

She regretted her words the moment they left her lips, for they both knew what was on his mind.

'If I have to.' Her mouth fell open at his bold declaration, words she was never expecting him to say out loud.

He reached out, pressing a finger beneath her chin to close her lips, just as the cheerful sound of Georgina's footsteps signalled her approach.

'Uncle Alex!' The little girl threw her arms up, and Alexander didn't hesitate, scooping her up in his arms and resting her on his hip.

'Good morning, Georgina. Did you sleep well?'

'Very well! And this morning Mrs Fields brought me milk and biscuits!'

'Excellent. Are you ready to go home?'

'Yes!'

Alexander shot Abbie a lingering glance, clearly frustrated by the interruption. She, however, thought it was for the best.

Though Georgina's arrival softened her mood somewhat, Abbie still had much she wished to say to her exasperating husband. His audacity in controlling her movements drove her to madness. His intentions might have been good, but something told her that he was not doing it just for Abbie's benefit but also for his own. She saw it in his eyes every time he looked at her – desire unmistakably reflected in those deep blue pools – and what frightened her the most was the possibility that he saw the same in her, no matter how hard she tried to hide it. The blush that always rose to her cheeks whenever he came near betrayed her every time.

She watched Alexander teasing Georgina, tickling her little belly until she shrieked with laughter, begging him to stop. Abbie was so absorbed by the scene that she didn't notice her aunt and Lady Charlotte approach until they stood on either side of her, both wearing whimsical smiles.

'Good morning, my dear,' Lady Charlotte said, her eyes glinting as she looked between Alexander and Abbie. 'I presume you slept well last night?'

Abbie gave her a questioning frown.

'You seemed quite besotted with your husband,' Lady Charlotte added with a knowing smile. The older woman was wearing a brown travel dress, her white hair tied up in a neat bun at the nape of her neck, giving her a natural air of elegance that only she could show. Leaning on her cane, she continued to look at Abbie with that mischievous twinkle in her eye. Abbie dismissed the comment with a wave of her hand and crossed her arms.

'I don't know what you could possibly mean,

Grandma Charlotte.' The woman patted her hand. 'Oh, you do, dear. The way you were looking at him says it all. Come along, Agatha.' She turned to Abbie's aunt, who kissed her on the cheek.

'I will see you when we return to London, darling.' Abbie kissed her back and watched both women as they climbed up into their carriage.

In a short time, the two women had rekindled their friendship, and her aunt appeared to be in better spirits as of late. Still, Abbie saw the lingering sadness in her eyes. She could see how conflicted her aunt felt inside, so she would have to keep a close watch on her. Abbie could not let her fall back into her uncle's clutches ever again. The woman's fear had long overridden her will to leave that rat of a husband. For Abbie could clearly see it wasn't a blind affection what made her go back to him but how terrified she was of the consequences of her actions. But now, under Alexander's protection, he couldn't harm her. Abbie knew – without him needing to say it – that Alexander would never allow it.

Waiting by the carriage steps, Alexander offered his hand. As Abbie placed hers in his, she looked up and met his devouring gaze. 'I don't want to argue, Abbie.'

'Then you'd best stop provoking my ire at every opportunity, sir.' Ignoring his exasperated grin, she climbed into the carriage and settled herself next to Georgina.

***

Abbie couldn't help but feel a chill as they turned onto Oxford Street. She had not returned to London since the murder of her parents, and the memory of the situation in which she had left the bustling city filled her with immense sadness.

As the carriage moved through the crowded streets, Abbie found herself unable to stop thinking about how different the shops looked. The excitement she used to feel when she accompanied her mother on shopping trips, or when they paused for tea at her favourite tea room, had vanished – leaving a hollow ache in its place. Now, it was nothing more than a distant memory of a life that had once been perfect. She wondered if she would ever feel that kind of happiness again – if she would ever smile as she had in those days.

The noise of the city began to fade as they left the commercial heart behind and entered Mayfair. His parents' house, though it was large and handsome in its own right, would never compare to the stately homes that lined this prestigious corner of London.

As they approached the park's edge, the carriage came to a halt, and the coachman opened the door to let the passengers out.

Her head lifted upwards in admiration at the sight of Alexander's residence.

The entrance to the two-story high building was located at the side of the house, leaving the front façade unobstructed to allow one to properly admire the gardens overlooking Hyde Park. For a moment, Abbie felt overwhelmed. From now on, this would be her home – and she didn't know how she would adapt, or if she would ever be able to think of it as hers.

Alexander stepped out first, assisting Georgina and then offering his hand to Abbie. But instead of releasing her once she was safely on the ground, he kept hold of her, drawing uncomfortably – dangerously – close.

'How long do you think you'll be vexed with me, Abbie?'

She looked at him, lifting her shoulders with a smile of feigned innocence. 'That, my lord, is a mystery.' And with that, she slipped her hand free from his and walked ahead, following Georgina, who had taken off towards the house, skipping joyfully and urging Abbie to follow her.

CHAPTER 14

Looking through the window of his study, Alexander found himself distracted, reflecting on all that had changed since he was last in this house. For a long time, it had been just him; his parents lived in the countryside with his younger sister, and rarely came to the city, preferring the fresh air of Shropshire. Which reminded him – he hadn't yet informed them of his marriage to Abbie, and he knew they would not be pleased about his news. After all, he was to be the future Duke of Clarence, and there were responsibilities that came with that title. But he would be able to explain to them his reasons for keeping them in the dark. There had been no cause to place them in the same danger he and Abbie now faced.

His mind now was wholly fixed on protecting Abbie and Georgina, and he hoped his father would come to understand why he had chosen not to involve them.

With Georgina, he had begun to experience the first changes in his life – but now, with Abbie, the house had come back to life in a way that stirred memories from his boyhood, when his parents would entertain guests throughout the season. It felt like a home again. And he could see the rest of the household was as pleased by it as he was, for the sadness that had descended on them all since Everleigh's death was slowly lifting from his shoulders. It was as if Georgina and Abbie could bring light even to the darkest of times.

The hustle and bustle coming from the corridor was

unusual in a house that had known such stillness for years – quiet and longing for the activity of the past. Alexander had grown accustomed to that pleasant noise, which, for some reason, made him feel truly back at home once more. Shaking his head and smiling faintly, he turned and sat at his desk, reaching for the stack of correspondence that had accumulated during the weeks of his absence.

Immersed in reading the letters, he did not hear the knock at the door – until it opened, and the very woman who had been keeping him awake at night peeked through.

'Alexander?' Abbie said, pushing the heavy door open.

She wore a homely pale green dress that, despite its simplicity, enhanced her beauty in a way that set his senses alight – as though he were a teenage boy again. Her hair was tied in a neat bun at her nape, and he longed to see her cascade of curls, just as he had on their wedding night, only a week ago.

'So, the mystery is solved?' he teased.

She arched a brow, irritation flickering her expression. 'And to which mystery would you be referring?'

'The mystery of when you would stop being vexed with me, of course.' He grinned, but Abbie rolled her eyes and, ignoring his comment, asked,

'Where can I put my father's books?'

Noticing how she lingered near the door, avoiding the space where he sat, Alexander rose and crossed the room to meet her. She stiffened slightly as he closed the distance between them, so he paused a few feet away, not wishing to drive her off. They remained there in silence, watching each other breathe, until at last she broke it. 'Well? Are you going to tell me or not?'

He blinked. 'Tell you what?'

She placed her hands on her hips and let out a sign of

exasperation. 'Where can I leave my father's books…?' He could see he had annoyed her once again.

'You may leave them here.'

She glanced around with a faintly suspicious expression, avoiding his eyes – until he tilted his head to catch them. 'You don't trust me?' he asked softly.

'I don't know yet,' she replied, hesitant but honest. He didn't take offence at her words. Trust would take time after everything she had been through, and he knew that no matter how many times he assured her she could rely on him, his words alone would never be enough. He would have to earn it – patiently, steadily – until she trusted him as wholly as he trusted her.

'There is always the library, if you prefer,' he offered. 'I can give you a key. No-one will disturb you there. It is one of my mother's favourite places in the house.' He watched the tension ease from her shoulders. She nodded gently.

'Thank you. I would appreciate that.'

She turned to leave – but then stopped, turning back towards him.

'You mentioned your mother.'

'Yes?'

'I just realised – I don't know very much about you.'

'We certainly don't know much about each other,' he agreed. 'But that's something we might remedy. What would you like to know?' He gestured toward the sofas by the fireplace, inviting her to sit.

She glanced at them, and for a moment, he feared she might flee. But to his relief, she crossed the room and sat down.

'Where are your parents?' she asked as he joined her, settling opposite.

'They live in the countryside, near Ludlow. My mother grew weary of London, and since she much preferred the quiet, she decided to remain there. My father – well, there is little he would not do to please my mother's wishes.' He smiled fondly.

But her expression had gown pensive.

'What is it?' he asked. She hesitated, as if searching for the right words.

'Hearing you speak of your parents… it seems to me they love each other very much.'

'Yes, they do.' It was he who raised an eyebrow this time, encouraging her to continue.

'I don't know… it just surprises me.'

'And why is that?'

'Because you married without love.'

Before he could respond, the door opened and Thomas entered. Alexander couldn't tell whether he was relieved or annoyed by the man's appearance.

'My lord,' he said with a bow, 'a young man is here to see you. He carries a letter from Captain Colton.'

Alexander rose at once. 'Show him in, Thomas.'

The butler hurried away, sensing the urgency in his voice. Abbie turned to him, surprised by his reaction. 'What is it?'

'Derek. I've been waiting for him to send word of any advancement in our investigation.'

'Your cousin?' she asked.

'Yes. He came to Everleigh Manor the day we met and returned to London to find out more about Philip Braxton.'

Before she could question him further, Thomas returned with a boy who stepped forward and presented a sealed letter.

'Good afternoon, my lord. I am Marty, sir – the captain's cabin boy. He sent me to deliver this to you in person.'

Using the letter opener, Alexander broke the seal and

read quickly.

My journey to London has led me to interesting information down south. It may be of use to our project, which I shall share as soon as I see you.
Until then, take care.
C

'Where is Captain Colton now?'

'In Portsmouth, sir. He left this morning and told me to find ye. If ye weren't in London, I was to go to Everleigh Manor. Goo' thing ye were here, sir. Oxford is a tad far fer me.' The boy grinned.

'Thank you, Marty. Thomas – see him to the kitchens, please. Make sure he gets something to eat while I write a reply.'

But before they could leave, the boy added, 'There's another thing, sir. The captain told me to say that *The man* is going to Drury Lane.' Alexander didn't need to ask who he was referring to. It was clear that Marty didn't know either – Colton had likely omitted that information to avoid putting him in danger.

'Thank you, Marty. Go along now.'

As the boy was led away, Alexander returned to his desk and began to write. Abbie came to stand opposite him, her hands resting lightly on the wooden surface. 'What did the message say?'

He looked up and handed her the note. After reading it, she frowned. 'This doesn't say much, Alexander.'

'It says enough for me to understand.'

'And who is *The man*?'

'Braxton. And he's going to the theatre this evening.'

At the mention of his name, her face went pale, her eyes flaming with a fury that reflected the hatred burning within her. He could almost see the storm emotions surging through her, like a volcano about to erupt. She turned abruptly, and Alexander followed, grabbing her arm and gently pulling her back.

'Where are you going?'

'To change,' she said, defiant.

'And why would you do that?' he asked, even though he knew what the answer would be.

'Because I can't go to the theatre looking like this, can I?'

He shook his head. 'Oh no, you're not going anywhere.'

'Are you going?'

'Yes, but–'

'Then so am I.' She raised her chin stubbornly, daring him to disagree with her.

'Oh no, you are not. Abbie, it could be dangerous.'

'Well, I have my strong husband to protect me now.' She tapped his chest with a mocking smile. Before she could withdraw her hand, he caught her fingers in his. To his surprise, she didn't pull away.

'Abbie…'

'You are not leaving me here. I'm as invested in this as you are. I'm not afraid of him.'

'You should be. This man is dangerous. I won't put you in any more danger, Abbie. Those men will have no qualms about killing you if they get the opportunity.' She yanked her hand back and started pacing the study.

'And you think I don't know that?' she shouted. 'I saw my parents die in front of me! I saw what they tried to do to Georgina – not to mention what they nearly did to me.' Her voice broke. The memory of that filthy man laying his hands on her was too vivid. She shook her head, but her next words were steady. 'I won't hide anymore. I need this to end. And the only way is to show him we won't run. We have to make him nervous, make him slip up.'

Alexander hated the idea of putting her in harm's way – but she was right. Braxton had remained silent for too long. Seeing them together might make him question how much they knew and force his hand, making him reveal his next move.

He ran a hand through his hair with a sigh. 'Do you have a dress to wear?' He said, giving in reluctantly. She crossed her arms and nodded, the gesture quiet and victorious.

'We leave at seven.'

'I'll be ready.' She paused by the door and without turning, added softly, 'Thank you.' Then she ran from the study. He shook his head, unable to help the small smile that curved his lips. Her bravery astounded him.

***

The clock struck seven as Alexander walked down the staircase to find John waiting at the bottom.

'Is everything ready?'

'Yes, my lord. The carriage is waiting, and two men will escort us to the theatre.' That afternoon, after they had decided to attend the theatre, Alexander had still not been convinced about taking Abbie with him. In the end, he had deemed it necessary to arrange an escort, in case Braxton chose that moment to strike. He would not risk Abbie suffering again because of that bastard.

'Do you trust them?' he asked, fastening the last of his cufflinks.

'Yes, my lord. Captain Colton recommended them.'

Alexander nodded and placed a hand on John's shoulder. 'Perfect, where are they from?'

But John did not answer. He had gone silent, his eyes fixed staring just over Alexander's shoulder. Frowning, Alexander turned – and time seemed to stop. Coming down the stairs was Abbie, descending each step with the grace of a queen.

She wore a deep burgundy gown with a square neckline that left her delicate collarbone and shoulders exposed. A fine muslin wrap, darker than the dress, covered her arms, but the translucent silk only served to enhance the allure of her skin beneath. He watched her as though the world had slowed in order to allow him to savour the moment. Gently, he took her hand to help her down the last few steps, and he did not miss the opportunity to raise her gloved fingers to his lips.

'You look incredible,' he said. And as he watched her cheeks flush, something stirred within him – something that had no name but burned fiercely in his chest. Abbie awakened a feeling he couldn't define. Lowering her head in thanks, she whispered.

'Thank you, my lord.'

He stepped closer, his hand resting lightly on her lower back as he bent his head to whisper in her ear. 'Alexander. Call me Alexander. I thought we had agreed on that already.'

And, as any husband might, he kissed her cheek. He breathed in the soft scent of roses as though it were his last breath – and he felt her tremble beneath his touch. Was it possible that she felt just as unsteady in his presence as he did in hers?

Pulling back, he met her gaze and smiled. 'The carriage awaits us, my darling.' He extended his hand to invite her to walk before him.

John stood by on horseback, alongside the two men Derek had sent, ready to accompany them. Billy, Alexander's coachman, tipped his hat in greeting.

As Alexander helped Abbie into the carriage, she asked. 'Are they coming with us? Is this truly necessary?'

'I will take no chances where your safety is concerned,

Abbie.' She nodded and, lifting her skirt, stepped into the carriage.

Now, seated opposite each other, Alexander could not help but stare at her. Half her face was cast in shadow, the other lit faintly by moonlight, and the sight made him long to take her in his arms and kiss her full lips until the world ceased to turn. Still gazing out the window, Abbie broke the silence, pulling him from his lustful thoughts.

'Are you certain he will be there?' She clutched her reticule as though the little piece of red fabric might protect her.

'Yes, I am. Colton has men everywhere. If he said Braxton would be there, then he will be. What I don't know is whether he'll be alone or in company.' She nodded and glanced at him.

'What are we going to see.'

He blinked. 'What do you mean?'

'I mean, what play are we seeing?'

'I'm not sure. Does it matter?' He said, confused.

'No… not really. I'm sorry. I'm just nervous. When I first met Braxton, I didn't know who he truly was, and now… now I don't know how I'll react.'

He leaned forward in his seat, taking her hand in his. He wished she weren't wearing gloves – for he yearned to feel her bare skin beneath his touch. 'He won't lay a finger on you, Abbie.'

She looked down at their joined hands, and he was surprised to feel her fingers tightening around his. 'I know. But what if I can't control myself? There are so many things I want to say. I want to…'

He lifted his other hand to her cheek, gentle and steady. 'We must both refrain from revealing what we know, Abbie. We cannot risk alerting him.'

Meeting his gaze, she nodded and leaned back, slowly

withdrawing her hand from his. She turned her attention once more to the bustling streets of London beyond the carriage window.

He had not confessed it out loud, but he harboured the same doubts. He, too, questioned whether he would be strong enough to contain the fury that surged in him whenever he thought of Braxton – of what the man had done to his family. For that is what Abbie, Georgina, and he had become now. A family. And he would protect them with his life.

***

The carriage stopped in front of the Theatre Royal on Drury Lane. Numerous carriages lined up to unload glamorous passengers, all excited to step inside. The women looked beautiful in their elegant gala dresses, ready to impress. The men, dressed in expensive frock coats, walked with pride, capturing the ladies' attention.

Alexander, dressed in an elegant black and white suit, stood out as the most handsome among them. When he stepped out of the carriage, Abbie couldn't help but notice the admiring glances of the women around him. Their looks stirred an unexpected pang of jealousy in her, confusing her more than she cared to admit.

As she had walked down the stairs earlier that night to meet him, she remembered how her pulse had quickened, stealing her breath. He looked at her – so intense and unwavering – unsettling her to her core. She feared something was growing inside her, an affection that warmed her entire body whenever she so much as thought of him.

Alexander helped her descend from the carriage, lacing her hand into the crook of his arm. As their eyes met, the world ceased to exist. For a moment, everyone around them vanished into thin air.

Softly, he whispered, 'Ready?' She nodded, centering her thoughts on what lay ahead. She was about to face the man who had ordered the brutal murder of her parents.

Upon entering the grand lobby, Abbie's breath caught at the beauty of the space. The walls, painted in soft cream, were finished with intricate mouldings that glowed under the lamplight, despite the lateness of the hour.

A sparkling chandelier hung from the soaring ceiling, presiding over the ascent of the red velvet-wrapped staircase that made guests feel like royalty as they ascended to their seats, eager for the play to begin.

As they approached the stairs, a middle-aged woman with brown hair streaked elegantly with grey came towards them, a good-natured smile lighting her oval face. There was something about her serene, confident manner that instantly put Abbie at ease. Alexander bowed and returned her smile.

'It has been a long time since you graced the theatre, Lord Crawford. How is my dear friend Lady Charlotte?'

'She is well, Mrs Garrick. She stayed at home this evening. We travelled from Everleigh Manor yesterday and she needed to rest, but I'm certain she would be delighted to join us next time.'

'Do send her my regards and tell her I shall call on her soon. I was deeply saddened to hear about her son. Such a tragedy. And so young!'

'Thank you. I will be sure to pass on your condolences.' Abbie could see the woman's sincerity; she appeared genuinely affected by the loss.

'But where are your manners, boy? Are you not going to introduce me to this lovely young lady?'

'My apologies,' he said, a mischievous glint dancing in

his eyes. 'Allow me to present my wife, Lady Abigail Crawford. Abbie, this is the legendary Mrs Garrick.'

'Oh, stop teasing me, boy – 'legendary' indeed!' She playfully tapped him with her fan, chuckling. 'I was merely a marvellous dancer.' She turned to Abbie with a warm smile that coaxed a soft giggle from her. 'And... as much as I loved my late husband, I still prefer you call me by my given name – Eva Marie, darling. Call me Eva Marie.' She beamed at Abbie. 'A pleasure to meet you, girl. I didn't know you had wed, Lord Crawford. Have you been keeping her a secret, my lord?'

Tightening his hold on Abbie's waist, he replied, 'Not in the slightest, my lady. We were wed only a week ago and haven't yet had the chance to inform many people. It was a small, intimate wedding with only close family. But rest assured, hiding my wife is the last thing I would do. I couldn't be prouder – or more surprised – that she agreed to marry me.'

Eva Marie eyed him with playful suspicion, then smiled. 'Well, young man, I must say you have excellent taste. Your wife is a rare beauty indeed.'

'That, my lady, I am quite aware of,' he said, gazing at Abbie with such intensity it sent a shiver through her. She returned the look, and something sparked between them.

'I can see you're quite taken with her, so I'll let you go enjoy the play. But please, Lady Crawford, next time my dear Charlotte joins me for tea, do come along. I'd love to hear all about how you managed to catch this young man.' Abbie hesitated, wondering how she might explain a marriage of pure convenience. But what would it matter? They were already lying to everyone – what was one more person?

'Please, call me Abbie. It would be my pleasure, Eva Marie.' The older woman smiled, patted her hand in farewell, and turned to greet another guest.

They continued on to their box, and when they arrived, Alexander held aside the red velvet curtains to let her pass. In any other circumstances, she might have appreciated the box's prime location. The view of the stage was excellent, and for the briefest of moments, she almost forgot why they had come.

There were ten seats in the box. As the first guests entered, Alexander introduced her to each one. Without fail, all reacted the same: surprise at not having heard of their marriage.

As a middle-aged couple turned to greet someone else, Abbie seized the opportunity to whisper, 'If we are going to remain up here, how will he know we're present?' She leaned closer, but before Alexander could answer, his face tensed, and his gaze fixed on something over her shoulder. Then she knew.

A chill ran down her spine as she turned to see Philip Braxton enter, cane in hand, his expression as arrogant as ever.

When his eyes landed on her, they shifted from surprise to irritation, his icy look piercing through her. As though sensing her rage boiling in her veins, Alexander rested a steadying hand on the small of her back, silently giving her the courage to stand her ground.

Braxton forced a smile and approached them slowly, like a predator circling its prey. Ignoring Alexander completely, he addressed Abbie.

'Miss Clarkson! What an unexpected surprise. I thought you were still in Oxfordshire.' He bowed and lifted his hat in greeting – then froze when he noticed Alexander's hand resting intimately on her waist.

Without a word, he turned to look at someone behind him, fire in his eyes.

Uncle Harper squeezed through the curtain, red-faced and short of breath. He froze when he met Braxton's gaze.

'What…' he began but stopped abruptly when he saw Abbie. Braxton raised a brow at her flustered uncle, and Abbie seized the moment. Clearly, her uncle hadn't informed him that the two of them had wed.

'Good evening, Mr Braxton. What a pleasant surprise,' she said, flashing a bright, false smile. 'I believe you haven't met my husband, Lord Crawford.'

'Your husband?' Uncle Harper joined Braxton, his gaze darting towards the exits as if he wanted to run away.

'Uncle Harper, you didn't tell Mr Braxton about our wedding?' She shook her head, clicking her tongue. 'Tsk, tsk, tsk.'

She looped her arm around Alexander's and gazed up at him with affection.

'We met only a few weeks ago, but we fell so deeply in love, we couldn't bear to be apart.' She turned her wide, innocent eyes on Braxton. 'I assumed Uncle Harper would have shared the good news. I'm sorry you had to find out this way, my lord.'

She could have sworn his eye twitched with fury.

'I was not made aware of your nuptials, Lady Crawford. I must say, I am quite… heartbroken by the news. If you'll excuse me.' He turned sharply, and without a word, Uncle Harper scurried after him like the snake he was, the perfect coward.

As the two men departed, Abbie surged to follow, but Alexander gripped her waist firmly and whispered, 'Let it go, Abbie. You've rattled them. That's enough for now. Braxton will be far more preoccupied with your uncle's betrayal than with us.'

'I just want to–' she hissed, grabbing her reticule tightly.

'Abbie?' he asked, eyeing her clenched hands.

'Yes?' she said, still staring at the curtains.

'Please tell me you're not carrying a knife in that reticule.'

'I am not carrying a knife in my reticule.'

'Abbie…' his tone was warning, making her see he didn't believe a word she said. She rolled her eyes as she confessed.

'I'm carrying a pistol,' she muttered. He spun her to face him, eyes wide. She stared back calmly into his blue orbs. 'As you said, I'm in grave danger. I must be prepared. Sometimes, you see, I do listen to you.'

'Don't play clever with me, Abbie. You are in danger, but I'm here with you! Besides, you cannot enter a theatre with a pistol in your reticule!' he hissed.

She could see the vein in his temple throbbing as he controlled himself to not raise his voice in public. She laid a hand on his chest to calm him, but immediately regretted the contact. The heat of his body radiated through her glove, and she quickly withdrew it.

'It's just a small one,' she said, trying to sound nonchalant.

'Abbie...' His tone darkened.

'Fine. Next time, I won't put it in my reticule.'

He ran his hands through his hair sighing, recognising defeat once again. 'You are impossible.'

'I'll do what I must to get justice for my parents, Alexander. And not you, nor anyone else will stop me from doing so.' He must have seen the fire in her eyes, for he gently stroked her arm, and said:

'Come, let's try to enjoy the rest of the evening. Truce?'

She nodded; there was no point in fighting with him here. He wasn't the enemy – not tonight.

They took their seats at the back of the box and as the actors began to perform, Abbie fixed her gaze, grateful for the distraction and trying to forget her encounter with

Braxton.

The first line echoed through the theatre, anchoring her to the present moment.

'I declare, I never saw you look so grave before!—This must be some very important secret, that can occasion your Lordship to look so very dismal!'

CHAPTER 15

A week had passed without any sign of what Braxton's intentions were. Since their encounter at the theater, the men Alexander had assigned to follow both her uncle and Braxton, had brought no news. It looked as if, all of a sudden, the earth had swallowed them whole, leaving no trace of their existence.

Captain Colton, on the other hand, had found a lead on the missing cargo, but again, he remained vague in his findings, fearing their correspondence might be intercepted. Abbie could only be impressed by their cleverness because this message– just like the one they had received a week prior – contained only the phrase *'I will be in London soon, my friend',* followed by a sequence of numbers. Alexander had deciphered Colton's message using a book, and now they both awaited his imminent arrival with bated breath.

Meanwhile, Alexander helped her sort through her father's documents and Everleigh's belongings, but to no avail. Nothing they found offered further insight into whatever it was Braxton sought.

Abbie sat on her bed, closed her eyes and breathed deeply. The thought of what Braxton might be plotting chilled her to the bone, for she knew he would not leave matters as they stood. He still needed whatever her father had hidden – and he believed they possessed it.

Shaking her head, she pushed the thoughts aside. She needed air, something to clear her mind. Rising, she went downstairs to find Alexander, for, much to her annoyance, she had promised to inform him when she went out.

She opened the study door, but finding the room empty, she turned to look for Thomas – and was startled to find him already behind her.

'Oh, Thomas!' she gasped, placing a hand to her chest. The butler looked alarmed, nearly making her laugh.

'I am deeply sorry, my lady.' Abbie waved her hand, dismissing his apology.

'Don't fret, Thomas. I was just looking for Lord Crawford. Do you know where I might find him?'

'He has gone out, my lady. He said he would return by lunchtime.' The voice came from behind Thomas, and she moved to find John approaching. Abbie eyed him suspiciously.

'Did he mention where he would be going?'

'No, my lady. But he told me to assist you if needed.' Raising a brow, Abbie crossed her arms.

'Did he now?'

John returned the look with a mocking smile. 'Yes, my lady.'

She rolled her eyes, frustrated. *So, he may come and go as he pleases, yet I must obey orders and remain under guard?* She considered telling John she needed no assistance, but as with everyone in the house, he was simply following Alexander's instructions. Instead, she offered a saccharine smile and nodded.

'Thank you, John. I'll let you know if I require anything.'

With a graceful turn on her heel, she gave them both a polite nod before disappearing through the door that led to the kitchens. She would help Jane with whatever she was baking and hope the task would distract her at least until Alexander returned.

The rich aromas wafting from the kitchen greeted Abbie as she pushed open the heavy door. The first thing she heard was Georgina's laughter. Seeing her at the table with Suzie, making everyone laugh, warmed Abbie's heart.

'I *can* eat a whole cake by myself, Jane! You just make one, and I'll show you!' Georgina declared proudly.

Suzie couldn't contain a chuckle and pinched her rosy cheeks. 'Oh, little one, what Jane's afraid of is that you'll eat all her desserts and leave none for the rest of the household!'

Jane laughed. 'That's right, Georgina. You've quite the appetite when it comes to sweets, and I'm afraid your uncle will be none too pleased if I can't provide him with dessert.'

'Well, he certainly doesn't need it, Jane,' Abbie giggled, captivating Georgina's attention.

'Abbie! You're here!' Georgina cried, turning at once. 'Tell them how much I love cakes!'

She ran to Abbie, and she picked her up, kissing her cheek. 'Oh, I think they already know, darling.' She set her gently back down on the floor.

Georgina turned back to Jane, resting her little hands one atop the other and her chin upon them, looking up at Jane with puppy-dog eyes. 'Please?' she begged sweetly.

They all burst into laughter. Jane smiled at her, clearly defeated by her charm. 'Alright, little one. I'll bake you a cake – but only if you're a good girl and do everything Paige tells you. Deal?'

'Deal! I'll go and do it right now!' Georgina squealed, dashing from the kitchen with a skip in her step, leaving everyone grinning behind her.

'I do love that little girl,' Jane said fondly, and kept

knitting the dough she was working on.

'She's a treasure, isn't she?' Abbie agreed.

'How are you?' Jane asked.

'Fine, thank you. What about you? How are you finding your new kitchen?'

Jane smiled. 'I must say, I'm impressed with its advancements. The pulley wheel is marvellous, and they've even built a cavity above the fire just for bread. Very impressive indeed. I'm just missing some of my utensils. Clearly, no-one's done much baking in this kitchen.'

'I don't think anyone's done much of anything in this house as of late. Alexander's family hasn't lived here for quite some time.'

'That explains it.' She paused, looking at Abbie. 'Are you alright?'

Abbie sank onto a bench beside Suzie. 'Yes... I'm just restless. I cannot bear staying indoors for one minute longer. I miss Oxford. I long to go for a ride, but riding through the streets London is nothing compared to galloping across the fields near Redwood House.'

Suzie frowned. 'Lord Crawford would not be pleased if you ventured out on horseback, my lady.'

Abbie rolled her eyes. 'Oh, Suzie. Please don't call me that.'

'But you are a lady now,' Jane teased, shaping the dough and placing it in a wooden bowl. 'Nothing you can do about that now.'

'No, there isn't. But at least in this house, I would like to be just Abbie. Please.' She squeezed Suzie's hand with a pleading smile. The maid returned the gesture with a warm nod.

Jane started rummaging through a cupboard and huffed in frustration. 'There are so many things missing in this kitchen! Look at this pie mould – it hasn't even any engravings. If I bake anything in this, it will be the most boring-looking pie in London.'

Abbie straightened, a spark of eagerness in her tone. This was the perfect excuse for her to leave the house without John questioning her.

'We could go to my house on Berkeley Square and pick up your kitchen utensils.'

'That would be wonderful! I've a few things there that would be very useful to have here. I can be back in just a couple of hours.'

'I'll go with you. I need a few things as well,' Abbie added. She didn't, but no one needed to know that.

Suzie placed a thoughtful hand on her mistress' arm. 'Are you sure?'

She had realised, even before Abbie, that returning to the townhouse might open the door to the memories she had been trying to escape for almost a month.

Abbie covered Suzie's hand with her own and offered a small smile. 'I'll be fine, Suzie. But thank you for asking.' Suzie nodded and stood up.

Jane dusted the flour from her hands. 'Brilliant. I'll leave the dough to rise by the hearth, and we can be off.'

But Suzie looked uncertain, and began, 'Lord Crawford will not be pleased, my–' Abbie lifted an eyebrow in warning, and Suzie quickly corrected herself. '–Mrs Abbie.' She nodded in approval and waved away Suzie's concern as she walked to the door.

'I'm sure my darling husband won't mind. Besides, we'll ask John to escort us.' As she got to the door she turned around impatiently and looked to Jane. 'Well? Are you coming or not?' Jane laughed and followed her out.

Much to Abbie's amusement, the long speech she had prepared to convince John of their outing proved entirely unnecessary. As she opened her mouth to begin, Jane interceded with a smile and simply asked if he would be so kind as to accompany them to Berkeley Square. As if enchanted, John's stern expression softened into something unexpectedly tender. There was no mistaking the cause – Jane had clearly cast her spell. For that expression was one only a man besotted will show. Without hesitation, he left to ready the carriage.

Abbie grabbed Jane's arm and pulled her making her turn and face her.

'What was that?'

Jane lowered her gaze, feigning innocence. 'I don't know what you mean.' But the smile tugging at her lips and the flush on her cheeks betrayed her. It was evident from her reaction that a spark had most certainly been kindled.

'I will drop the matter for now,' Abbie warned playfully, 'but not for long. I'll fetch my reticule and be down in a moment.'

A few minutes later, they were on their way to Berkeley Square. True to her word, Abbie immediately resumed teasing Jane about John – though without much success.

'There is nothing to tell, Abbie,' Jane insisted. 'We simply enjoy each other's company. Don't start imagining things.'

Abbie chuckled. 'Oh, I'm not imagining anything, Jane. I've never seen that look in John's eyes before.'

'What look?'

'As if he'd bring the world to your feet!' They both burst into laughter.

But as Berkeley Square came into view, the jovial conversation fell away into silence. The townhouse stood on the west side of the square, its windows catching what little sunlight broke through the London haze, illuminating the rooms that faced the street. But to Abbie, the light no longer held the same warmth.

They descended the carriage in silence, helped by John and Abbie slowly lifted the latch on the black iron gate to the small front yard. As they reached the steps, the front door opened. Jasper, the caretaker, stood there with a broad smile on his face. He had stayed behind with his wife, Bridget, to care for the house in their absence, as they always had done after her father's business had concluded in the city and the family returned to Oxford.

'Good morning, my lady,' he said, bowing low. Abbie returned his smile.

'Good morning, Jasper. I apologise for having come unannounced,' she said as she arrived at the top step.

'No need, my lady. This is your home. Suzie sent word of your arrival to London.'

'Thank you, Jasper.' She stepped into the entrance hall with a heavy heart. The air felt thick, and the very act of breathing became more difficult as they walked through the house. It wasn't that the house was untidy, for it was as clean and well-kept as ever. But the memories of that horrific night lingered like shadows in every corner. The horror still haunted in these walls.

It was a strange feeling; she had stayed here for a few days after the attack, yet somehow, returning now felt harder. As if all the pain and grief had been lying here in wait, ready to come like a wave, crashing over her heart anew. Her eyes fell on the door to her father's study – it was still closed – and she was grateful for it. She wasn't ready to face that room yet.

She hadn't even realised she was staring at the closed door until Jane touched her arm.

'Abbie?' she asked, looking at her friend with a sympathetic look on her face, covering her hand with hers.

'Don't worry, Jane.' She took a deep, calming breath and Jane gave her arm a gentle squeeze.

'I'll be in the kitchen. It won't take long.'

As Jane disappeared through the kitchen door, Abbie turned toward the staircase. Sensing John was following close behind her, she stopped and turned. 'I don't need you to guard me, John. I do believe I'm quite safe here.' He grinned.

'Oh, my lady, I'm not concerned for your safety. I'm concerned for mine. Lord Crawford will have my head if I fail to follow orders.'

Her brow arched. 'And what orders would those be?'

'That I shall not take my eyes off you, my lady.' An exasperated huff escaped her lips.

That husband of hers was truly trying her patience. Still, knowing John would obey Alexander's command no matter what she said, she rolled her eyes and continued to climb up the spiral staircase.

Suzie had already packed everything they would need before they left for Redwood House, but she still paused in front of her mother's room before entering. The knot in her stomach tightened as she placed a hand on the doorknob.

The soft morning light poured through the window, casting a gentle glow on the rose-coloured walls, making them look brighter. Like so many other times before, the mirror on her dressing table reflected her image, unchanged – and yet everything *had* changed. How many times had she sat here with her mother, watching her prepare for a dinner party or special event? Her heart ached with the memories of those quiet, cherished moments that she had always taken for granted.

She walked slowly to the dressing table and sat in the overstuffed chair, upholstered in a beautiful floral print. Abbie ran her hand over the delicate wood. Her mother's jewellery and perfumes were still where they had been left more than a month ago, and though everything looked the same, the reality was that everything was drastically different. Tears formed in her eyes, and when she saw John's sympathetic face reflected in the mirror, she quickly brushed them away.

Abbie opened the jewellery box, revealing her mother's beautiful treasures. She had never been a woman who wore extravagant ornaments; she preferred discrete and elegant jewels. That was just what her mother had been – discrete and elegant. Abbie took into her hands a fine gold choker with a small ruby finishing the delicate work. A beautiful piece that her father had given to her mother on her last birthday. The love they had for each other was truly unmatched. She opened her reticule and placed the necklace inside, but before closing it, she noticed a small note tucked within. As she took it out, she remembered the circumstances in which she had been given it.

Jeremy Bates
Chancery Lane
Lincoln's Inn

She had completely forgotten about the Bates' son and his involvement with her father. Excited to have a clue to pursue, she almost screamed out loud. But seeing John standing nearby, she reined in her emotions. If he suspected what she was planning, he would never allow her to go anywhere without Alexander.

The sensible part of her told her to return to the house and wait, so they could go together. But as always, her impulsive side prevailed. Now she needed to find a way to distract John, as she knew he would not allow her to visit Chancery Lane without Alexander's approval. After all, her dear husband had instructed him to follow her everywhere, precisely for fear that she might do exactly what she was about to do.

She looked around and her gaze settled on her mother's favourite perfume – *Lily of the Valley*. She opened the almost empty flask and inhaled deeply, closing her eyes. It smelled of her mother. It felt like a sign, as if it was guiding her where to go next. Mr Floris' perfume shop was on Jermyn Street, and from there, she could flag down a coach to take her to the lawyer's chambers. She had been there with her mother many times and remembered the shop had a passage leading to the alley behind, she could use it to escape.

She turned to John. 'I would like to go to Jermyn Street, John.' The look in his eyes betrayed unmistakeable suspicion, so she played the only card she could think of. Lifting the flask, she said, 'This was my mother's perfume. And I would like to buy more. I miss her terribly, and this fragrance reminds me of her.' It was true, she told herself. Even so, she whispered a silent prayer to her mother, asking forgiveness for using her memory to trick the man – especially since she knew John would likely be reprimanded if Alexander discovered the truth.

Don't get caught, then, she thought, offering John a timid smile.

He shook his head, but he finally relented. 'But afterwards, we must go straight home, my lady,' he warned.

'Of course, John. Straight home.'

They met Jane at the bottom of the stairs. She was struggling with more pots and kitchen utensils than she could carry in her small hands, and John immediately rushed to help her.

'Thank you, John,' she said, smiling at him.

'You're welcome. I'll take them to the carriage.'

'We are going to Mr Floris' shop.' Abbie announced.

Jane raised a questioning brow, clearly confused. 'Why?'

Abbie pinched her arm. 'Because I need more of my mother's perfume.' Then, lowering her voice, she whispered in her friend's ear, 'Don't ask. I'll explain later.'

Jane gave her a subtle nod of understanding, and once they were settled in the carriage, she couldn't contain her curiosity any longer. 'Why are we going to Mr Floris' shop?'

'I need to visit a lawyer, and John will not let me alone for a second.'

'And why do you need a lawyer?'

'I don't. I just want to ask him some questions. Please, Jane, I need your help.' She didn't want to mention Jeremy yet – not until she was certain it wasn't dangerous.

'You are going to get into trouble, Abbie.'

'That shouldn't surprise you by now, Jane.'

Jane shook her head, but she smiled. She knew her better than anyone.

'Thank you,' Abbie said, taking her friend's hands.

'Where is it?'

'Gray's Inn.'

'But that's nowhere near Floris' shop, Abbie.'

'It's not too far if I take a coach.'

'And how do we explain being gone for so long?'

'You're not coming. You need to keep John entertained.'

'And how do you suppose I'll do that?' Jane asked with a smirk.

'You just need to talk to him. Distract him, only for a little while. Come on, you two like each other – and don't even bother denying it!' she warned as Jane opened her mouth to protest. But she closed it with a sigh.

'Fine! But you need to hurry. If you take too long, I'll send John to come and find you.'

'I am quite certain John will realise I've gone in ten minutes or less, but that's no matter. I just need enough time to get to Gray's Inn. After that, you can tell him when he asks. Say I told you he could come and pick me up from there. I don't want to get you in trouble, Jane – so tell him the truth.' Abbie gave her a dazzling smile.

Jane frowned. 'How will you get out of the shop without John seeing?' Abbie's smile widened. 'I wandered off once when I was little, during one of my mother's visits. There's a staircase in the back that leads to the basement – and from there, out to the alley. Trust me.' Abbie felt very positive about her plan.

Nestled behind the bustling thoroughfare of Piccadilly, the small shop on Jermyn Street had become quite a favourite amongst London's high society. Even the Queen, it was said, succumbed to the allure of the perfumer's floral concoctions. Abbie couldn't recall how her mother first discovered it, but she remembered well that, ever since her father had purchased the first bottle, no other perfume would do.

As the carriage pulled up in front of the shop, Abbie turned to Jane. 'I just need a small head start. Then if John asks you, you can tell him where I've gone.'

Jane sighed. 'One of these days, you'll get me into real trouble, Abbie.'

She was about to reply when John opened the door and offered his arm to help them down. With a final look at Jane, Abbie walked into the shop, leaving her friend to work her charms on John.

The soft jingle of the bell that hung on the door announced her arrival. The shop had grown from a modest room into a refined boutique, with elegantly carved shelves and delicate bottles housing the most exquisite fragrances – from exotic citrus limes to the sweet vanilla bean. It wrapped every visitor in a sensory embrace.

A clerk was speaking to two elegantly dressed ladies, their attire marking them as women of status. When he spotted her, he gave a discreet signal, and immediately, a dark-haired young woman with beautiful sparkling eyes appeared. Abbie recognised her at once as the perfumer's daughter, who sometimes helped in the store and had often attended her mother.

The girl approached with a gentle smile. 'Good morning, my lady. How may I be of service?'

'Good morning.'

Abbie took the flask from her reticule and showed it to the girl. 'I would like to purchase this perfume, please.'

'Lily of the Valley. An excellent choice, madam.'

'I think so, too.'

'If you'll wait here, I'll fetch it for you.'

'Oh, I was wondering…' Abbie paused, her voice softer, 'would it be possible to see where you make the perfumes? You see, this was my mother's scent, and she always wanted to see the flowers you use to create such a divine smell. She died a few weeks ago.' Abbie looked at the young woman with a knotted brow, and wiped a fake tear from her eye. She felt a pang of guilt for using her mother's memory in vain. *But surely, she would understand that I'm doing this for her*, she convinced herself.

The gesture achieved its intended effect, and, looking at her with sympathy, the girl leaned in and lowered her voice. 'I shouldn't do this, but I understand your pain, my lady. I lost someone dear to me not long ago as well.'

Abbie smiled at her, guilt rising in her chest. 'Thank you…'

'Elisabeth, my name is Elisabeth.'

'Thank you, Elisabeth.'

'Follow me, before my brother sees us.'

Elisabeth led her to the back of the shop, opened a

door and invited her through. A heady wave of aromas enveloped Abbie as she stepped inside. Several chests stood open, filled with bottles of all sizes, ready for the perfumer's delicious creations. On the table stood a set of scales and a thick recipe book. She scanned the room until her eyes found what she sought: the stairs to the basement. Elisabeth's voice reminded her that she was not alone.

'This is where my father makes the perfumes.' She went to one of the chests, retrieved a fresh bottle of Lily of the Valley, and handed it to Abbie, who slipped it into her reticule. 'My father's out just now but he'll return any minute, so we must be quick.'

'Yes, of course.' Abbie gave her two shillings and smiled. Then she gestured to the stairs. 'Oh, do you also have a basement?'

'Yes, ma'am. That's where we store the flowers.'

'And does it have a back door?'

'Yes…' Elisabeth's voice grew cautious. 'My lady, we should go. My father will be here any moment.' Abbie sighed, deciding to trust in the girl's kindness.

'Elisabeth, I need to leave the shop without being seen.'

'But, my lady…'

Abbie touched her arm. 'There is a man at the door whom I wish to avoid.'

'Are you in danger?'

She nearly said yes but she had misled the girl enough. 'Not exactly. The truth is… I'm going to see someone my guardian would never approve of.'

Elisabeth's eyes softened with understanding – as misplaced as it was. Abbie realised the young woman had assumed it was a lover's meeting.

'But what shall I say if they ask for you?'

'A friend is covering for me. I promise no-one will

trouble you.' After a moment's hesitation, Elisabeth nodded, finally giving in to her request.

'Follow me.'

Abbie trailed her down to the basement. The girl listened carefully to check there was nobody around and signalled Abbie to follow her, ensuring they were as quiet as possible.

They moved carefully through the many crates of supplies until they reached the door that led to Ormond Yard. Elisabeth turned the knob and peeked out, turning to her, she gestured with a hand for Abbie to come closer.

'Thank you, Elisabeth. If anyone asks, say I left through the front. Say it with confidence, and no-one will doubt you.' The girl nodded, and with a final hush, gestured for her to slip through the door, closing it behind her.

Abbie wanted to run, but that would attract too much attention, so she kept her pace steady. Once she reached Piccadilly, she tried to hail a carriage but found none available on the busy street.

Someone tugged at her skirt, and she stepped back abruptly, fearing it was a thief. When she turned around, she had to look down – for the one who had grabbed her was a small boy, his face smudged with soot, his clothes half-ragged. He looked up at her, smiling shyly. 'Can I help ye, m'lady?' he said with a little bow.

Abbie studied him for a moment then decided he posed no threat. 'I need a coach.'

'I can get it for ye, miss!' He darted into the road, causing Abbie to gasp as she feared he'd be trampled by one of the oncoming carriages crossing Piccadilly. But to her amazement, he succeeded in stopping one. Though the coachman unleashed a torrent of insults at the boy, once he allowed him to speak, the man looked at her and motioned for her to approach.

'Where are you going, girl?'

'To Gray's Inn, sir,' she replied, stepping closer to the carriage.

'I can take ye.'

Abbie looked inside her reticule and saw she had only just enough to cover the fare for the carriage. She turned to the boy. 'I don't have any money for you now, but do you know where St. James' Place is?' The boy nodded. 'If you walk there from Hyde Park, you'll see a white house on the corner. Go there tomorrow, and I will give you your reward.'

The boy grinned. 'Thank ye, m'lady.'

'What's your name?'

'Nicholas, m'lady.'

'Well, Nicholas, thank you. And don't forget to come tomorrow.'

'No, m'lady.' He gave her a quick bob of his head, doffing his cap, and Abbie turned to the carriage door.

'Jump in, girl! I don't have all day!' the coachman barked.

She gathered her skirt and climbed in as quickly as she could, nearly losing her balance as the driver spurred the horses on before she'd even sat down. Steadying herself, she finally sat with a sigh of relief. The first part of the plan was complete. Now, she hoped Jeremy would be able to answer the many questions that were plaguing her.

The heavy traffic on Shaftesbury Avenue slowed their progress. *It would probably be better to walk back, that is, if John doesn't find me first.* She knew she would face trouble later, but that was something to worry about afterwards.

When they finally arrived at Gray's Inn, she practically threw the money at the coachman in her haste. She passed through a stone arch that led to a small courtyard. One of the walls bore numerous wooden boards inscribed with lawyers' names, but there was no sign of

Jeremy Bates.

Abbie looked around for someone who might assist her. At the arch's entrance leading to the main courtyard stood a sentry box, and within it, a man – either half asleep or half drunk – who sat with his head resting on one hand. He looked at her with little interest.

'Excuse me, sir.' He lifted his gaze, still propping up his chin with his hand. He looked her up and down and didn't bother to reply, merely raising a brow in question. Abbie swallowed her irritation and forced herself to remain polite. 'I am looking for Jeremy Bates. I was told he lodges here – he's a lawyer.'

The man let out a braying laugh. 'A lawyer, you say? Ha! That boy is merely a servant to Sir Romilly!'

'Do you know where I can find Sir Romilly?'

'He's not here.'

'And when will he return?' Abbie was beginning to grow exasperated with the man's smugness.

'How would I know? You'll have to ask Jeremy.'

Abbie rolled her eyes. 'Well, will you at least tell me where I can find Jeremy?'

'Where else? In Sir Romilly's lodgings! Foolish girl,' he muttered, closing his eyes again, clearly finished with the conversation. Her patience already fraying, It was clear he wasn't going to be of any use. Abbie turned and passed through the arch into the central courtyard, scanning the engraved boards until she found the one she was looking for.

Sir Samuel Romilly, Lawyer for the City of London.
Second floor.

She climbed the narrow stairs and knocked softly at the door. When no-one responded, she knocked again – more firmly this time, her patience getting to the end of its tether.

'I'm coming!' called a voice from within the room.

At last, the door opened, and she recognised the kind eyes of Jeremy Bates. His hair was no longer a wild tangle of red curls; instead, it was sleek and neatly tied at the nape.

'Miss Abbie! What a surprise! Please, come in!' he said with a smile.

'Thank you, Jeremy.' The chamber was simple, yet elegant and tidy. There wasn't much furniture displayed in the room, apart from a large mahogany table and a much smaller, more worn desk in the corner – where Abbie presumed Jeremy worked – the room was sparsely furnished. At the back, a half-open door led to what she assumed were Sir Romilly's lodgings. She found herself wondering where Jeremy slept.

'Please, Miss Abbie, have a seat.' Jeremy pulled out a chair by the larger desk for her. 'Can I offer you something to drink?' He sat opposite her.

'No, thank you, Jeremy. And forgive me for arriving unannounced.'

'Oh, miss, do not apologise. I was expecting you.'

'You were?'

'But of course! Your father said you'd come – though he never said when. It's fortunate you've come now, miss, as we haven't been long back from France. Do you know, Sir Romilly asked me to accompany him on his Continental Tour? I couldn't believe it at first, but he did. And oh, Miss Abbie, it was an incredible journey. We went to France, Switzerland–'

Abbie couldn't contain her surprise. 'Wait, Jeremy.' Abbie lifted a hand, interrupting his enthusiastic ramble. Jeremy was a lovely young man, but once he began talking, he seldom stopped. 'What did you say about my father?'

'Why, the will your father asked me to draft. It was the first one I'd ever done. He trusted me with it,' he said, puffing his chest with pride.

He stood, walked to his small desk, opened a drawer and retrieved a leather pouch, which he handed to her. 'He said to give this to you when you came to collect it.' He beamed. 'I don't quite know why he didn't give it to you himself, but he made me swear not to tell anyone. I suppose it's like the old days – you remember? He used to make me hide clues for you to find. Are you sure you don't want anything to drink?' His cheerful tone confused her. 'How is your father anyway?'

'Jeremy… don't you know?' Abbie asked confused. 'Have you heard from your parents?'

'Oh yes, miss. They've sent letters, but I haven't had time to open them yet. Why'd you ask?'

Abbie drew a deep breath. 'My parents were killed four weeks ago, Jeremy.'

His face turned pale – paler than before – and he sank back into his chair. 'What? What happened?'

'I don't know yet. That's what I'm trying to find out. When did you draft this for him?'

'Not long before I left – about six weeks ago, I believe.'

Abbie stood and began to pace, the leather pouch clutched tightly in her hands. She has just begun to undo the seal when a knock at the door startled them both.

'Sir Romilly?' came a voice she recognised instantly. Abbie rolled her eyes and groaned. *What on earth is Alexander doing here?*

Jeremy opened the door and towering almost a head taller, Alexander filled the doorway.

'Good morning, sir. How may I be of service?' Jeremy asked.

His severe gaze swept past Jeremy to find her.

'Don't bother, Jeremy. He's not here for you,' Abbie cut in. 'Let me introduce you to my annoying husband.'

The moment his eyes met hers, Alexander's expression darkened. Brushing past an astonished Jeremy, he stormed into the room.

'What on earth are you doing here, Abbie?'

'I might ask you exactly the same thing, *Alexander*,' she replied coolly, lifting her chin high in defiance.

'I came home to find you had gone. I went to Berkeley Sq and was told you went to Jermyn St. Imagine my surprise when I arrived at the perfumery and learned you weren't there either. John almost had a heart attack.'

'As you can see,' she said, spreading her arms and bowing, 'I am perfectly fine. And if you're here, it is because Jane told you where I was.'

'Do you not understand the danger you're in, Abbie?'

'I found something – and needed to follow where it led.'

'And why you didn't tell me?'

'Oh? Like you told me you mean? You left the house this morning without a word. Am I just supposed to sit at home waiting, while you disappear on your own secret missions?'

'Yes!'

'Well then, my lord, you married the wrong woman if you think I'm going to sit around idly, while someone gets away with murdering my parents!'

'I didn't marry you by–'

'–choice?' she interrupted. 'That's what you were going to say, wasn't it? Well, neither did I!' She turned to storm out, but paused when she saw Jeremy staring at them both in disbelief.

'My apologies for the scene, Jeremy.'

It was only then that she noticed the young man's eyes had welled with tears. 'Mr and Mrs Clarkson are... dead?'

he asked quietly.

Abbie placed a hand on his shoulder and gently guided him to sit. 'Yes, Jeremy.' He sank into the chair, wiping his reddened eyes.

'Oh, he was so very kind to me. Do you know, Miss Abbie, it was your father who found me this job? I told him I wanted to be a lawyer, and instead of laughing at me, he said, 'Boy, you can be whatever you want to be.' Two weeks later, he told my parents that he'd found me an apprenticeship here in London. He was a good man. Can you tell me what happened, Miss Abbie?'

She looked at Alexander before turning back to face Jeremy.

'We don't know yet. That's what we are trying to find out. In the meantime, for your own safety, it's best you don't mention our visit.'

'My master and I are going to Wiltshire this afternoon.'

'Good. Go with him – and say nothing to anyone.'

'I won't, Miss Abbie.'

'Take care, Jeremy.'

Alexander waited for her to leave the room, then followed her down the stairs. As they passed the sentry, Alexander stopped and addressed the man, who now looked at him with a lot more respect than he'd bothered to show her.

Alexander reached into his pouch, drew out several coins, and held them up. 'We were never here,' he said, his voice cold. The man's eyes widened at the sight of the generous sum. But before he took it, Alexander demanded, 'Do you understand?' The man nodded eagerly.

'Yes, my lord. I never saw you.'

They stepped into the carriage. Alexander's furious gaze bore into her. He ran a hand through his hair and shook his head.

'Why didn't you tell me you had found something?'

'I didn't know until I got to my parent's house.'

'Come on, Abbie. Do you expect me to believe that?'

'I'm telling the truth!'

'And you just decided to come here without me?'

'I didn't *decide* to come without you – it just happened! Besides, you left the house this morning without telling me. Did you consider telling *me* where you were going?'

'That's different.'

'No, it isn't.' Tired of the argument, she turned her attention to the leather pouch resting in her lap.

'What is that?'

'I haven't looked at it yet. Jeremy said it's a will.'

He knocked twice on the carriage roof, signaling the driver, and they began their journey home.

Abbie untied the knot, unfolded the documents, and confirmed it was indeed her father's will. She inspected it all carefully. The properties and money were left to her – but most importantly, the document named her aunt, and only her aunt, as her legal guardian in the event of both her parents' deaths.

She noticed Alexander watching her impatiently. She handed him the will and as she did, a letter slipped from between the pages. She picked it up and saw her name written in her father's elegant hand. Her heart pounded as she broke the seal.

My dearest Abigail,

If you are reading this, it means that I am gone. Please live, my dear girl and bring peace to the spirit of your honoured father. This will be the first chapter of your new journey. I hope you find what you are looking for.

Love, Papa.

She turned the page to see if there was anything written on the back. Nothing. Just this? Were those the last words her father had to say to her?

She looked at Alexander, who was still studying the will. Without glancing at her, he said, 'Your uncle couldn't have forced you to wed after all.'

Abbie raised an eyebrow. 'What is that supposed to mean? Are you now regretting forcing me into the marriage I didn't want in the first place?'

'Good god, woman! I never said that – and I didn't force you to do anything. As I see it, you're better off with me than with Braxton.'

She turned her head towards the window. By the time they arrived home, it was late, and the sun was beginning to set. She opened the door and hurried out of the carriage. John was waiting for them nervously by the entrance.

Alexander's voice echoed from behind her. 'Next time, check the back door. She can be clever when it comes to escaping places,'

Abbie smiled meekly at John and paused in front of him. 'I'm sorry, John. I didn't mean to get you in any trouble.' He didn't speak but gave a curt nod, accepting her apology.

She entered the house, followed closely by a furious Alexander, who managed to catch her just as she reached the stairs, grabbing her arm.

'Can you just stop running from me? We need to talk!' He pulled her into his study. She wrenched herself free and moved away from him.

'What do you want?'

Ignoring her exasperation, he asked, 'What does the letter say?'

'Nothing. Absolutely nothing.'

Tears welled in her eyes as she handed him the letter.

'Three lines. That's all he had to say to me. No reason why he was killed. No explanation for any of this. Nothing!' She tossed the letter at him, and he caught it before it hit the ground. 'Nothing,' she whispered, her voice hollow.

Alexander read the short letter and looked at her. He handed it back and began pacing the room.

'I want you to stop putting yourself in harm's way, Abbie.'

'I didn't do that. I just went to see Jeremy. That can hardly be considered dangerous, Alexander.'

'You should not have gone alone.'

'I wouldn't have gone alone if *you* had been with me! I wouldn't have gone alone if you hadn't left without saying where you were going this morning! But no, of course not. *You* may do as you please – and I must stay still until you decide otherwise.' She threw up her hands, exasperated. 'I haven't left this house in a week! I don't know anything – and you want to stop me from finding out why on earth my parents are dead? *Why* they had to die? And most importantly – *who did it?*' She was trembling, the anger inside her so intense she feared she might shatter into pieces.

'You act like you must do everything on your own, without taking into consideration they were *my* parents! I deserve to know what happened to them! I lost *everything* that night – don´t you understand? Everything!'

'If I understand? *Of course* I understand! I lost my best friend. And now I'm raising his orphaned child, knowing full well I can never take his place. Don't tell me I don't care!'

He stepped closer. Their bodies were so close, she could feel the heat radiating from his skin. 'I care more than you could possibly imagine, Abbie. We are in this together.'

His voice was deep, low, and it sent a shiver down her spine. She could so easily lose herself in those blue eyes. She shook her head, trying to clear the confusion he always stirred in her.

'Then why don't I *feel* like we are?' The words landed with weight, heavy on her shoulders.

He reached out and gently caressed her cheek. 'Then we need to change that.'

With that cryptic reply, he turned and left the room, leaving her again with many more questions than answers.

How can he be so infuriating… and so utterly charming at the same time?

She looked down again at the brief letter her father had left her, upset and confused at such a short note with no apparent meaning. The air in the room had grown cold, and a chill brushed over her skin. Her gaze drifted to the liquor cabinet in Alexander's study and she decided to pour herself a glass of brandy. She'd never tried it before, but her father always claimed it helped warm him up.

She swirled the glass, watching the amber liquid slide around the sides. At the first sip, she nearly coughed as it burned its way down her throat – but it did what it was meant to do. She sat in front of the fireplace and let the brandy soothe her frayed nerves.

Sometime later, Alexander returned to the study. 'What are you doing?'

'Drinking,' she said flatly, stating the obvious as she lifted her glass. She pushed herself up to her feet using the arm of the chair and almost lost her balance.

'How many have you had?'

'Two?' She waved her hand vaguely.

'That's enough for you.' He took the glass from her hand.

'Why?'

'Why is it enough?'

'No,' she said, raising her voice and stepping closer. 'Why are they gone? They've gone forever and left me here. Why did he have to get involved in something so dangerous? They left me alone! *With you!*' She pointed at him, her body swaying back and forth like a pendulum.

His expression shifted. 'With me?'

'Yes, with you.' Abbie jabbed a finger at his chest. 'Look at you – all handsome – and I can't stop thinking…' she covered her mouth with her hand.

'Thinking what, Abbie?' She shook her head. 'I'd better go to bed.'

She turned too quickly and stumbled, nearly falling – until Alexander's strong arm caught her around the waist. Before she could protest, he swept her up into his arms.

Abbie looked directly into his eyes, and without thinking, she reached up to stroke his cheek. 'Lord Crawford… you are very handsome.'

'And you, Lady Crawford, are very drunk.'

'Yes, I am,' she murmured, resting her head on his shoulder as he carried her to her room.

CHAPTER 16

'Mrs Abbie?' Suzie's voice had always brought joy to Abbie. There was something in her soft, melodic tone that could always calm her – but not this time. This time, it felt as if someone was beating a drum, mere inches from her ear, provoking an excruciating pain that made her reach blindly for the pillow beside her. She covered her head, attempting to block out the increasing throb in her skull.

She let out a growl that, had she not known it came from her own throat, she might have believed it belonged to a wild animal. Mortified that Suzie had heard her, she pressed the pillow harder against her ears.

'Mrs Abbie?' Suzie stood by the bed, touching her shoulder with care. Cautiously, Abbie peeked from beneath her fluffy shield.

'What time is it?' she moaned, retreating once more beneath the pillow to block out the bright sunlight invading the room.

'It is ten in the morning, my lady. Lord Crawford requested that we bring you tea and something to break your fast. He also said you were not feeling well last night. Is that right, my lady?'

Last night.

'Oh, no.' Abbie exclaimed, burying her head under the pillow again. *No, no, no.* She felt the heat rising to her cheeks as she remembered the inappropriateness of her behaviour the night before. Her behaviour, her boldness, touching his cheek and... did she tell him he was handsome?

'Oh, Lord.' She whispered remembering her actions.

Why on earth had she thought she could handle the drink? She'd never had more than a single glass in her life.

'Are you all right, Mrs Abbie? Are you still feeling unwell? I can come back later if you prefer.'

Abbie removed the pillow from her head and looked up at Suzie's concerned face. 'No, I'm not unwell.' Lowering her voice, she said. 'Just... embarrassed.'

'Are you sure? You look a bit pale.'

'I have a headache, that's all.'

Suzie had brought a tray with tea and sandwiches and left it on the side table. When Abbie sat up and rested her back against the pillows, Suzie handed her a cup.

'Here. This will make you feel better.'

Abbie drank the comforting tea and tried to banish the image of Alexander carrying her up the stairs, her body pressed against his.

'I'll bring you a basin of water to refresh yourself. Hopefully, that will help as well.'

'Thank you, Suzie.'

Once alone, she shook her head and settled back down into bed. She set the cup back on the tray and let her thoughts drift to the cryptic message that her father had left.

'If you are reading this, it means that I am gone. Please live, my dear girl and bring peace to the spirit of your honoured father. This will be the first chapter of your new journey. I hope you find what you are looking for.'

She had read it so many times that she had it memorised by heart. Was that really the only thing he had to say to his only daughter? A few meaningless lines? She felt a fresh stab of pain in her chest, mingling with anger for his lack of words.

Suddenly, something stirred in her memory. Familiar words. Repeating the phrase out loud, she said to herself.

'Bring peace to the spirit of your father.' She sat up straighter in bed. 'I hope you find what you are looking for.' Her eyes widened.

She threw back the covers and jumped from her bed with excitement, her heart racing. As she burst out of the room, she nearly collided with a confused Suzie, who was about to enter her room with the basin of water. She didn't stop.

She flung open the door to Alexander's study without knocking. He sat behind his desk, looking up with an expression of amused curiosity.

He cleared his throat. 'Are you fully recovered, my dear?' Ignoring his teasing, she asked bluntly,

'Where's the letter?' She scanned the room and spotted it beside the chair where she'd sat the previous night.

'I knew it!' she exclaimed, nearly bumping into Alexander as she turned to face him.

'Knew *what*, exactly?' She stepped back from his solid form and held up the letter.

'Bring peace to the spirit of your honoured father,' she quoted, pointing to the words. 'Chapter One: A journey. Peace to the spirits of my honoured parents.'

Alexander looked at her, puzzled. 'Am I supposed to know what that means?'

He raised an eyebrow, expecting a clarification.

She groaned, exasperated. 'Those are the first lines of *Cecilia*!' His expression remained blank. It was clear he was still as confused as before receiving the information. 'Fanny Burney?' she prompted. Still nothing. Abbie's mind raced out of control as she began to pace the room, her thoughts spilling out aloud. 'How did I not see this sooner?'

She stopped and faced him. 'I have always loved the work of Fanny Burney. *Cecilia* is one of my favourites. My father is sending me a message – he's telling me where to look.'

'And where is that?'

'Back in Redwood House. I have a copy of *Cecilia* in my father's library. I think he left something for me something inside the book. Don't you see? We have to go back to Redwood House!'

The use of *we* startled her – and him. When had she begun to think of them as a unit? And yet, she noticed a subtle shift in his expression, something she couldn't quite name.

'How are you so sure you'll find something in that book?' He wasn't dismissing her, but Abbie could sense the doubt in his voice.

Abbie sighed, brushing hair from her face with her fingers. 'I'm not, Alexander. But what else do you propose? We have no leads to follow. We've searched everywhere and found nothing that connects Braxton to my parents' deaths – or Stephen's. So, unless you have a better idea, please say so. I'd be delighted to hear it.'

They stared at one another until Abbie broke the silence again. 'I am certain my father would never have written such a simple farewell. Never. There must be a reason why he chose those words. And I think the answer is inside that book.' She held his gaze, barely breathing.

To her surprise he looked down at the goodbye letter in his hand, then nodded. 'I'll ask John to prepare the carriage.'

It took her a moment to process his response, but when she did, she hurried to add, 'The carriage will delay us. If we ride, we can be there by nightfall.'

'Very well. But may I suggest you change?' He smiled, devouring her with his gaze, taking her from her bare feet to her long, loose hair cascading over her shoulders.

Suddenly aware of her attire, Abbie crossed her arms over her chest and took a step back, retreating from the heat in his deep stare.

Turning on her heel, she made for the door, clutching her chemise so she wouldn't trip – when a sudden thought stopped her cold. She didn't remember undressing the night before. A rush of heat surged through her – from embarrassment to suspicion. She turned around, to look at Alexander with fire in her eyes.

She snapped, 'Who undressed me last night?'

'I did,' Alexander replied calmly, meeting her gaze without a hint of remorse. Before she could launch into an outraged tirade, he changed the subject. 'We need to hurry if we want to arrive before nightfall.'

Abbie had no doubt that the heat in her face was now visible – since she felt her cheeks burning. *He had undressed her.* But his attitude made it clear that he showed no inclination to apologise. As she had just won a battle – she wasn't about to risk him changing his mind. She chose to save her indignation and desire to argue with him for another time.

'I won't be long.' She hurried out, trying to steady the flustered storm inside her.

As she made her way up, Mrs May, Jane's mother, was going upstairs and turned to face her.

'Oh, my dear, I was just coming to see you. There's a boy who says he helped you with a carriage yesterday and that you promised to pay him. His name is Nicholas. Is that true?'

'Oh, yes! Please give him something to eat and tell him to wait. I'll be right down.'

'The poor thing is quite thin. Something to eat

wouldn't hurt. And perhaps a bath too!' she said as she headed for the kitchens.

In her room, Suzie helped her to change into a riding dress. Abbie had learned, in recent weeks, just how dangerous her situation truly was. Without hesitation, she opened the trunk where she'd hidden her father's pistol and a knife. She tucked the heavy firearm safely into her bag and slid the blade into the hidden pocket sewn between the folds of her skirt.

Knowing the ride would be long and arduous, she pulled on a pair of breeches beneath her skirts. Suzie watched, wide-eyed. 'Stop looking at me like that. It's going to be a long ride, Suzie.' The maid shook her head but, in the end, she smiled – hardly surprised anymore by her mistress' choice of clothing.

Abbie went down to the kitchen, where she found a hungry Nicholas, who was eating a stew that Mrs May had prepared for him. She smiled, watching the poor boy devour every last spoonful.

'Do you like the stew, Nicholas?'

Seeing her, the boy jumped to his feet and smiled. 'Yes, milady. It's delicious.'

'I'm glad. Now, I owe you some coins for your kind assistance yesterday.' Abbie took some coins from her purse and gave them to the boy, whose eyes widened in surprise.

'But milady, this is too much.'

'Well, I thought you might be able to help around the house with some chores. Would you be interested?'

'Yes, milady! Of course! Thank you very much.' Abbie smiled at him sweetly. 'Where do you live?' The boy lowered his head. 'Here and there, milady.'

With that simple answer, Abbie understood that the boy had nowhere to stay. 'Where are your parents?'

'I don't have any.'

Abbie looked at Mrs May, who was looking at him with pity. She had taken Jane in as a child herself.

'Would you like to stay here? I'm sure Mrs May can find you a room.'

The boy's face lit up. His eyes glistened with emotion. 'Yes, I would like to, milady.'

'Well, that settles it. I must go now, but I'm leaving you in good hands.' She said, looking at the cook.

'Yes, little one. You'll see how well you'll be here. The first thing will be to bath you!'

Abbie laughed at the look of displeasure and left the kitchens for the stables, hoping to find what they were looking for at Redwood House.

***

Alexander followed Abbie's hurried exit with his gaze. After carrying her to bed the night before, sleeping had proven elusive. All he could think about was the feel of her soft, sleeping body pressed against his as he carried her up the stairs. Undressing her had tested his self-control more than anything ever had. This woman was pushing him to limits no other had ever reached.

Her behaviour had him confused. She seemed constantly braced for a quarrel, yet any time he drew closer, the barrier she insisted on erecting between them would crumble before his eyes. He couldn't help but wonder if he would ever succeed in tearing it down completely.

He called for John to ready the horses, and the man returned a few minutes later.

'My lord, everything is ready for our departure.'

'John, I need you to stay here.' Alexander saw the displeasure flicker across the man's face, but as always, he obeyed without question. 'I do not trust anyone else to guard Georgina and Aunt Agatha. We will return the day after tomorrow. I will rest easier knowing you are here to protect them.' With a firm squeeze to his shoulder, Alexander conveyed his gratitude.

'With my life, my lord,' the man replied with solemn pride.

'Thank you, John.'

Alexander placed his pistols in a satchel, along with some supplies Jane had prepared for the journey, before making his way down to the stables. Abbie arrived shortly after, dressed in a dark green riding dress, her hair neatly tied in a bun at the nape of her neck. She stepped into the stables with a bag in hand.

Her head tilted as she caught sight of Hettie in her stall and she turned to look at him. 'Do you think I will ride side-saddle for fifty miles?'

'I wouldn't dream of it, Abbie,' he said with a twitch of amusement. 'Marcus has gone to fetch another saddle for you. But I will ask you to ride side-saddle until we are out of London. I do not wish to attract attention before we leave the city.' She rolled her eyes but didn't say a word. He knew well enough she didn't care what people thought of her – but they both understood that drawing attention now would only alert those who might already be watching.

A few minutes later, they were riding through Hyde Park on their way out of the city. Once free of the city's prying eyes, Abbie swung her leg over and rode astride, and together they quickened their pace, eager to reach Redwood House before sundown.

They exchanged no words until they stopped along the way to rest the horses. They found a small river near a clearing just outside the town of Beaconsfield, and Alexander retrieved bread and some cheese from his saddlebag, offering some to Abbie before guiding the horses to the river to tame their thirst.

He leaned back against a tree, watching her. 'What do you think you'll find in that book?'

'If I'm honest, I don't even know if there will be anything inside. But if there is, I sure hope that it will be something that will help us answer at least some of the questions we have. One thing I do know – my father went to incredible lengths to ensure no-one found that information but me.' Alexander nodded silently and chewed his bread. He carried the same doubts and hopes that she did.

Once the horses had rested, they packed the leftover food and continued the journey. It was almost five in the afternoon, and the sun had begun its descent. Though they had a few hours of daylight left, they would need to rely on the moon to light their path before the evening was through.

With ten miles to go, they passed into the dense shade of Chiltern Forest. The leafy canopy allowed little light, slowing their progress. Alexander glanced at Abbie. She rode tall and proud, like an Amazon stepped from the pages of a Greek myth. The exertion had left a flush on her cheeks, and her hair had loosened from its bun, allowing several blonde strands to fall around her face. She looked even more beautiful than before – if such a thing was possible. The urge to reach out, to loosen the rest of her hair and feel its softness between his fingers, was almost overwhelming.

'What happened the day Stephen died? I realised I'd never asked you.'

Her voice broke the spell. It took him a moment to return to himself. Abbie turned to look at him, raising an eyebrow in expectation. He cleared his throat.

'Stephen's steward came to bring me the news of his death. At first, I refused to believe it were true. He was an excellent rider – the odds of him falling from his horse were slim, to say the least.'

'You didn't believe it was an accident.'

'No. I asked the authorities to investigate, but they claimed there was insufficient evidence to suggest it was anything but a tragic fall.'

'So, they didn't investigate at all?'

'No. I still remember the constable's face as he dismissed me – he didn't even have the decency to meet my eye.'

'Did you check the saddle?' Abbie asked.

'Yes. Nothing appeared out of the ordinary. They said he simply fell, hit his head on a rock. A man found him and brought him back to Everleigh Manor
, but it was too late.'

'And his horse?'

'Next to him.'

'Really?'

Her raised tone caught his attention. 'Yes. Why?'

'Well, as you said, an experienced rider wouldn't fall unless he was riding at high speed and the horse had spooked for some reason. And if that had happened, the horse would've already been halfway to the house by the time he was found. He wouldn't still be standing there next to his body. I remember I fell once, while training Hettie. Luckily, I had no major injuries, just a few bruises. But Hettie galloped so fast I couldn't catch her. I had to walk nearly a mile before I found her grazing peacefully in a field near the house.'

'That's–'

A sharp snap of a branch cut him off. He raised a hand, signalling for Abbie to halt. They scanned the trees, seeking the source of the sound. It could have been a wild animal – but the tension in Alexander's gut was too familiar to ignore after many years of experience in the field.

His fears were confirmed when another branch cracked behind the dense tree line surrounding them and a guttural scream broke the silence. Two men, one on either side, burst out from the darkness of the trees, pointing at them with matching pistols.

Alexander couldn't distinguish their features – since both wore scarves covering their faces. The man in front of Abbie was short and round-bellied, dressed in a dirty shirt full of holes from wear. His greasy black hair fell to his shoulders, and his eyes were fixed greedily on Abbie. His pistol aimed squarely at her head.

The man facing Alexander was taller and stockier, his clothes did not appear as worn as his partner's, a hat obscuring his hair. Only his dark eyes were visible above the bandana that was pulled tightly over the bottom half of his face.

Alexander reached for his pistol, but the short man jerked his head towards Abbie, and barked, 'Tsk-tsk-tsk, not a good idea. Try it again, and I'll shoot her first. Toss it – now!' He pointed with his head to the floor. Alexander assessed the situation. He had no choice. Slowly, he threw the pistol to the ground.

'Dismount.' The man barked again, louder this time. 'Both of ye. Off – now!' Alexander looked at Abbie, and they both obeyed the man's command. She dismounted cautiously, never taking her eyes off the man pointing a gun at her.

'Step forward.' They did as they asked.

'What do you want?' Alexander asked.

'Shut up!' the tall man snapped, striking him across the side of his head. Alexander stumbled but regained his balance. Abbie screamed, stepping towards him.

'No!' But the shorter man raised his pistol again, stopping her mid-step. She froze, the barrel mere inches from her face.

Alexander shook his head, wiping blood from his cheek. Seeing the blood smear on his hand, fury surged in his veins. He wanted to break the man's neck with his bare hands.

'Speak again, and I'll put a bullet between your eyes,' the taller man growled. He nodded towards the horses, and his partner began ransacking their saddlebags.

'Nothin' here,' he muttered.

The tall one tossed a sack at their feet. 'Empty yer pockets.' Alexander complied slowly, emptying the pockets of his coat item-by-item, dragging out his movements, buying time to think about what to do next.

The other man approached Abbie, attempting to search her. She slapped his hand away and stepped back.

'Dare to touch me again, and I'll make you regret the day you were born!' she snarled.

The man pointed his pistol at Abbie again, angered by her reaction. 'Empty yer pockets, wench!' he barked.

'I have no pockets, you fool!' Abbie spat back.

They had to end this, and soon, or they would never leave the forest alive. Alexander turned to his attacker and said,

'You have the money. Now go.' The tall man's eyes wrinkled. 'What do you want?' Alexander asked again.

'From you? Nothin'.' Just as he was lifting his pistol to shoot him, they both heard a sharp scream at their backs. 'What in the devil–?' the bandit exclaimed.

Abbie had stabbed the short man and was now grappling with him, trying to take his gun. Alexander acted quickly to take advantage of the distraction. He batted the tall man's pistol aside and punched him hard. The man staggered. Alexander snatched his fallen weapon and fired – striking him square in the chest. The man's body fell with a dry thud, lifeless at his feet, sprawled across the muddy road.

He spun around. Abbie was still wrestling with the small man for the gun. Alexander charged forward, but before he reached her, the gun discharged and the echo sounded through the forest. He ran towards Abbie, grabbed the attacker by his filthy shirt and punched him with all his strength. The man dropped backwards, unconscious.

Abbie stood panting, looking at the knife in her hand. Blood dripped down from the blade, tinting her hand. 'Are you hurt?' Alexander asked, still catching his breath. She turned her head toward the man lying on the floor. When she still didn't respond, fear that she could be hurt struck Alexander so hard, his heart nearly stopped. He began to inspect her, searching for any sign of injury, until finally, she raised her gaze to meet his.

'The blood is not mine.' Still unconvinced, he asked,

'Are you sure?' She must have heard something in his voice, for she reached out, touched his face, and made him look at her.

'Alexander, I am not hurt,' she repeated in a whisper. They stood there, eyes locked, until their breath began to steady. He placed a hand on her waist and pulled her close, resting his forehead against hers.

A groan coming from the ground snapped their attention to the man lying unconscious. Alexander crouched beside him and shook his shoulder to wake him up.

'Hey, open your eyes.' The man stirred, blinking twice as he fought to remain conscious.

'Who do you work for? Who sent you?' The man coughed, spitting blood from his mouth. He shook his head and looked at Alexander.

'He'll kill me.' Alexander glanced at Abbie. It was clear this was no ordinary highway assault. Someone had sent these men – most likely to kill them.

'You'll die if we don't get you help soon,' he said. 'So, with that in mind, I'll ask you again. Who hired you?' But before the man could answer, his eyes rolled back, and he fell still. 'Damn,' Alexander muttered, beginning to search his pockets.

'This was intentional?' Abbie asked.

'I'm afraid it was.'

'Do you think they knew about my father's letter?'

'Probably.'

'But how? We haven't told anyone about it.'

'I don't know.'

'Have you found anything?' She asked as he finished searching the man.

'No,' he said, gesturing to the other ruffian. He moved to the man's body, knelt, and began searching his coat.

Alexander rifled through the man's pockets and found a leather pouch. It clinked when it landed in his hand. He opened it, letting its contents drop into his palm.

'Ten pounds.'

'That's quite a substantial amount for a man of his means.'

'Agreed.'

Something else was inside the pouch, and he pulled out a small object, passing it to Abbie.

'This is me!' she exclaimed. 'My father had this miniature portrait done a few years ago. He kept it in his office at the London house. How did they get this?'

'I don't know,' Alexander said, his voice tight with frustration. There was nothing else among their possession to suggest who had hired them.

'How did you know someone hired them?' Abbie asked.

'When I asked them what they wanted, one of them said, 'From you, nothing.' They came for you. And that portrait proves it.' He gathered the pistols and slung both into his saddlebag.

'Let's go. I'll send a message to the constable in the morning. We're only a few miles from Everleigh Manor. It's best we sleep there tonight and finish the journey tomorrow.' Between the long ride and the assault, Alexander could see the fatigue etched in Abbie's face and felt relief that, for once, she refrained from arguing with him.

It took them less than thirty minutes to reach the stables of Everleigh Manor. As they arrived, a sleepy Luke appeared from the back rooms where he slept.

'My lady, we didn't know you were coming. My lord.' He added, bowing to them both. Alexander dismounted and helped Abbie down from her saddle. 'We were on our way to Redwood House when we were assaulted,' he said. Luke's eyes widened in alarm.

'Are you well?' He addressed Abbie, not Alexander – something that made Alexander smile, knowing how easily she had won the hearts of everyone at the house.

'Yes, we're fine. Would you mind tending to the horses, Luke? I am sure my wife would love a hot bath. Where is Mrs Watson?'

'She went to see her sister, sir. She left but an hour ago. She said she'll return in the morning. But I can boil the water and take it up, sir.' Alexander handed Luke the reins, but before he could respond, Abbie spoke.

'Don't worry, Luke. I think we can manage. Take care of the horses and go back to sleep.' The young boy looked to Alexander for confirmation.

'You heard my wife. We'll be fine. Thank you, Luke.'

They went into the house, and Alexander turned to her. 'Are you sure you're not hurt?' Abbie met his gaze.

'I'm not hurt, Alexander, just covered in dirt.' He straightened, letting out a breath.

'Good.' His tone was sharper than he intended, edged with something beyond control. Abbie threw him a puzzled look.

'What is wrong with you?' He strode into the study, and she followed him close behind. 'Alexander! I'm talking to you!' He stopped abruptly and turned, retracing his steps until she was right in front of him.

'This time was too close! I should have hired guards to accompany us. I never should have agreed to travel in such haste.'

Abbie, frustrated, moved even closer. 'You think they wouldn't have attacked us with guards? And why are you angry with me? This isn't my fault!'

'I know it isn't!' His voice rose again.

'Then why are you shouting at me?'

'Because you could have been hurt, Abbie!'

He heard it then – in his own voice – the pain and fear for what could have happened. His heart pounded like a drum, reverberating inside his chest. Something changed in her expression, her voice softened. 'But I wasn't,' she whispered, laying a hand on his arm.

He gasped. Her hand came away stained with blood. He followed her gaze to his arm and saw a drip of blood on his coat, now tainting her hand. She stared at it, then met his eyes.

'But *you* are!'

'It's nothing, Abbie.'

'Why didn't you say anything?'

'I'm telling you Abbie – it's nothing.' Without waiting for permission, she seized his other arm and pulled him towards the kitchen.

'What are you doing?'

'I'm going to have a look at your arm.' Alexander allowed himself to be led, a smile forming on his lips.

In the kitchen, she went to the hearth and revived the

amber ashes, bringing the flames back to life as they enveloped the logs, she added one by one. A pot of water already sat warming above the fire. She ladled some into a basin and soaked some clean cloths.

Alexander couldn't stop watching her. The sure way and the efficiency with which she moved, taking charge of the situation.

She turned to him and stepped closer, beginning to remove his coat and he let her. His waistcoat followed. Then, each layer of clothing, got her hands closer to his skin. He followed with detail the movements of her hands as she undressed him, enjoying the closeness of her body. She smelled of flowers – soft, familiar. It was though, in this short time, the floral scent that was so characteristic of her, had become home. She was home.

But when her hands brushed the last barrier of clothing he had, and he felt them touch his torso, the sensation was more than he could bear. If he didn't stop her now, he sure wouldn't be able to control himself.

'Stop,' he said, his voice rough. She looked at him, lifting one of her perfect eyebrows.

'I need to see your arm. Do not start being shy now, Alexander.'

He growled.

'What is that supposed to mean?' She placed her hands on her hips.

'Just let me do it.' He grabbed the collar of his shirt and pulled it up just as Abbie turned back toward the fire.

***

Abbie shook her head. She was surprised by the disappointment she felt when he stopped her from removing the last piece of clothing. She wanted nothing more than to see what was underneath, but his refusal to let her continue made her realise that she might have gone a little too far, crossing an intimacy line he did not wish to breach. She turned her attention to the task of fishing the cloths from the hot water and placed them on a tray to let them cool, before attending to her patient.

Once they were ready, she turned – and the shock of his exposed chest made her catch her breath. Recovering from the impression of seeing him half naked, she rested the tray beside him and focused her efforts on his wounded arm. Thankfully, it was only a scratch, and soon the wound was clean. She put a bandage around his arm, tightening the fabric as gently as she could.

Satisfied with the result, she turned to wash her hands. But feeling the exasperation rising within her, she couldn't help but blurt out her thoughts. 'Why on earth didn't you tell me you were hurt?'

'Because it didn't hurt at the time. Not much, anyway. Besides, as you can see, it was nothing.' His charming smile was capable of disarming even the most stubborn maiden, and she was no exception.

Still, refusing to concede, she accused him: 'But it could have been.'

'Is that concern I hear?'

Abbie turned away and concentrated on washing her hands, not wanting him to see her expression, that must be showing the tangle of feelings now rising inside her. Staring into the water, she said, practically in a whisper.

'You could have been killed.' She turned to face him, anger in her eyes. 'You shouldn't have risked your life for me!'

As if to emphasise her words, she raised a hand, aiming for his uninjured shoulder. He caught her wrist before she could strike, and rising from the table where he had been leaning, drew her closer.

In a low voice that awakened all her senses, he said,

'And I would risk my life a thousand times more – for you.'

It wasn't only his words, but the deep stare into her soul that made her shiver. In that moment, she could no longer restrain herself. Abbie slid her hand behind his neck, threading her fingers through his black locks and drawing his head down to meet her lips. And as if ignited by her fire, the passion they had long contained was released.

They let go of all the anger, fear, and tension that had grown between them for weeks. In that moment, no-one else in the world mattered – only them.

His arms wrapped around her waist, pressing her against the hard plane of his chest. Feeling the hardness of his muscles against her breasts, combined with the sensuality of his kiss, sent an unfamiliar current rising from the centre of her being, spreading like lightning through all her limbs. With a swift movement, he changed their position, lifting her to sit on the kitchen table and parting her legs to draw her closer to him. As he pressed against her, Alexander let out a guttural sound, quickening her breathing. His left hand held her firmly to him, while his right rested at her neck, guiding her into the depths of his mouth.

Their breath came faster, feeling the anticipation and increasing desire. Slowly, his hand drifted down her neck until he reached the top of her breasts. When he caressed her nipple through the fabric, Abbie held her breath as she felt the touch of his eager hands awaken the most delicious sensations in her. Alexander intensified his kiss, sensing what she needed even more clearly than she did. The brush of his tongue against her own increased the pleasure beyond anything she had ever imagined existed.

The burning she felt between her legs became increasingly fierce and consuming. Alexander was leading her to the edge of a precipice she had never before approached, and though she did not know what lay beyond it, she longed to get to wherever he was leading her.

He lowered his mouth to her ear and gently captured her lobe between his teeth. She moaned, wrapping her legs around his waist, needing him impossibly close.

As if he sensed the desperation growing inside her, his hand slipped between them and lifted her skirt, sliding upward along her thigh. In that instant, Abbie wished with all her might that she didn't choose to wear the stupid breeches– for more than anything, she needed to feel his hands against her skin, more desperately than she wanted to admit.

Alexander paused and looked at her, amused. Without a word, he held her gaze, caressing her thigh as Abbie's breathing grew and his hand got closer to the centre of her passion. When he finally reached it, a gasp of pure pleasure escaped her lips. She saw the fire ignite in his eyes with an uncontrollable flame as he claimed her mouth once more.

His kiss synchronised perfectly with the rhythm of his hand. Increasing the pace of his caresses as her breathing became more agitated.

The ecstasy that followed overtook her completely. She cried out, and Alexander drowned out her moans by covering her mouth with his own, until something, exploded inside her shattering her from within. Abbie clung to his neck, feeling the world disappear beneath her.

Slowly, her breathing calmed, and she found the strength to lean back against the table and look at him. 'I didn't know…' she began, but before she could finish, the creak of the heavy kitchen door startled them both. Alexander swiftly pulled her skirts down to cover her.

If young Luke had any notion of what had just occurred, he showed no sign of knowing. Instead, he merely said, 'My lord, the horses are already in their stables. And I lit the fire in your chamber. Will you be needing assistance with anything else?'

Alexander cleared his throat, gathering himself to respond to the young man. 'That will be all, Luke. You may go to sleep now. Thank you.'

'As you wish, my lord. Good night, my lady.' He bowed to Abbie and left, closing the door behind him.

When he was gone, Alexander looked at Abbie – and they both burst into laughter. He reached out and tucked a loose strand of hair behind her ear, his fingers grazing her neck.

'Shall we go upstairs?' he asked softly.

With her cheeks still blushing from the pleasure he had given her only moments ago, Abbie nodded. Feeling the heat building up again with only that light touch on her neck.

Alexander took her hand and guided her upstairs to his chamber.

She stood in front of the fire, concentrating on the flames, and when she felt Alexander behind her, she leaned into him, allowing his arms to enfold her.

'I have been waiting for this moment since the day I met you,' he whispered in her ear, making her shiver from head to toe. She turned her face to meet his gaze.

'So have I.' She saw the surprise in his eyes.

'You hide it very well, my lady.'

'I don't need to anymore.' And turning fully to him, she wrapped her arms around his neck, drawing him down to her waiting lips. Alexander's hands moved swiftly, unfastening the laces of her dress until the fabric slipped from her shoulders and lay sprawled on the floor around her feet, leaving her in nothing but a thin chemise, almost transparent against the dancing lights coming from the fireplace.

He lifted her into his arms and carried her until they stood beside the bed, facing each other. He removed the pins from her hair, letting it cascade over her shoulders.

'You are so beautiful.' His hand touched her hair with such tenderness, Abbie felt her heart swell in a way she had never known.

Placing a hand under her chin, he lowered his head, claiming her lips – at first, slow and tender, until the flame inside them rose to uncontrollable levels. Soon, they lay on the bed, needing everything from each other – until the flame turned into fire, carrying them to pleasures neither of them had ever dared dream of.

CHAPTER 17

Alexander woke to the warmth of Abbie's body pressed against his. Her arm was draped across his chest, her leg resting over his. As he looked at her, memories of the night before stirred vividly in his mind. The passion with which Abbie had responded to his caresses had ignited something deep within him.

Since the day he had seen her riding into the front yard at Everleigh Manor, something had awakened inside him – and as the days passed, the desire to have her close, to touch her hair, to feel her bare body against his, had grown into something far beyond mere lust. But not even in his wildest dreams had he imagined that she would reciprocate him with such sensual urgency, nor with the same desperation that had tormented him during the weeks they'd lived under the same roof. With that first kiss, he had known she had been longing for him just as much as he had longed for her.

Her blonde curls were spread over the pillows like a waterfall of golden water. He reached out and gently ran his fingers through her locks, catching one between his thumb and forefinger. It felt like silk against his rough skin. She looked like a nymph; her bare breasts peeking out from beneath the sheets, and the sight of her stirred him once more. Even though they had spent hours exploring one another's bodies, Alexander knew he would never have enough. He wanted her like this – in his arms – for the rest of their lives. His need for her surpassed any desire he had ever felt for a woman before. No-one had captivated his interest or his desire like Abbie had, not even Georgina's mother.

Alexander kissed her forehead, and Abbie responded with a soft purr, shifting in his arms and opening her eyes sleepily to meet his gaze. He took the opportunity to place a hand at the nape of her neck and draw her to him for a gentle kiss, bringing his lips close to hers. She received him without shame and responded with the same passion.

As the kiss broke, he looked into her eyes. 'Good morning.'

She smiled and replied, 'Good morning.'

'How are you feeling?'

Her smile widened. 'I feel different. But mostly, I feel...' she paused, '...hungry.' She laughed at his lascivious look. 'I mean hungry for food, Alexander. Can you only think of one thing?'

'How can you blame me? When I have a goddess in my arms, resisting temptation is near impossible.' He kissed her again and lifted her so she lay atop him, trapping her in his embrace. 'But this time, I shall be benevolent – if only because I need you to regain your strength... so we may continue doing my new favourite thing.'

'And what might that be?'

'Making love to you.' He grabbed her bottom and pressed her against his hardness, drawing a moan from her.

'I think that has also become my favourite thing to do,' she murmured, planting a quick but passionate kiss on his lips before rolling off him. 'But, my dear husband, we have things to do.'

'You are cruel, my lady. You tempt me with your kisses and then leave me aching for your touch.' She wrapped a bedsheet around her body and, standing at the edge of the bed, looked over her shoulder with a mischievous smile.

'I promise, my lord, our marital games shall resume later. But first, we must go to Redwood House.'

He wished, just for a moment, that they could forget why they were back in Oxfordshire, and escape the nightmare they were both living. He looked at her and saw the same wish reflected in her eyes. But they both knew they had to face reality and continue their search for the truth. Until they did, they would forever be looking over their shoulders.

He folded his arms behind his head and nodded. 'I shall see if Mrs Watson has returned and can prepare something for us to eat before we leave.' He got out of bed, pulled on his breeches from the floor, and stepped into his dressing room to retrieve a clean shirt. Then, returning to her, he wrapped his arms around her waist and kissed her temple before reluctantly leaving the room.

As he entered the kitchen, delicious aromas invaded his senses, making his stomach growl. Mrs Watson stood by the hearth, focused on removing a steaming pot from the top rail. He knocked lightly on the doorframe, and she turned in surprise.

'My lord!' she exclaimed, setting the pot on the kitchen table.

'Good morning, Mrs Watson.'

'Good morning, my lord. Please forgive me for not being here yesterday. I wasn't aware of your arrival until Luke told me this morning.' Alexander smiled, brushing off her apology.

'Think nothing of it, Mrs Watson. We were on our way to Redwood House and hadn't planned to stop here, but our plans changed at the last moment.'

'Luke told me you were attacked! Are you and Lady Crawford well?' Her gaze dropped to his arm, and her eyes widened. He followed her line of sight and saw the fresh blood that had seeped through his shirt, leaving a red stain on his arm.

'Yes, we're fine,' Alexander said, touching his arm. 'It's only a scratch, Mrs Watson. And Lady Crawford did a good job taking care of me.' Seeing the worried gaze of the cook, he decided to change the subject. 'Was your sister well?'

'Yes, my lord. I hadn't seen her in weeks and wished to spend some time with her and the children.' Alexander knew how close the two sisters were.

'I'm glad to hear that.' He nodded towards the pot she had left on the table. 'What's that? It smells wonderful.'

She lifted the lid to reveal a loaf of freshly-baked bread. The rich, yeasty aroma filled the kitchen. 'That looks delicious, Mrs Watson.'

'I'm afraid I don't have much to offer this morning, my lord – only a bit of cheese. So, I thought some warm bread would at least make the meal so at least you can have something more filling.'

'Thank you. That was very thoughtful. I am sure Lady Crawford will appreciate it. She's positively ravenous this morning. Would you mind taking it up to our chamber? And some water, please. We need to leave for Redwood House as soon as we can.'

'Of course, my lord.'

'Thank you, Mrs Watson.'

He left the kitchens and made his way to the stables, where he found Luke brushing Hettie. 'How are they doing?' he asked the young man, concerned the journey had worn the horses too thin. He and Abbie treated their horses with the utmost care and after the long journey, he would not be surprised if they needed to rest a bit longer.

'They're recovering well, my lord. A good leg massage, plenty of water, and some bran mash with salt will have them as good as new. I also gave them some apples – they seemed to enjoy it, sir, especially Hettie.'

Alexander smiled in relief and stroked Hettie's head, who greeted him with a cheerful whinny and a toss of her mane. 'Your father taught you well, Luke.'

'Yes, my lord. But please, do remind him of that when you're back in London.'

Alexander laid a hand on the boy's shoulder. 'I will. But I am certain he's proud of the young man you've become – even if he doesn't say it often.'

The lad smiled at him. 'Thank you, my lord.'

'My wife and I will be leaving shortly for Redwood House. Could you ready the horses?'

'Of course, my lord.'

'Thank you, Luke.'

When Alexander returned to the house and opened the bedchamber door, he could not hide his disappointment to see Abbie fully dressed.

'I think I prefer you naked,' he said as he stepped inside.

Abbie stood at the mirror, finishing braiding her hair. She turned and smiled at him as she tied the end with a lace, but her expression changed when she turned and saw him.

'You're bleeding again.' She walked to him.

'It's nothing, Abbie. I'll change the shirt.' She began unbuttoning his shirt and tugging it free from his breeches.

'And ruin another one? Let me change the bandage first, Alexander. Arms up.' He obeyed with a grin, clearly enjoying her care.

'As you wish, my lady.' He lifted his arms, looking at

her with desire.

'Do not even think about it, my lord,' she said, laughing.

'I do not know what you are talking about, my dear.' She raised an eyebrow, unconvinced, and turned her attention to the bloodied bandage on his arm.

'Your wicked grin gives you away, my lord. You do not have to say anything for me to see that you will want us both to stay in this chamber the rest of the week.'

'Or the month,' he murmured, teasing her, whispering in her ear. She laughed and brought over the basin and fresh cloths that Mrs Watson had provided. Gently, she peeled away the bandage.

'It's healing nicely, but the wound has reopened.' He slid a hand around her waist and pulled her closer to him.

'I can't imagine how that might have happened.' Abbie shook her head.

'Too much exertion, my lord.' His laugh echoed through the room.

'Well, if that's the case, I will gladly endure the pain – for I must say, making love to you is the most rewarding exercise, my dear.' He kissed her neck.

'You're a rake,' she teased. 'Now, let me finish dressing your wound, or we'll never make it to Redwood House.'

As he looked at her, he saw a shadow of sadness pass over her features. 'What is troubling you?' She said nothing, focusing on her task. 'Abbie.' He slipped a finger under her chin, lifting her face to look at him.

'I'm afraid we won't find anything of worth in the book.'

'Your father was a clever man, Abbie. I can only agree with you that he would never have left you such a short, meaningless message if he knew it might be the last thing you'd ever receive from him. So let us not despair. Don't lose hope.'

She nodded, and he kissed her gently on the forehead. 'Let's go, then.'

***

Abbie's head was spinning with anticipation, though a part of her was afraid to discover her suspicions were nothing more than empty hopes. She urged Hettie to go faster, forcing Alexander to match her pace until they reached Redwood House. She couldn't wait a moment longer.

She pulled Hettie's reins as they turned onto the short road leading to the front yard, just in time to see Simon, the stable boy, running towards them, who was adamant about helping her dismount, but he had no chance – for before he reached them, Abbie was already knocking on the front door, her anxiety to get inside impossible to contain.

Mrs White opened the door to the unexpected visitors. 'Abbie, darling! What a pleasant surprise! I thought you were still in London?' She embraced her lovingly and smiled warmly. Then she turned to Alexander. 'Good morning, my lord.'

Alexander dipped his head in greeting towards the housekeeper. 'Good morning, Mrs White. Apologies for not sending word of our arrival. We left in haste.' He offered her one of his most charming smiles –so disarming, in fact, that poor Mrs White blushed at the mere sight of it.

'Oh no, my lord. There is no need for apologies. This is your home,' she replied, said, dismissing his concerns. Abbie smiled at the flustered reaction of the woman who had helped raise her. She had never seen Mrs White so agitated, but how could she blame her? Alexander had that effect. Abbie herself had felt it from the very first day they met – the weakening of the knees, the constant flush running through her body.

'But come in, please! May I get you some tea?' the housekeeper offered.

'No, thank you, Mrs White,' Abbie said over her shoulder, already halfway down the corridor. She could no longer restrain her desire to confirm what she had suspected. She ran towards the library, knowing Alexander would be close behind.

Abbie stood in front of the door that led to the library, and taking a deep breath to gather enough courage, she turned the doorknob and stepped into the room.

The darkness inside enveloped her. Without hesitation, she crossed the space to open the curtains, letting in enough light to reveal the shelves packed with books filling every wall of the room. She pulled another of the heavy curtains aside, and just as she prepared to draw the next curtain, she felt Alexander's stoic figure close to her body, his hands already reaching to assist her.

'Find the book. I'll take care of this.'

She nodded her thanks with a smile and walked over to the wooden shelves that lined the room, filled with books of all colours and sizes. Her father had once tried to classify them by subject, but over time they had been hopelessly mixed without any specific pattern.

Everywhere you looked there were science books, mixed with poetry and mathematics. The lack of order would make the task more difficult than expected. But Abbie was determined to find what she was looking for, even if she had to examine every book on the shelf.

She slid the wooden ladder, attached to the top rail, along the length of the shelves until she reached the far end. She climbed the ladder and began going through them one by one, murmuring the titles under her breath.

'Remind me – what was the name of the book?' Alexander asked from the bottom of the ladder.

Abbie looked down at him. '*Cecilia*, by Fanny Burney. You can start on the lower shelves. If I remember correctly, I think the cover was brown with the title engraved in gold, though I wouldn't rule out it being another colour.'

'I'll keep my eyes open,' he replied, and they both resumed their search, going through the volumes one by one.

After what felt like an eternity, they had made it only to the centre of the shelves when Alexander picked up a book and several documents slipped from its pages.

Hearing the rustle and his surprised exclamation, Abbie turned quickly.

'Did you find it?'

Alexander bent down to retrieve the papers from the floor and began to read through them. Looking up, he shook his head, making her hopes crumble.

'No, it appears to be the purchase contract for Redwood House – between Alan and a man named Miles Claybrook. But the transaction was made through a London betting house. It says here that the house was wagered to cover a debt and your father bought it for half its value to the betting house. He paid forty thousand pounds for the estate and gave Miles Claybrook a house in Devon, along with four thousand pounds in cash. Considering the lands and the size of the house, Redwood House estate is worth at least a hundred thousand.'

Abbie climbed down to take the documents Alexander held out to her. She looked through the contract, surprised.

'I didn't know my father bought the house from a gambling house. Do you know who Miles Claybrook was?'

'I've never heard the name before. Forty thousand pounds is a large sum for your father to have...' Abbie raised an eyebrow and Alexander raised his hands. 'I am not suggesting anything – I'm just asking.' She handed the documents back to him and slid the ladder further along the shelves.

As she climbed, she said. 'Well, to answer your question, it's not odd that he had that money. My grandfather was a man of some means, so I imagine my mother's dowry was considerable. That, along with the success of my father's business, must have been enough to buy the property.'

'That makes sense.' He placed the papers on the desk by the window and continued his search.

An hour passed, and Abbie was starting to lose hope when, finally, she spotted it. With an exclamation of excitement, she stretched out her arm to reached for the book.

Just as she remembered, the book was brown and had a hard leather case. Along the spine, the engraved golden letters read 'Cecilia'. With the tip of her finger, she pulled the book towards her until it slid out from in between the other books that surrounded it. It was wedged in tightly, and when she held it, it felt heavier than she recalled.

Alexander was already standing at the base of the ladder. She reached out her hand for his assistance, and he took the opportunity to pull her into him, catching her in his arms until she was pressed against his chest. Looking into his eyes, and her excitement still coursing through her body for having found the book, Abbie kissed him before he set her down on the floor. Without wasting another second, she crossed to the desk and opened the book. 'I knew it,' she said triumphantly.

Alexander came to stand beside her, looking over her

shoulder.

'My father used to play a game with me when I was young,' she explained, smiling at the memory. 'He would leave clues in books for me to find – just a hint as to which one, as it was up to me to decipher where it was hidden.' She could still remember the laughter and joy of those childhood games, the thrill of finding a treat or hidden toy. It had been years since they last played, but her father had known she would remember.

Inside the book, instead of pages, was a hollowed-out compartment filled with folded documents. Her father had cut into the book, creating a secret pocket. She looked at Alexander and began laying the contents out on the table.

The first document she unfolded was an insurance policy on a vessel, signed by an insurance broker named Richard Wilkes. She handed it to Alexander.

'Who is Richard Wilkes?' she asked.

'He's the man I told you about. When Stephen called to tell me what had happened, I put him in contact with Richard. He'd handled insurance for me in the past, and I knew we could trust him to be discrete.' Alexander examined the paper. 'This proves the cargo was insured.'

'But I don't understand. Why would Braxton go to the trouble of hiring a fake insurer. It doesn't benefit him.'

'It would if he sold the cargo and declared the ship lost at sea. His company's insurance would cover the cost of a new vessel, and he'd come away without a loss – in fact, he'd make a considerable profit, considering it was Stephen and your father that financed the shipment.'

'But why go to the lengths of killing three people? I don't know, Alexander… I find it hard to believe that someone would want to wipe out an entire family for a few thousand pounds.'

'Men have killed for far less – especially if they feared

their secrets were about to be exposed.'

'I know, I'm not that naïve. But I feel there is something more to this story that we're not seeing.' She couldn't say exactly why, but something about it all felt... wrong.

Abbie continued sorting through the documents. Among them were three neatly folded letters, all addressed to her father from Lord Everleigh. She picked one up and began to read aloud.

January 29th, 1787

Dear Alan,

I received word of the Brigantine Tyrrell's arrival at port early this afternoon. Captain Walters sold the furniture to a Spanish merchant and expects to sell him more on his next trip.

Mr Braxton plans to load the next furniture delivery as soon as The Brigantine is ready to set sail. He has suggested we increase the purchase on this occasion to raise our profits. I will be at New John's tomorrow at noon. I hope to see you there and discuss this further.

Yours sincerely,
Lord Everleigh

Abbie passed the letter to Alexander, who had just finished reading the insurance document. 'This is the first shipment. It's dated a month before Stephen had the accident.'

She handed him the letter and opened the second one, reading aloud.

February 15th, 1787

Dear Alan,

I have been informed of something concerning our last shipment. Meet me at New John's tomorrow morning.

Yours sincerely,
Lord Everleigh

Abbie looked up at Alexander. 'This must have been when Colton contacted him about what he'd heard at that tavern.' She handed him the second letter and unfolded the last one.

February 22nd, 1787

Dear Alan,
They know. I will leave for Everleigh Manor tomorrow at first light. Meet me there.
Yours sincerely,
Lord Everleigh

Everything was becoming clearer now.

'Stephen realised Braxton knew about the insurance policy with Richard Wilkes and headed to Everleigh Manor to meet my father. They must have arranged for my father to keep the documents at Redwood House, then when Stephen was killed, he hid them – and went to Jeremy Bates under the pretext of drafting a new will, and to conceal a message for me.'

'That's what it looks like. They insured the cargo while it was still at sea. The insurance papers were drafted on the 17th of February, and the shipwreck was reported in the newspapers on the 20th of February – so the policy is valid.' Still, Abbie couldn't shake the feeling that something was amiss about this situation.

'Even with all these documents, we still can't prove that Braxton is responsible for my parents' and Stephen's deaths. Nothing here implicates him directly with their deaths. There isn't even a clear motive. All we have is speculation based on Stephen's letters.' She sighed, disheartened.

Alexander began pacing the room, considering her words. 'We could – if we find the cargo,' he said, turning back to look at her.

'How would that help?'

'This shipment was unique. They transported high-quality furniture – luxury items. If they sold it, there must be a trail. That sort of furniture is only accessible to those with significant means. If what we think is true, I doubt they'd waste the opportunity to profit by letting it sink in the middle of the Atlantic. Derek has been following leads – I'll send him a letter asking him to look for luxury furniture sold under questionable circumstances.'

Abbie placed the documents back on the table. 'We need to make him pay,' she said softly. He pulled her into his arms to hug her tight, and she let herself be held, allowing his warmth to anchor her.

'We will. I promise you that. Don't disappear, Abbie. The fight is not over – and we'll get to the bottom of this.' She rested her head on his chest, wrapping her arms around him as she tried to contain the fury rising inside her.

Money. All of it, for money. Her parents. Georgina's father. Murdered for the greed of one man. How could it be possible? Now, nothing would stop her – not until Braxton was brought to justice.

Not until he paid for everything he had done to their families.

CHAPTER 18

'I don't think we'll find anything else between the pages of these books, Abbie,' Alexander said from the opposite side of the room. Abbie could barely see the top of his head, almost buried behind the piles of books he had been rifling through.

After finding the documents her father left for her, they had set about searching the rest of the library, hoping to uncover anything further that might shed light on the intricate mystery they were attempting to unravel.

Abbie had chosen the floor as her place of work; with her legs crossed, she worked through book after book, running her finger over the pages and fanning them open. The rustling sound filled the room – until she reached the final book and snapped it shut.

Silence enveloped the room. Feelings of frustration and emptiness accompanied the absence of sound surrounding her like a cloak, making her heart ache. The weight of the past few weeks had left her exhausted, and as much as she tried to hide it, it was becoming increasingly difficult to bear.

She let out a sigh and looked up to meet his gaze. 'I think you're right.'

Alexander raised his head from behind the books, smiling. 'Could you repeat that, Lady Crawford? I don't believe I heard you properly.' His playful grin made her shake her head.

'I don't think that's advisable – for it would only

inflate your ego, my lord. Otherwise, I'll end up with a peacock strutting at my side for the rest of my days.'

Alexander laughed walked over to where she sat, standing in front of her.

Abbie looked up at him. In so little time, the man in front of her had managed to dispel the cloud that seemed to follow her everywhere since her parents' death. And, despite herself, she was beginning to accept that the feelings growing inside her were as strong as those she had witnessed between her mother and father.

Alexander sat down beside her, crossing his legs in front of him. They both stared at the half-emptied shelves of the library.

'I must admit, I'm very impressed with your father's ingenuity,' Alexander said. 'I wouldn't have thought of leaving the trail of clues that he so cleverly left for you.'

Abbie smiled as childhood memories stirred.

'My father loved playing mystery games with me. He'd hide clues around the house for me to find and as I grew older, the puzzles became more challenging. But I must say, he's outdone himself with this one.'

She focused her attention on a loose thread on her skirt, trying to control the pain that arose inside her every time she thought of her parents and wondered when it would stop. She wished with all her might that she could remember the wonderful times they had spent together without the sharp sting of grief piercing her heart.

She felt his hand cover hers – a silent gesture of support. She took a deep breath, not wanting to burden him with her sorrow, and asked quietly, 'Do you think what we've found will be enough?'

Alexander entwined his fingers with hers. 'It's a start.'

Abbie rested her head on his shoulder.

'I suppose so. But we still don't have any concrete evidence against Braxton.'

'Perhaps not, but I'm sure that the Admiralty will at least take the case into consideration now. With their resources, we'll have a better chance of finding the proof we need.'

'I hope so.' She knew the documents they had found were important, but part of her feared they still wouldn't be enough to bring Braxton to justice.

He lifted her chin gently with his fingers until her eyes met his. 'It will be.'

She felt the warmth of his lips against hers, filling her with a hope she never thought was possible to convey with a kiss.

When his lips parted from hers, their gazes lingered. Time seemed to halt – leaving only the two of them in the world. Her hand found his cheek, asking him without words to kiss her once more, and he did not hesitate to oblige. His tongue caressed hers with slow, sensual movements that only awakened the deep desire she felt for him.

Her heartbeat quickened with every kiss he gave her, and his strong touch fuelled her longing, her need for him growing more and more urgent. With one swift motion, he lifted her onto his lap, drawing a surprised gasp from her.

She held his face between her hands, feeling their hearts beat in unison. It felt as though her body had no will of its own when it came to this man. The walls she'd built around herself had crumbled to pieces, leaving her defenceless to the gaze that made her weak at the knees.

'What are you doing to me?' she said in a whisper.

'I could ask you the same thing,' he replied. Placing a hand on her back, he pulled her even closer still. Their lips met once more, pressing their bodies against each other. Alexander's hand slipped up her thigh, raising the temperature of the room, but their desire was soon thwarted when they heard a knock on the door followed by a familiar female voice.

'Mrs Abbie? I thought you might like something to eat, darling.'

Mrs White's voice was like a bucket of icy water. Alexander couldn't hide his disappointment and let out a groan of annoyance. Abbie let out a breathless laugh, but the truth was that she felt the same frustration as him. Their lips parted, but Abbie didn't move from her position. She rested her forehead against his, waiting for her breathing to settle.

'This habit of getting interrupted isn't healthy, Abbie.' She placed a hand on his chest, feeling his racing heart. Giggling, she kissed him softly.

'I agree,' she murmured, then rose to her feet.

Abbie smoothed her skirt and tucked a stray curl behind her ear, before walking to the door to let Mrs White in. She paused and turned to look at him with a raised brow.

'Are you planning to stay on the floor and let Mrs White wonder what we've been doing?'

'She's a grown woman, Abbie. I think she knows exactly what we've been doing,' he replied as he stood up. Abbie let the housekeeper in, who came in carrying a tray with tea and sandwiches carefully cut into small triangles.

'I thought you two must be starving. You've been in here for hours now!' The woman looked around the room, taking in the sea of disarrayed books. Her expression changed to one of surprise to concern. Placing her hands on her hips, she exclaimed, 'What on earth have you been doing here, child? You haven't left a single book standing!' Abbie laughed at the housekeeper's reaction.

'We'll put everything back, Mrs White. In the haste to find the book I wanted; we didn't realise what chaos we were creating.' But seeing the doubtful gaze in the woman, she added. 'But don't worry, Mrs White. Lord Crawford has kindly volunteered to return every single book back where it belongs.'

It was Alexander's turn now to arch a brow, but he said nothing. and she simply smiled at him innocently with a playful gesture. He shook his head but didn't contradict her.

'That's very nice of you, Lord Crawford,' Mrs White said with approval.

Alexander stepped forward and slipped an arm around Abbie's waist. 'Anything for my lovely wife.' The woman smiled with loving eyes.

'Well then, let me know if you need anything else, darling.'

'We will, Mrs White. Thank you for the sandwiches.' Abbie replied, before the housekeeper left the room.

Alexander glanced down at her, his hand still comfortably resting on her hip. 'Every single book?'

'If I'd told her I was going to be the one cleaning this mess, she wouldn't have believed me. But I knew she wouldn't say a word if you were the one cleaning up.'

'I have the feeling this isn't the first time you've played this trick on poor Mrs White.'

'Me?' She widened her eyes innocently and placed a hand on her chest. 'Never.' He let out a chuckle, clearly not convinced, while she dropped to her knees to start with the long process of putting the books back on their shelves.

It took them at least another hour to put the final book back into place. By then, the light was beginning to fade, and the first shadows of evening crept across the floor.

'It's getting late. We should leave tomorrow with the first light. We can be back in London by the afternoon,'

Alexander said, leaning back against the bookshelf.

She agreed, but thinking of the dangers of travelling back without an escort made her doubt the safety of the journey. Whoever had sent the two men who attacked them would, by now, know of their failure. And if they were alone, they risked it happening again.

'We should hire someone to accompany us to London.'

Alexander nodded. 'I know three brothers who live in the village – the Dawley brothers. I'll send them a message. I believe they were planning to return to London in the next few days.'

'And who are these Dawley brothers?'

'They're part of Colton's crew. I sailed with them during my years in the army.'

Only then did she realise how little she knew about her husband's life before they met. 'I didn't know you served.'

'It was years ago,' he replied curtly. His tone alone told her enough – it was apparent he didn't want to talk more about it. And while she had to respect his wishes, she couldn't help but want to know more. Still, she decided not to press the issue, for things between them had improved considerably, and truth be told, she was enjoying this newfound intimacy.

'Do you trust them?' she asked. That, in the end, was what mattered most. Given the recent attacks, and the certainty that someone close to them was providing information about their whereabouts filled her with doubts about the people around her.

'I do. They've saved my life on more than one occasion.' He closed the distance between them and grabbed a lock of her hair between his fingers before cupping her cheek.

Abbie closed her eyes, leaning into his touch with a

soft sigh.

'I won't let anything happen to you,' he whispered.

Opening her eyes, she smiled. 'Nor will I.'

***

It was barely dawn when Abbie and Alexander began their journey back to London. When they reached the main road, they found themselves facing three large men, each riding a mare as rugged and tough as their owners. From their resemblance, Abbie guessed these must be the brothers Alexander had spoken of.

'Good morning, my lord,' the three men said in unison, like a well-practised chorus.

'Good morning. Peter, Walter, David.' Each brother nodded as his name was spoken. Peter wore a stern expression, a faint scar cutting through one eyebrow where the hair no longer grew. Yet despite his appearance, Abbie did not feel threatened by him. Walter, by contrast, had a gentler look which, despite his considerable size, conveyed a strange and reassuring calm. The last brother, David, wore a permanent cheeky grin that instantly put Abbie at ease.

'Are you not going to introduce us?' Peter asked.

'Gentlemen, allow me introduce Abigail Crawford – my wife.'

David jumped in his saddle. 'You married? Man! We thought you'd never go down that road after–' He was abruptly cut off by Walter delivering a sharp jab to his stomach to shut him up. Abbie glanced at Alexander, confused, only to find him staring hard at David with a warning look. The mystery of his secretive past grew when she saw his reaction.

'What did you do that for?' David gasped.

'Please excuse him, Lady Crawford,' Walter said with

a charming smile. 'My brother is not accustomed to speaking in the presence of a lady. It's a pleasure to meet you.' Peter raised an eyebrow at Walter's words but remained silent.

'Enough of this,' Alexander cut in. 'We have a long way to go, and if you don't mind, I'd like to start the journey today.' With that, he spurred his horse forward, leaving the others looking at the back of his head.

Abbie cleared her throat. 'My apologies for my husband, gentlemen. It seems his manners have loosened of late. Thank you for accompanying us to London – we appreciate your time.'

'I like her,' David said to his brothers. 'My lady, the pleasure is all ours,' he added with a flourishing bow. Abbie heard a snort and turned to see Alexander waiting for them down the road.

'Shall we?'

His sudden shift of mood only increased Abbie's curiosity. She smiled at the brothers, with only one thing on her mind: to find out what Alexander was so diligently trying to keep from her. The three brothers took up position – Peter at the front with Alexander, while Walter and David flanked Abbie as though guarding a precious treasure.

After a while, seeing Peter and Alexander deep in conversation, Abbie seized the opportunity to question the brothers, slipping her inquiry into casual conversation.

'So, where did you all meet?' David leapt at the chance to speak, like a young boy thrilled to be the centre of attention.

'We've known each other since we were but wee ones, my lady. Captain C and my lord here,' he said, nodding at Alexander, 'used to stay at Everleigh Manor during the summer breaks from that fancy school – what was it called?'

'Eton,' Walter supplied.

'That's it! Eton. First time we saw them, Peter lobbed an egg at Alexander.' David laughed. 'Oh, he was furious, my lady. He jumped the fence between the estates and punched Peter so hard he fell on his a–'

'On his back, my lady. He fell on his back,' Walter interjected quickly, shooting his brother a warning look. He then took over from his brother and continued the tale. 'After they'd both cooled down, they started talking and we all became fast friends. We spent every summer getting into mischief. Stephen's father wasn't too happy about it – thought the little lords shouldn't mix with low-born lads like us.' He shrugged. 'But Lady Charlotte, bless her, managed to convince the old man to let us play together. She's a remarkable lady. Have you met her?' Abbie smiled warmly.

'Yes, and I do agree with you – she is indeed wonderful.'

'When Alexander and Captain C joined The Argo, we followed them,' Walter went on, lowering his voice to a whisper. 'We couldn't let these two go off alone – they'd never have made it back alive.' Abbie smiled at the remark. She wanted – no, *needed* – to know more about her husband's life. And David and Walter seemed more than willing to share every detail.

'The Argo?' she prompted, continuing her gentle interrogation while praying they wouldn't realise her intentions.

'That was the ship for the second battalion of the third regiment of His Majesty's army, my lady. They were assigned there, and we volunteered. The war with the French had just begun, you see, and from what I could tell, neither of the sirs was particularly interested in settling down.'

'And Lord Everleigh?' she asked, her curiosity growing.

'Well, he was interested in settling down,' Walter said with a knowing grin.

'Interested?' David looked at his brother. 'He was more than–' But once again he was interrupted by Alexander's deep voice.

'Enough with the tales, David. Stop boring my wife with your stories.' David chuckled, clearly enjoying how much he could provoke Alexander.

Alexander halted his horse and twisted in the saddle to face them. His unfriendly demeanour took Abbie by surprise. She couldn't understand what part of that story could have been the reason for his mood swing– but one thing was clear: she needed to learn more about why Stephen had chosen to stay in England while Alexander chose to leave.

'We are going to stop in that clearing to rest the horses,' Alexander said, nodding towards a path through the woods where the trees parted to reveal the remains of past visitors. As they guided the horses closer, Abbie heard the sound of a nearby stream, making it an ideal resting place for both them and the horses. They dismounted and unpacked the food Mrs White had kindly prepared for the journey.

As she sat on a fallen tree, Abbie listened to the men speak about their most recent voyage with Captain C, which Abbie learnt was how the crew called Derek Colton, Alexander's cousin.

'We had a rough return from Spain,' Walter was saying. 'The storm nearly destroyed The Isabella – but she's strong. The finest vessel we've ever sailed.' He turned to Abbie. 'You should come and see her one day, Lady Crawford. There's nothing like her.'

Unfamiliar with the seafaring talk, Abbie asked. 'The

Isabella?'

'Yes, my lady. That's the name of Captain C's ship.'

'And you refer to it as *her*?'

'But of course!' David chimed in. 'All ships are female, my lady.'

'And why is that?'

David opened his mouth, eager to reply, but it was Alexander who answered her question.

'There are many theories,' he said, 'but the most popular is that the ship takes on feminine qualities. By naming it after a woman – the beauty, grace and strength – blesses the men who sail her. She will guide them to port and return them to their loved ones.' His eyes were fixed on her as he spoke, and once again, the world vanished around them. She had almost forgotten the others were present until Walter resumed the conversation.

'Has he told you what happened when we docked in a French port near Calais?'

Abbie wanted to scream. *Has he told me? I hardly know anything about this man!* But before she could even reply, Alexander intervened once more.

'I think we should get moving,' he said, offering a hand to help Abbie to her feet. When she looked into his eyes, she could have sworn he told her without words: *I will tell you everything.*

CHAPTER 19

By the time they arrived in London, the sun was hiding behind the buildings west of the grey city. Dirty and exhausted from the journey, the party of five stopped at the back entrance of the manor where the stables were located.

Alexander felt the weight of the long ride in his bones as he climbed down from his horse and walked over to help Abbie dismount.

They had barely exchanged a word throughout the journey. The two younger Dawley brothers had captured Abbie's attention almost from the moment they left Redwood House, and knowing David and his indiscreet nature, her current mood was most likely triggered by something he had mentioned to her.

Her expression told him enough as she dismounted before he could reach her, glancing over her shoulder with a look he recognised all too well. Without a word, she led Hattie into her stall. Marcus Finney, the horse master, arrived in haste to take care of the mare. With a curt nod, she thanked him before turning to the three brothers, who, sensing something was amiss, had fallen uncharacteristically silent over the last few miles.

'Thank you again, gentlemen, for accompanying us on our journey. You are more than welcome to stay the night – you must be tired after such a long ride.'

Walter took a step forward and spoke on behalf of the three. 'It has been an honour, my lady. We thank you for your hospitality, but the captain is expecting us.'

'At least have something to eat before you leave.'

'We won't say no to that, my lady!' David called, poking his head out from behind his brother's broad shoulders.

'Good,' she replied with a faint smile. 'Good night, gentleman.' Then, turning to Alexander with a swift curtsy and an unmistakable cool tone, she added, 'Alexander.'

With that, she turned on her heels and headed to the house, leaving the men baffled by her abrupt departure. All but Alexander – he knew precisely why she was upset with him. He turned to David.

'When are you going to learn to keep your mouth shut? What did you say to her?'

'What are you talking about?' David raised his hands, clearly confused by his accusation. Walter gave him a look.

'What world do you live in, brother? He is talking about you nearly telling her about Catherine.'

'But I thought...' David's expression shifted to one of concern.

'You thought wrong,' Alexander snapped, cutting his words short.

Peter, who was leaning against a stable door, finally spoke. 'Well, my friend, it's about time you told your wife.'

'I know that, Peter – but it wouldn't have been half this difficult if your brother hadn't opened his mouth!' Peter raised one brow at Alexander's agitated tone but said nothing.

'Never mind,' Alexander muttered, sighing. 'Go inside and ask the cook to get you something to eat. And try not to empty the larder. I've no idea how your mother managed to feed the three of you. Where are you staying?' he added.

'At The Devil's Tavern,' Walter replied.

'When is Derek coming back?'

'Tonight, as far as we know. He told us to meet him there.'

'Good. I need to speak with him as soon as possible.'

Walter laid a hand on Alexander's shoulder. 'We'll let the captain know.' He turned to his brothers, nodding towards the servant's entrance. 'Come on, I'm starving.' Alexander watched them disappear through the door, then shook his head and set off to face his wife's wrath.

As he walked through the door, Georgina's cheerful voice echoed throughout the house. She was speaking in her usual rapid-fire manner, sharing one of her adventures. Abbie held her in her arms, smiling and nodding at the little girl as if she understood every word. The sight of them together warmed Alexander's heart, and a smile rose to his lips as he fixed the tender image in his memory.

'Have you been getting up to much mischief?' Abbie teased, gently pinching the little girl's nose. Georgina gave an exaggerated look of offence.

'Me? Nooo,' she replied, her green eyes sparkling with mischief.

The moment Georgina spotted him, her eyes lit up with joy. She begged Abbie to put her down and then ran straight into his open arms.

'Uncle Alex! You're back!' she cried, leaping into his embrace. He lifted her high in the air, making her giggle in delight. 'I missed you, Uncle Alex.'

'But it's only been a couple of days.'

'I know, but I always miss you.' She hugged him tightly and then looked back at Abbie. 'Did you miss me too?' Abbie stepped closer and stroked Georgina's cheek.

'Of course I did.'

From the top of the stairs came a familiar voice. 'Now,

Georgina, it's time for bed,' Paige called, using the same usual joyful tone she always reserved for the little girl.

'But they've just arrived, Paige! And I want to know where they've been!' She looked up with a pleading expression. Her big brown eyes could melt anyone's heart. Alexander knew first-hand the power of that look – but Paige, it seemed, had developed an immunity.

'Hey,' he called gently, and Georgina turned to him. 'We'll tell you everything tomorrow.'

'You promise?'

'I promise.'

He lowered her to the floor and kissed her on the cheek. 'Good night, sweet pie.'

Georgina ran to Abbie, who crouched down to give her a hug. 'Night-night!' the little girl called as she dashed upstairs.

'That girl has enough energy for ten,' Alexander said, following her with his gaze. 'Indeed, she does.'

He turned to Abbie, ready to speak, but she addressed Thomas, who was waiting just behind him. 'Thomas, would you be so kind as to ask Suzie to prepare a bath in my room, please?'

'Of course, my lady.'

'Thank you.' She smiled and began to ascend the stairs, but paused with one foot on the first step and looked back at Alexander. 'Good night.'

He couldn't let her leave without saying something. 'Wait.' He took her hand and gently turned her towards him.

'I'm tired, Alexander,' she said without looking him in the eyes.

'I know, but I would like to speak with you first. I don't know what David said, but I can explain–'

Abbie pulled her hand from his and crossed her arms over her chest. 'David?' she repeated. 'You think I'm upset because of something David said? You are unbelievable!' She didn't give him a chance to speak. 'This isn't about David – it's about you!'

'What on earth are you referring to?'

'Every time they started talking about…' she paused, searching for the words. 'Gah! I don't know what! But it's as clear as the sun rises in the east that there is something you don't want me to know!'

'Abbie–'

'No. You know what? It doesn't matter. I'm too tired to talk. I'll see you tomorrow.' She turned away and practically ran up the stairs.

***

She went to the bedroom and waited until two maids brought in the copper bathtub.

'Can you place it near the fireplace, please?' Abbie only wanted to sink into the water and fall asleep there. The girls smiled at her and moved the tub closer to the hearth.

She needed to unwind after the long journey. Her muscles were tight from the effort of keeping pace, and more than anyone, she had longed to reach London from the moment they'd left her home. Another assault like those of the previous days, and she wasn't sure she'd survive it.

Suzie arrived shortly after, followed by the girls with steaming buckets of water. Suzie helped her undress until only her chemise remained. 'Would you like me to assist with your bath?'

'No, thank you, Suzie. I'd like a bit of time to myself. It was a long journey – and quite a crowded one, if I might say so.'

'Of course, my lady. Do not hesitate to call me if you

need anything.'

'Thank you, Suzie.' She curtsied before leaving, closing the door softly behind her.

Once she was finally alone, Abbie immersed herself in the hot water, letting its warmth soothe her aching limbs. Suzie had added a few drops of rose essence to the water, and now the gentle scent surrounded her, enveloping her senses. She rested her head on the tub's edge, allowing the water to calm her body with its sweet caress against her skin.

But the most challenging thing was trying not to think about Alexander or the woman he had closed his heart to. What could have happened to make him go to the extent of recruiting into the naval service, taking on such dangerous missions on the high seas? Had he loved her that much?

She closed her eyes, trying to ignore the unexplained pain she now felt in her chest, though she knew full well the source of that pain: none other than the man she had fallen in love with.

She must have dozed off, for she didn't notice Alexander's presence until his deep voice echoed through the room, sending a shiver down her spine.

'Ask me.' Startled, she instinctively covered her chest and looked around, finding him next to the hearth.

'What are you doing here?'

The daylight had faded entirely, giving way to the darkness of the night, leaving only the flickering glow of the flames to illuminate the room. She looked back at his face, lit by the red and yellow flames from the burning logs dancing across his features, making him look dangerously handsome.

'You want to know – so ask me. I won't lie to you.'

Abbie stared down at the water, drawing her knees up close to her body. She didn't need to ask what he meant.

Taking a deep breath, she formulated her question.

'Why did David say you would not marry after… after what?' Her voice trembled. Part of her feared what the answer was going to be, so she continued to stare at the water, creating circles with her hand, letting the warm liquid slide through her fingers. 'Was it because of a woman?'

Alexander rested his hand on the mantel shelf and remained silent so long that Abbie thought he would never answer her question. She looked up at him and watched the dim light take on the masculine features of his face. His jaw tight with tension, but releasing a breath of resignation, he finally spoke.

'Catherine,' he said, turning to face her. 'Georgina's mother.' Abbie looked at him and saw a shadow fall over his eyes. He sat on the stool by the fire and started to tell her the story, his gaze lost in the flames.

'We met as children. She lived next to my father's estate. Her mother and mine were close friends, and they often visited our home, so Catherine and I created a special bond from early on. But as is nature's way, my feelings for her changed once I was old enough to recognise and appreciate the woman she had become. She was no longer the girl I would spend my days climbing trees with or stealing biscuits from the kitchen with. No.' He shook his head, a wistful smile softening his face, 'I wanted to be with her in a different way. Her beauty captivated me as much as her tenderness – she was all joy and light. Georgina has the same glowing smile, you know? And the same rebellious spirit.'

He went quiet again, and Abbie heard herself whisper, 'What happened?' Alexander looked at her, and her heart ached at the pain in his blue eyes.

'Stephen came to stay with us one summer, and it was undeniable; the first time they laid eyes on each other, that was it; you could almost see the sparks between them. She never looked at me like she looked at him.' He ran his hand through his hair, long-carried memories resurfacing. 'I had never spoken of my feelings for her, so it would have been selfish on my part to mention it to either of them. It didn't take long for them to get engaged, and not long after the wedding, I left.'

'What happened after?'

'Colton and I were at sea for four years when we heard of Catherine's death in childbirth. I blamed Stephen for a long time – until I saw him one day, visiting her grave, and I saw his grief. Then, when I saw Georgina in his arms… nothing else mattered any more. She looked just like Catherine.' His smile reflected the pain he felt in remembering that moment.

'From that moment on, we both tried to be as we had been before, to be the friends we were. But something had broken between us; it was too difficult. We were polite, but never as close as we were when we were young.' He shook his head. 'I regret that now, I didn't give him the chance I should have. She wasn't destined to be with me. I wasn't destined to be with her.' He rose and walked to the tub, kneeling beside her.

Abbie hugged her legs tightly against her chest, unwilling to meet his eyes. He had loved Catherine with such intensity. How could she compare to a love like that?

He gently took her chin between his fingers and tilted her face to his. Like a raging sea, the intensity of his blue eyes shook her to the core. When he spoke, she knew their hearts were beating as one.

'I was destined to be with you.'

She could feel the tears forming in her eyes. Letting go of her fears, her doubts, and whatever made her doubt his feelings, she placed her hands on either side of his face and drew him to her. The kiss they shared was full of love, passion, and longing – a longing for each other and a shared need to erase the past and not look back. She wanted to make his pain vanish, to release him from the pain he suffered all those years ago. Rewrite his story and set him free.

He kissed her with the same fervour, his hand sliding down her back, caressing her soft skin and pulling her towards him.

'The water's still warm,' he murmured against her neck, trailing kisses along her neck.

'Yes,' she whispered. Taking her trembling reply as an invitation, he undressed and stepped into the tub behind her.

She shifted to make room, allowing him to slide his legs to either side of her. She leaned back against his muscular chest, basking in the warmth of his embrace and the strength of his arms. A soft hum of pleasure escaped her lips as his hands caressed her.

Though she couldn't explain it, Abbie sensed there was more weighing on his heart than Catherine's death.

'It wasn't your fault.'

Alexander looked down at her. 'What wasn't?'

'Stephen. It wasn't anyone's fault.' She turned to meet his gaze, resting her head on his shoulder. 'We always think that when someone dies, we didn't do enough to show them how we feel. That we could have done more. There is always more. Something we didn't say, something we didn't do. But the truth is – they knew.' She realised that what she was saying was also true for herself. 'He knew you would be there for him. That's why he left you his most precious treasure – his daughter. What more proof do you need of his trust?'

Alexander pulled her closer, his voice a whisper. 'Thank you.' Then, he added quietly, 'Your parents knew it too, Abbie.' He kissed her temple, and they remained there, wrapped in each other's arms, just enjoying the shared peace until the water turned cold.

Alexander climbed out and wrapped himself in a towel, then lifted her gently from the tub. She kept her arms around his neck and took the opportunity to kiss him, as he held her naked body in his arms. The sweet touch of his lips against hers made her forget the world outside – and now the only world she wanted was the one they had created together. He set her down and wrapped her in the bathrobe, which rested on the chair next to the bathtub.

As he tightened the sash around her waist, his gaze swept the room with a frown. 'All your belongings are in this room.'

'Yes, they are. Why is that relevant?' she asked, following his eyes.

'Because I want them to be in *our* room.' She slid her arms around his neck, puzzled. 'I thought we'd have separate rooms. My parents did.'

He tightened his arms around her and whispered. 'Oh, no. I want to go to bed with you every night and wake up every morning with your soft body next to mine. And if you stay here, I can't do that, can I?'

Abbie smiled. 'I suppose not.'

'Then it's settled. Tomorrow I'll ask Thomas to move your things to *our* room. Would that please you?'

She beamed. 'Very much.'

His lips lowered to claim hers in a loving kiss that made her feel like she was floating, and she rested her head on his shoulder. The flickering candles and the soothing water had lulled her into a sense of peace she hadn't known in far too long – and she wished she could stay in that state of serenity, embraced in his arms. Closing her eyes, she dreamed that it was possible.

***

The following day, they were breaking their fast with Georgina and Aunt Agatha in the dining room when her aunt began to eye her suspiciously.

'Is something amiss, aunt?'

The woman giggled. 'Oh no, darling – you just look… different.'

'Yes! I noticed that too,' Georgina exclaimed, feeling very important for having picked up on it first. 'It's like you're shining,' she added, stuffing her mouth with fruit.

Abbie's cheeks flared crimson, and Alexander couldn't help but chuckle. For which Abbie repaid him with a sharp kick to the shin beneath the table, throwing him a warning look to underline her displeasure. He groaned quietly in pain but made no effort to hide the mischievous smile that lingered on his face.

'What? She's right.' Leaning in, he added softly by her ear, 'And may I add that you look deliciously beautiful this morning?'

The colour in her cheeks deepened another shade. How could he make her burn so quickly, simply by whispering in her ear? But the truth was, the intimacy they had found had made her life a lot easier. Avoiding him for fear he might discern her feelings had become exhausting. Now, she no longer needed to hide the depth of her desire for him.

Georgina's voice interrupted her thoughts.

'Abbie, can we play afterwards? You said we would play today.' She whispered this in imitation of her uncle, ignoring the fact that everyone around the table could hear her. Abbie smiled.

'Of course, darling. I cannot wait,' she whispered

back.

The sound of a cane tapping against the marble floor announced Lady Charlotte's arrival. Dressed in an elegant green dress, she entered the dining room with her usual bright smile, bringing light into the space. Georgina jumped to her feet and ran to her grandmother.

'Grandmama!' She hugged her legs, and Charlotte affectionately patted the top of her head.

'Hello to you, too, my dear. I've missed your hugs.'

'Me too!'

Alexander rose and moved a chair for her, kissing her cheek before returning to his place at the head of the table. 'To what do we owe the pleasure, Grandma Charlotte?'

'Darling, are you suggesting I can't visit my favourite granddaughter whenever I please?' Georgina climbed into her lap.

'Of course you can! Isn't that right, Uncle Alex?' He smiled at her and then looked at the older woman.

But Abbie noticed the spark in Lady Charlotte's eyes. She hadn't merely come to see Georgina – she wanted to know what they had discovered. Alexander seemed to notice this, too.

'I would never stop you from seeing your favourite granddaughter,' he replied smoothly. The older woman smiled at them, but when she set her eyes on Abbie, she lifted an eyebrow and gifted her with an inquisitive smile. She said nothing, though her knowing expression said plenty. How could everyone notice?

After breakfast, Aunt Agatha informed them she would retire to the drawing room to work on her embroidery, kissing Abbie on the cheek before leaving. Abbie watched her go, still worried about her.

She had tried to talk with her aunt about her uncle, but the woman had refused, still gripped by fear of retribution should he ever find out she'd spoken of the horrors that had taken place behind the closed doors of their home. No matter how often Abbie reassured her she was safe now, she still flinched whenever she heard an unfamiliar male voice in the house.

Georgina came to her side, 'Can we go and play now?' But Lady Charlotte stepped in before Abbie could answer.

'Darling, would you mind if I stole Abbie for a moment? You can go and start preparing your room. Would that be all right, my sweet?'

Disappointment flickered across Georgina's face, but she recovered quickly. 'I'll take all the dolls out! You're going to love it!' she said, her excitement bubbling over. She ran from the room, her skipping steps echoing as she called for Paige to follow her up the stairs.

Lady Charlotte turned her attention to the remaining adults. 'Now – do you have any news?' she asked, resting both hands atop her cane. Abbie and Alexander exchanged a glance.

'We do. We found something that might help us. Would you like to see it?'

'But of course! What are we waiting for?' Alexander's laugh filled the room. Helping her to her feet, he guided her to the study, with Abbie following behind.

Once she had settled onto the sofa, Alexander handed her the documents. She examined them one by one, nodding as she read. 'This is more than what we had. But still…' Abbie sat beside her.

'We know it's not enough to implicate Braxton.' The woman laid a hand gently over Abbie's.

'No, darling, it's not. But it's a good start.' She turned her attention back to the documents and, holding one up, showed it to Abbie. 'Is this the deed to Redwood House?'

'Yes. Why, Lady Charlotte?'

'Grandma Charlotte, darling.

'What is it, Grandma Charlotte?' Abbie repeated, smiling.

'Thank you.' She returned her attention to the papers.

'I know this name. Miles Claybrook.' She studied the deed again, then clicked her tongue and chuckled. 'I remember now – of course. The Claybrooks. His father was a prominent merchant, and young Claybrook inherited the business and fortune after his father's death. Miles married well – the daughter of a Duke, no less. But the Duke had no money. So Miles brought the fortune, and she brought the title and connections to the London elite.' She continued. 'But after a few years, the business began to fail. His largest client was American, and when the war came, everything stopped. The man lost everything and tried to gamble it back – but with no luck. He took his own life. His wife was pregnant at the time and died during childbirth. Those poor children…'

'He had children?' Abbie asked.

'Oh, yes. A young son and a baby girl, too, although he never got to meet her. No one knows what became of them after. I see here,' she said, pointing at the deed, 'that your father gave them a house in the country. Perhaps they remained there. It was such a tragedy.' She shook her head and returned the documents.

'Your father was a thoughtful man, my dear. He never spoke a word about what he did for that family. But sometimes we can't help those who don't want to be helped.' She patted Abbie's hand with gentle affection. Abbie smiled in response. Her father had been a good man – she didn't need anyone to tell her that, for she already knew. He had been kind, generous, and always willing to help those in need, regardless of who they were.

'So, what's next?' Lady Charlotte asked Alexander.

'I'll go to Whitehall tomorrow.'

Lady Charlotte raised a brow. 'To see Mr Nepean, you mean? Not sure I like that man.' Abbie sensed an unspoken history between them, and Alexander gave a knowing nod.

'Lady Charlotte, I assure you – if he had found anything earlier, Mr Nepean would have helped us. But there was no proof of the scheme until now. I believe that with these documents, he'll have a better idea of where to look and who to ask.'

'I hope you're right, darling. Well, I'll leave it in your capable hands.' She extended her hand for Alexander to help her rise. 'I'll be upstairs with Georgina.'

'I'll join you shortly,' Abbie said, unwilling to break her promise to Georgina – but first, she had questions for Alexander.

Once Lady Charlotte had left, Abbie could no longer hold back her curiosity. 'Who is the man you were speaking of?'

'Evan Nepean. He's the Under-Secretary of State for the Home Department.'

'And how do you know him?'

'I've worked for him before.' Abbie stared at him, clearly unsatisfied with such a vague reply. Raising her brow, she silently invited him to continue.

'Derek and I brought him information during the war.'

'What exactly does this man do?'

'He's in the business of knowing everything.'

'About who?'

'About everyone that walks this earth. He has a spy network bigger than you could imagine.'

'And you're one of them?'

'Not anymore. Back then, Derek and I passed him intelligence about British ships confiscated by the Spanish and the French. We helped bring the crew back home safely.' He sat next to her and took her hand. 'If that cargo was sold – he'll be the one to find it.'

Abbie could only hope, for all their sakes, that he was right.

CHAPTER 20

Alexander couldn't recall how many times he had gone through the documents they had found inside the book. He wanted to ensure he hadn't missed any detail that might help them unmask Braxton's true intentions, but as far as he could tell, nothing else directly incriminated him.

Sitting behind his desk with his feet crossed atop the wooden surface, he was now reviewing the vessel's insurance papers and comparing them with the version drafted by Braxton's broker. The forgery was of excellent quality. If they hadn't investigated the man and discovered that no bank was backing the insurance, they might never have uncovered the scam. Nothing else appeared to be out of place.

He was beginning to suspect that the only way to obtain the necessary evidence would be to break into Braxton's offices at the port. But if they were caught, proving Braxton's involvement would become even more difficult. They needed something more to bring the bastard down.

'Have you *married*?'

At the sound of the familiar voice, Alexander lifted his head from the documents in his hand. Captain Derek Colton stood leaning against the doorframe, one brow raised, his incredulous expression giving away his surprise.

'Well, well, look what the tide has brought in.' The

captain cocked his head, still waiting for the answer to his question, which Alexander ignored, lowering his legs off the desk, he stood up to greet his cousin.

'You were starting to worry me – I hadn't heard from you in days,' Alexander said as the men embraced. The look on Derek's face made it clear that avoiding the question would not deter him from demanding an answer.

'Oh no, don't you dare try to dodge it. You've married? And to none other than Abigail Clarkson. I thought she hated you?' Alexander's lips curled into a smile.

'How did you know?'

With an innocent expression, Derek settled into one of the sofas, arms folded. 'I have contacts.'

'Georgina told you.'

Colton burst out laughing. 'First thing she did as soon as Thomas opened the door.' With Georgina in the house, secrets were impossible to keep. 'The only thing the Dawley brothers told me was that you had a surprise for me. But marriage never crossed my mind, cousin. So? What happened?'

'Things changed.' Alexander crossed to the drinks cabinet and poured two glasses of port.

'I've only been gone a couple of weeks!'

'A lot can happen in a couple of weeks, Derek.'

'I can see that. But how did you go from hate to love? That must be a fascinating tale.'

Alexander didn't turn around, but the word struck him. *Love.* Was that what this was? It had been so long since the last time that now it was difficult for him to identify the feelings that Abbie aroused in him. But he knew it wasn't mere lust. It was far more than that.

'Georgina and Abbie were kidnapped a few days after your last visit.'

Derek leaned forward, concern flashing across his features. He loved Georgina as dearly as Alexander did. 'Were they hurt?'

Shaking his head, Alexander took a sip of his drink. 'Abbie managed to hide Georgina and helped her escape into the forest. But if I hadn't arrived in time…' His blood boiled at the memory. The danger they'd both been in – and the terrible consequences of what the bastard holding Abbie had nearly done to her before Alexander had burst through that door. He shook his head, banishing the terrible thoughts from his mind. 'After that, the only way to protect her was to keep her under the same roof.'

Derek eyed him knowingly. 'I don't think it was strictly necessary to marry to protect her, cousin.' Alexander chuckled.

'That is what she said. But Alan would have come back from beyond the grave to haunt me for the rest of my days.'

'If I'm being honest, I'm a little offended I wasn't invited.'

'There wasn't time. Besides, it wasn't that kind of wedding, Derek.'

The words came out softly, an attempt to mask the depth of emotion he'd felt when he'd decided to marry her – not just from a desire to protect her, but from a need. A need to keep her close, no matter the cost. And it had turned out to be one of the best decisions he had made in his life.

'So, my friend, what kind of wedding *was* it?' Alexander was about to reply when a female voice interrupted.

'Yes, Alexander, what kind of wedding *was* it?'

Both men turned to find Abbie standing in the doorway, arms crossed, waiting for his answer. How long had she been standing there?

Her head tilted slightly, her expression unreadable – but her eyes… her eyes were smiling at him, shining like stars in the night sky.

Alexander rose and closed the distance between them. Ignoring both their comments, he placed a hand at the small of her back and kissed her cheek. Then he took her hand and led her further into the room to meet Derek.

'Cousin, allow me to introduce you to my wife – Lady Abigail Crawford. Abbie, this is my cousin, Captain Derek Colton.' Derek rose and bowed to her with exaggerated ceremony.

'At your service, Lady Crawford.'

She tilted her head. 'Thank you, Captain. It's a pleasure to meet you. I understand you've been of great help in looking into the death of my parents. For that alone, you have my deepest gratitude.'

'You are most welcome, my lady. Though there's still much to do before we bring down the bas–' Alexander coughed deliberately to stop him from saying something inappropriate, and he corrected himself. '–him,' Derek amended with a sheepish grin.

Abbie smiled. 'I don't require coddling, gentleman. You can call him for what he is, a bastard. And please, call me Abbie.'

'Only if you call me Derek.' He gave her a warm smile before turning to Alexander. 'I like her.' Alexander laughed.

'Wipe that rakish grin off your face, my friend – and stop flirting with my wife.' Derek raised his hands in a gesture of peace.

Alexander guided her to the sofa. Perhaps he was more possessive than he ought to be, but reason rarely prevailed where Abbie was concerned. 'Let's sit down, so you can tell us what you've been up to these past few weeks. Any new findings that might help us?'

Derek's devilish grin widened. 'We have one of Braxton's men.'

Alexander's eyes widened and urged him to speak. 'How?'

'When I returned to London, I began asking discreet questions around the port – nothing that might alert Braxton. Then, a week ago, I found someone who had bought furniture from a sailor in the south. I travelled to Hollington, and after visiting nearly every tavern in the area, I found a sailor spending an impressive amount on ale. The man had been drinking for hours, and it didn't take long before he started boasting about a bit of business he'd done with some of his fellow sailors. He'd sold some furniture without anyone noticing.'

'But how did they bring it back to England?'

'It never left England, Alex. *The Viola* departed London but stopped at Bulverhythe Beach, where they unloaded the goods to a band of smugglers before continuing. This sailor was tasked with transporting the cargo to a warehouse in Hollington. But greed is a powerful thing. He couldn't resist keeping a set of beautiful tables – small enough to hide, but worth a good twenty pounds.'

'So, they hid the cargo and sank the ship?' Alexander's brow furrowed, struggling to make sense of it all.

'Oh no,' Derek said, shaking his head. He leaned forward, resting his forearms on his knees. That familiar glint of mischief danced in his sea-weathered features – Alexander had seen it many times before. The lines around his eyes, deepened by years at sea, and at that moment, reflected the anticipation of the effect that the following words he was about to say would have. 'They *sold* the ship.'

His grin finally reached his eyes, and Alexander felt

the full weight of what he meant. Abbie touched his arm, drawing his attention; confusion reflected in her gaze.

'Why are you both smiling like wolves around prey?'

'Because…' Alexander said, 'they've just given us the proof we need to expose their conspiracy. A shipment is easy to hide – even if you find it, you can't prove it's stolen goods. But a ship? That's another matter entirely. Wherever it is, there'll be a trail. And with that, we'll find it.'

Abbie looked at Derek. 'And do you know who bought it?'

'Not yet. But I've got my First Officer asking questions in every tavern. It won't be long before we learn something useful.' As though a cloud had lifted, and finally, the sun was showing enough light to see hope rising through, Alexander relaxed in his seat.

'Where is this sailor now?'

'I left him with the brothers at The Devil's Tavern,' Derek replied with a chuckle. 'They know how to persuade a man to confess everything – even give up his own mother – just by looking at him. And bless this poor soul, I don't think he'll resist for long. I paid the innkeeper handsomely for a private room, far from prying ears. They'll send word the moment they get something worthwhile.'

Alexander knew the three brothers were expert interrogators, though fortunately for the sailor, their methods were usually subtle. *Usually*.

It was a skill Derek had taught them himself.

Abbie said nothing, but he could see her body tense beside him. He wanted to assure her that the sailor would not be harmed, but he couldn't make that promise. Instead, he reached out for her hand and turned to Derek.

'It's time to pay a visit to Nepean. He has a web of

spies vast enough to track any ship that sets sail from here – or anywhere in international waters. With that sailor's confession and the documents we found, it should be enough to compel him to get involved and begin an investigation.'

Derek looked puzzled. 'Which documents are you referring to?'

Alexander stood and retrieved the papers from his desk, handing them to Derek, who skimmed through them, his eyes widening with surprise. 'Where did you find these?' Before Alexander could speak, Abbie answered.

'In my father's library. They were hidden inside a book.'

'Inside a book?'

His smile showed evident admiration, clearly impressed by Alan's ingenuity. He looked between them, holding up the documents in one hand. 'This tells the whole story of what happened. Good find, Abbie,' he said, giving her a wink.

'We should go to Whitehall today. I don't want to waste a single moment.'

Derek nodded, and Alexander's heart pounded knowing once again how fortunate he was to have a cousin, a friend, willing to walk through fire for him and his family. There was no-one more loyal than Derek Colton. Abbie rose from the sofa with purpose, but before she spoke, Alexander already knew what she was going to say.

'No,' he said, answering her unspoken question.

'No? What do you mean, *no*?' Her honey-coloured eyes locked on his, fierce and unrelenting. That gaze alone nearly made him surrender to whatever she asked of him. But this time, he couldn't. And unless he gave her a compelling reason, he knew she would march into

Whitehall herself, with that same fire blazing in her eyes, determined to convince the Under-Secretary to help them.

'Abbie, please don't argue with me on this. Nepean is a reserved and deeply cautious man. If we bring someone unfamiliar into his office, he may refuse to help us altogether.'

'Not even someone as beautiful as you,' Derek interjected, attempting to ease the tension but unsuccessfully. The look Abbie shot him could have frozen a lake. Alexander almost pitied him; Derek hadn't yet learned the fire that burned inside his wife– or what she was capable of when provoked.

Alexander shook his head and stepped in to rescue Derek, who was now raising his hands in surrender, though the smirk on his face remained.

Facing her fully, Alexander took her hands in his. 'If it were up to us alone, we wouldn't hesitate to take you. But this must be handled delicately. Please, trust me when I say this is the only way.'

He could see her battling the frustration inside of her, and at last, she closed her eyes and let out a quiet sigh of surrender. 'I trust you. But come straight back. Don't leave me waiting long – or I *will* come after you.'

He leaned in and kissed her cheek, whispering close to her ear. 'I wouldn't dream of it.' He loved the way her body reacted whenever he did that, the subtle shiver that ran through her as if lightning had just grazed her soft skin. 'Thank you for trusting me,' he murmured.

'You are welcome,' she replied. And the sound of her barely audible voice sent that same lightning through his skin.

Derek coughed politely, breaking the spell between them. Alexander brushed his thumb over the palm of her hand, then turned to collect the documents from Derek

and placed them inside the hidden drawer on his desk.
'You're not taking them with you?' Abbie asked, surprised.

'One must be careful when dealing with Nepean. We'll tell him what we know first. Depending on his reaction, we'll decide whether it's safe to show him the evidence.'

'You don't trust him?' she asked, worry flickering across her features.

'I trust him… until I don't.'

They called for Thomas to bring their coats, and Abbie walked them to the door. Standing on her tiptoes, she leaned close until her mouth was just inches from his.

'Be safe,' she whispered – and kissed him.

Unlike the kisses they'd shared in the past, this one was full of a love he'd never dared to imagine could exist. And he answered her with the same tenderness, brushing her cheek with his thumb. Resting his forehead against hers, he whispered hoarsely, 'I'll be back for dinner.' He kissed the tip of her nose, then left with Derek.

***

Derek sat opposite Alexander in the spacious carriage, his legs stretched out in front of him. Even on dry land, he preferred the comfortable clothes he typically wore aboard his ship. Before leaving, Alexander had suggested that he wear something more suitable for visiting the Under-Secretary. Derek had reluctantly agreed to wear one of his frock coats, occasionally grumbling about the discomfort of the outfit. He turned from the window to address him.

'Do you think he'll help us?' he asked, his expression tinged with concern.

'I don't know. But if he doesn't, we might have to go

above his head.' Derek's brows lifted.

'You mean sending a request to the King?' He shook his head. 'If convincing Nepean is hard, I can't imagine the King's response would be any different, Alexander. That is – if he responds at all.'

'I don't need to send a message to the King – only make Nepean *think* we will, if he refuses to help us. I think that'll be enough to force his hand,' Alexander said, a glint of amusement in his eyes.

'That might work just fine,' Derek replied with a grin. Alexander hoped he was right – for he couldn't think of any other option.

The carriage pulled up at the north entrance to Whitehall Palace. The King had not used the palace as a residence for several years, and the old buildings now housed various institutions, including the Home Office – where they were headed.

The footman opened the door. Alexander glanced at Derek before stepping down. He saw in his cousin's eyes the same uncertainty that was coursing through him. They nodded to each other, and Alexander turned to climb down the short steps of the carriage.

John, who had accompanied them at Abbie's insistence, was speaking to one of the guards stationed at the doors of the vast white stone building. When he turned back to them, his expression was twisted in displeasure, and he did not hesitate to let the guard know, throwing the guard a withering look over his shoulder.

He approached Alexander and said grimly, 'We can't leave the carriage here, my lord.' Alexander laid a hand on his shoulder.

'Wait for us around the corner, John. Hopefully, we won't be too long.' Still grumbling,

John gave a curt nod. 'I will, my lord.'

Derek and Alexander approached the entrance of the

building, the great wooden door flanked by guards on either side. The hall inside was a large chamber preceding the inner offices where the clerks worked. One of them appeared through a doorway, juggling a precarious stack of papers. At the sight of the visitors, he nearly dropped them all. Managing to stabilise the bundle, he blinked in surprise.

William Devaynes, an esquire employed among the clerks, was one of many who assisted Nepean in his daily tasks. For that reason, he knew the full extent of the missions that Alexander and Derek had undertaken – and had never shown much fondness for the latter.

Alexander had never learned the cause of Devaynes' animosity toward the captain, but every time he encountered him, the man stared at Derek with eyes full of loathing.

'Good afternoon, Devaynes,' Alexander said.

'My lord! This is… unexpected. How may I be of service?' His exaggerated bow was directed solely at Alexander. The deliberate disdain he showed Derek caused his cousin to snort in amusement.

'We're here to see Mr Nepean.'

Devaynes looked confused, and Derek couldn't hold his tongue. 'You know… the Under-Secretary? Your *boss*?' Only then did Devaynes acknowledge his presence, glaring at him with venom in his eyes. Alexander had no time nor patience for the squire's games and brought the man's attention back to him.

Devaynes finally broke his stare. 'Did he know you were coming, my lord?'

'No,' Alexander replied curtly. The squire hurried to nod. He guessed his tone had been enough for the thin man to realise who he was talking to. His face paled a tone lighter, and he cleared his throat.

'I shall inform him at once, my lord.'

Once he'd gone, Alexander couldn't contain his curiosity any longer. 'What on earth did you do to the poor man?' Derek feigned innocence.

'*Me*? Why would you assume I'm the one to blame?'

'Because you're grinning like a devil and the man looks ready to explode in anger?'

'It was an honest mistake,' Derek replied with mock sincerity. Alexander narrowed his eyes, and Derek's smile widened. 'I didn't know she was his wife.'

'And I'm sure he doesn't believe you were innocent.'

'No, he doesn't.'

'I hope your rakish behaviour hasn't compromised our cause, my friend.' Derek's smile faded. With all his faults, he was loyal to the core. The thought that his actions might ruin their chance at justice clearly weighed on him.

'So do I.'

As they waited for Devaynes to return, Alexander thought of all the times he and Derek had served Nepean faithfully, providing 'particular services', as the Under-Secretary liked to call the information they provided through the years. There had never been an issue, but Alexander wasn't sure that if they had been in trouble, he would have rushed to their aid—not if their interests didn't align with his own.

Now, it was time to see if Nepean would return the favour. Until they were sure of his support in taking down Braxton, Alexander wouldn't show him the documents – they were their only leverage.

'What's your plan?' Derek interrupted, stopping the chaos of thoughts crashing about in his mind.

'I need to convince him it would be in *his* best interests to help us bring Braxton down. And also make him believe it was his idea.' Derek chuckled.

Devaynes returned several minutes later – probably

because Nepean wanted to make them wait. Another of his petty games was to remind them that, though not of their social class, he still held enough power to keep a lord waiting. 'Mr Nepean will see you now, my lord.' He said, his sombre face was stiffer if that was possible. Gesturing with his hand, he motioned for them to follow.

As they entered the office, Alexander glanced around. He had never visited Nepean at Whitehall before; they had met once, briefly, in Greenwich, but then most of their contact had been through letters. The room was sombre but well appointed. A large table in the corner was scattered with maps and letters – no doubt correspondence from his many spies across the country.

The Under-Secretary sat behind a carved wooden desk. At two and thirty, he had been appointed by the King himself permanent undersecretary, an achievement that few had reached at such a young age. His fair hair, now dusted with grey, was tied at the nape of his neck. He rose, his cold gaze assessing them.

'Lord Crawford. Captain Colton,' he said. 'To what do I owe this... *unexpected* visit?' The emphasis made it clear he disapproved of their appearance in his office without the appropriate protocol. Alexander ignored the slight and sat opposite him without waiting for permission, crossing his legs in a manner he knew would irritate the man. Nepean clenched his jaw and sat down again, glaring.

'We've found documents proving Philip Braxton was involved in the deaths of the Duke of Everleigh, Alan Clarkson, and his wife.'

Nepean raised an eyebrow, surprised. 'Well? Show me.'

'We didn't bring them here. We have come as a courtesy to you. We understand this is not a usual matter for your office, but we thought it right to inform you –

especially given our prior conversation.'

'It is not that I *refused* to help you when you came to me before, Lord Crawford,' Nepean said. 'But Mr Braxton has an impeccable reputation. I could not, in good conscience, launch an investigation without solid proof against such a prominent citizen.'

'Prominent citizen?' Derek scoffed. 'That man seeps filth from every pore.' Nepean's eyes raked over him in disdain.

'And how have you come to that conclusion?'

'We captured one of his men,' Derek replied, arms folded.

Alexander stepped in. 'He confirmed what we suspected. Braxton's second shipment was never going to leave England. They sold the ship, and the cargo was transported to Hollington and then passed on to smugglers.'

'You have proof of all this?'

'We have letters between Everleigh and Clarkson. Plus the ship's insurance paperwork, dated two days after its departure.'

'Why two days later?'

'Because Braxton had forged an insurance document for the cargo. Alan and Everleigh discovered it in time and commissioned a legitimate one.' Still seeing no change in Nepean's impassive gaze, Alexander decided it was time to force his hand.

He stood up and nodded to Nepean, who then also rose to his feet. 'Mr Nepean, time is of the essence. This man is planning something bigger. Do you really believe Braxton orchestrated all of this just for a few pieces of furniture? I certainly don't. There's something bigger at stake here. He must have some hidden agenda that we are not seeing. My niece and Alan Clarkson's daughter were kidnapped, and I was nearly killed two days ago…

They will keep going until someone stops them.' Seeing his countenance did not change, Alexander finally said.

'Thank you for your time, Under-Secretary.' Alexander turned to leave. Derek arched a brow and quickly regained his composure when he realised Alexander's intentions. He gave a curt bow to Nepean, then followed Alexander's lead. But just as they reached the threshold, Nepean called out.

'Where are you keeping this sailor?'

They turned. Alexander fought hard to control himself, making sure the smile inside didn't show on his lips that Nepean had taken the bait.

'At The Devil's Tavern,' Alexander replied. 'With three of Captain Colton's men.'

Nepean narrowed his eyes at Derek. 'I would say that's a bit unorthodox – even for you, Captain. You could've been arrested for assaulting the man.'

'It's a good thing I wasn't, then,' Derek said with a grin. His cocky response was rewarded with a glare from Nepean, but curiosity had finally bested his pride.

'I'll begin enquiries. Bring me the sailor and the documents. We'll interrogate him. Speak of this to no-one.'

They both nodded. 'Thank you.' And they left before he could change his mind.

Alexander and Derek emerged through the main entrance, forcing themselves not to show any of the joy that was rising inside.

'Careful, my friend, or you'll be taking over Nepean's role as master of manipulation.' Alexander snorted at his mockery and headed towards the carriage.

'I'll bring the documents. You pick up the sailor – we'll meet back here in a couple of hours.'

As they turned onto Northumberland Avenue, where John waited, another carriage suddenly veered into their path. Two men leapt out before it even stopped. Alexander stepped back, reaching beneath his frock coat to grab his pistol. He didn't need to look at Derek to know he was doing the same. But before either man could act, a man came from behind and struck Derek in the head, slamming his body hard against the building's stone wall.

Alexander watched his friend fall to the ground, rage rising inside him like a tide as he watched Derek's body still on the floor. He turned to confront the man behind him, grabbing him by the lapels and landing a solid punch to the face. The thug crumpled.

He was ready to strike again when a sharp pain exploded at the back of his skull. Warm blood started running through his hair and down onto his neck. His hands flew to where blood had begun to flow, wetting his hands. His vision blurred as two arms dragged him towards the carriage and pushed him unceremoniously inside.

The world was going dark around him, enveloping its cold cloak around his mind, even though he fought hard to keep his eyes open. Darkness closed in.

I need to live, he thought, before everything went black.

CHAPTER 21

Abbie, pacing around the room, kept glancing at the longcase clock that stood in the drawing room. Made of dark wood and decorated with delicate gold patterns on either side of the tall structure, she couldn't help but look every time she reached the edge of the room. The slow movement of the clock's hands echoed around her, making time pass far too slowly for her liking.

It had only been two hours since Alexander and Derek had left for Whitehall, and although she had no reason to be alarmed, a knot had formed in her stomach, as if something wasn't quite right. *I should have gone with them,* she told herself angrily. At the very least, she could have waited in the carriage. She didn't need to enter the Under-Secretary's office, but then she wouldn't be pacing, on edge, waiting for him to return.

'Why did I listen to you?!' she said under her breath, frustrated.

'Did you say something, darling?' asked her aunt, who was sitting on the sofa reading. That was practically all she had done since they'd arrived in London. She hadn't stepped outside once, and whenever anyone suggested going for a walk, she would excuse herself, claiming she was tired. But Abbie knew that wasn't the real reason she didn't want to go out. She glanced at her aunt with a sad smile, wishing she could help her overcome the fear she carried.

'Nothing, Aunt, I didn't say anything.'

'Child, if you keep pacing around the room like a caged lion, you'll wear out the carpet. Please sit down. I can't concentrate with all your incessant movement.'

Abbie nodded and sat down next to her. 'I'm sorry, Aunt. I can't help but think that I should have gone with them.' Her aunt closed the book and placed it in her lap.

'And what good would that have done, Abbie?' Abbie shook her head.

'I don't know. All I know is that until Alexander returns, I won't be able to calm down.'

She buried her face in her hands, resting her elbows on her knees. Her shoulders slumped beneath the weight of all that had happened over the past few weeks. But she couldn't let her anxiety cloud her judgement – not now, when they were so close to unmasking the man who had placed everyone she loved in danger.

She couldn't afford to lose her composure now. As if in answer to her turmoil, her aunt's hand came to rest on her arm, grounding her, drawing her out of her spiralling thoughts.

'I see that, in the end, it wasn't as terrible a union as you once thought, dear. You've grown fond of him.' It wasn't a question – it was evident to anyone who looked at her that something had shifted since their return from Redwood House.

Fondness, Abbie thought. No, what she felt for Alexander wasn't mere fondness – it was something far stronger, far more consuming. Just thinking about him made her entire body prickle fiercely, as though fire coursed through her veins, consuming her. Her heart raced just imagining those blue eyes looking at her with an intensity no-one else had ever shown her before. She knew their feelings for each other had changed drastically since they had finally given in to the passion they'd been holding back for so long – but fear kept her from giving voice to what she knew was already growing inside her.

A loud knock on the front door made her jump out of her seat. She turned to her aunt with a smile.

'Finally!' she exclaimed, picking up her skirts as she hurried from the drawing room.

Thomas seemed just as eager, striding briskly towards the entrance. But when the butler opened the door, both their faces turned pale. At first, her eyes saw John – but then the air turned as cold as a winter's night when she saw who he was carrying. Derek had one arm slung over John's shoulder, but it was John's arm around his waist that was keeping him upright.

'Captain Colton!' Thomas exclaimed, stepping to Derek's other side and wrapping his arm around the man's shoulders to help him stand, struggling to hold the nearly unconscious man up.

Derek could barely support his own weight. His head leaning forward and blood dripping down his neck, staining his white shirt crimson red. With great effort, he raised his head and met Abbie's gaze. The fire that had warmed her blood just a few minutes ago as she thought of Alexander faded just as quickly. 'Where is he?' Her voice trembled, her heart already bracing for the worst.

'Abbie…' he tried, but the words faltered, and whatever strength remained drained from him. He nearly collapsed. Abbie pushed her fears aside and clung to reason.

'Hurry. Take him to the drawing room,' she ordered.

The men dragged him inside, and Aunt Agatha sprang from her seat, her book falling forgotten to the floor. Her face was as white as snow. 'What happened?' she asked, voice shaking.

'Aunt, please go to the kitchens and ask for a basin of water and some clean cloths.' The older woman stood there frozen, eyes locked on the blood trailing from

Derek's head. 'Aunt! Please! Now!' Abbie felt terrible shouting at her, but this was no time for gentleness. She would apologise later. The older woman rose from her stupor and ran to the kitchens.

'Thomas, send for the doctor.'

'Yes, my lady,' he said, turning sharply and hurrying out.

Abbie knelt beside Derek and placed a cushion under his head. 'What happened?' she asked, looking to John.

'Lord Alexander and the captain were assaulted,' he said, a mix of rage and shame in his voice. She recognised it – she knew too well what he was feeling, the sense of responsibility for being unable to prevent the attack. She was more than familiar with those feelings herself.

'Where is Alexander?' she asked, dreading the answer.

'We were ambushed just as we left Whitehall,' Derek said weakly, attempting to sit up, but his weak body refused to obey. He sank back onto the sofa. 'Two men jumped from a carriage and blocked our path. Another attacked me from behind and knocked me down.' He paused, grimacing.

'And Alexander?' Her hands trembled as she waited for Derek to continue. 'I was barely conscious, but I saw them put him into their carriage.'

'Was he hurt?'

'I don't know. He wasn't moving.' A gasp escaped her trembling lips. 'Abbie, if they'd meant to kill him, they would have done so there. He was alive.' He squeezed her hand, the motion making him wince. 'I'm sorry.' He whispered in between the pain.

'It's not your fault, Derek,' she said softly, gripping his hand in return. Abbie went to the cabinet and poured a glass of whisky, pressing it into his hand. Then she turned to John, sensing that Derek was too weak to continue talking.

'We were just around the corner with the carriage when we spotted Lord Crawford and the captain. I saw the other carriage but thought nothing of it – until I saw him,' he said, nodding towards Derek, 'slam into the wall and fall to the ground. I ran towards them, but they were already leaving by the time I arrived. We came straight here.' He lowered his head. 'I'm sorry, my lady. I should have been there.'

Abbie shook her head. 'You could have been hurt as well, John. Don't punish yourself for something you couldn't have possibly prevented. We all know who's to blame – and it isn't you, either of you.' He nodded, though his eyes betrayed lingering guilt. She doubted he would let the feeling go until Alexander was found.

'Do you have any idea where they took him?' she continued.

John shook his head. 'I don't know. But I'll find out, my lady.'

'Yes, we will,' Derek added, trying to sit again, but as soon as he moved, he touched his head, pain reflected in his green eyes. Abbie laid a hand gently on his shoulder and gently pushed him back to the sofa.

'You need to rest now. We will find him – but we need you healed so you can help us.'

Her aunt returned, followed by Suzie, who carried a basin of water and a basket of clean, white cloths.

She left them on the floor beside Abbie, handing her the basket. She carefully turned Derek's face to the side so she could locate the wound at the back of his head. He flinched at her touch. 'You need to stay still, Derek.'

'Yes, Captain,' he murmured, attempting a smile. Abbie tried to smile back, but the knot in her stomach wouldn't allow it. Once she found the cut, she dipped a cloth into the warm water and began to clean the blood away. It didn't appear deep, but it was enough for the blood to flow steadily. She pressed the cloth against it, hoping it would hold until the doctor arrived.

'Thomas, has word been sent for the doctor?'

'Yes, my lady. I sent Billy with the carriage – he'll return soon.'

Colton grasped her hand. 'I'm deeply sorry, Abbie. I'll find him.'

'We will, Derek.' She placed a reassuring hand on his shoulder, not knowing if the words of encouragement were for him or herself. She fought with everything she had against the terrifying thought of never seeing those blue eyes she had come to love. She immediately pushed the idea out of her mind and made a silent promise: *I will find you.*

At last, Billy burst into the room with the doctor, urging him to hurry. Doctor Walshman crossed the threshold, carrying his briefcase in his hands.

'My lady! Doctor Walshman is here,' Billy called out breathless, his youthful face mirroring the concern they all felt.

'Thank you, Billy,' Abbie said. The boy gave a quick bow and left the room.

Abbie remembered that name. He had been the doctor who had treated her on the day her parents died. The doctor was in his late thirties, and his affable face and spirit contrasted with the seriousness of his profession. She stood to greet the doctor, and he nodded at her with a timid smile.

'Miss Clarkson. It is a pleasure to see you well.'

'Thank you, Doctor Walshman. I only wish it were under better circumstances.'

'Agreed, my lady. So, since this is not a social call, how can I help?'

Abbie turned to look at Derek, and when the doctor saw the captain lying on the sofa with a bloody cloth pressed to his head, he rushed to his side.

'What happened to you, now?' The physician sat on the sofa beside his patient with a knowing sigh.

'It's a pleasure to see you again, my friend.' Said Derek, settling into the sofa. 'And by the way, she's Lady Crawford now. Clever Alexander got married without telling anyone.'

'Married?' The Doctor was as surprised as everyone else and looked at her with a raised eyebrow.

'Yes. It's complicated.' Abbie glanced between the doctor and Derek. 'You two know each other?'

'I had to suture this stubborn man more times than I can count. I was the appointed doctor aboard the vessel where the captain and Lord Crawford served. His lordship has always been the more sensible of the two – but this one,' he added, gesturing at Derek as he opened his doctor's bag, 'this one had a particular talent for attracting danger in those days. Or perhaps I should say, he still does.'

The doctor began to examine the wound, brushing aside strands of golden hair now tainted with blood, eliciting a groan from Derek.

'No need to be so dramatic, William. I just slipped.' Derek muttered with a cheeky grin.

'Captain, how many times have I heard that? This isn't the first time, nor will it be the last, that you've 'just slipped'.'

Derek's smile quickly faded as the doctor began to clean the wound more thoroughly, draining the colour from his face. The cut, though no longer bleeding heavily, was deep enough to require stitches. 'Ouch!'

'Don't be so dramatic, Derek,' the doctor replied dryly, tossing his words back at him. Derek managed a faint smile despite the pain, and Abbie couldn't help but be surprised that, despite being prostrate on a couch with his head bleeding, the captain still had a mischievous sense of humour.

'Is he going to be alright, Doctor?' she asked.

'It looks like a minor concussion, and he's going to need stitches. Nothing to worry about, my lady.' He retrieved a small bottle from his bag. 'Drink this.'

Derek raised an eyebrow. 'What is it?'

'Laudanum. You're going to need it, my friend.' Derek looked at Abbie and then back to the doctor.

'No, no laudanum.'

'Don't try to impress Lady Crawford with your bravery, Derek. This is going to hurt.'

He shook his head once more. 'I can't.'

'Why not?' the doctor asked, glancing from Derek to Abbie. 'What's going on?'

Derek looked back at her and then said simply, 'Alexander has been taken, William. I can't take laudanum – I need a clear head to find him.' The concern on the doctor's face reflected his regard for her husband.

'What happened?'

'It's a long story.'

'I think we'll have time,' he said, turning to Thomas. 'Could you bring us some whisky? He'll need it for what I'm about to do.' He started preparing his equipment. 'Let's hear it, then.'

Derek accepted a glass of whisky, then began recounting the events of the last few months.

When the pain became too much, Abbie took over, describing the nightmare that had consumed their lives. She told him about her parents, the repeated attacks, and now Alexander's kidnapping. She sank onto the sofa and buried her face in her hands, the weight of everything finally pressing down.

A gentle hand rested on her shoulder. Lifting her head, she saw her aunt's worried expression. 'Oh, child.

I didn't know. I'm so sorry.' Tears welled in her brown eyes – those same warm, loving eyes Abbie had always associated with her mother. She took her aunt's wrinkled hand with her own and squeezed it gently.

'You have nothing to apologise for, Aunt. I didn't mean to burden you with my problems, not when you have your own to deal with.'

She grabbed her chin and made her look at her, and Abbie saw a strength that she hadn't seen in a very long time. It was the look of a lioness protecting her cub.

'My husband tried to marry you to the man who hurt your parents. A man who may well have murdered them, from what you're saying. He knew Braxton wasn't a good man, and yet he still tried to hand you over to him.' Her voice quivered with fury as the truth set in – that her own husband might have had a hand in her beloved sister's murder. 'There's nothing else to deal with. I know you were worried I might go back to him. You don't have to worry any longer.'

The steel in her voice gave Abbie hope. She felt relieved, for she could see her aunt was finally free. The invisible string that had bound her to a man who had never deserved her had snapped. The shame, fear, and guilt had begun to fade, and Abbie could see how the darkness that had clung to her for all those years had vanished, leaving behind a woman who had reclaimed her dignity—someone with the courage to claim what was rightfully hers.

Her freedom.

She squeezed her aunt's hand. 'I am glad to hear you say that, Aunt.'

'That should do it,' said Dr Walshman. Both women turned their attention to the men.

When Derek tried to sit up, the doctor placed a firm hand on his shoulder and pushed him back onto the sofa.

'Oh no. If you start moving now, the stitches will come out, and I'll have to do it all over again.' Seeing Derek's defiance, Abbie decided to intervene.

'Please, Derek. Listen to the doctor.' Reluctantly, he stopped resisting and allowed William to bandage his head.

Once finished, the doctor began packing away his instruments. 'Any idea where they might have taken him?' As he finished the sentence, a knock came at the door – and Billy appeared, young Nicholas at his side.

Abbie stood. 'Any news, Bil–' She stopped short as she saw Nicholas' face and the swelling around his eye. She rushed to him. 'What happened to you?'

She knelt before him, inspecting the growing bruise with gentle fingers. 'I was downstairs in the kitchens when a man knocked at the servant's entrance, my lady. I told him he should go, that you were busy. But he pushed the door open, and it hit me in the eye. I tried to stop him, but he threw me to the ground and said that if I cared about my master's life, I should give you this note.'

The boy held out a sealed letter, and Abbie didn't hesitate. She snatched it from his hand and broke the seal.

Bring the documents, and you will see your husband alive.
Midnight at Allhallows Stairs.
Come alone.
PB

As she read the message, Abbie's heart began to pound uncontrollably. It took her several deep breaths to calm herself before she looked back at the boy.

'Do you know the man who gave this to you?' He shook his head.

'I don't know, Lady Abbie.' The boy twisted his beret

in his hands, clearly on the verge of tears.

'It's alright, Nicholas,' she said gently, resting a hand on his small shoulder. 'Can you describe the man?'

'He was tall and very big, my lady. A giant! And he had a scar on his face. Here.' He traced a line across his left cheek with his fingers, and Abbie knew instantly who it was. She would never forget the horrid brute who had almost killed her the night her parents died.

She looked over at Derek, who extended his hand. Abbie gave him the slip of paper, and as he read it, his expression hardened. She straightened her back with fresh resolve, and he shook his head as though he already knew what she was thinking. 'No.'

'Do you have a better idea?'

'Alexander will kill me.'

'He's going to die if we don't do what they say, Derek!' There was nothing he could say to dissuade her from going after Alexander. She would do anything to bring him back. Anything.

He looked back at the note again, then at the clock. 'Abbie, the tide will be going out at that time.'

'So?'

'Allhallows Stairs lead to the Thames. That means that they'll be taking you east. If they're not telling you where Alexander is, the only reason to meet you there is to get you onto a barge and take you down the river. That way, no-one could follow without being seen. Damn it, Abbie, it's too dangerous!'

'I won't let him die!'

'If I don't know where they're taking you, I can't protect you!'

Their heated exchange was interrupted by Aunt Agatha's trembling voice. 'Harper has a warehouse in Wapping.' They both turned to look at her. She was staring at the letter, her hands shaking. 'He's there,' she said.

'How do you know, Aunt?' Her aunt passed her the note. 'There's a mark in the top corner.' Abbie inspected it more closely and saw a faint black stain. She looked up at her aunt, confused.

'I went to the new warehouse with your uncle about a month ago. He was in one of his rage moods that day – he shoved the table and spilt ink everywhere. I tried to clean it up, but the ink soaked through a stack of clean paper, staining the corners.' The room fell silent.

To prevent her aunt from reliving more painful memories, Abbie asked softly, 'When did he buy the warehouse?'

'January, I think? He said an investor gave him the money.'

'Where?' Abbie managed to control the quickness of her tone, a flicker of hope growing inside of her.

'It was near the eastern side of the docks. By Wapping Pier.'

'I know where that is,' said Derek.

'Could he be there?' Abbie asked, turning to face the captain.

'Braxton has his offices at the Exchange. Taking Alexander somewhere with no direct link to him would prevent any association with his crimes. Your uncle is the perfect front for that.' He tried to sit up, and both Doctor Walsham and Abbie urged him to stop, but he waved them off and leaned back against the cushions. 'You cannot go alone, Abbie.'

She hated to admit it, but he was right. Going alone without a plan would be reckless. 'We have to try, Derek.'

'What if they're not taking you there? What if Alexander isn't there? You absolutely cannot go alone. I'll go with you.'

'They were very clear in their instructions, Derek. I

have to go alone. And you said it yourself – no-one can follow me without being seen.' She started pacing in front of him.

'I'll go with John and the brothers and wait nearby.'

'You're not well enough, Derek.'

'Your husband will have my head on a spike for this, Abbie. I can see that there's no convincing you not to go, but know this – there's no point in you trying to convince me either.' His fierce determination to protect her warmed her heart. She couldn't take that from him. At last, she gave him a slight nod.

Abbie saw the glint of satisfaction in his eyes – the look of a captain falling back into command. 'You cannot give them the documents. If you do, you'll have nothing left to bargain with.'

'Thomas will come with me to the crossing,' she said, turning to the butler, who proudly accepted the responsibility. 'He'll stay hidden with the documents. If Alexander isn't with them, I'll tell them I won't hand anything over until I've seen him.'

'You'll need someone else to wait on the stairs to keep watch unseen and give Thomas the signal when he sees you are both safe.'

Nicholas stepped forward. 'I'll do it, Lady Abbie.' She reached out and gently ruffled his hair.

'It's too dangerous, Nicholas.' The boy stood tall, his chin raised in resolve.

'I'm not afraid. They won't find me, milady. I am good at hiding.'

'I know you're, but–'

'Abbie, the boy is right,' Derek cut in.

She didn't want to risk another innocent life – least of all a boy who had already endured so much – but there was logic to what they were saying. If they believed Nicholas was the one bringing the documents, they wouldn't hurt him.

She closed her eyes and let out a slow breath, then looked at the boy. 'You're a brave boy, Nicholas.' Looking around the room, she saw the worry on every face – but more than that, the determination to do whatever was necessary to bring Alexander home. She smiled at them all, deeply grateful to be surrounded by such loyalty.

'We have time.' They had four hours to prepare for whatever awaited them in that warehouse. 'Thomas, could you bring something to eat?'

'Of course, my lady.'

She turned to Suzie. 'Come, I need to change.' Abbie felt all eyes on her as she left the room. She climbed the stairs, each step weighed down by fear and purpose. Her room was already fading into darkness when they entered. Suzie lit the candles, then opened the wardrobe and turned to her.

'The blue dress, please, Suzie.' The maid retrieved the dark blue gown and laid it across the bed – the same bed where, that very morning, she had awakened beside Alexander's warm body. She wanted that moment again. She wanted it every morning, for the rest of her life. She needed him back.

Suzie touched her shoulder, silently showing her understanding. 'Come, my lady. Let's get you ready.' *Ready*. The word sank deep in her heart. She had to be ready for whatever this evening would bring.

Once dressed, Abbie opened a drawer in her dressing table and withdrew her knife. She held it in her hand for a moment, feeling its weight. She would do anything to save the man she loved. Sliding the blade into her secret pocket, she looked at Suzie.

'I'm ready.'

CHAPTER 22

Abbie looked at the faces of the two figures sitting across from her in the carriage, illuminated only by the dim glow of the few streetlamps that lined the streets of London. Young Nicholas wore a serious expression, his hands nervously fiddling with the lapel of his jacket. The boy was visibly anxious, but despite the fear he projected, he sat upright, embodying the courage that filled his small frame.

She felt a surge of gratitude for having found such a loyal boy, willing to stand by her in such strange and dangerous circumstances. She only hoped she had made the right decision – that no-one would suffer as a result of their actions, and that she wasn't, in trying to solve one problem, creating a far bigger one.

Thomas, on the other hand, appeared perfectly composed. He laid a comforting hand on the boy's shoulder. 'You're a brave boy. I applaud your courage, Nicholas.'

Nicolas' eyes flickered with appreciation for the older man he had grown to admire. From the day Abbie had brought him into their home, the butler had ensured that the boy lacked for nothing – especially the affection he had so desperately needed.

She addressed them both, doing her best not to let her nerves show. 'Remember: when we arrive, I'll go to meet them alone. Thomas, you'll stay in the carriage and come back in half an hour. I don't know if they have any more men nearby, so don't stop until you're well away. And above all, don't let them catch you. Nicholas, you'll hide at the beginning of Allhallows Lane, and if anything happens, run straight to the house and ask for help.' They both nodded.

The remainder of the journey passed in silence. Each passenger was lost in their own thoughts – but Abbie's were fixed on one person alone: Alexander. She had to find him, no matter what.

As they neared Allhallows Stairs, Abbie knocked twice on the roof of the carriage to signal the driver. She heard Billy jump down from his seat and open the door for her. She looked at Thomas and Nicholas one last time, noting how Thomas's features twisted in worry.

Abbie felt the weight of the responsibility she was placing on the man's shoulders, but she saw no other way to bring Alexander back.

'Thomas,' Abbie handed over the insurance documents they had found. 'don't return for at least half an hour.'

'Yes, my lady. Please take care of yourself,' he added, surprising her by taking her hands in his. Abbie squeezed them gently to reassure him.

'I will. And I'll bring Alexander back with me. I promise.' She prayed those words would prove true.

Billy helped her out of the carriage, followed by Nicholas, and she could feel his gaze fixed on them as they walked away, disappearing around the corner that led to the Allhallows Stairs.

Leaving Nicholas hidden behind some bins, she headed towards the river.

At the far end, two figures waited, their outlines still against the murky glow of the Thames. A lantern in one man's hand threw a small, steady light, glinting on the wet stone and catching briefly on the shifting water below.

Her fears were confirmed when she recognised the scar on the man's face watching her approach. A crooked smile twisted the corner of his mouth as he said, 'We meet again.' His voice dragged her back to that dreadful night. It was the same menacing tone she'd heard all those weeks ago. Jack, she remembered.

The lantern's light also illuminated his grotesque features – the same ones that had haunted her many nightmares. The old scar on his right cheek now had a twin above his left eye, the cut not yet fully healed. A dark flicker of satisfaction passed through her – at least she had left him a scar for the rest of his life.

She realised she'd stopped walking, standing frozen at the top of the alley. Her body was refusing to get any closer to that man. But when she saw his smile widen – recognising the fear that she was trying to contain – it gave her the strength to take another step forward with all the confidence she could gather. She would not let him have the satisfaction of seeing her cower before him. Steeling her body, she lifted her chin and met his gaze without flinching.

When she was only a few steps away, his eyes swept over her from top to bottom and then glanced behind her.

'Have ye come alone, poppet? She nodded.

'Yes, I have. Where's my husband?' He stepped closer. Abbie stood firm, staring at the giant, lifting her chin even higher.

He laughed. 'Your husband's not here.' He lifted a hand to touch her, and she slapped it away.

'Don't you dare touch me, or you shall regret it,' she hissed, glaring at him with fire in her eyes. His laughter stopped abruptly, and he looked her up and down with a dark scowl.

'You're in no position to give orders.'

Without wavering, she hissed with every piece of rage contained inside her. 'It's not an order – it's a promise.'

She had no idea where that strength in her voice came from, for inside she was trembling, but she held his gaze, defiant. A voice rang out from behind him.

'Enough, Jack!' Jack turned, and the lantern's glow shifted to reveal the pale, sharp features of another man. 'If you want to see your husband, Lady Crawford,' the newcomer said, 'give us what our boss seeks.'

He was thin and wiry, with his black hair tied back in a ponytail. His clothing was not as ragged and dirty as Jack's, but still bore the marks of a man who lived on modest means. His tone was commanding – he was clearly the one who was in charge that night. But Abbie didn't flinch.

'Not until I see my husband,' she replied, her voice unwavering.

Jack clicked his tongue and shook his head from side to side. 'Tsk-tsk-tsk,' the sound hissing from his teeth like a viperous snake. 'It doesn't work like that, poppet.' Abbie turned to face him.

'Do you really think I'd hand over the documents without seeing my husband first?' Jack paused and looked back at the thin man. 'As soon as I see my husband,' she continued, 'I'll bring you the documents. Not a moment before.'

The black-haired man frowned. 'Your husband isn't here, Lady Crawford. But I'm curious – how do you plan on bringing the documents? Are you certain you're not carrying them with you?' The man gave Jack a knowing look, who grinned and took a step towards her with his hands out, clearly intending to search her – even beneath her dress. Abbie raised a hand, stepping back.

'Don't even think about it,' she warned. 'I've already told you that I don't have them with me. When I see that my husband is alive, someone will bring them. But unless they see both of us unharmed, they will not come.'

Jack's grin returned, revealing a row of rotten teeth. 'Or I can force you to tell me until you start talking. I can be very persuasive.' Abbie's eyes spat fire.

'Then you'll be wasting your time. I've given strict orders not to come unless they see us both.' She paused. 'Alive.'

The word hung between them – an unmistakable warning that killing either of them would achieve nothing.

Jack stared at her, as if weighing up his options. His rotten toothed grin that followed made her stomach churn. It revealed the violent thoughts of a man utterly without a soul.

Finally, the other man made his decision. 'So you want to see your husband, Lady Crawford? No problem, our boss would like to see you too. We'll take you to him, won't we, Jack?'

'Of course, Gus.' And grabbing her elbow, he forced her down the stairs. 'This way.' Abbie yanked her arm away, feeling his vile touch burn her skin like hot irons.

'Don't touch me, you ignorant fool.'

The insult made him bristle. He grabbed her again, dragging her closer until their faces were nearly touching. 'I could do more than that if ye don't get in the boat right now. If it were up to me, I'd have taught ye a lesson long ago. But unfortunately, I've been ordered not to touch ye… For now.' His last words were spoken inches from her face, and the fetid stench radiating from his entire body made her turn her head in disgust.

'That's enough, Jack,' Gus snapped. 'Get her on the boat. We don't want to keep the lady waiting – she'll be eager to see her dear husband.'

Jack tightened his grip on Abbie's elbow and shoved

her down the final steps that led to the river. The tide had gone out, leaving behind a shoreline of sand, pebbles, and other unidentifiable debris that glinted under the moonlight. They helped her into the small boat, and after pushing the raft off into the river, Jack leapt aboard with surprising agility, causing the little boat to rock sharply. Abbie clutched the bench to steady herself and stared at the two men. Jack, with his back to her, began to row, while the thin man named Gus sat opposite her, the lantern resting at his feet, staring at her with fixation. Its dim glow lit his angular face, casting shadows that made him look like a living skull.

The Thames, at that hour, was a dark ribbon of treacherous waters. As Derek had predicted, the tide was going out, carrying the barge swiftly down the river. Jack rowed in front of her, hardly making any effort as the current helped them navigate with speed. If her aunt had been correct, they would soon arrive at the warehouse complex in Wapping. Or so Abbie prayed with all her might.

No words were exchanged among the boat's occupants, for which she was grateful. The less they spoke, the less chance there was of betraying the fact that she had some inkling of where they were headed – or somehow reveal that Derek and his companions might already be in wait, ready to rescue them.

They passed beneath London Bridge, and Gus began to steer towards the north bank. As they neared the shadowed docks and imposing warehouses, Abbie found herself praying silently. She had never been to that part of London before, and in the dark, she probably wouldn't have recognised it even if she had. She looked over her shoulder as they approached a small wooden pier.

'Do you know what they used to call this place, poppet?' Jack asked, his voice thick with malice.

'Execution dock. Maybe we'll come back later so you can get a better look.' Gus chuckled at his remark, but instead of feeling fear, Abbie felt a flicker of hope. They were indeed heading for her uncle's warehouse in Wapping.

The sand brought them to a sudden halt, and Jack climbed out. 'My lady,' he sneered, and with an exaggerated politeness, he lifted her by the waist and practically threw her onto the muddy bank. She landed without grace, boots sinking into the mire. She scowled at him – it was evident he had done it on purpose. A few more inches, and he could have placed her on solid ground. She struggled to free herself from the muck, thankful she'd chosen her sturdy boots instead of the delicate slippers, or she might have lost them entirely. When she finally reached firmer ground and felt pebbles beneath her feet, she made her way cautiously towards the stairs, feigning reluctance so they wouldn't suspect she was precisely where she wanted to be.

She hoped that she had delayed them long enough for Derek to reach the Dawley brothers and organise Alexander's rescue.

Jack seized her arm again, squeezing so hard she was sure he'd leave a bruise on her skin. She longed to strike that smug grin from his face. The weight of the knife hidden against her thigh gave her a small, fierce comfort. Grateful neither of them had thought to check whether she was armed.

Gus secured the boat to one of the dock's posts and followed them up the steep steps. The brick buildings were shrouded in darkness and could barely be made out in the dim light that illuminated the streets. Once at the top, Jack forced her to turn right onto the cobbled street. It was deserted, save for a couple of drunken sailors who slowly walked towards them, struggling to keep up straight. One glance at Jack, and he quickly reconsidered, pulling his friend to the far side of the street, as far away from him as possible.

They hadn't walked more than a few yards when he forced her down a narrow alley. He pressed a hand into her back and pushed her forward, making her stumble.

She recovered quickly and kept walking until he grabbed her shoulder, stopping her in front of a red door. Before pushing her inside, Jack leaned in, his breath hot against her ear.

'As soon as the boss is done with you, it'll be my turn, bitch. I've been dreaming about what I'm going to do to you ever since that night.'

Abbie didn't flinch. She refused to let him see her fear; the thought of being in his hands made her stomach churn. But it wasn't only fear – it was fury, pain, and rage that boiled within her, making it difficult to contain them.

She raised her chin and said, 'If you touch me, I assure you that I won't hesitate to leave a mark on the other side of that wretched face of yours' He squeezed her shoulder painfully hard, forcing her to hold her breath.

'Soon, bitch. You'll pay soon.' And opening the door, he dragged her into the building.

The interior was dim and reeked of damp, old wood and rancid decay, making her wrinkle her nose in disgust. She squinted through the gloom and realised they were in a warehouse. The side doors must have once allowed for the delivery of goods.

The vast space was strewn with sacks scattered all over the floor and stacked wooden crates, towering higher than a man's length. Dirt piled in the corners, and she was sure she heard rats scurrying back and forth across the large warehouse.

A single light illuminated the way to the back, revealing a staircase leading to the upper floor. She scanned the shadows, trying to find any sign of Alexander between the filthy boxes.

Jack's hand pressed into her back again, urging her to move forward. Just as they reached the stairs, he leaned in once more.

'Looking for your husband, are ye? He's not here. But don't worry – he's close by. Though I should warn ye… your hubby isn't as handsome as he was when he first arrived.' His laughter echoed through, chilling her blood.

Abbie spun around and shoved him. 'What have you done to him, you damned bastard?' A storm of panic overtook her, like a blizzard that froze her from the depths of her heart. He brushed her hands away like she was nothing and grabbed her by the throat, his face inches from hers.

'Just gave him what he deserved for putting a hole in my arm. But I don't know if he'll be as lucky as I was… last time I saw him he–'

'That's enough, Jack.'

He glared at her one last time, then, releasing her from his brutish grip, he nodded towards the stairs and pushed her forward.

The upstairs level was nothing but an empty space with a single line of light at the end of the room. But looking closer, Abbie realised it was a door, slightly ajar. Like moths to a flame, the three of them made their way towards it.

Jack gave her another rough push, sending her crashing into the door. She stumbled inside and grabbed the edge of a table to steady herself. When she looked back, Jack's eyes were no longer on her – they were fixed on someone behind her. 'Here she is, Mr Claybrook.'

Abbie's eyes widened. That name – the one that had raised so many questions when they had found it on the deed to Redwood House. She turned, and the face she saw was all too familiar: Philip Braxton. He looked her up and down as he sat behind a large desk that dominated the room, the arrogance in his cold gaze sending another chill through her body.

Abbie looked him in the eyes with the greatest confidence she could muster.

'My dear Lady Crawford. What a pleasure to see you again.'

'The pleasure is not mutual,' she said coolly, resisting the urge to draw the knife from its hiding place.

Braxton stood up from his chair and strolled around the desk to face her, folding his arms with infuriating calm. 'My dear, a young lady ought not to be so rude.'

Ignoring his comment, Abbie asked him. 'Why did he call you Mr Claybrook?'

'Oh dear, he wasn't addressing me.' Abbie blinked in confusion.

'Jack was speaking to me.' The voice came from the shadows at the back of the room, where a corner was surrounded by darkness. A figure moved forward, emerging into the lamplight. With his plump body, August Williams stepped out with a confidence she had never seen in him before. Gone was the stammering wreck who had once visited her home. Abbie thought she had imagined Williams speaking without a stutter all those weeks ago, and when he opened his mouth again, she confirmed that it hadn't been in her imagination.

She looked from one man to the other in confusion, and Williams approached Abbie and said with a rage she had never seen in anyone else in her life.

'I am August Claybrook. The true owner of Redwood House – the house your father stole from mine.'

***

Alexander felt the cold cobblestones against his

cheek, the chill oddly soothing against his bruised face. He lifted a hand to touch his eye, but the clink of metal reminded him sharply of where he was. He looked at his wrists to see the iron shackles tight around his raw, scratched skin. He was unsure whether the damage was due to his own attempts to escape or from his captors hauling him up to make it easier for them to torture him.

He pushed himself upright and leaned his back against the wall. A single candle flickered beside a guard who was settled into a deep slumber, grunting occasionally as he slept. The other man had left only a few minutes before, but not without casting him a look of disgust as he went. That one had been the first to strike him upon arrival.

Fragments of memories returned to him. He concentrated on gathering all the pieces, and slowly everything became clear:

They had dragged him from the carriage with a sack over his head and hauled him to a warehouse. He couldn't say where they were, but he would have sworn he'd heard the sound of a river nearby. They brought him inside a building and shoved him to his knees before tearing the sack from his head. He blinked, adjusting his vision to the poor light illuminating the space.

Slowly, as the blur cleared, his gaze focused on the figure standing before him. Fury flooded him. With a roar, he lunged forward with his hands raised, determined to hit the smirking man. Philip Braxton had stepped back, but before Alexander could reach him, a fist slammed into his stomach, knocking the breath from his lungs. He crumpled, gasping, the pain burning deep from the inside. When he finally managed to draw breath again, he glared up at Braxton.

'You'll pay for this, Braxton.'

'Lord Crawford, you are in no position to make threats.' Braxton signalled to the second man who stood behind him. 'Rick, chain him.'

The man obeyed at once. The cold metal encircled his wrists, and a length of chain rattled as it was drawn taut above him. Then, the other brute yanked it upwards from somewhere behind him, dragging his arms overhead and forcing him to his feet, his toes barely brushing the ground. Once the chain was secured, the larger of the two men came to stand before him.

His face was vaguely familiar – one scar running across an eye, and a fresher wound above his brow. His memory stirred, and a slow smile formed on Alexander's lips. This was the man who attacked Abbie – and the one she had marked in return.

'What's so funny?' he growled. He didn't wait for a reply. His fist cracked across Alexander's jaw; he felt the iron taste in his mouth as the blood started pouring from his lip. Jack grabbed a fistful of his hair, pulling his head back. 'I'll wipe that smile off yer face by the time I'm done with ye.' Alexander spat a mouthful of blood at his feet, then looked him square in the eye and smiled again.

Jack raised his fist once more, but Braxton barked, 'Enough!' Alexander saw the struggle in the his eyes, but he relented, stepping aside to allow Braxton to approach.

'Lord Crawford,' Braxton said calmly, 'I think it's time we ended this nonsense. Don't you agree?' The casual tone, so indifferent when referring to the atrocities he had committed, made Alexander's blood boil.

'And to which nonsense are you referring?' he bit out. 'If you mean the killing you've ordered to cover the crimes you have committed, then I hardly think the word 'nonsense' is the appropriate term for it.'

Braxton's mouth twisted. 'All this could have been resolved without bloodshed, Lord Crawford. But you and your companions have consistently refused us a simple document. I can only blame their stubbornness for what befell them.' He paused to look at him from top to bottom. 'So, the question is – will you be as obstinate, or will you have more sense and help me bring those documents into my possession?'

Alexander's voice was hoarse but defiant. 'I'm a bit tied up at the moment. And as your men had already discovered, I don't have them with me.'

'Yes, that was rather disappointing,' Braxton said, glancing at Jack and Rick and shaking his head. 'But not to worry. This time, we'll make sure we get them. You see, I believe there's a woman who wouldn't hesitate to do anything for the man she loves.'

'Don't you dare touch her!' Alexander surged forward, the chains pulling taut, biting into his wrists.

Braxton arched a brow. 'Ah, so the sentiment is mutual.' He smiled malevolently. 'How delightful. I must admit I was rather put out when you took what was rightfully mine. And for that, Lord Crawford, I shall allow our friend Jack to take his revenge. After all, you did nearly kill him.' He turned away with a dismissive wave. Jack didn't hesitate a second before his heavy fist landed squarely into Alexander's stomach.

Braxton walked away, saying over his shoulder. 'Do what you please – as long as you don't kill him.' He paused. 'I want her to see him first.'

'With pleasure, sir.'

Again, a steely fist impacted into Alexander's stomach, his breath leaving him just as instantly. The next punch, this time to the left side of his head, impacted against his eye. He dropped into a semi-conscious state where his thoughts wandered, focusing only on Abbie and the fear of what they might do to her. A final blow reduced his sight to a narrow slit. Fog crept through his mind. His knees buckled, and he hung by the chains, unable to support his weight. Everything after that was a haze.

'Jack, if ye keep going, yer gonna kill him.' It was Rick's voice who said it in a weary tone, not too worried about what the bastard was doing to him. Jack must have seen the truth of it, for he finally relented. The tension in the chains released, and Alexander dropped heavily to the floor. He could feel the warm stickiness of blood pooling around him as his palms hit the ground.

Together, they dragged him into a dark room and let him fall with a crash as soon as they released their grip. Alexander groaned and used the wall to steady himself, shaking his head to expel the blur that now filled his vision.

'I will kill you,' he croaked.

But Jack's laugh lingered long after he disappeared through the rotten door that separated him from his freedom. Rick secured the chain once more and then slouched into the corner of the cell, watching him with disdain. Alexander struggled against the restraints, the iron claws digging into his wrist, rubbing against his sore, wounded skin.

'You'll only make it worse if ye keep trying,' Rick muttered. That lack of emotion in his tone gave Alexander little hope he might appeal to his humanity – but perhaps money would convince him...he needed to try.

'I will pay you handsomely if you release me.' Rick paused, picking at his teeth. He seemed to consider it for a moment, but then shook his head and didn't bother to reply, crossing his legs in front of him and closing his eyes.

Alexander's strength gave out. He collapsed onto the cold stone floor of his cell, consciousness slipping away.

And that was all he remembered.

Now, with a new guard soundly asleep in his stool,

snoring like he was in the most comfortable bed, Alexander finally had the clarity to start thinking about how to escape. He needed to get out of there.

He looked around, scanning for something sharp to break the lock, but there was nothing useful – just a few sacks that looked like they contained grain. The keys hung from the guard's belt, but he knew the chains holding him to the wall were too short to be able to reach him. But if he was able to trick him into coming closer, he might at least have a chance to steal the keys by using the chains as a weapon.

He was thinking through the possibilities when a shadow passed beneath the door. His heart clenched. Could it be Jack again? He rose shakily, preparing himself to fight if need be.

But the door didn't open. A sharp rap on the door roused the guard, who jolted upright.

'Who's there?' he barked.

But no reply came from the other side. He approached the door cautiously, and as he was going to open, it slammed with force against his face, breaking his nose at the impact.

Alexander had never been so glad to see his cousin. Derek darted inside, clamping a hand around the guard's throat to stifle his cry. He tightened his grip harder and harder until the man sagged, unconscious, and then lowered him gently to the ground. He looked at Alexander.

'Did you miss me?' he asked with a grin. Aside from the fact that Derek's white shirt was now streaked with dried blood and that he had a bandage around his head, Derek looked remarkably intact. Alexander felt a rush of relief.

'Never been happier.'

He tried to step forward, but his legs buckled. Derek

caught him and eased him back down. 'What the devil happened to you?' Derek muttered, alarmed. Seeing Derek's worried gaze, Alexander could only imagine how he must look. Probably as bad as he felt. But, he only had one thing on his mind.

'Where's Abbie?' Derek avoided his gaze and busied himself, looking around the room. 'The keys are on his belt.' He rolled the man over and fished them free, talking as he worked.

'Let me tell you something about your wife: she's just as stubborn as you are, my friend. Brilliant too! So determined, and incredibly resourceful!' He slid a key into the first lock.

'Where is she, Derek?' Alexander rasped. Derek still didn't look at him. 'Derek!'

The captain sighed and finally met his eyes. 'She's on the other side of this warehouse.'

'You brought her here?' Finally free, Alexander grabbed his arm, fear and fury mingling.

'I didn't exactly *bring* her, Alex,' Derek said, raising an eyebrow. 'She was quite adamant about coming to your rescue. She came up with the whole plan herself – she went to distract Braxton while–'

'You let her go alone?!' Alexander now gripped his jacket and faced him, trying to keep his voice low, though he burned with the urge to shout. He wanted to throttle Derek for risking Abbie's life like that, but Derek didn't flinch. He simply placed a hand on his shoulder, wincing slightly.

'Let her? I'm lucky she let *me* come. Do you really think I could have persuaded her? Honestly, I think she would have drugged me just to keep me out of her way.'

Alexander released him, recognising the truth in his words. Once Abbie had set her mind on something, there was no stopping her. And the fact that she was risking her own life for him filled him with equal parts pride and dread. With determination, he braced himself against the wall and rose to his feet, breath coming short from the effort. Derek moved to help him.

'Careful now.'

'I'm fine,' Alexander said, steadying himself with a hand on Derek's shoulder. 'Just a bit bruised, that's all.' Derek grabbed his waist to help support him all the way to his feet.

'I would believe you,' Derek muttered, 'if I could see your left eye.'

'Never mind that. Tell me what happened, Derek.'

'The short version? After they took you and kindly left me for dead, John found me and got me back to your house. Later, we received a message from Braxton – documents in exchange for your life. They wanted Abbie to deliver them. Alone.' He paused. 'The choice wasn't hard to make for either of us.'

'Did you follow her here?'

'No. They brought her by river – so we weren't able to track them. But thankfully, Aunt Agatha knew about this warehouse. We came first to find you, but we waited until she arrived before I came in.'

'Where is she now?'

'She went inside with two men.'

'And where are the documents?' asked Alexander.

'She wouldn't give them over without seeing you first.' Alexander smiled. 'At any moment, they'll come to fetch you. We need to move fast.'

Derek opened the door, checking that the hallway was empty. Supporting him carefully, they slipped out of the room. Using the crates and boxes scattered across the storage room for cover, they moved swiftly towards the back exit, avoiding detection.

The fresh night air filled Alexander's lungs, sobering

his foggy mind. Outside, John and two of the Dawley brothers – Peter and David – were waiting in the shadows. John kept watch through a grime-smeared window, while the brothers flanked either side of the door.

'Sir, nice to see you alive,' said Peter. Alexander gave a low chuckle and shook his head from side to side.

'Thanks, Peter.'

'Barely, I'd say. That eye looks nasty,' David added, earning a slap from his brother. 'What? It does!'

'You can keep teasing the poor man once we're all back at the house with a glass of port,' Derek muttered, setting Alexander gently against the brick wall.

He turned to John. 'Did you see where they took her?'

'Yes, Captain. They all went upstairs – on the opposite side of the warehouse. There are boxes and sacks everywhere. We can slip in through the back and use them as cover.'

'Good. Lead the way, John.' He looked back at Alexander. 'Can you stand on your own?'

'I've been worse.'

'That's not what I asked.'

'My wife is in there risking her life to save me. I can stand just fine.'

'Hey, calm down, man. I was only asking.' Derek handed him a pistol. Alexander wrapped his hand around it, grip tightening, ready for whatever they found behind those doors.

As John had said, the space inside was cluttered with boxes and sacks, providing plenty of places to hide. As Alexander rested against one of them, he noticed the seal branded into the wood. 'Whose warehouse did you say this was?'

'Abbie's uncle. Why?'

Alexander studied the emblem more closely. 'This is

the cargo, Derek.' He glanced around. The same seal – Everleigh's coat of arms – marked every crate. 'So, I guess her uncle helped them, too. That fucking snake, I'm going to kill him.'

John gestured silently to get his attention, pointing at the floor a few metres ahead. 'I don't think you will need to.'

Alexander crept forward to where John was crouched and looked down. There, crumpled in an unnatural heap, lay a body. The legs twisted grotesquely; the neck bent at an impossible angle. Harper Truscott, Abbie's uncle, lay dead on the floor. Rats were already swarming around the corpse, eager to strip the remains, and the stench was unbearable – he had been dead for a few days at least.

John wrinkled his nose, repulsed by the smell. 'I doubt his widow will miss him.' No-one disagreed with him.

'Let's keep moving,' Derek whispered, taking the lead once more.

The staircase at the far end of the warehouse was dimly lit from above, casting a faint glow that led them through the labyrinth of boxes. They halted at Derek's signal when a female figure crossed the upper level along a corridor between the rooms. 'Is that…?' Derek murmured.

'No,' Alexander said quickly. He knew the shape of his wife's silhouette too well to be mistaken. They waited until she disappeared from view, then resumed their climb, silently closing the distance.

With no small effort, Alexander climbed the stairs, one painstaking step at a time. At the top, he heard voices echoing from the adjoining room – and one of them struck him like a bell.

Abbie.

Her vibrant, defiant voice was unmistakable, guiding him to her like a beacon. He turned to Derek, nodded, and together they pressed forward, prepared to take down anyone who stood in their way.

***

Abbie looked from one to the other, still perplexed by the information she had just received. Williams' stutter – or whatever his name was – was gone; there was no trace of the taciturn and insecure accountant she had always known. All that remained of that man was the cold, sinister look that had always made her shiver every time he'd laid eyes on her.

'Mr Williams?' she questioned.

'Claybrook. My name is Claybrook. August Claybrook.'

Abbie shook her head. 'Claybrook? Like the man who owned Redwood House?' He stepped closer, making her retreat, only to find Jack's chest behind her, which made her jump to the side and against the wall.

'But that's not possible, he died years ago.' His eyes darkened at her words.

'He was my father. And your father killed him.' Abbie shook her head. 'What are you saying? My father didn't kill anyone!'

'Well, actually, he did.' Abbie was surprised to hear a female voice from the doorway.

'Jane?'

Abbie looked at Claybrook. 'What is she doing here? Let her go!' She tried to go to her, but Jack touched her shoulder.

'Do not move.' Slowly, she realised Jane had entered of her own accord and was now standing side by side with August Claybrook.

'Jane?' The word was just a whisper; she couldn't believe her friend had betrayed her. August looked at

Jane and placed a hand on her shoulder.

'Why?' Abbie wanted to cry. The pain she felt in her heart was unbearable, like a knife piercing through her soul. 'It was you all this time?' The pain faded as rage took over. 'You helped them get into the house! You helped them kill my parents! They gave you everything, Jane. How could you do this to them? You killed them!' Abbie saw a flicker of guilt in her eyes, but it faded just as quickly.

Jane lifted her chin. 'That wasn't supposed to happen, but it's their own fault. They should have given us the documents when we asked.'

'He was going to give them to him!' Abbie turned to point at Jack, who didn't even react.

'Enough of this! I don't have all day.' Claybrook was starting to grow impatient.

Abbie turned to look at him, her anger surging as she saw Jane standing beside that snake.

'You will pay for everything, Williams. In this life or the next. I promise, you will pay.'

'Claybrook,' he said coldly. 'My name is Claybrook. And you are the one who will pay. Your father took everything from me.'

'What are you talking about?'

'He took our house and ruined my father!' Claybrook shouted, but he quickly regained his composure.

'My father didn't steal anything from yours.'

'Yes, Abbie, he did.' This time, it was Jane who spoke.

'Jane, I don't know what this bastard has told you, but his father–'

Jane interrupted her and stepped forward. 'Our father.'

Abbie looked at her, confused, and shook her head. Looking at both of them, she suddenly saw the similarities between August and Jane: the dark eyes, the thin nose – so out of place in August's chunky body yet elegant on Jane's.

'You're his sister? Your father was Miles Claybrook.'

'Yes. And your father left him in ruins.'

'That's what he told you?'

'That's the truth.'

'No, it's not.' Abbie turned to Claybrook. 'You lied to her so she would betray us?' She looked at the woman who had once been her friend. 'It seems he forgot to mention that your father gambled away your house and lost it. And that my father bought his debt and then gave him another home – which he also gambled.' Jane began shaking her head.

'That's not true.' She looked at her brother, but he didn't bother replying.

'Enough! Where are the insurance papers?'

Abbie took a deep breath, trying to keep her emotions in check. She had too much at stake to lose control now. If she didn't remain calm, she might lose the chance to get Alexander back – and that, she couldn't bear even considering. She straightened her back.

'Where is Alexander?' she asked, lifting her chin.

'The insurance first.' His wicked smile sent a shiver down her spine.

'I don't have it with me.'

Williams looked to Jack, frowning. Before he could reply, she added, 'Once Alexander and I are back at Allhallows Stairs, I've arranged for someone to bring the insurance document in exchange for us. Not before.' Given no other option, Claybrook growled to Jack.

'Bring him. But I'm not so sure you'll recognise him.' His smile chilled to the bone.

As Jack left, Jane turned to her brother. 'Is it true what she says?' He turned to face his sister. 'So what if it is? Redwood house is still ours by right!'

'But you told me Alan killed our father!' Abbie began to edge closer to the door as they argued, hoping they wouldn't notice, when a sudden gunshot rang out from the other side of the door. Everyone turned as a man crashed and fell through the door into the middle of the room, with a gaping hole in his chest.

Stunned by the sight of Jack's dead body, Abbie watched Derek step through the doorway, raising his pistol directly at Braxton – who had already drawn his weapon. But the captain fired first, hitting him cleanly between the eyes. They saw him fall, head-first to the ground. Without wasting a second, Derek rushed to grab the pistol that Braxton dropped, but Claybrook got there first, bending down to pick up the weapon.

Instead of aiming at Derek, he turned the gun on Abbie. She stared at him, bracing for the impact, not expecting Jane to leap in front of her with a scream.

'No!'

But Claybrook had already fired. Jane turned slowly to face Abbie, her hand pressed to her stomach. She lifted her hand, and both women looked at the blood seeping through her fingers, staining her pale blue dress a dark purple. Abbie rushed to catch her as her legs buckled, and they collapsed together onto the floor. Jane looked up at her.

'I'm sorry.' And the light left her eyes, leaving only the pale, lifeless body in Abbie's arms.

'Nooo!' August's scream tore through the room as he seized Abbie by the hair, pressing a knife to her throat. 'Step away!' he shouted at Derek.

His attention fixed on the captain, he didn't notice the figure entering behind him. Abbie didn't waste a moment. She reached into her pocket, pulled out her own knife, and drove it into Claybrook's leg. As his grip loosened, she leapt forward, just as the thunder of a pistol shot echoed through the room. His body fell to its knees with a heavy thud.

Derek rushed past her, and she turned to follow him with her eyes. He stomped on Claybrook's hand, forcing him to drop his weapon.

'Bastard! Let me go!'

'It's over, Williams. I'd love nothing more than to put a bullet in your chest, but that's not how we do things. Newgate will suit you just fine – for the rest of your miserable days.'

'I'll kill you! I'll kill you all!' he raged, trying to rise, his eyes bloodshot as he turned his fury on Abbie. She saw Derek lose his patience – and before anyone could stop him, he punched Claybrook in the jaw. The man collapsed, unconscious, leaving only the heavy quiet of shared relief.

Abbie looked up, her eyes filling with tears of joy as she saw her husband standing in the doorway. But joy quickly turned to fear when she saw how unsteady he was. She ran to him, catching him just as his knees buckled, and they sank to the ground together. Wincing in pain, he raised his arm to touch her cheek.

'Are you hurt?' Abbie shook her head, relief washing over her.

'Me? No. Oh my love, what have they done to you?'

Tears streamed down her cheeks as she caressed his face, careful not to touch his swollen eye. He brushed her tears away with his thumb.

'You said, 'my love, " he murmured. His comment made her smile. Wiping her tears, she leaned closer to his lips.

'Yes, I did,' she whispered, kissing him tenderly.

Only then did she notice that John, Peter, Derek, and David were all watching them. Alexander raised an eyebrow.

'Are you going to leave me on the floor all day?'

Derek laughed and helped him to his feet. 'How are you feeling, my friend?'

'Like I'm ready to go home.'

Alexander glanced at the bodies strewn on the floor. 'So, Williams is Miles Claybrook's son?'

'Yes. And Jane was his sister. You heard?'

She looked at her friend lying lifeless on the ground. John knelt beside her and gently closed her eyes. Abbie hadn't realised how close they'd grown until she saw the pain in his expression. 'I'm sorry, John.'

'Don't tell her mother what she did, my lady,' he said, eyes pleading. Abbie nodded. Telling Mrs May the truth would only break her heart. After all, in the end, Jane had saved her life. She at least owed her that much.

'No-one will tell her. You have my word.' He nodded his thanks. Derek broke the silence.

'Peter, find us a carriage. I doubt Alexander can ride in this state. You can explain everything later.'

'Derek, can you send someone to tell Thomas and Nicholas? I don't want them to worry.'

'Of course, Abbie,' he said with a nod and looked at Peter, who left the room to follow his orders.

John was covering Jane's body. "I'll take care of this," he said, looking at the bodies.

Everyone could see that he wouldn't allow anyone else to look after Jane, and no one contradicted him.

Abbie couldn't take her eyes off her husband.

'Let's take you home.'

CHAPTER 23

Abbie settled into the carriage next to Alexander, gently urging him to rest his head on her lap. She could see how the jolting of the carriage wheels against the cobbled streets made him feel every wound and bruise now covering his body. With every jolt, he held his breath, waiting for the pain to ease before slowly relaxing back into her lap.

'We are almost home.' Every time Alexander winced, she felt as if the pain was being inflicted on her own flesh. She could feel every cut, every wound, and her anger towards the people responsible for his suffering grew by the moment. Even knowing that they had finally received what they deserved, the consequences of their actions would linger long after the wounds had healed.

Another bump in the road made him hold his breath and squeeze his eyes shut. Seeing that he wouldn't open them again, Abbie shifted him gently.

'No, no, do not fall asleep. Keep your eyes open, Alexander. Stay with me.' She wasn't well-versed in medicine, but she knew enough to know that if he lost consciousness before seeing the doctor, he might never wake.

It seemed like an eternity until he finally opened his dark blue eyes, and relief washed over her as she saw him trying – albeit with difficulty – to force a smile. Abbie released the breath she had unconsciously been holding.

His deep voice was now barely more than a hoarse

whisper. 'I am not going anywhere,' he said, lifting his hand to caress her cheek. 'My love.' Tears slid down her face, and she bent to kiss his forehead.

'You had better not, my lord. I have grown used to you now, and I cannot be bothered to find another husband. It would be the most tedious task,' she said, smiling through her tears.

She carefully brushed a strand of hair from his forehead, making him focus his gaze on her. 'Tell me what happened,' she said gently.

Alexander breathed deeply, and she saw him gathering the memories of the day.

'After visiting Nepean, we left Whitehall to reach the carriage where John was waiting for us, but before we could reach it, we were attacked. I saw Derek on the ground, but I didn't have time to do anything before someone struck me with something sharp and, half-unconscious, I was thrown into a carriage. I don't know how long it took to reach the warehouse, but they dragged me inside, and Braxton appeared shortly after.'

Abbie caressed the side of his head next to his swollen eye. 'Did he do this to you?' she asked, gritting her teeth in anger.

'No. I doubt that man had the courage to do such a thing himself. Braxton was the sort of man who had others do his dirty work for him. No, this was courtesy of the one who broke into your house.'

'Jack.'

'Yes. This was his way of getting revenge for the hole I left in his arm before he escaped. Braxton just wanted to know where the insurance papers were.'

'It was lucky you didn't have them with you.' But his expression beneath the bruises was one of doubt.

'They wouldn't have brought you into this, Abbie.'

'I believe that was their intention all along, Alexander.

When I met them at Allhallows Stairs, they did not object to my request to see you. They wanted me to be here. Claybrook wanted to see my face when he brought you before me.'

'So Williams was actually Claybrook?' Alexander asked.

'Williams' real name is August Claybrook; Miles Claybrook's son.'

'The man who lost Redwood House?' Abbie nodded. 'I don't understand. Why would he want to hurt you?'

'He claimed Redwood house belonged to him – that my father tricked his and stole everything. He blamed their misfortune on my parents. And Jane… Jane was his sister,' she said, her voice tinged with sorrow. Someone that she had trusted for years had betrayed her in the most painful way, and now that she was dead, there would be no closure. 'Claybrook lied to her. I know it doesn't justify what she did, what she helped them do, but she believed my father had killed hers. I don't know… in her place, perhaps I would have done the same.'

'I don't believe that. You would never be able to betray a friend without knowing the truth.'

'How do you know?'

'Because I know you.' He squeezed her hand gently, and his certainty gave her comfort. His belief in her made her feel as if she had finally found the family she thought she had lost forever.

'Thank you,' she said with a smile, before continuing to fill him in on everything she'd learnt in the past few hours.

'Claybrook used Braxton and my uncle to trick them into participating in the business.' She paused, a sudden thought striking her.

'My uncle?' Alexander shook his head.

'We found him among the boxes at the warehouse. He'd been dead for at least a day.' Abbie nodded, thinking of how she might break the news to her aunt – but she doubted it would grieve her. That man did not deserve a single tear from her.

'I don't know exactly how they orchestrated it all, but I believe he used Braxton to lure Stephen and my father into the scheme, with the ultimate goal of making my father lose everything – as revenge for what he believed he had done.'

'Derek is taking Claybrook to the Under-Secretary. He will uncover the truth. If anyone can make someone talk, it's Evan Nepean. And I imagine he's particularly invested in learning how a man with admiralty approval became involved in the brutal murder of a nobleman – along with so many others. He'll take it as a personal offence.'

They finally reached the house, and when the carriage stopped, Thomas immediately opened the door as if he had been waiting at the entrance for their arrival. The butler looked relieved to see both passengers alive, but his face turned pale when he saw the state Alexander was in.

'My lord!' he exclaimed, dismayed. Nicholas stood behind him, peeking out from behind.

But Abbie had no time to explain; the doctor needed to see Alexander at once.

'Hurry, Thomas, we need to get him inside.' Billy appeared beside Thomas, and between the two of them – and not without great pain from the patient – they helped Alexander down from the carriage and into the house. Abbie followed them to the drawing room, where Dr Walshman and her aunt were waiting. They both sprang to their feet at the sound of the commotion.

'Lay him on the sofa,' said the doctor. Alexander lifted

his head. 'Hello, William,' he said as they settled him down.

'Alexander.' The doctor nodded, kneeling beside him and preparing to tend to his wounds.

'It looks worse than it is,' Alexander added with a wince as the doctor started unbuttoning his shirt.

'I doubt that, but nice try,' said Dr Walshman. He turned to Abbie. 'I need to assess the damage and stabilise him before we can take him upstairs. I'll need water and bandages. Thomas, help me with his shirt.'

Alexander let them undress him to the waist. The general gasp in the room made him glance down at the dark bruises forming across his abdomen. Abbie sat beside him, holding his hand as the doctor examined him, gently pressing along his ribs and chest, asking him to breathe. Each breath contorted Alexander's face in pain.

'How is he?' Abbie asked anxiously.

'I don't believe there's internal damage, but he's cracked a rib. Fortunately, it's not broken – but he's going to need bed rest.'

'And his head?'

'I'm fine, Abbie.'

'Look at you, Alexander. You are not fine,' she said firmly. The doctor took the bandages Paige had brought, placed Alexander's arm across his abdomen and began wrapping him to immobilise the area. When he finished, he looked to the butler.

'Help me get him upstairs, Thomas.'

Getting Alexander up the stairs was no easy task for anyone involved. Not wanting to wake Georgina, Abbie saw him bite his lip several times to keep from swearing while holding his breath. By the time they reached their room, Alexander had lost most of his strength and would have collapsed to the floor if not for the two men holding him on either side. Abbie watched the ordeal, frustrated by her inability to ease his pain. Once laid flat on the bed, they removed his boots, and William turned his attention to Alexander's swollen face. His nose was twisted into an awkward position, split between the eyes.

'Stay still,' he warned, and Alexander obeyed, stifling a cry of pain as the doctor repositioned his nose.

'Damn, William. You could have warned me!' The doctor ignored him and continued his examination.

'I find it more effective when I don't warn my patients – less time for them to complain about what I'm about to do.'

'I bet you've had your own nose broken for that very reason.'

'They usually pass out after I do, but you, my friend, are quite resilient.'

He finished inspecting his face and head. 'It doesn't look like they've broken anything else. But your ribs are bruised – so there could be some damage I can't yet detect. I'll have to wait for the swelling to go down to see if there's anything to worry about.'

'Thank you, Doctor Walshman,' said Abbie.

'It has been my honour to patch him up.' He began collecting his things. 'Make sure he doesn't go to sleep in the next hour. And give him this once the hour has passed.' He handed her a small bottle. 'It's laudanum.'

Alexander groaned from the bed. The doctor turned to look at his patient.

'You need to sleep. If you don't, it will take much longer to heal. This will dull the pain, at least through the night. A few drops won't make you lose consciousness, but it should ease the pain enough to let you sleep.'

Abbie took the bottle and nodded. 'He'll take it.' The doctor smiled.

'I'll come back in the morning. But if he gets worse, send for me. You should try to rest as well, Lady

Crawford – it's been a long day.'

'I will try.' She walked the doctor out of the room, meeting the butler as he returned with a tray of hot broth and bread for Alexander. 'Thank you, Thomas.' He set the tray on the bedside table and turned to her.

'Would you like something to eat too, my lady?' The thought of food made her stomach turn. She shook her head.

'No, thank you, Thomas. But if you could ask Suzie to bring up some hot water from the kitchens, I would appreciate it.' Her own words brought Jane and her mother to mind.

'Where is Mrs May?'

Thomas' expression hardened. 'John sent word with Walter Dawley that he was taking Jane to the funeral parlour, so Billy has taken Mrs May to see her.' Abbie closed her eyes and placed a hand to her chest, imagining the pain the woman must be feeling.

'What have you told her?'

'Not much, my lady. We said the ruffians had kidnapped her... and that she died where Lord Crawford was found.' She nodded, relieved no-one had told the woman the truth of what her daughter had done.

'Please let me know when she returns.'

'I will, my lady.' He bowed and left, closing the door softly behind him. She stared at the door, lost in the memory of her friend – a friend she now doubted had ever truly been as caring as she once believed.

'Abbie, it is not your fault,' said Alexander from the bed. Abbie turned and saw him struggling to sit up.

'Careful!' She rushed to help him rest his back against the pillows.'I know it's not,' she said, 'but I cannot help but struggle with it. She betrayed us in so many ways, and yet... before Claybrook appeared in our lives, she was my friend. I know she was. But these past months, she's done terrible things. My heart feels split in two – I don't know whether to feel sorrow or fury.' She pulled a chair next to the bed and sat down, picking up the bowl of steaming broth.

'It's too soon to say. We should wait until Derek comes back with more information.'

'I hope he doesn't take long.'

'Hopefully not. Do I really need to eat? I don't feel like I could hold anything down.'

'Doctor's orders. You haven't eaten, and you need your strength to recover,' she said firmly, allowing no room for debate.

'I don't know if I'd want you as a nurse,' he said, amused.

'Well, you'll just have to put up with it. I'm not going to let you starve. Here.' Seeing that he couldn't manage with the bowl himself, Abbie sat on the bed and lifted a spoonful to his lips. Even the simple act of swallowing the amber liquid seemed to cause him pain, so she took care not to rush him, afraid of doing more harm than good.

Once satisfied with how much he had eaten, she set the tray down on the table by the door and returned, moving the chair closer to sit by his side. But before she could sit, Alexander said, 'Not there. I need you here, beside me.' He opened the covers with his free hand and patted the mattress.

'But I might hurt you.'

'It'll be worth it,' he said with a smile.

She moved around and carefully lay beside him. He opened his arm so she could nestle in the crook of it, holding her close. Once settled against him, she listened to the slow rhythm of his heartbeat, and for a brief moment, the tension faded. He was home, safe.

But the peace did not last long.

As the sun's rays bathed the room in light, Alexander's temperature rose to dangerous levels. So much so that, in a delirious state, he began to pronounce her name in desperation. The sheets were soaked with sweat.

'Alexander?' she whispered, but he didn't answer. He shook his head from side to side as if trying to escape some invisible horror. His face had swollen further – he was now nearly unrecognisable. Abbie jumped from the bed and ran to call from the door. Within minutes, Thomas and Suzie appeared.

'My lady?' Thomas asked, alarmed.

'Alexander has gotten worse. I need Doctor Walshman at once.'

'Right away, my lady.' Thomas rushed off without another word.

Suzie stepped forward. 'What do you need from me, Lady Abbie?'

'Bring cold water and cloths. We need to bring down his temperature.'

'Yes, my lady.' Suzi hurried to carry out her instructions.

Fortunately, the doctor arrived within half an hour and quickly examined Alexander to determine the source of the fever.

'It appears the infection is internal,' he said gravely, 'but I'm afraid there's nothing I can do. We will have to wait for the fever to pass and help his body fight it with cold compresses until his temperature returns to normal.'

It was not the news Abbie had hoped for, but squaring her shoulders, she refused to succumb to despair. She began following the doctor's instructions to the letter – just as everyone else in the house did.

No matter how hard she had to work, she would help him find his way back to her.

CHAPTER 24

Alexander tried to open his eyes, but the task felt arduous, as if all strength had evaporated from his body. After several attempts, he finally managed to part his eyelids in a thin line.

Blinking to dispel the blurriness clouding his vision, he gradually brought the room into focus – and recognised it as his own. The curtains were half drawn, allowing a dim light to bathe the space. He had no notion of how much time had passed; his last clear memory was of Abbie lying beside him. After that, everything had become a blur, haunted by dreams – or perhaps nightmares – of Claybrook attacking her.

Searching for a familiar face, he looked around the room until his gaze landed on Abbie. She sat slumped in a chair next to his bed, her head resting on her arms, which she'd crossed like a pillow. Her golden hair spilt over her shoulders, and it was clear she had remained by his side for hours.

He reached out and gently stroked her hair. As if touched by a hot iron, Abbie woke with a jolt and sat upright, startled. Her face bore the strain of sleepless nights, and the shadows under her eyes told him it had not been mere hours – but days.

The sight of her eyes shining with joy struck him deeply. With effort, he lifted a hand to caress her cheek. Abbie leaned into his palm.

'You're back,' she whispered. He opened his mouth to speak, but his throat was so dry that no sound emerged. In a hoarse voice he barely recognised as his own, he pleaded,

'Water.' Abbie hurried to bring a glass to his lips. 'Slowly, and small sips.'

As the liquid passed from his mouth, he felt as if the water was a river that had washed over a desert. The harsh dryness subsided, and he drank gratefully. When he raised a hand to wipe away a few stray drops from his chin, he realised his beard had grown. Clearing his throat, he tested his voice. After a moment, he asked, 'How long has it been?'

Abbie set the glass down on the table. 'Three days. There were times when we thought we were going to lose you.'

He squeezed her hand. 'But I'm still here.' She rested her head on his shoulder.

'Yes,' she whispered. 'How are you feeling?'

'Breathing hurts.' He looked down at the white linen bandage across his chest, securing his arm to his torso. His abdomen was blotched with purple and green bruises. Though he could now see her, his left eyelid remained swollen, obscuring part of his vision. 'But the important thing is that I *can* breathe, right?' He tried to lighten the mood, for he could see the worry lingering in her gaze. 'I'll be better soon, Abbie.'

'You'd better be. I won't spend the rest of my days prostrated at your bedside, sir.' But even her feigned reprimand couldn't mask the depth of feeling in her eyes. He could tell she cared for him – perhaps just as profoundly as he did for her.

Shaking her head, she stood from his side, 'I need to let everyone know you're awake. Especially Georgina. The poor thing has been worried sick for three days, coming by every day to ask after you.'

Alexander's expression tightened. The idea of

Georgina suffering for his sake disturbed him, but Abbie placed a hand on his shoulder.

'I didn't let her see you until yesterday, once the worst had passed. She only saw you sleeping peacefully. She's a strong girl, Alexander.' She kissed his forehead. 'I'll be back with something to eat. You need to regain your strength, my dear husband.' He let out a small chuckle, which turned into a wince. 'Try to rest,' she said, and he watched her leave the room.

Not long after Abbie's departure, a soft knock sounded at the door. Without waiting for a reply, it opened just enough to reveal Georgina's little face peeking through the gap. 'Uncle Alex?' she asked cautiously.

'Georgina!' His voice brightened at the sight of her. 'Come here, sweet face.' She ran to the bed but stopped herself just short of climbing up.

'I might hurt you, Uncle Alex!'

'You won't.'

She threw her arms around his neck, and though the movement made him hold his breath, he concealed the pain. Her embrace was the best medicine he could ask for. He stroked her hair with his hand and rocked her gently, trying to calm her trembling.

'Shhh, I'm alright, Georgina.'

'But you almost died,' she said between sobs.

'Me? Oh no, darling. It will take more than that to kill your uncle. I'm a strong man.'

'I came to see you every day, but you were sleeping all the time.'

'I was just resting so I could hug you.'

She leaned back to look at him, her cheeks streaked with tears. 'Dr Walshman said you were too stubborn to die.'

'And he was right.'

'You won't leave me, then?'

'Never.'

'Promise?'

'I promise. Now, tell me – what have you been doing these past three days?'

***

Abbie opened the door to the kitchen, and the unexpected sight of Jane's mother at the stove stopped her in her tracks. 'Mrs May?' The cook lifted her head, her eyes red from crying. The pain reflected in her expression broke Abbie's heart.

'I'll leave if you want, my lady. I'll understand.'

'Oh, no – please. You mistake my surprise, Mrs May. I wasn't expecting you to be here, that's all. I think you should be resting, taking care of yourself. You don't need to be here.'

'I just can't stop thinking about what she did.'

Abbie blinked. The woman knew? As far as she was aware, no-one in the house had told Mrs May the truth of what had happened a few nights ago, nor of Jane's involvement. The cook must have seen the confusion in her eyes. 'I know what she did, Lady Abbie.'

She dried her hands on her apron and sat at the large wooden table on the kitchen side. Abbie sat beside her. 'The night you left to rescue Lord Crawford, she was packing her clothes. When I confronted her, she told me she wasn't my dau… my daughter.' Her voice broke into a sob. She wiped the tears from her eyes. 'She always knew she was an orphan, but never, in all these years, had considered herself less for not being blood related. And then she left. She said to go with her real family. The true owner of Redwood House. I realised then that all the misfortunes that had happened were because she'd been helping those men.'

She buried her face in her hands. Abbie felt her pain as if it were her own. She had known this woman for over twenty years and couldn't let her daughter's last memory be one of disgrace.

'She was manipulated into thinking the worst of us, Mrs May. She saved my life in the end. That's what I'll remember – and you should, too. Her final actions showed the real Jane.'

'It's going to be difficult. And what she did to you…' The woman couldn't even meet her eyes. But Abbie tilted her head, gently catching her gaze.

'It *will* be difficult. But you must remember the good things she did – and she did many. Please don't forget that. I've already forgiven her.'

Mrs May looked at her with gratitude. 'Thank you, Lady Abbie.'

The kitchen door opened, and Abbie's aunt entered, dressed in a pastel blue gown. Abbie froze at the sight. It had been years since she'd seen her aunt wear anything but dark colours.

'Aunt!' she exclaimed. 'You look… beautiful!' The woman waved away the compliment gracefully and changed the subject.

'I just came back from your husband's room. He looks much recovered.'

'Oh dear!' said Mrs May, rising quickly. 'He must be hungry!'

'Don't worry, Mrs May. I can prepare something for him,' said Abbie, not wanting to place a burden on the cook.

'Nonsense, my lady. I'll prepare a proper meal to help him recover.' She headed for the cellar to fetch supplies. Her aunt sat beside Abbie and took her hand.

'Let her be, darling. She needs to keep busy.' She

touched Abbie's cheek. 'You look tired.'

'I am, but the worst is over. I predict I'll sleep for days after I take Alexander something to eat. How are *you* feeling, Aunt?' Aunt Agatha folded her hands in her lap, twisting her skirt between her fingers. When she spoke, it was barely above a whisper.

'Guilty.'

'Guilty?' Abbie echoed, startled, raising her voice more than she intended. Her aunt flinched slightly and responded defensively.

'Yes, darling. Guilty – because I feel relieved.' A part of her had assumed that no one would be affected by her uncle's death. But now, hearing her aunt admit to feeling relief – and the guilt that came with it – Abbie understood just how complicated grief can be, especially for someone as kind-hearted as her aunt.

Abbie took her hand, struggling to find the words that might offer comfort and help her break free of the abuse she had endured for years.

'He was a horrible man who got what he deserved.'

'But he was my husband, Abbie.'

'A real husband wouldn't have treated you like he did. What would you say if Alexander treated me like Uncle Harper treated you?' Her aunt's eyes widened as the truth struck her, suddenly understanding that what she had suffered over the years was not acceptable.

'I would be furious.'

'You're free now, Aunt. You don't owe him anything. You don't need to mourn him. You don't need to feel guilty for the freedom you now enjoy – it is your right and it always was. He took that from you. Now don't let him steal a second more of your life.'

Tears welled in Aunt Agatha's eyes. She squeezed Abbie's hands. 'Thank you, darling.'

Abbie wrapped her in an embrace and said, 'You don't

have to thank me, Aunt. We're family. We protect each other – always.'

Sudden shouts from upstairs startled them both. They exchanged a glance, then hastily ran from the kitchen to see what was happening. When they reached the entrance hall, they found a striking woman, about her aunt's age, standing in the entrance. Her dark hair was streaked with silver, but that did nothing to diminish her glamorous air. Beside her stood a tall man – nearly Alexander's height – whose features were immediately familiar.

'Where is my son?' he demanded of Thomas, agitated. 'He gets married and doesn't even have the decency to tell his parents? He's going to hear me!'

'Calm down, Henry,' the woman said, placing a hand his forearm. 'Let's speak to the boy before you start shouting.'

'He is *not* a boy anymore, Susanna! And why are you so calm?'

'Because we are surrounded by strangers,' she said softly, 'and you're making a spectacle, dear husband.' The remark made Abbie smile. She stepped forward, her aunt by her side.

'Your grace?'

The older man blinked at the unfamiliar voice. 'Do I know you, girl?'

'Not yet. But your son has spoken of you.'

'And why would he do that?'

'Because I'm his wife.'

Alexander's mother stepped forward, letting her husband recover from his surprise.

'Dear, it's very nice to meet you. I'm Susanna, Alexander's mother.' She took Abbie's hands and kissed her cheek warmly. 'Please forgive my husband – he's just shocked by our son's sudden nuptials.'

'Shocked, you say? I wasn't shocked – I was *furious* that

my eldest son didn't even introduce us to his future wife! What's your name, girl?'

'Abigail, your grace. I do apologise. But there wasn't much time.'

'You're with child?'

Alexander's father clearly had little restraint, and Abbie blinked at his bluntness. 'No, my lord, I'm not. It's... complicated. Perhaps it's best if we go and see your son – so he can explain everything.'

'Where is he?' asked Susanna gently.

'Upstairs, in our bedchamber.'

'He's in bed at this hour?'

'He suffered a...' Abbie didn't want to scare them. '...a small accident. The doctor advised him to rest for the day. That's all.' She knew they'd realise the truth once they saw him, but she couldn't bring herself to be the one to explain that their son had nearly died – because of her. 'I'll see if he's awake.' Her aunt touched her hand.

'I'll get some refreshments in the drawing room.'

'Thank you, Aunt.'

Hurrying upstairs, she heard her aunt's voice in the distance, kindly introducing herself to Alexander's parents and leading them away. Abbie needed a moment alone with Alexander before facing his family. She didn't want to explain to his parents how they had gotten to the point of marriage. Or at least she didn't want to do it alone. Opening the bedroom door, she found him on his feet – with Georgina's help. 'What on earth do you think you are doing?' she cried.

'I heard voices. A man was yelling.'

'I *told* him, Auntie Abbie!' Georgina chimed in. 'But he said he needed to see who was yelling.' Said Georgina, barely managing to help her uncle. Abbie rushed to his side and gently eased him back on the bed.

'And for that, you think getting out of bed is a good

idea? I *will* tie you down to the bed myself if you try this nonsense again!'

'Abbie…' Alexander warned, but she wasn't finished.

'Your parents are here. And they are not pleased about our marriage.'

'My parents? How did they find out?'

Before she could answer, his father stormed into the room with his wife just behind him. The woman gasped at the sight of Alexander and his bruised body.

'Alexander, dear!' Abbie took Georgina's hand and stepped back as Susanna rushed to her son's side. 'My child – what happened to you?'

'Son.' His father's voice was thick with emotion. He placed a hand on Alexander's shoulder. 'Who did this to you?'

'It's a long story. It looks worse than it is, Father.'

'But look at your face!' Susanna exclaimed.

Abbie leaned down to whisper in Georgina's ear. 'Let's leave them to talk.'

Looking over her shoulder, she led the girl from the room, leaving Alexander to explain the last two months of their lives.

CHAPTER 25

The mystery of how his parents had learned of their marriage was quickly solved. It had been Grandma Charlotte who, assuming they were already aware of their nuptials, had written to them after his kidnapping, urging them to come to London. He knew her intentions had been good, but he dearly wished that he had been the one to tell them.

The conversation with his parents went precisely as he had expected. Though he knew his reasons for keeping them in the dark about the difficulties of the past few months were valid, it did little to placate his father. As head of the family, the duke believed it was his duty to protect those under his care. Alexander now understood that sentiment well – for it was how he felt about Abbie and Georgina.

Explaining to them the difficulties they had faced in the past few months had not been an easy task. Wanting to spare them unnecessary worry, he provided only a brief account, avoiding the lurid details – from Stephen's death to his own kidnapping just days before. Even so, with every word, his mother's eyes widened between disbelief and worry for the situations they had to endure.

On the other hand, Alexander could see in his father's face that, despite feeling the same sorrow as his mother, the man was offended that his own son hadn't come to him for help

'Father,' Alexander said gently from his bed, 'it would

only have put you in danger – you, Ma and Juliet. I wasn't willing to risk losing you as well.'

'I understand your reasoning, son,' his father said, placing a hand on his shoulder, 'but I cannot help but feel I ought to have been there for you.'

'I know if I'd written to you, you would have come at once. But in this case, the fewer people who knew, the better.' His father nodded, albeit reluctantly. His brow remained furrowed, thick eyebrows drawn together, deep in thought.

Alexander recognised the expression – it was the same look he had seen many times when his father disagreed with someone, and since he would soon express his true feelings, Alexander encouraged him to talk. 'What is it?'

The duke did not answer immediately; he took his time until he couldn't hold it any longer, and raising his arms to emphasise his words, he exclaimed.

'But did you have to marry?'

His wife looked turned on him at once, piercing him with her gaze.

'Henry! But of course, he had to marry her! What did you expect – for our son to leave the poor girl abandoned and unprotected? We raised him to be a gentleman, did we not?' She turned to Alexander, giving his hand a gentle squeeze. 'You did well, darling. She's very pretty – and spirited. I like that.'

Alexander smiled at his mother, grateful as always for her steadfast support. But when he looked back at his father and saw that he still had a doubtful expression, he was puzzled. His father was not the sort of duke who clung to status or entitlement. He had worked very hard to avoid the arrogance so common among the peerage.

The idea that having a title placed you above anybody else was something his father had always abhorred. Alexander knew his hesitance had nothing to do with

Abbie's lack of social status. It had to be something else.

'Speak your mind, father. You've never held your tongue – don't let this time be the first.'

His father hesitated once more, clearly struggling with what he was about to say. At last, he spoke. 'How sure are you that she wasn't involved?'

Having someone doubt Abbie's loyalty sparked a fury inside Alexander unlike anything he had felt before. To question her – after everything – was intolerable. 'She saved Georgina and risked her life to rescue me,' he snapped. 'That's how I know she wasn't involved. Not to mention, she lost her parents and almost died herself. Is that not reason enough to trust her?'

His father could say little, for the loyalty she had shown was, without a doubt, something he deeply admired. At last, he nodded, conceding the point. She was part of their family now, and Alexander would not tolerate anyone questioning her. Not even his own father.

A soft knock at the door interrupted the moment and broke the tension between them. Alexander looked up to see Georgina peeking through the crack. When he signed for her to enter, she opened the door fully, revealing Abbie standing behind her.

Georgina ran to the bed and looked at her uncle curiously. 'How are you feeling?'

'Much better now that you've come to visit. I haven't properly introduced you. Georgina, these are my parents.' She turned to them with a polite smile.

'Very nice to meet you.' Then she offered a graceful curtsy.

'The pleasure is all ours,' said Susanna, smiling warmly at her.

Abbie stepped forward, a letter in her hand. 'Forgive the interruption – Derek sent a message, and I thought you might want to read it.' She handed the letter to

Alexander.

Susanna stood and moved closer to Abbie, reaching out to take her hands. 'Darling, thank you for what you did for my son. Alexander has told us what you've been through. I am so very sorry for your loss.'

'You're welcome,' Abbie replied with a gentle smile. 'But to be fair, he didn't leave me too much choice. I've gotten used to him now.' His mother laughed, turning to her husband with a look of fond amusement.

'As I said – I like her.' And in that moment, they all burst into laughter.

***

Slowly, the newly discovered routine was finally established in the house.

After several days– during which Alexander nearly exhausted Abbie's patience with his repeated attempts to get out of bed – the inhabitants of the house joined forces to contain the stubborn husband and prevent him from worsening his condition. With their combined efforts, they managed to keep him still until the doctor finally permitted light activity. He began with short walks, first around the room, then later in the week, around the house and garden.

Now, a week after that terrible night, they were all gathered in the drawing room, awaiting the arrival of Captain Derek Colton. He had sent word with Peter Dawley that he would be arriving that afternoon with news from the Admiralty, and so Abbie had called everyone involved to hear what he had to report.

Seated on the sofa that crowned the room, her aunt looked radiant in a yellow dress, embracing every second of her newfound freedom. Grandma Charlotte was visibly delighted to see her long-time friend shine once more, just as she had done years before she met her late husband.

Alexander's parents were entertaining Georgina with stories of a young Alexander, recounting the many times he had earned punishments for his mischievous behaviour – stories which her husband vehemently denied.

'Father, if you keep telling her all that, she'll think I was a rascal!' His mother waved off the comment with a fond smile.

'Not a rascal, my dear son. Just a bit mischievous. And still, you've grown into a fine man.'

'Thank you, Mother,' Alexander replied, pressing a tender kiss to her head.

The ringing of the front bell resonating in the house silenced the room. All eyes turned towards the hallway, expectant. At last, Derek entered, flanked by the Dawley brothers and John, who followed a step behind. Derek raised an eyebrow and scanned the room with amusement.

'What a reception! Were you all waiting for me?' he teased.

'What do you think?' Alexander retorted, walking towards his cousin with the help of a cane. 'We've only been waiting a whole week for you to bring us news.'

'You're awfully irascible, cousin – and you look absolutely terrible, by the way.'

Though the swelling had gone down, Alexander's face still bore multicoloured bruises tainting his skin, which showed the severity of the beating he had received.

'As always, you're so considerate with your opinions,' Alexander said dryly.

'What can I say? I have a gift,' Derek replied, grinning at the room.

Abbie had not known Derek well before all of this,

but she was quickly learning that his calm, light-hearted nature had likely saved him from many difficult situations – and just as likely gotten him into a few as well.

Alexander eyed the Dawley brothers and raised a brow. 'And why on earth are you dressed as if you're about to meet the Queen?'

'Because they wanted to look presentable for your wife,' Derek quipped. Alexander snorted, though Abbie noticed the smile that tugged at the corner of his mouth despite the exaggerated gesture.

Just then, Derek noticed Alexander's parents. 'Aunt! Uncle! I didn't know you were in London.' He shook his uncle's hand and kissed his aunt's cheek.

'We had to come,' said the duke with mock severity. 'Our son got married without even inviting us.'

'I know. It was so very rude of him.'

'Uncle Derek!' Georgina ran to him and threw her arms around his neck.

He lifted her into the air, making her giggle. 'Hello, cherry face. How have you been?'

'Very good! It's so fun having everyone at home!'

'I can see that. Hey, would you do me a favour?'

'Of course!' The girl's enthusiasm enthralled everyone in the room.

'I'm *very* hungry. Could you go to the kitchen and ask for something to eat?'

'Yes!' she replied in delight, skipping off to the kitchens.

Once Georgina left the room, Abbie stood up, unable to hold her curiosity any longer. 'Please, do not leave us wondering a moment longer, Captain. I beg you – tell us what has happened.'

'For you, my lady, I will.' They all found seats, filling every chair and sofa in the room and waited eagerly for Derek's account.

'After what happened in the warehouse, we took Claybrook to Nepean, and the little weasel started singing like a canary.' There were murmurs of surprise and anticipation. 'He was indeed Lord Claybrook's son. When their father died, he left Jane at Mrs May's doorstep. He'd discovered that she was your new cook,' he said, glancing at Abbie, 'and thought he could leave her nearby until he was ready to return. For years, he planned his revenge on your family, Abbie. He joined the Hawkhurst gang – a smuggling group with ties all along the coast. Once he had the connections he needed, the plan began to take shape.

'First, he recruited your uncle – who, thanks to gambling debts and his access to your family, was an easy target. But he needed someone with shipping routes. That's when Braxton's misfortunes began. He lost two ships at sea – ships that Claybrook and a Spanish pirate crew had intercepted. With the money he made from selling Braxton's cargo, he approached Braxton, offering financial help until the man was so entangled that he couldn't go to the authorities. Knowing your father lacked the capital for such a large venture, they also brought in Stephen – who, according to Claybrook, the old Lord had failed his father and thus also his son deserved to suffer.'

Abbie was shocked to hear the lengths the man had gone through to avenge his father.

'Once they tricked them into investing, the operation started. The first shipment was successful. But when Stephen and your father realised the deception and insured the next cargo at sea, all his plans were thwarted. The Spanish pirates refused to return the ship, and in a desperate attempt to recover that insurance, they lost control.'

Derek stood and crossed the room to pour himself a

drink. Silence had fallen over those present, waiting expectantly for Derek to continue.

'Claybrook is now in Newgate, awaiting trial. But rest assured, he will not be leaving that prison alive. Nepean doesn't take too kindly to being deceived, and Braxton and Claybrook have both earned his fury. The Under-Secretary of State for the Home Department does not forget a betrayal.'

He took a sip, then added, 'Claybrook named every single associate, and that is where we have been this past week. Helping Nepean apprehend them all, and they're now behind bars.'

A collective breath of relief swept through the room. Abbie reached for Alexander's hand and held it, finding comfort in his touch.

'Where are you headed now?' asked Alexander.

'I'm putting *The Isabella* back in the water. Nepean wants me to hunt down the Spanish crew that took Braxton's ship. We set sail for Spain in two days.'

'Good luck, my friend – and thank you.'

'We're family. What is family for, if not to get involved in each other's troubles?'

Abbie laughed at his sense of humour despite everything. 'We thank you nonetheless, Derek. Without you, we could not have stopped Claybrook or his men.'

'It was a pleasure, Abbie,' he said, bowing with a roguish smile. 'Now, I believe it's time for some food, don't you think? I, for one, am starving.'

'Me too!' said Georgina, re-entering the room. 'Thomas is bringing sandwiches!' She jumped into her uncle's lap, full of joy.

'That sounds delicious, cherry face.'

Abbie looked around the room. Seeing everyone enjoying each other's company made her feel that she had found the family she had lost. Nothing could replace her parents' love, but the love of the people around her now brought a peace she hadn't thought possible.

Alexander leaned down to whisper in her ear. 'Now we'll definitely have time to get to know each other better.'

Abbie met his gaze, smiling. 'It's customary to do that *before* the wedding, you know.'

'Well, it's never too late, my love. Never too late.' He pressed a soft kiss to her lips. As Abbie looked around at the happy faces of those she loved, one of her father's teachings rose in her memory:

There are moments in life that, for some reason, remain engraved in your heart, as if they had happened only yesterday.

And Abbie knew – this moment would remain in her heart forever.

THE END

Coming next...

We will follow in the footsteps of Captain Colton, whose voyage will take him in search of a Spanish ship.

There, in the middle of the ocean, an unexpected encounter with a woman from the Cantabrian coast will change the course of his life.

Their turbulent first meeting will force them to confront not only the adversities of the sea and their enemies, but also the storm of emotions that begins to stir between them.

A NOTE TO THE READER

Thank you for accompanying Abigail and Alexander to the end of this story.

As an independent author, every reader matters more than you can imagine. If this historical romance filled with mystery, secrets, and passion moved you, an honest review on Amazon and Goodreads can make a tremendous difference. It helps other readers discover the book and allows this story to continue reaching new hearts.

Thank you for your time, your reading, and for being part of this journey.

Your opinion is the greatest support this story can receive.

With gratitude,

Lucy Alvarez

Follow me on Instagram: @lucyalvarezauthor

Acknowledgments

The path to creating this book has been full of challenges that, without the help of many people, would not have been possible to overcome.

To my sisters, Elisa and Andrea, for being there for me in my most difficult moments and never letting me fall. You have been my rock.

To my parents, for teaching me to fight passionately for what I want and to never give up in the face of adversity. Thank you for everything you have given me.

Thank you, family, for the love you give me every day.

To my friends, to all those wonderful women who accompany me on this marvellous journey that is life. Thank you, my little witches.

To Rocío, for encouraging me to keep writing when that writer's block that all writers know overwhelmed me, making it difficult for the words to flow. Your art has been an inspiration.

To my colleagues at Slow Horses, thank you for the support you have given me over these years and for patiently listening to my endless stories about the tales I found.

To the British Library and the Bodleian Library, for offering me a world of knowledge and inspiration that I will never forget.

And, especially, to my son, Alejandro. You have just arrived, and you already illuminate our lives with your light. Thank you.

Printed in Dunstable, United Kingdom